# JOHN LEE JOHNSON FROM TEXAS

*The Man from Texas*

CONN HAMLETT

WestBow
PRESS
A DIVISION OF THOMAS NELSON

ISBN: 978-1-4497-2781-9 (e)
ISBN: 978-1-4497-2783-3 (sc)
ISBN: 978-1-4497-2784-0 (hc)
Library of Congress Control Number: 2011917376

WestBow Press books may be ordered through booksellers or by contacting:

WestBow Press
A Division of Thomas Nelson
1663 Liberty Drive
Bloomington, IN 47403
www.westbowpress.com
1-(866) 928-1240

Printed in the United States of America
WestBow Press rev. date: 11/14/2011

# CHAPTER ONE

It was early May of 1864 and a group of Confederate troopers was assembled in a copse of trees not far from the crossroads several miles south of Lexington, Tennessee. The crossroads led south to Selma and west to Henderson and east to Nashville.

Captain Ben Grover ordered them dismounted and to gather around. He had a gray-slouch hat that shadowed his dark eyes. His gray mustache hung drearily down his jaw line. "Gentlemen, we've got a grave situation here." He paused and pointed with his gloved hand toward Lexington, Tennessee. "This Federal general out of Memphis, a General Sturgis, is sending out patrols to find General Forrest. He is trying to ascertain if he is in West Tennessee or in Mississippi." He raised his eyes from the shadow of his brim and looked around. "He ain't gonna find nothing but pain."

Captain Grover spat some tobacco juice on a cluster of Johnson grass. He continued, "What we have here is two-Federal scouting patrols. One's coming down this road shortly and the other's coming from Jackson toward Henderson." He chewed some more and spat some more then said, "We're going to stop the one from Lexington." His eyes tightened, "Or die trying."

He shrugged and forked a thumb over his shoulders. "Now

Captain Sullivan is setting up an ambush between Jackson and Henderson. I think at Pinson. But his task is considerable harder than ours. He's facing a whole lot of men."

He spat again and then his eyes settled on the big Texan, John Lee Johnson. "And he don't have John."

All eyes turned in some form or another to John Lee Johnson. He was six-inches over six-feet and had shoulders a yard wide. He had an athletic body and a handsome face covered in three-day whisker stubble. He had two-Navy Colts on his hip and two in his belts. John's eyes were shadowed by his black slouch hat. He acknowledged the compliment by dipping his head and licking his lips.

The captain continued. "Now here's what we got to do." He nodded toward the north toward Lexington. "We got to put this patrol out of business. "If we fail," he paused and held up his index finger for emphasis. "They'll catch Captain Sullivan here in a trap trying to get to Savannah."

His eyes narrowed as he panned the faces of his charges. "But we ain't gonna fail." He chewed some more and nodded to the woods around them. "I want everyone of you to go into the woods and empty hisself out." He shook his head side-to-side. "I don't want any farts or someone breathing heavy because he's ate too many green apples."

He smiled and spat again. "Now when you boys are all sanitized and everything, I want you to take some canteen water and clean out those noses. Any sneezes could make my wife a widow."

He straightened and put his hand on his own Navy Colt and pointed to the trees on each side of the road. "When you're all done with that and that means in ten-minutes, you get yourselves on each side of the road and stagger yourselves so you won't shoot each other when we fire across."

He reached to his saddle and lifted out his Sharps rifle. Bring these and use 'em when you have used up those Colts."

He nodded toward the trees. "I expect you swinging jacks in about ten-minutes."

Billy Taylor, a sixteen-year old boy, was waiting on John when he emerged from the woods. Billy had tousled blonde hair and dark-blue eyes. His eyes, shadowed under his black hat brim, were filled with admiration for the big Texan. "John, you ever notice that the captain always singles you out?"

John ignored the question and changed the subject as he slapped Billy on the back. "How old are you, Billy?"

Billy flashed a big grin. "Twenty-one is what's on record."

John laughed jokingly. "I thought you were a lot older than that." John knew he was sixteen or thereabouts. He let the matter drop.

They both walked to their horses and both John and Billy pulled theirs Sharps out and moved toward their respective positions.

As soon as the men had all gotten their rifles, several soldiers who served as hostlers took the horses to a hiding place. John turned and watched over his shoulder. They had done this so many times; it had become second nature.

He looked across the corduroy road and saw the captain behind a bole of a tree. He noticed in a few minutes that most were almost invisible among the trees and shadows. John was three-feet from Billy, who was holding his pistol muzzle up.

They stood there approximately ten-minutes among the bird chirpings and buzzing of bees. They then heard the sound of a clattering wagon coming down the trail.

The hay-filled wagon soon came into view. The driver was wearing a farmer's straw hat and a one-gallus overall. He was no farmer but private Milton Sewell from Florence, Alabama. As the two-horse team went by, Milton with his head down, held up three-fingers meaning the Federals were three-miles back.

It seemed like an eternity but in twenty-minutes, they could hear the sound of horses. They were trotting at a leisurely pace.

As they got closer, the sounds of harness and shod hooves could be heard.

Captain Grover's eyes went to his right. He had Landis Tully there with his sawed-off shotgun. Landis's job was to jump in front of a patrol and cut loose with both barrels and then hightail it to the trees. Captain Grover's eyes moved to his left. There he had Eugene Tate, who was to jump behind the patrol with his greener and blast away.

The initial shock would freeze the patrol and the men on both sides would commence firing.

The men became anxious and tense. Fingers were sweaty in the trigger guards. Eyes narrowed or widened. Breathing shallow and expectant. They waited.

The captain of the Union patrol was looking at his pocket watch as they made their way between the trees. He was riding to the left of a soldier, who was supporting the regimental guidon.

The Union cavalry seemed bored and sleepy.

The clippety-clopping of their mounts became more magnified as they became centered in the ambush.

Captain Grover nodded at Landis Tully, and he jumped from the bushes and leveled his shotgun. Both barrels bucked and bellowed from the force of the shot, and he sent the Union captain and the guidon carrier wheeling from their horses. The quick and unexpected shots sent shock waves down the line of horsemen.

From the rear, Eugene Tate jumped into the road and fired both barrels and sent two-troopers flying forward through the air.

From both sides of the trees, Navy Colts began blasting, and orange and yellow flames erupted from the dark shadows. The Union cavalry were whirling their mounts and reaching for their revolvers.

Both Landis Tully and Eugene Tate made their way back to the safety of the trees and reloaded. They turned their loaded shotguns back toward the milling and confused troopers.

The Union patrol gave up loud shouts mixed in fear and anger. They overcame the shock of the surprise attack and began firing back. The zing of balls were zipping through the trees and nipping leaves and thudding into tree trunks. But they received worse than they were able to give. They were totally exposed and their tormentors were hidden. Horses were yanked around sending mouth foam splaying from their bits. It was a desperate cacophony of wild primal screams, the neighing of frightened horses and unending gunfire.

John gritted his teeth and entered the fray. He began firing like clockwork and his Colts were taking a toll. With each shot a Federal was hit or was falling. He kept firing and firing until he heard the ominous click of empty. He ditched his empties and reached for his reserves.

Through the fog of gunsmoke, one seasoned and observant Union trooper was able to see who was levying the heavy damage upon his men and took aim and sent a ball that missed John by inches. He cocked the hammer once more and aimed carefully at the big man who was firing like a deadly machine.

Billy, who had been working his Navy sixes, heard the pistol ball whiz by like an angry hornet in the space between him and John. He saw the Union soldier level his weapon. He realized John did not see the threat. He jumped from his cover and fired several rounds. They missed The Union cavalryman, who felt the furrow of air as the shots nipped at his tunic and barely missed his head, turned his attention to Billy and fired.

John saw a strip of bark fly from the first shot, but he heard the ominous 'slunk' of lead as the second-shot hit Billy. Billy groaned and sank to his knees. John caught sight of his comrade on his knees and then watched helplessly as he keeled over to his side.

He then caught sight of the trooper. Both looked at each at the same time through the thick haze of gunsmoke. John sent two-shots that drilled into the man's chest. The Union trooper jerked painfully in the saddle and tried desperately to hold on to his saddle horn. He suddenly collapsed and toppled to the road but not before sending an errant orange shot into the earth as he fell.

John was reaching for more cylinders for his Colts as he glanced at Billy's dying form. He grimaced at the sight. He pushed it from his mind the best he could. He quickly loaded and leveled his pistols for more shots.

Thick clouds of cordite wafted above the troopers' heads. The sounds of men cussing and screaming merged with the sounds of angry gunshots.

The incessant and violent gunfire continued, but the fierce fusillade was dimming the courage and the spirits of the patrol and soon the survivors threw up their hands in surrender.

The gunshots subsided and soon the gray and butternut soldiers revealed themselves to the Union patrol. They emerged from the shadows with drawn weapons and hard-eyes.

John holstered his weapons and leaned down to check on Billy. He did not have to check long. He could tell by his glassy-lifeless eyes that he was dead. He straightened and took a deep breath. He did not weep for him or any other comrade because he would be crying all the time, but it did take a toll on him.

He turned his attention to the dead and wounded Union soldiers in the road and the downed horses. He caught the look of Captain Grover walking toward him through the carnage. The captain looked through the weeds to see the dead body of Billy Taylor.

The captain asked, "You all right?"

John nodded, "Yeah, I'm all right."

The captain looked more fully at the dead body of Billy Taylor. He shook his head in sadness and said, "You were fond of that lad."

"Yes, I was."

The captain nodded solemnly and took in air. "Where was he from?"

"Gainesville, Arkansas." John looked off and continued, "He

always bragged about it. Said he had family there. A father I think."

The captain did not linger. He walked away and began organizing his men and prisoners.

John turned and looked at the corpse of his dead comrade once more. He took in a lung of air and started walking toward the road.

He saw a wounded Union soldier being cradled in the arms of one of his comrades. The soldier's shoulder was bleeding. The man turned his pale, pained face toward John as he emerged from the shadows of the trees. The trooper knew instantly that this was the man who had inflicted so much damage on them all. He croaked out, "Who are you, soldier?"

John wordlessly knelt and examined the man's bloody shoulder and pulled out his handkerchief and gave it to his friend. The surprised trooper quickly pressed it to his bleeding comrade's wound. John examined the man's wound and satisfied it was not death-threatening raised himself to full height and answered," I am John Lee Johnson from Texas."

As he walked away, the wounded soldier with his hand pressed on the handkerchief, wanly turned his head and asked, "What did he say?"

His friend sighed and answered, "He said he was 'John Lee Johnson'." He paused and then his words lingered ominously. "He ain't from Texas, though. He is from Hell."

John walked through the mangled bodies of the wounded and dead to the front of the Union line. When he reached where the Union captain was he stopped when he heard him moan.

John leaned down on one knee and lifted the upper torso of the captain up and with his free hand took the top off his canteen and gave him a drink. The captain had blood rivulets running from each corner of his mouth. His eyes were glassy, but he could still speak. John poured water into his bloody mouth. The captain rinsed his mouth, and spat out the tainted water. He nodded that he would drink the next water. He swallowed the next offering and nodded his head when he finished. John lowered the canteen and placed to top back on.

"Who are you, soldier?"

"John Lee Johnson from Texas, sir." He quickly replied with military courtesy.

The captain was silent for a moment and continued, "I should have seen this coming. It was too quiet."

John said nothing. He peeled back some of the captain's military blouse and examined the wounds. It did not look good.

The captain caught the look of sadness in John's eyes. He realized he was dying and knew this was the best he could hope for in the situation. He asked, "I'm going to ask you a favor."

John looked into his eyes. He had heard death wishes before and it always perplexed him. Favors for a dying man were a solemn thing and was not to be taken lightly. He wanted to ease him back to the earth before he could speak, but seeing the desperation in his eyes he held him tightly and nodded his head. No matter how many times he had seen a dying man it still troubled him. "I'll do what I can, Captain."

The captain looked down at his pants pocket. "I have a pocket watch that I want you to give to my brother, Cyrus."

John caught the direction of the captain's eyes and reached down and pulled the watch out. He looked at it and back at the captain. "Where does Cyrus live?"

"In Ironton, Ohio."

John's eyes widened and he breathed in deeply. "Captain, I." But before he could say anything else the captain died in his arms.

John slowly lowered his body back to the road. He sighed and looked on the back of the watch and saw the words 'Judge Randolph Schofield'." He supposed that it was the captain's father or grandfather by the age of pocket watch.

He was still standing when a line of captured Union soldiers walked by him. One soldier, a burly sergeant, broke ranks and walked menacingly toward him. The Confederate corporal who was in charge of prisoners gave chase and was extending his hand to brusquely pull him back into the line when he caught John's eyes. The corporal merely licked his lips and dropped his hand. He returned to his detail and left the Union sergeant with John. The prisoners passed by curiously looking at the big Texan and the brawny Union soldier. The sergeant looked at the dead captain and then cast his suspicious eyes on John and the pocket watch he held in his hands.

"He was a good captain." He snapped unsmilingly.

John nodded," What was his name?"

"He was Captain Benjamin Schofield."

John sighed and looked at the watch. "He wanted me to deliver this to his brother, Cyrus."

The sergeant's eyes remained skeptical. "Are you going to do that?"

John shook his head as in indecisiveness. "Well, I ain't a thief if that's what you're thinking."

The sergeant then asked abruptly, "Then what are you?"

"I'm a soldier." He paused and looked into the sergeant's eyes fully. "Just like you are."

Corporal Blanchard returned and stood with John. "Is this man bothering you?"

John shook his head 'no'. "He just wanted justice for his captain."

When he heard John's words and the kindness in them. The sergeant's skeptical eyes softened. He dropped his head in thought and wiped a tear. He extended his hand. "Maybe I was wrong about you soldier."

John shook his hand and Corporal Blanchard trundled him off to the band of prisoners gathered near the trees.

Captain Grover, who was giving orders and being in all places at the same time, saw John mulling over the pocket watch. He walked up to him and nodded at the timepiece. "Was that the captain's watch?"

John nodded 'yes' and sighed audibly. "He asked me to deliver it to his brother." He looked over into the eyes of Captain Grover. "In Ironton, Ohio."

"How in the hell are you going to do that?"

"That I don't know."

The captain slapped him on the shoulder. "Well, it's like this, I know better than try and talk you out of it. You're too good of a man, but that will be one hell of a promise to keep."

John nodded soberly and pocketed the watch. He was walking toward the tree line when he saw Milton Sewell drive up in the now empty wagon. The prisoners were herded into it and he stood and watch them ride away. Another wagon appeared from the side road to pick up the remaining ones.

The Union sergeant, as he loaded himself in the wagon, waved at John. He felt he had judged the big Texan right. John nodded at him and watched him ride off

John observed Corporal Blanchard going through the pockets of the Union dead. He and one private were in charge of collecting money from the dead soldiers to give to the Confederate widows. But he would not be giving them the Union captain's pocket watch.

He next saw Billy being lifted up and taken away. He could see the locks of blonde hair through the weeds as the soldiers carried him away for burial. He twisted his lips in a grimace and reached down and picked up his canteen.

John was about to head for the remuda of horses when he heard the captain call to him from across the way. "John, you head for Savannah and get those submerged boats up. We'll be leaving for Mississippi in the morning and we need to cross the Tennessee River. I want you and two-squads to take care of it."

John acknowledged the order with a nod and started to turn when the captain called to him again. Wordlessly Captain Grover walked up to him. He looked him in the eyes and whacked him on the shoulder. "You're one damned good soldier." He paused and added, "But more importantly you're one damned good man."

John looked over to his left to see the dead Union captain being carted away. He turned back to look in his own captain's eyes. The terrible violence and the sense of responsibility began to weigh on him. "I try, Captain, I truly try."

John and the two-squads made their way across the open space toward the horses.

The captain stood watching them and then turned and cast his eyes in the direction of Henderson, Tennessee.

Corporal Blanchard came along side of him and saw where the captain's eyes were directed. "You worried about Captain Sullivan?"

He turned and looked into the corporal's eyes. "You damn right I am. Now mount up and let's head to Henderson and see what we can do to help."

John and the soldiers rode the rest of the day and made Savannah about sundown. They extricated the heavy boats from the water and drained them. They applied some tar to some cracks and made them shipshape to handle both men and horses.

They finally bedded down at midnight. John used his saddle as his pillow Texas style. Some of the others caught on and started using theirs too. He slept fitfully however. The loss of Billy Taylor at such a young age was troubling, but he had lost many comrades in battle. He was bothered by the inherent promise he made to the dying Union captain too. But it was as though something more ominous was in the air. He did not understand his premonition. He just knew he could not sleep. He wished he were back home in Texas.

He was awakened by a rooster crowing just before the sun came up. He sat up and threw back his blanket and started to the cook's wagon.

Fred Batson was the cook. He had an avuncular look: slim,

friendly and old with a bad haircut. He gave John and the others who were creeping through the light blue morning a metal plate filled with eggs and a hot cup of coffee.

John made his way back to his tree and sat down. He polished off the mound of eggs and drank the hot coffee greedily. He reached into his pocket and fished out a cheap cigar. As he was lighting it, his eyes moved to the uneven road and the mounted soldiers moving along it. It was the other patrol and they looked worse for the wear. He stood and began moving toward them to offer assistance. Others joined him in walking to meet their comrades.

Some were bent over their saddles. There were a number of empty saddles too. He could make out both Captain Grover and Sullivan. Both looked exhausted. It was apparent that there had been a mighty struggle and by the looks of the command it was hard to tell who came out on top.

Captain Sullivan handed his reins to John and with weary eyes and tired voice said, "It was one tough assignment. They were many and we were few. I wished a dozen times in the battle that you were there." The weary captain dismounted stiffly

John stood and watched Captain Sullivan move his gaunt body toward the mess wagon. He then turned and took the reins of Captain Grover's horse. The captain moved his leg wearily to the ground and then the other. He shook his head and said, "They drove the Federals back but he took a lick hisself."

"What happened?"

The captain pointed in the direction of Captain Sullivan. "The Federals had about three-times the men the one coming out of Lexington had.

"He jumped them and they jumped back. He managed to down enough of them to send them back to Jackson but they'll be headed out after him early." He paused and added, "And us."

John led both horses over to the hostler and handed him the reins. Ned, the hostler, shook his head. "These hosses are worn out. They must have rid all night."

John nodded, "They did, Ned. They had a hard time."

Ned sighed, "Well, General Buford is waiting across the river. We have to get these horses across soon but," he pointed at the jaded mounts covered in sweat foam, "These horses need two-days rest at least." He added thoughtfully, "I hope the Yankees leave us alone for awhile."

John nodded and walked back to his tree and sat down and took a heavy drag on his cigar. He was about to fall asleep again but through his sleepy lids he saw a strange sight that brought him alert again.

He saw two-troopers leading a mule with a scrawny kid aboard. The skinny bumpkin looked awfully familiar. He had squirrel-red hair and bony but broad shoulders. Then it hit him broadside. It was his cousin, Russell, from Baileysboro, Texas. John tossed his blanket aside and stood by the tree as they led the mule toward him.

The two-cavalrymen pulled the mule up to his tree and one of them leaned forward, "Howdy, John, we got us a man who claims he knows you."

The other trooper joined in. "This gomer was in Savannah asking about you and claimed he was your cousin."

John nodded and walked around to where Russell was. He looked up and down the sorry mule he was on and back at his half-starved cousin. "Russell, what in the hell are you doing here?"

The two-surprised troopers hearing these words released the mule and rode over to the hostler.

Russell slid down the mule and pulled the stubborn animal as he slowly followed John toward his tree. "We got trouble back in Texas, John."

John wanted to ask 'what?' but he could look at Russell's face and could see he had not had eaten anything in a spell. He had dark circles around his eyes and he looked faint.

He took the crude reins from Russell tied them to a low limb and picked up his metal plate and mug and led his starved cousin to the Batson food wagon.

After Russell had eaten a heaping plate of eggs and grits and had a piping hot cup of coffee, he sighed, sat down and leaned back against the tree and accepted eagerly a cigar from John.

John sat beside him tossing pieces of a stick on the ground and then asked, "Now what's going on in Texas?"

Russell sat silently for a while. It was obvious by his trembling lips and the quick intake and exhaling of breath that his message was bad. He finally composed himself and began talking, "My dad and yours were killed by a group of land swindlers called the Purvis brothers."

John sat stunned. The news hit him like a wood mall. He recalled his restless night. He frowned and tossed all the bits and pieces of stick he had in his hand. "What caused all this?"

"The Purvis brothers claimed that my dad and yours had paid their taxes in Confederate money. They were trying to evict them but when that didn't work, they killed them." He paused and said, "The Union now holds that part of Texas and they ain't giving it up." He tremulously continued. " They hold all the cards for now."

John took another drag off his cigar. He felt like crying and cussing but all he could do was sit in anguish. "When did all of this happen?"

Russell lit his cigar from a match proffered by John. "About four-months ago. Sheriff Nelson couldn't do nothing cause he is afraid of the Purvis brothers too."

John balefully stared straight ahead. He rose slowly with his eyes facing Texas. He usually remained silent when he was flummoxed by a situation. He cussed to himself. His eyes were slits of gray fire.

"What about Uncle Henry and Kiowa Bob?"

"The Purvis brothers bought out Uncle Henry's place and paid his taxes in Federal money and they chased Kiowa Bob off."

Russell sighed, "Uncle Henry ain't much of a fighter. He ain't in good health. I reckon he had no choice."

John knew that to be true. Uncle Henry stayed alive to take care of Russell and hold down the fort until he could get back. At least he hoped he was alive.

"Is Uncle Henry and Kiowa Bob alive?" He pointedly asked.

Russell nodded and picked up his plate and mug to go clean them. "Yes, when I left they were but not sure now."

Captain Grover, who was walking by, noticed the dour look on John's face. He stopped. He could tell that the skinny lad had brought bad news. He felt like he might be intruding, but he went over to the tree where John stood. John was staring at the horizon in a painful silence.

Captain Grover cleared his throat to announce his presence. "What is the matter, John?"

John exhaled through tight lips and turned toward the captain. "Some land swindlers killed my father and uncle."

The captain looked shocked. "What in the hell are you going to do about it?"

"I don't know yet, Captain." John looked deeply troubled. "I ain't sure about my army obligations."

Captain Grover's eyebrows arched. "You've served well beyond your enlistment, John. I ain't one to give advice, but if I was you, I would take my leave and go back to Texas."

John nodded and exhaled in relief. "I was hoping you would say that."

The captain looked at Russell as he approached with clean utensils. "Son, you go over to Ned and get yourself a decent horse and saddle and use that piece of," He paused and thought better of his words. "Well that mule for a pack animal."

As Russell headed for the hostler, the captain said loudly to his back. "And have the quartermaster give you a decent shirt and some boots."

He turned back to John. "You kill those sorry bastards, John."

John nodded, "I sure as hell will give it my best, Captain."

The captain stuck out his hand. "We'll miss you. Besides Forrest hisself, you're the best in our command."

"I'll miss you, Captain. There ain't many Captain Grover's in the world." He shook the captain's hand sadly. He had an idea it would be the last time. The captain had always been honest and most of all had been a true friend.

The captain nodded toward the west and said, "Well, all those preachers who never served don't know the hell we go through. The only way you can stand life is to drink and cuss and fornicate." He paused and shook his head. "There may be a better way but I ain't privy to it." He added, "And damn them polecats that would kill to steal. They deserve to die, John."

John nodded his approval at the captain's words. He looked at the river and the boats that were being loaded. He sadly said, "Looks like you have a river to cross, Captain."

Captain Grover turned and looked and then returned his gaze on John. "I've got a river to cross and so do you, so get to it, John."

He walked wordlessly away. John peered at the captain's back letting the moment pass through his chest. He looked at his comrades as they moved with purpose to the boats. He felt a sense of sadness. He had not only shared a lot of life and death and hellish battles with them, but they were the last hope of the Confederacy in the western theater. He knew it was a defining moment in his life.

His comrades looked back curiously at him too. They sensed something bad had happened. Today was a day of change. They were bothered that he was not joining them. His presence on the battlefield had always given them an edge. He had always given them a measure of confidence.

Corporal Blanchard eased up to the captain and asked him what was going on. The captain filled him in. The corporal whistled and said, "You know, Captain, I shore as hell would hate to be those damned land-grabbers."

The captain looked once more at the broad back of the Texan. "Them jaspers might not yet know it, but they might have just as well tried to give an enema to a brown bear." He paused. "They are dead men." With that said, he turned facing the other bank of the river. He knew the Yankees would be coming soon.

John brightened some seeing his cousin leading a dun horse with a Yankee saddle on it. He had on a brown-faded shirt and was smiling for the first time.

John went to retrieve his bay and after he saddled him and was about to put on the bridle when Fred Batson walked up and handed him a canvas bag replete with beans and hardtack.

"It ain't much but I heard from Captain Grover you're headed for Texas and want you to have something. We got some Yankee coffee but it has to last the boys." He then pointed to some of the men and horses being transported across the Tennessee River. Got to feed them boys." He smiled broadly, "But had to feed you too."

John thanked him and threw the canvas bag behind his saddle and he put the bridle on and mounted up. He and Russell rode north following the Tennessee River. John tried not to look at his comrades as he rode away but he caught sight of some of them with his peripheral vision. They seemed to be watching him.

They rode thirty-miles that day using the Tennessee River partly as a guide but later moved westward and past Parker's Crossroads. They were headed to Dyersburg, Tennessee and the ferry. Russell and John were making good use of their time except for the weary mule, which objected to the pace.

They camped that night among a small grove of trees that bordered a small stream. They tethered the horses and John started a campfire. He pulled out a skillet and put in some beans and they sat back against the trees and talked.

John pointed out that the mule was slow and asked Russell how much he paid for him.

"I paid four-dollars for that mule."

"Well, you paid four-dollars too much."

Russell nodded and said, "I probably did but he got me here."

"Well, he ain't hauling much. We ought to ditch him or sell him the first chance we get."

Russell did not say anything. But John could tell that remark bothered him some.

Russell was toying with a stick in his hand and looked over at the mule. "I've taken a liken' to that ole mule. I just hate to turn him loose. He'd die in no time or the wolves or coyotes would get him."

"There ain't any wolves in these parts and ain't never seen any coyotes around here neither, Russell."

Russell looked sad and John did not say anymore about it.

John handed him a plate of beans and a piece of hardtack. They ate silently for a small space of time and John kept noticing the sad countenance on Russell's face.

John realized that Russell had undoubtedly endured a great deal of inconveniences in order to reach him. He reasoned that even if the mule was more of a liability than an aid, he might as well just accept the fact that Russell was attached to him. He finished his beans and took Russell's plate to wash in the nearby gurgling stream.

He thought on his words and when he returned he looked at his sad cousin. He sighed and said, "You know, I have been studying on that mule. He might be useful after all."

Russell immediately brightened. He smiled and nodded and said, "I knew you'd come to your senses."

John turned to put the plates away in the provision sack. He rolled his eyes up some and then smiled to himself.

Later they were smoking cigars and drinking canteen water and lying back against the trunks of the trees. Russell looked over at his cousin and asked. "John?"

John turned toward him some and puffed on his smoke. "What?"

"How did you become like you are?"

John looked at him inquiringly and back at his cigar. "I don't follow you, Russell?"

"Well, everyone looks up to you and you ain't afraid of nothing and you're tough and you can fight and shoot." He paused as he took a drag off his smoke. "How did you get like that?"

"Well, let's get this straight. I'm afraid of some things. I don't like failure and not finishing a task. I don't like giving my word and not following through. When you give your word, it becomes an obligation."

Russell shook his head, "No, , I don't mean that. Them aren't real fears. I mean how did you learn to fight and shoot and things like that?

John shrugged and turned his eyes up to the stars. The firelight threw scintillating shadows over his face as he thought. "Well, when I was a kid, Kiowa Bob taught me about Indian moves and kicks. He used to beat the hell out of me. But I got better. When I got older I was takin' Kiowa Bob to the woodshed."

Russell smiled and said, "Kiowa Bob was pretty tough in the old days."

"He ain't bad now, Russell."

Russell digested John's words and then asked, "How did you learn to be so good with pistols?"

"That's an easy one. We had two-old gunmen who worked for us and they taught me about drawing and shooting and aiming damned straight. One was named 'Sid Jones.' He had a lightning draw and he taught me how to draw and to shoot.

The other one was named 'Jay Waters,' and he could knock a gnat off grits. I took the best of both of 'em and just applied it. They never liked each other but both liked me."

Russell smiled, "I remember both of those guys." His vision turned to the burning embers. "I reckon you've learned a lot more since being in the army."

John sighed and nodded, "Yeah, when I went off with John Bell Hood, I fought in Virginia for a spell and they had this wrestling champion there. "I wanted to wrestle him and he made me look like a pretzel." John laughed, "But I got better and got to where I could hold my own." John chuckled again and wiped his brow with a handkerchief. "But I never did beat him."

Russell seemed disappointed in that admission. "Did you ever fight anyone with fists in the army?

"You mean box?"

"Yeah, box."

"I fought some guy out of Nashville, Tennessee. He was a skilled pugilist as he called it. He used to work me over, but I got better and the last time we fought. I knocked him out."

Russell smiled at that one. "You see, John, that is why people like me look up to you."

"Why is that?"

"Cause you never start nothing but you sure can finish it."

John did not know how to respond to that so he said nothing.

Russell sighed, "I just ain't tough. I couldn't fight my way out of a paper bag."

John looked across at his cousin's profile. "I tell you what you can do and that is find the courage to ride miles across unknown states and territories to find me." He paused and continued. "And I'll tell you this, Russell, you're honest and kind and you ain't a liar and a cheat. You treat women well and critters well, and I am damn proud of you."

John let the words linger in the air and continued, "Paper bag or not."

Russell dropped his head in humility. "I guess it's late, cousin."

John added, "Yeah, it is and we got us a long ride tomorrow."

The next morning they had hardtack for breakfast and made their way across the rolling hills. They rode for half-a-day when the sky became like steel. Roiling gray clouds and grumbling thunder surrounded them.

John started to reach for his slicker but he remembered that

Russell did not have one. He knew if he offered it to Russell and he did not have one himself that his cousin would refuse to wear it. So, he left it in his war bag and just kept riding.

Russell looked up at the sky and grimaced. "John, it looks like it's going to come a gully-washer soon."

John looked up and remained silent. "Let's just ride and maybe we can come upon some shelter."

They rode another few miles when lightning sizzled across the sky like an electric- shattered branch. John frowned. He saw off to his left a soft dirt road and he turned his horse toward it.

They rode about a hundred yards and they saw an old house sitting in on the edge of a cotton field. It was unpainted and weatherworn brown. In places it had moss growing on the sideboards. Adjacent to the house, about 100 feet away, was an unpainted, rickety barn.

Sitting on the front porch of the house were three-people. Two were in cane-bottomed chairs: an old man wearing overalls and an old woman wearing a bonnet. The old man watched them warily and the old woman churned her butter wordlessly. The young boy was pale and unhealthy looking.

John and Russell rode up to the porch and John briefly doffed his hat at the woman. John looked up at the sky and then to the barn. "My name is John Lee Johnson. I'm from Texas. I've been fighting in the War and just wondered if we could stay in your barn till the lightning and rain stops."

The old man looked at John and then at Russell with discerning eyes. "You ride with Forrest?"

John not sure how to answer decided on honesty. "That I did."

He nodded his head 'yes' and then indicated by the tilt of his head for them to go ahead and camp there.

They rode to the barn and soon entered the cramped quarters. They dismounted and unsaddled their mounts and Russell found a rag and wiped down the horses and mule and stationed them in the rough-hewn stalls.

John fished out a cigar and walked to the barn entrance and looked up at the darkening sky and the first fat drops of rain. He stepped back and lit his smoke as he walked to one of the stalls and sat down with his back to a rough post.

They were making small talk and not saying anything of importance when they saw the small boy, who had been sitting on the porch, enter the barn with a rag on his head.

John said, "That ain't much of a rain hat you got on."

The boy smiled and pulled the rag off his head and said, "Yeah, but it's all I got."

John smiled and said, "That's good enough then."

The frail boy sat down next to John. He leaned back against a post. "You really a soldier?"

"Was a soldier."

"You look like a soldier."

John smiled and ignored the remark. "What's your name?"

"Zeke." He sighed and continued, "Zeke Fagan and that's my grandmother and grandfather you met on the porch."

John nodded, "That's a fine and graphic name."

Zeke shrugged and said, "I reckon."

John sat silently and took a good drag off his smoke. "How old are you, Zeke?"

The boy looked uncomfortably answering. "I'm twelve but look younger I know." He pointed to his chest. "I've got a bad heart and I ain't growed like I should have."

John did not give a response to that. He changed the subject. "You got a nice stand of cotton I noticed."

Zeke sighed, "Yeah, , I hate choppin' it though." He paused and shrugged his bony shoulders. "That comes later."

John nodded, "Bet you do at that." He added, "But at least you got cotton to chop."

Zeke stared at the ground and then his face tightened as he

looked back up at John. "I don't know how to ask you this but my grandparents have got a real problem."

"Oh, what kind of problem?"

Zeke's face screwed up some as he attempted courage. "You know how to use those guns?" His pale face was directed toward the Navy Colts at John's holsters.

John removed his cigar and spat a fleck toward the center of the barn. His eyes cut at Zeke. "Young fella, if you got a question, just ask it." John could see the indecision in the young boy's face. He softened his voice and asked, "Is it about your grandparents?"

"Yeah." He inhaled a breath of air and said, "We got this man down the road who steals from us all the time. He's took our mule and two of our hogs." He shrugged and said, "He's gonna starve us to death."

John sat thinking and looked back at Zeke. "Your grandpa got a gun?"

"He's got one but it ain't no good and he can't shoot."

John nodded his head in thinking. "And you want me to do something about this man?"

Zeke fished out a five-dollar gold piece. "If you get our livestock back, you can have this. My grandfather told me to give it to you."

Russell added in, "If we get your livestock back, he'll just steal it again."

Zeke did not know how to reply to that so he ignored Russell. "How about it, Mister?"

John looked uncomfortable. He was caught between feeling sorry for people he did not know and the mission he had facing him in Texas. He just stared ahead for a few minutes mulling over the situation. It was a long damn ways to Texas and they were just getting started. He did not relish those bastard Purvis brothers living on his father's ranch and claiming it as their own.

He started to say 'no,' but when he looked down at the painfully thin boy, he noticed that Zeke's fingernails had been bitten down to the quick. He observed that Zeke's shoes were worn-out and held together by tied rags and leather thongs. He knew that if he did not help the Fagan's that they would be even more destitute. He realized he could not say, 'no,' and live with himself. He figured those scurrilous Purvis brothers could wait another day or two.

He swallowed and looked at the rain pouring down and then over to Russell who was looking away. He recognized that Russell wanted no part in this matter.

Russell had endured the pain of the Purvis brothers and he wanted to get back. Russell understood the painful situation the Fagan's were in but he wanted it to be John's decision and not his. He figured John was going to give in and help the Fagan's. It was just his way. But he hoped it would be damn fast.

Russell heard John ask Zeke, "What's the name of the man who is stealing all your livestock?"

"Pig Patterson." The boy quickly responded.

John repeated the name, "Pig Patterson."

Zeke encouraged by John's demeanor continued, "He's sorry. He rides up and down the road and everyone is afraid of him. He bullies everyone and steals from everyone and no one is able to stop him."

John nodded, "He sounds like a bad hombre."

Zeke, who had never heard the term 'hombre' before, just shrugged and said again. "He's sorry is what he is." He paused and continued, "He shoots at houses when he's drunk. My granddad sometimes turns the kitchen table over and me and my grandparents hide behind it when he starts shootin.'"

"Where does this 'Pig Patterson' live?"

"Down the road about a half-mile."

John looked down at the five-dollar gold piece that Zeke still had clutched in his small hand. "You hang on to that and we'll see."

Zeke widened his eyes encouraged by the words. "You mean you'll help us?"

24

"I'd like to study on it some more, Zeke."

Zeke's bright eyes muted some when he heard him say that. "I sure hope you'll study right." His eyes tightened, "We need your help."

John looked at the steady rain and listened to it hit the top of the roof. He saw no reason to heighten the boy's anxiety when he was going to help him anyway. He leaned back and took a draw off his smoke and then nodded, "Okay, Zeke, when the rain lets up we'll go down to Pig's place and see what we can do."

Zeke stood up and his sickly eyes were animated. "I ain't supposed to run but I feel like runnin' to go tell my grandpa."

"You do no such thing, young fella, sit down until the rain lets up."

The rain lasted about another hour, Gradually the sun broke through and the air was cooler. Zeke lit out to tell his grandparents as fast as he could muster and then just as fast back.

They all stood and saddled their mounts and Russell let Zeke mount his mule. They found a bridle that would fit him and they all rode out the barn.

Henry Fagan, the old grandfather, was walking toward them, followed dutifully by his wife.

John watched the couple hobble toward him and he nodded at them.

Henry looked up at John. "I was hoping you'd help us. I kept that five-dollar gold piece and prayed every night that would God would hear us."

John inhaled a lung of air and nodded back at Henry Fagan. "I'm not sure I'm the answer to anybody's prayer, Mister Fagan. But maybe I can help." He was not sure the mule and pigs even equaled five-dollars, but he knew they needed his help.

Zeke pointed south and they rode away silently, Russell rode up beside John. "I ain't sure this is the smart thing to do."

John nodded his head in acknowledgement. "Yeah, but it's the right thing to do." He looked over his shoulder at the frail Zeke who was hanging on to the mule. "And right trumps smart every time."

The side ditches were filled dirty water and the road was muddy as they slogged along. The whole countryside was drenched. They rode until Zeke wordlessly pointed to a side road that went through a patch of weeds.

John turned his big bay onto the road and they went another quarter down the soggy path until he saw a small, unpainted house and a hog lot to the right about fifty-feet away and a mule tied to an oak tree.

Zeke whispered as if in fear. "That's our mule."

John rode up to the porch and looked over the sordid hovel. He looked over at the four-squealing hogs in the lot, and they looked like they had not been fed regularly. Since Pig had stolen their two-hogs, it appeared he had stolen some more.

Soon the door inched open and a large man eased through the door with a .44 in his hand. Pig was large and thick and his underwear top was streaked in grime. He had porcine features and a week of whisker stubble on his face. Pig's dark eyes were hooded by thick wooly-worm eyebrows. He, indeed, looked fearsome.

Russell gulped and grabbed hold of his saddle horn for support. His eyes went to his large cousin who seemed unfazed by it all.

Pig's voice grated on the ears when he asked, "Who in the hell are you?"

John thinly smiled and pointed to the mule. "I'm John Lee Johnson from Texas and I'm here to get a mule and two-hogs." He paused and looked at the hog lot to his right and added, "But since we're here, we will just take all 'em."

Pig tilted his head as though he had not heard correctly. He straightened his head and bulged out his chest when he said, "The hell you say."

John dismounted and said as he stood looking up at the man on the rotten porch. "The hell I do say."

Pig seemed puzzled by the actions of the stranger. He was used to being treated with extreme deference. "You and whose army?"

"You're looking at him."

Pig began a sneering smile. The whisker stubble parted to expose a series of nicotine-stained teeth. "Mister, do you know what in the hell you're doing."

" Yeah, I am talking to you, and frankly am tired of it. Get the damn mule, and gather the hogs, and do it now."

Russell looked at Zeke and Zeke looked back. There was fear in both sets of eyes.

Pig began a laugh of derision. "I've never broke a back of a Texan before."

John nodded and retorted. "I don't imagine you have ever broke anyone's back unless he was old or sick." He paused and added, "And you ain't going to break no Texan's back today."

Pig looked at the Navy Colts in John's holsters. He smiled his mirthless grin again. He leaned forward and placed his .44 on the soaked porch.

John looked at the weapon on the porch and up at the smiling Pig Patterson. He unbuckled his holster belts and looped them on his saddle horn.

Pig began the slow descent down the rotten steps. He placed his hands up and his fists looked liked hams. "I think I'm going to like this."

Pig was not as tall as John but his girth was more immense. He began to move forward menacingly. He shot out a quick jab that John deftly avoided. Pig jabbed several times and did not find his target. He frowned in his frustration and twisted his lips into a snarl.

John sent a hard left-jab that bloodied Pig's nose. Pig reached up and felt his bleeding nose and his porcine-like features hardened. "Mister, you better have a lot more than that."

John smiled and answered, "Oh I got a hell of a lot more than that, you sorry, pig-stealing bastard, and you are going to get every damn bit of it."

Pig waded in furiously. He was swinging wild roundhouses and hard jabs. John dodged most of them but he felt the force of the punches on his arms and shoulders when they did land. He backed up begrudgingly and let Pig continue his foray.

Russell was becoming concerned. Those hefty swings of Pig's were hard enough, if they landed, to drop an ox. Zeke was beginning to think he had made a mistake in asking for John's help.

John, who appeared to be in no hurry, eventually began to swing back and he landed several hard shots to Pig's body and the bully winced in pain.

Pig gulped air. He was becoming frustrated. He was beginning to develop a real need to kill the Texan. He began his wild offensive again. He fruitlessly charged several times, and tried to scoop John into his crushing arms, but every time he ran in, John punished him by hard meat-smacking punches to both his head and body.

Russell and Zeke's spirits brightened. John was hardly breaking a sweat and he looked like he was enjoying himself. Pig's left eye was beginning to swell and his nose was busted. His pride was wounded more than anything. He was determined to get back that confidence. He rushed, once more, but John calmly retreated hammering him with hard blows to the face and body.

Pig did manage to grab him by his shirt and hang on but was beaten severely for his efforts by hard raining blows from every angle. Pig endured the hard salvo and grabbed John in a bear hug. John could feel the strength of the man. He felt the hard squeeze, but he knew his opponent was desperate. John smiled grimly. He made the decision to end this silliness and get on back to Texas.

He angled his body and caught Pig between the legs and by doing so broke the hold and hoisted him up in the air, arms-length, above his head. He threw Pig like a bale of hay just inches from the steps of his porch. Pig landed heavily and all his confidence gone including his breath.

Russell looked at Zeke and gave a small grin. Zeke grinned widely back. Neither could believe the feat of strength they had just witnessed.

Pig sat up and moaned. He reached for his back, and his sheepish eyes moved up to John. "The mule is tied to tree, take the damn thing. I don't have Fagan's hogs. I ate 'em."

John shot a look at the hog lot to the right. "What about them?"

" I bought them from a Yankee patrol."

"You'll pay for the ones you stole and we'll take those just on general principles then."

"All I got is a dollar."

John said to Zeke over his shoulder. "How much is those hogs worth that he stole?"

Zeke said tremulously back. "They are worth two-dollars."

Pig gave a sneering look at Zeke. "You think you're smart now, but when he's gone what you gonna do?"

"I ain't gone yet." John quickly injected.

Pig looked up at John in pure hate. He began rising to his feet and reaching for his pocket. "Mind if I search for the dollar?"

Then John said, "Go ahead. We'll take that dollar and if you don't have any more. I reckon I'll take it out of your hide."

Pig rubbed his bloody face and sighed, "No, I've had enough."

Pig handed over the dollar and staggered a few feet and stood on shaky legs. "Just let me go check and see if I got anymore money."

John was watching him edge up the steps more groggily than he imagined him to be. He presaged Pig's next move. John reached for his Colt in the holster wrapped around the saddle horn.

Pig picked up the .44 on the porch and whirled quickly belying his girth. He was extending his hand with his finger on the trigger when he saw John's weapon spit orange and he felt a slug rip into his chest. His own weapon fired tearing up rotten splinters in the rotten porch. Pig collapsed and his eyes glassed over. His dying body fell down the wooden steps and lay in the wet weeds.

John walked over to Pig's corpse. The gun hand still extended from the dying bully. He removed the weapon and placed it in his canvas bag. He told Russell and Zeke to dismount and search the house for anything of value.

They inched up the steps with trepidation. Their eyes fixated on the dead man. They entered the hovel and John could hear them searching.

He hauled up the dead body and placed it over his shoulder and carried it to the pig lot. He tossed the body over the fence into the mud with a silky splatter.

The pigs, sensing the man was dead and since they were half-starved, started tearing into his body. They went into a feeding frenzy with loud squeals.

John started to his horse and untied the mule from the tree. He met Russell and Zeke coming down the steps. "Did ya'll find anything?"

Russell shook his head 'no.' "Just lots of whiskey jars and all of them empty."

John put on his holsters and mounted up. He sighed and straightened himself.

Zeke looked around and asked, "Where's Pig?" Then his eyes went to the milling and squealing pigs. He blanched and waited for Russell to lift him up to the mule.

Russell commented, "That might be some bacon you might want to avoid for awhile, Zeke."

When they got back to the Fagan's. Henry and his wife were sitting on the porch. Henry Fagan sat watching them lead in his stolen mule. John rode up to the porch and tossed him a dollar. "There's your hogs, Mister Fagan. You can't eat it but you can buy some more." He paused and forked his thumb over his shoulder toward Pig's place. "There's some pigs down the road that don't belong to anyone."

Henry's face's betrayed no emotion. He nodded and replied,

"I just know that you've helped us and a lot of other people as well. He was of the Devil's spawn."

His wife said shyly as she indicated with her wrinkled finger. "I got some vittles cooked up. We want you to eat with us."

John nodded and looked at Russell. "We could stand a good meal, Missus Fagan. Russell, here, is tired of my cooking."

They enjoyed a meal of corn bread, white beans, potatoes, and fried chicken and lots of spring water. Russell and John ate ravenously. They made some small talk about their trip to Texas and The Fagan's seemed interested in John's war effort and news of Forrest, but they were concerned about his travels home.

Henry turned his old eyes on John and said, "I know you're a man who can take care of himself, but be careful when you get near the Mississippi River. I had a nephew who was robbed and beaten there. And since the War, there ain't no law."

John nodded and thanked him for his advice. "I plan on being vigilant. And besides we ain't carrying enough to make it worth their while."

Henry stiffened momentarily and said, "I forgot myself." He slid across the five-dollar gold piece."

John shook his head 'no,' "You folks got to live too."

Henry said, "Please."

John looked up from his plate and caught the imploring look in the old man's eyes--a look begging for dignity.

John reluctantly dragged the coin across the table and put it in his pocket. He looked the old man in the eyes once more and simply said, "Thanks."

After the meal, John and Russell decided to spend the night in the Fagan's barn and so they adjourned themselves from the filling meal.

They made their way to the barn in the growing shadows and Russell took care of the animals. He unsaddled the horses and unloaded the small load from the mule. He both fed and watered them from the meager provisions of the barn.

They pulled out their bedrolls and used their saddles for pillow and lay smoking cigars. Russell seemed unusually taciturn.

John looked over at him and caught his features in the wan moonlight. "Anything wrong, Russell?"

Russell sighed, "When you killed Pig Patterson today, did it bother you?"

John studied for a spell and said, "No, he needed killing." He thought some more and continued. "At least I don't think it affected me but you never know."

Russell turned his head to try and read John's features, "What does that mean?"

John sighed and placed his hands behind his head as he concentrated. "During the War, I went with Longstreet to Tennessee and in a battle near Chattanooga, we had this sharpshooter from Elizabethtown, Kentucky, named 'Dewey Hoskins.' "

John took a drag off his smoke and exhaled. "During that battle, he shot thirty-one Union officers and soldiers." John turned to Russell to make his point. "These were legitimate kills too, not just some inflated figures. They were confirmed kills. He was decorated and cheered, told how great he was."

John turned his head back and looked up at the barn ceiling. "He seemed okay with it for a few days but he got to drinking and stopped talking and in a few days they found him wadded up in his blanket. He went crazy I guess."

Russell looked up at the barn ceiling too. "I can't see you doing any of that."

"Is that what you're worried about?" John paused, "How the killings are going to affect me?"

Russell answered, "No, I wasn't thinking of you at all. I was thinking about me."

John inquired, "How so?"

"Well, John, I've seen killing before; hell, I'm from Texas. I know that Pig Patterson fella needed killing too. But I know I've got to kill too and just wondered how I'm going to handle it."

John sighed and looked at his cigar. "Well, no one likes killing if he's got a lick of sense, but sometimes you've got no choice."

Russell inclined his head toward John again, "You think I can do it?"

John raised his eyebrows and exhaled. "Russell, we got a long ride and a sizeable chore ahead of us. "I would imagine, you'll be tested. If you are, I hope you can do it, because it could mean your life and mine."

Russell pulled his blanket up and lay for a long while with his eyes open. He knew that John had told the truth.

The next day at dawn, they pulled out from the Fagan's barn and made their way back down the wet farm road to the larger road and set their course to Dyersburg.

They rode all day and stopped to eat some hardtack and water their horses. They had made over thirty-five miles and John was pleased considering they were pulling the slow mule.

The spotted a grove of trees down by the river and made camp. Russell took care of the horses and mule and John made a fire and placed a skillet of beans on the fire.

They ate the beans and drank fresh canteen water. John went to his horse, which was tethered by the river, and pulled a holster and Navy Colt from his war bag.

He later handed it to Russell and said, "This is the area that Henry Fagan warned us about. I know for a fact that a lot of bad hombres prey on unsuspecting travelers around here."

Russell placed on the holster and checked the weapon. "Seems in good shape."

John nodded, "You keep it in good shape and it'll keep you in good shape."

John pulled his last two-cigars from his shirt pocket. "We got to get us some supplies soon and cigars are a must."

Russell accepted the cigar offered to him and dug for a match. "How much money do you have on you, John?"

John smiled, "Well, I don't have to pause and count it that is for damn sure." He looked over at Russell. We got about six-dollars."

Russell sighed, "Henry Fagan shore helped us out."

They sat and smoked and soon they let the fire dwindle and they bedded down. John was uneasy. He had lived on his instincts for so long, and his instincts were alerting him. It was like how a hen knows there is a fox somewhere out there. She cannot see him or hear but knows the fox is there.

He had heard tales about this area, and he knew that many men without character, cut loose by the War, were roaming the countryside robbing and killing to make a living.

John rolled and tossed and would sit up and listen. He heard one of the horses make an uneasy nicker. He knew horses did not normally make sounds at night unless their rest was interrupted.

He crawled from his blanket. He decided to bolster up his sleeping gear by placing a hat at the end and fluffing up the blanket to give the appearance of someone sleeping.

He looked at Russell but decided to let him sleep. He slipped behind the bole of the tree where he had all his provisions propped up. He waited and listened. He was about to think it was his imagination and over-anxiety when he heard the sound of weeds being swished against.

John pulled his Navy Colt from his holster and canted his head to aid in his hearing. He heard several sounds that convinced him that human predators were indeed sneaking up.

He swiveled around to see if anyone was coming up behind him. He heard nothing in that direction and ascertained they were moving in front of him. He hunkered down and leveled his pistol.

His eyes narrowed when he heard the scuff of a boot on rocks. He kept his eyes peeled on any moving shadows that might appear beneath the dark trees, which appeared almost as black as the night sky.

Presently he saw three silhouettes move forward. They were

spaced and he knew they were not bringing cigars and beans. He could make out that the man in the middle was taller and seemed to be the leader. They edged stealthily closer. They became emboldened and soon strode up to the edge of the campfire.

The dying embers betrayed the one in the middle's appearance. He had on a deacon's hat with an extreme-wide brim and a small crown. His face was wedge-shaped with a cruel mustache that surrounded his thin lips.

He hand moved up from his side brandishing a silver-plated .44. The skulker looked first to Russell and secondly to the bulky-shape of John's bedroll.

John stood from his sitting position and his voice broke the spell. "Howdy, Gents."

The one in the middle was startled and his eyes went to his left and right making sure his henchmen were in sight. He looked back at John and a greasy smile began to spread on his features.

"Howdy, Stranger, I am the Reverend Simon Finley and like old King Saul I'm looking for my lost sheep."

John nodded knowingly. "I think old King Saul was looking for his lost asses and I think you've found them."

Simon Finley dryly answered as he looked once more to his left and right. "I stand corrected. He was looking for his asses at that."

John's voice was definitely unfriendly as he countered, "It is mighty strange to see a reverend looking for animals in the night. That is usually reserved for sorry-ass bastards. They're the ones usually looking for people to kill and take their belongings." Simon's oily smile again surfaced, "You got us all wrong, Stranger, we was looking for some coffee and maybe some beans."

John answered, "We don't have any coffee and we don't have no more beans." He paused and said, "And besides you would find our coffee really bitter."

Simon nodded slowly as if in thought. His menacing voice droned, "But you might want to make a contribution." He paused and looked in the direction of the tethered horses. "We don't mind some horses and some solid coin."

John's anger was building. "Look, I know you're a thief and you know you're a thief. So, let's get down to it. Use those damned pistols or take off running. I ain't missing sleep over a two-bit thief." John paused and looked at the two-sinister men on opposite sides of Simon. "Or thieves."

Simon's smile disappeared. "I think you're right. I find you an obstinate bastard, Stranger." His smile returned, "As far as running, if you'll look," Simon made a dramatic turn of his head to the right and left. "You'll see there are three of us and one of you." Simon dropped his head in mock thought. He snapped his fingers as though he had received an epiphany. "Oh, yeah, sleeping beauty over there."

John stepped out from the tree. He had two-Colts in his hand.

Simon and his two-cronies bent forward to meet the challenge.

Before Simon could react, Russell rolled from his sleeping bag and his hand was filled with his Navy Colt. He fired a roaring shot that streaked orange a foot-long in the darkness. The man on Simon's left yelled like a woman. The pistol ball and hit him in the left-eye and his hat went sailing through the air.

Simon and his crony, momentarily stunned, raised their weapons to fire at Russell only to see that John's Navy Colts were bleaching the night air with yellow-orange deadly flames. Simon, hit high in the chest, staggered backwards and then took another shot in the groin. John nailed his companion in the forehead and his skull popped like a cantaloupe. Simon gurgled and fell on his back in the dark weeds just out of campfire glow.

John walked over to the dying Simon. "Looks like you picked the wrong damn camp to rob." He sneered the last word with relish, "Reverend."

Simon grimaced with the pain. "Who in the hell are you anyway?"

"I'm John Lee Johnson from Texas."

Simon gasped, "I need water." He sighed, "You got me good. Have mercy on me."

John nodded at him, "I intended to get you good. You're just taking a long damn time to die. You can ask Jesus for mercy cause you ain't getting none from me."

Simon's last breath was a ghastly death rattle.

Russell walked up to John with his pistol in his hand. John looked down at Russell's revolver. "You ain't gonna wad up in some blanket are you?"

Russell looked at his shaking hand. "No, reckon not." He looked more squarely at John. "What're we gonna do with these yahoos?"

"I'll tell you what we're gonna do. We're going to go through their pockets and get all the money they have and find their horses and sell them cheap."

Russell nodded and holstered his Colt. "What're we gonna do with their bodies?"

John shrugged and ignored the question.

"You need a hat, Russell." It was not a question but a statement. John reached down and picked up the Reverend's hat. "Here."

Russell looked at the hat and back up at John. "I always heard wearing a dead man's hat was bad luck."

"It is only bad for the dead man." John quipped, "I've got one myself."

Russell nodded and put on the deacon's hat. "Fair enough. We don't wear 'em like this in Texas, but we ain't in Texas."

The next morning they stacked the dead bodies like cord wood and Russell took Simon's boots and tried them on and liked them. They found ten-dollars hidden among the thieves' pockets.

John found the thieves' horses but they were substandard and were not worth selling so he took their saddles and bridles and placed them on Russell's mule and shushed away the confused horses.

Around nine-o'clock they mounted up and rode toward the Mississippi River. They came across a mercantile store about five-miles down the road.

They strode up to the porch and tethered their horses to the hitch rack and strode up the steps.

The owner of the store, Mister Lessing, was plump and bald and wore Ben Franklin-type glasses. He greeted them and then his eyes fell on the holstered twin-pistols of John. He became nervous but John assured him that he was no thief.

He gave a nervous laugh and began to fill their order. He placed beans and cigars and bacon on the counter. He reminded them he had no coffee. "The blockade has cut us off from coffee."

He looked a lot easier when John paid him the two-dollars due. He relaxed and looked John up and down. "You look like one of those men that have rode with Forrest." He looked around John and out through the door at John's bay and the Sharps rifle in the boot.

"I rode with Forrest and damn proud of it."

Mister Lessing remonstrated with both palms up. "Oh, I support the Cause. I was just wondering if you mean to cross the Mississippi."

John nodded, "We're headed for Texas."

Mister Lessing leaned in as if he were telling a secret. "Joel Starks, the owner of the ferry, he doesn't like Forrest and he is an avowed Unionist." He looked left and right, although there were no customers, and continued. "He'll refuse you if he thinks you're a Confederate."

"Well, I sure in hell don't plan on swimming the Mississippi River."

Mister Lessing smiled, "No, reckon you don't at that." His smile dissipated, "But his is the only ferry in these parts unless you go up to Illinois."

"I ain't going to Illinois either."

Mister Lessing stood arms akimbo and chewed on his lip. "I think you're going to have a problem."

John ignored his remark and asked him if he wanted to buy some used bridles and saddles.

Mister Lessing gave him two-dollars and they rode away even with the store.

They rode down a dirt road that had a sign that read 'Ferry' written in curlicue letters. They soon reached a shack near the levee. In front of the shack sat the dour Joel Starks in a cane bottom chair. Sitting on the ground were a number of seedy looking characters who worked for Starks.

John rode up in front of Joel Starks and indicated with the tilt of his head that he needed to go across. Joel, who was a thin middle-aged man, sat scowling up at him. "We don't take Rebels nowhere."

John sat for a moment and replied, "I'm through with the War. I need to get to Texas. And I need to get there fast."

Joel leaned forward in his chair and spat some tobacco juice in front of John's horse in a display of disdain. "I don't guess you Rebels hear real good. I said I don't take Rebels nowhere."

John dismounted and walked to the spot where the glob of tobacco juice wetly lay. His eyes looked down and then back up at the narrowed eyes of Joel Starks. "You'll take me across."

Amused sarcasm filled the face of Joel Starks. "Now why in the hell would I do that?"

John looked over the rough looking characters watching him with mild amusement. He let his eyes stay on them for a moment and then back at Joel Starks. "Cause I will beat the hell out of you and all these no accounts if you don't."

"You hear that, boys, he says he'll 'beat the hell out of all you no accounts.' "

Several got to their feet right away, and others feeling that the ones standing were enough took their time. They figured the big man was full of hot air. They grabbed some clubs and began moving forward. Their uniform of the day was stained underwear tops and whisker stubble.

John did not wait for them to get to him. He pole axed the first one with a hammering jab and sent him sprawling. He grabbed the next two and banged their heads together. He started chasing the next one but he threw down his club and ran. The others backed up, and just stared maliciously at him but made no move toward him. They came to the conclusion very quickly that he was not full of hot air.

John turned to Joel Starks. "You're next, you Yankee loving bastard."

Joel Starks' cheek was filled with a cud of tobacco. His eyes were wide and filled with fear. "Now hold on. You say you're out of the War?"

"That's what I said the first time."

Joel shrugged and said, "I guess I didn't hear that part."

John made no reply. "I'll pay the proper fee. I just need to get across."

Joel Starks stood and motioned for his men. "Hell, let's get this Texan home. He's out of the War."

John paid him three-dollars and soon he was leading his horse aboard a sizeable ferry. Russell rode up the gangplank and pulled his slow mule.

The men gave John a wide berth. They looked at him out of the corner of their eyes but it no longer was malicious but a healthy respect.

They poled a fourth of the way. And then a side paddle kicked in and they began to move more quickly. Joel Starks was at the helm. He stared straight across the river and never once glanced down at the big Texan.

One of his men, the one who received the first-punch moved closer to John and tried to make small talk. He said, "This is the most narrow place on the river till you get up to Illinois".

John nodded but made no reply. He was not interested in being friendly or making conversations with turds.

They landed and they dropped the gate and John and Russell rode up the gangplank and into Missouri.

Russell chuckled when they were out of eyesight and hearing. "They shore changed their way of thinking."

John merely nodded, "Yeah, it's funny how that works."

They rode through the flatlands of the Mississippi delta and saw lots of marshland and felt the bite of many mosquitoes. Dark brooding cypress trees sat in pooling green-foamy water. They rode on any passable road they could find and soon in a day's ride found some sandy loam. There were enough dry-bed roads to make their way toward Honersville, Missouri.

However, they did not reach their destination that day. They spent the night building a fire and cussing mosquitoes, but bright and early the next morning, they were on their journey again. They reached Honersville about noon, and as they were moving down the road they saw a strange sight.

In a yard off to the left they saw a ramshackle house and a grove of mulberry trees. In one of the mulberry trees was a man holding on for dear life. At the foot of the tree was an attractive woman shaking her fists at him and screaming and squalling in a high-toned manner.

John stopped his big bay and turned his body to see better what was transpiring. He looked at Russell quizzically and Russell looked back shaking his head as to agree.

John turned his bay toward the scene and he and Russell rode toward the woman. She ignored John and Russell for a long time and continued her tirade against her husband who was cringing at the top.

John interrupted her caterwauling with a question. "Ma'am, what's going on here?"

She flipped a few hairs out of her face and tossed them back over her head. She turned reluctantly to the two-strangers and said, "My man's seein' another woman."

"I ain't neither," the husband shouted down.

The woman ignored his answer and turned more fully to John and Russell. "He sneaks down to Mavis Jackson's house and diddles her when he thinks I am busy."

"I went down there to eat, Roberta Jean. You can't cook."

"I can cook, you liar."

He shook his head violently from the top of the mulberry tree. "I ain't messing with Mavis Jackson. She just can cook and I was starvin'."

"You just come down out of that mulberry tree. I'm gonna whop the tar out of you, you sorry ass."

"Now don't start cussin', Roberta Jean, the kids are listenin'."

John and Russell's eyes immediately went to the porch of the shack and saw three-tow headed kids watching intently. They were not crying and apparently had seen scenes like this before.

John looked up in the top of the tree. "What's your name?"

"LukeyDean."

John nodded and said the name "LukeyDean" aloud to himself and looked over at Russell who was shrugging again. John turned his attention to LukeyDean. "Why don't you come down from that mulberry tree and take your beatin' like a man."

LukeyDean's eyes grew wide in disbelief. "Are you kiddin' me? She'll beat the daylights out of me."

Roberta Jean ran her fingers through her light-brown hair and exhaled loudly. She looked up at John and Russell and said, "If you help me get him down, I'll fix you a plate of beans and potatoes."

LukeyDean shouted down at them. "Don't do it. She can't cook."

Roberta Jean started crying. "He's sorry and mom told me he was no account, but he's my man sorry or not. He's just got wandering eyes is all."

"I ain't got no wanderin' eyes, Roberta Jean."

"I loved you then and I love you now, and I ain't diddlin' Mavis Jackson."

"You promise, LukeyDean?"

"I promise, Roberta Jean. I love you and love you only."

She dropped to her knees in the soft sand and began weeping. "I love you too, LuckeyDean."

John rolled his eyes and shook his head. "Why don't you get down from that blamed mulberry tree and be a man about it."

"Mister, you don't know her like me. She's still gonna beat me and I really don't like being beaten."

John looked down at the forlorn woman crying on her knees. He looked back up in the tree. He said to Roberta Jean while his eyes stayed glued to the quaking LukeyDean. "Those beans and potatoes still go if we get him down?"

She stopped heaving for a moment and looked up at John and nodded her tousled head.

John reached down and pulled out his Colt. The hard ratcheting of it being cocked caught LukeyDean's ears.

"I'm coming down, Mister, I'm coming down. Hell yes, I'm coming down."

LukeyDean shucked down that tree like it was afire. He stood in front of Roberta Jean and she jumped from the ground like a panther and began pummeling him on the shoulder and head.

LukeyDean, while hunkered over and receiving the raining blows looked up at John and said, "See, , I told you."

She gave him a tailing kick as both started walking toward the house.

John and Russell were invited in and sat down while she finished cooking the beans. The house was definitely in need of serious repairs. The door was barely on the hinges and the windows had burlap bags to keep the flies out. The chairs had missing spokes in the back and the table had one-leg shorter than the others.

After the introductions were made and they sat talking, John's eyes moved over each family member. He watched covertly as

Roberta Jean set the table. She had an intelligent face, and when her bullet-headed husband made a stupid remark, which he did quite often, she would shake her head either in disgust or to clear the slate for the next idiotic statement.

She had a youthful face and figure and he knew she could not be too old, but he sure was not going to ask how old. He wondered how a woman like that could have ended up with her such melon-headed husband.

The oldest child, Mary Kate, who was nine, had pretty blonde hair and very alert blue-eyes. He noticed when her father said something ignorant, as he was apt to do and quite often, she would either look to her mother in a form of embarrassment or she would stoically sit and avert her eyes from her father as to shush away his awkwardness.

The second-girl, Romelle, was eight, had blonde hair like her sister and had equally alert brown eyes. She would look at her father when he spoke, and when she heard something silly or stupid she would drop her head and break into a wide grin.

The boy, TobyDean, was six, and like his sisters had blonde hair. His blue eyes were intelligent and bright but he lacked the discernment of his siblings. His attention was focused on John and Russell and his eyes would move from one to the other.

LukeyDean was constantly talking and telling his 'big' plans for the future. His eyes moved back and forth to Russell and John and occasionally to his wife.

John shut him out mentally and just focused on the meal that was being placed in front of him. The 'shucky' beans were not cooked well and the potatoes were burned entirely too much. The cornbread had no constituency and would crumble at the first pressure of hand or mouth.

Apparently Roberta Jean had never heard of seasoning or she did not have it.

They all ate silently and without complaint. LukeyDean's eyes were darting to his two-new acquaintances to see if they were registering any form of offense. When they worked their way through the half-cooked beans and the burnt potatoes, and did not complain, LukeyDean did likewise.

Later they made their way to the porch and sat down. The four adults took the major spacing and the kids stood behind them and just stood and listened as the 'big folks' talked. John made it a point to sit as far from LukeyDean as possible. He figured if he were talking to LukeyDean and a stranger walked by, the stranger might not know who the fool was.

LukeyDean looked down at John sitting on the far left and said, "I wouldn't mind one of them cigars you have your pocket there, John. I'm sure you would not mind sharing an after-dinner smoke."

John sadly but wordlessly pulled a cigar out and handed it to Russell to hand to the great philosopher.

LukeyDean leaned forward after receiving the cigar and looked down at John and asked, "Where did you get this cigar?"

John said in a bored monotone. "Tennessee."

LukeyDean held up the cigar and inspected it and looked to his wife who was reaching for a match. "Tennessee, gosh, someday I'd like to go there."

Russell looked at John out of the corner of his eyes and John looked back. They both figured Tennessee was about twenty-five or thirty miles away. They would have made it to Honersville the first day but had gotten lost in all the swamps and trees.

Roberta Jean torched LukeyDean's cigar, and he puffed contentedly. "Yessiree, now this is one fine cigar. I aim to go to Tennessee someday and see all those fine horses and dogs they got over there."

He looked boldly at Russell and John. "Now someday I'm going to build this place up and clean it up and make a money maker out of this forty acres."

John noticed the Johnson grass and weeds were just one foot from where LukeyDean was sitting but he made no comment. "I'm a fierce worker once I get up and get going, Roberta Jean will tell you that."

He looked at Roberta Jean and asked, "Ain't I, hun?"

She shook her head in the affirmative and exhaled.

John noticed Mary Kate suppress a half way smile and place her hands on her mother's shoulders.

LukeyDean extended his hand with the cigar in it and extolled. "Once I get on my feet I aim to go to Paris, Italy and look around and see some things."

Russell interrupted and said, "I think you mean, Paris, France, LukeyDean."

LukeyDean ignored the correction and kept on talking. Mary Kate smiled but when she caught John noticing her smiling, she dropped her head and looked off rather than betray the fact that she knew her father was a windbag.

John, who could take little more and the fact that it was pushing two-o'clock, stood and asked LukeyDean where his water pump and trough were.

LukeyDean pointed to a cluster of trees about an eighth-mile away. "I put the pump over there to get it away from the toilet."

He turned abruptly to Roberta Jean and asked, "Why don't you help him lead his horses down there and let me sit and talk to Russell." LukeyDean took a heavy drag off his cigar and looked at it in his hands. "All the way from Tennessee, I do declare."

John noticed the quick smile on Mary Kate's face and this time she looked square at John and smiled larger. She figured if he were leaving it was all right to reveal the knowledge that her father was a moron.

John smiled back at Mary Kate to let her know he knew her father was a moron too. He led his bay and Russell's horse and Roberta Jean took the mule and they walked side-by-side toward the pump.

Roberta Jean sighed and looked up at John. "You got a woman?"

He cut his eyes at her and shook his head 'no.' "War, I'm afraid makes widows out of wives and makes girlfriends lonely or with short memories."

She gave a soft laugh. She looked up him and said, "You know you ain't a bad looking man even without a bath and shave."

He smiled but hardly knew how to respond to that so he did not.

She looked straight ahead when she stated, "I sure do envy you ridin' off and just goin' down the road."

He looked at her and asked, "Why do you envy that?"

She let the words move out of her mouth slowly and apparently with much thought behind them. "You can just go down the road and see new things and experience new things. You're movin' and doin' and livin.'

John caught the sadness in her voice. He looked down at her and thought twice about asking but he did anyway. "Is it tough, Roberta Jean?"

Her eyes moved up to his with a certain understanding. She knew he knew her life was limited. "John, sometimes at night when it rains or I can hear the wind moan goin' through the trees or blowin' under the house, I just get so lonesome."

When he did not answer, she continued, "It's like my youth is goin' away on invisible winds and all those dreams I used to have are disappearin.'

He sighed and looked at her. Her eyes met his and she made a half way effort to smile. "I guess you think I'm silly and probably silly for marryin' LukeyDean."

"No, I don't think you're silly at all."

She studied his face and then smiled a sad smile. "You do think I'm silly for marrying LukeyDean."

He shook his head and said, "I can't go around making judgments like that."

She looked straight ahead and started talking. "I was a doctor's daughter. My dad had Honersville and part of Arkansas on his circuit. I used to go with him and help him out. When I was fifteen, I got boy crazy and met LukeyDean at a dance.

"We started kissin' and I did not want to stop and he didn't either and I ended up in the family way. My mom told me to just have the baby and not put up with LukeyDean. But my dad told me he didn't want a bastard for a grandchild."

He looked down at her and said, "Roberta Jean, why are you telling me all of this?"

She shrugged and shook her head. She looked away but he could tell she was wiping a tear. She walked a bit farther and said, "I guess I just wanted to tell you because I like you and I needed to tell someone."

She sniffed some and looked straight ahead. "When I was fixin' those bad beans, I noticed you lookin' around with those solemn gray eyes and was wonderin' what you were thinking. I had a pretty good idea."

She smiled and looked up at him and said, "You think LukeyDean is not too smart and I'm smart and you're wonderin' why I put up with him?"

He did not reply to that. She looked at him with the saddest eyes he had seen in any battlefield.

"John, I just don't want to end up in some church cemetery with a cheap wooden cross and my name on it --and the whole thing covered in bird droppins--and to have existed and never lived."

He inhaled air and exhaled deeply but did not give her a reply but her words stayed with him.

John and Roberta Jean were at the trough and they watered the animals wordlessly. As they turned to go back to the porch, the horses blocked their view from the house. John took Roberta Jean's hand and placed a gold dollar in it. His hand covered hers for as long as he could without drawing attention from the porch. It was like one human reaching out to another human. He could not cure her loneliness, but he sure in hell could show her it mattered to another person.

They both walked the animals back to the porch. Russell was bored and looking at John with 'let's get out of here' eyes. John caught the exaggerated smile of LukeyDean and his son, TobyDean. He figured if the son wanted to know how to grow up and be a windbag, he was learning from the master.

Romelle smiled at him and waved a sad one-finger-at-a-time goodbye. Mary Kate did not smile---she looked at her mother and ran to her and they both dabbed tears.

John and Russell saddled up and pulled the reins around, and he and Russell made their way back to the road.

As they rode along, Russell asked, "Why did Mary Kate cry when we left?"

John simply said, "She knows things."

Back in Texas, Bill Purvis was sitting in the Texas State Saloon with his brother Michael. Bill Purvis was a very muscular individual with broad shoulders and thick arms. He had honey-brown hair and blue eyes. His face was rounded and pudgy. He was in his middle-thirties. He wore a wide brim white hat with a tall crown. He wore a black vest over a light-blue shirt and around his waist was a black gun belt bordered in white leather stitching. The .44 had white grips and he kept five-rounds in it at all times.

His brother Michael was a handsome man with an ever- ready smile. He had a dainty almost feminine face. He was short in stature but was well built like his brother. He wore a black hat with shorter brim than was the custom. He was the gunman of the two and was not shy about using his .44 when called upon. Or not called upon. The smile on his face was an insolent smile. It was the smile of someone who was overly proud. It was that smile that infuriated most who did not like him and that number was large.

Bill Purvis was sitting tossing poker chips idly while listening to the rinky-dink piano in the background. His eyes roamed over the few patrons in the room, and then over to Henry Johnson who was tending bar. His eyes lingered there and narrowed and then he cut them to Michael who was observing him.

Michael's eyebrows arched up as he asked, "What's been eating at you lately?"

Bill Purvis plinked a poker chip on top of another one and then said, "Have you ever heard of a man named John Lee Johnson?"

Michael squinted his eyes in thought and tilted his head as to assist in memory. "No, don't reckon I have." His eyes suddenly filled with recognition. "Is he a Johnson that is kin to the Johnson's we evicted?" After saying the word, 'evicted' he gave a leering grin.

Bill Purvis tossed another chip onto the pile in front of him. "He is the only son of Ed Johnson."

Michael shook his head negatively and shrugged. "Well, I've never heard of him." He reached for his schooner of beer and drank a gulp and then let his eyes return to his brother. "What about him?"

Bill Purvis sighed and let his eyes fall again on Henry Johnson who was talking to a cowhand at the bar. "I heard he was a bad hombre and that Russell Johnson had left to get him."

Michael gave that insouciant smile and laughed, "Where did you hear such a thing?"

Bill Purvis tossed another chip and pursed his lips. "Kiowa Bob was in town the other day and got lit up and was bragging to Ferlin Henderson over at the mercantile store that Russell had taken off to Tennessee to get his cousin."

"Does that really matter?"

"Well, I talked to Charley Danton, (the tax assessor and trustee of Bailey County), and he told me that this John Lee Johnson was hell on wheels. He told me enough that it definitely concerned me."

Michael hooted and dropped his beer mug firmly on the counter. "Charley Danton is scared of his own shadow and besides this John Lee Johnson is just one-man. Russell is just a silly-ass kid and he isn't a threat."

Bill nodded and said, "You're probably right." His eyes returned to Henry Johnson, Ed and Roy Johnson's brother. "But I just like to make sure."

Bill caught Henry's eyes and motioned with his mug that he wanted another beer. Henry nodded and soon presented a fresh beer in front of Bill Purvis.

Bill looked up into the eyes of the florid-faced Henry Johnson. "I haven't seen your nephew in town lately."

Henry features betrayed nothing as he shrugged. "If you're talking about Russell, he's gone to Galveston to get a job."

Bill leaned forward and his voice had an edge on it. "Wonder if I told you that Kiowa Bob told Ferlin Henderson that Russell had gone to fetch his hell-fire cousin to come home and avenge his dead father and uncle."

Henry straightened and fought both anger and fear. He was angry, that Kiowa Bob had let slip a confidential secret. He knew that his own life was hanging by a thin thread. And that he sure as hell had better choose his words carefully.

He stood there surrounded by the gay notes of the rinky-dink piano and the unrelenting stare of Bill Purvis. "I would say that it's the words of a drunk half-breed." Henry tried to keep his composure and his dignity but he was seething inside. He shrugged and lied, "Besides his cousin is in Virginia."

Bill nodded wordlessly and Michael kept his sarcastic smile plastered on his smug face. Henry looked down at the beer and asked, "Is that all?"

Bill looked at the beer and back up at Henry. "No, that's not all." He pointed a gloved finger up at Henry and said accusingly, "I put your two-brothers in the ground because they couldn't obey the law. I let you live because you had the good sense to sell out."

Henry's blood pressure soared and he inwardly glowered but his face never changed expressions. He knew and everyone else knew that his two-brothers were killed for their ranches and that issue of paying their taxes in Confederate money was a reprehensible ploy used by the Purvis brothers and their amoral uncle, Colonel John Purvis.

Bill's face became more severe as he kept the gloved finger pointing up at him. "If you're lying to me about Russell going to Galveston, I'll kill you so fast that your head will spin."

Henry nodded and turned and walked away. He went to the bar and positioned himself there and feverishly wiped glasses and mugs. He never allowed his eyes to move up and catch the glaring eyes of the Purvis brothers. Michael curiously looked over at his brooding brother. "What are you thinking?"

Bill's expression softened some and he tossed the remaining poker chips into the pile before him. "I think if there's something to all of this, he'll go find Kiowa Bob. He probably will want to wring his neck." He then paused and turned his hands up and looked at Michael. "If there's nothing to it, he'll go to his rooming house and just cower there."

Michael nodded and smiled, "How about if I put 'All-Night' Roy on his tail and see what happens?"

Bill stood and smiled. "Now you're thinking, brother."

Henry Johnson watched as the two-brothers exited. He had presaged that they would be watching him, but he did, indeed, want to strangle Kiowa Bob for divulging his plan.

He was standing and barely wiping out the beer mugs when Otis Quigley, the owner, came up and patted him on the shoulder. Otis knew that Bill Purvis had put the fear of God into Henry. He could tell by his shaking hands and florid face.

"Henry, if you need to go, I'll pull your shift."

Henry looked over at his boss and appreciated the kind eyes. "I don't have any place to go, Otis."

Otis took his eyes off his friend and let them go to the batwings, which were through swinging with the departure of the Purvis brothers. "I miss the old days and wish for better days."

Henry nodded wordlessly. He did not want to say too much. The Rocking P cowhands were dotting the room. He sighed and listened to the piano as it cranked out one happy song after another in an unhappy setting. He decided to work till midnight and then slip down to Chili's and get his horse and pay Kiowa Bob a visit.

Two hours later, Bill and Michael Purvis rode into the old ranch that had once belonged to Ed Johnson. It was the headquarters of the burgeoning Purvis Empire.

Bill gave his horse to the hulking Monk Danielson, his powerful personal guard. Michael tied his mount to the hitch and they moved up the steps into the ranch house.

Bill stopped his brother with the back of his hand before they entered the living room. "Go get Harley and Slade Rawlins. Tell them to go and shadow Kiowa Bob. I want you to discover what 'All-Night' Roy found out by following Henry Johnson."

Michael asked, "You really worried about this John Lee Johnson?"

"Little brother, we didn't get this far without looking at the little things. I would like to know more about this John Lee Johnson for sure. I just don't want to look over my shoulder later on and say 'if I had just done this or that.'"

It was midnight, when Henry Johnson placed his apron on the surface of the bar and nodded 'goodnight' to Otis and left the back way. He proceeded behind the saloon building and with the intent to make it to Chili Thomas' livery stable. He knew he might be followed, but it was late, and he did not want to go to his boarding room for the night. He was too keyed up and he knew he might be prone to mistakes, but he head-strongly headed to his friend's business.

As he paused to let his eyes adjust to the darkness, he heard a distinct 'pssst' noise of someone beckoning him. He turned warily toward the dark alley running between the saloon and Purvis' Mercantile Store. He hesitated between briskly walking away or confronting the source of interest. He swallowed and moved stealthily to the shadows.

When he walked into the heavy darkness, a hand grasped his

shirt and yanked him into one of the recesses of a side door. He was nose to nose with Sheriff Nelson.

The sheriff placed one-finger up against his lips to indicate silence and whispered. "'All-Night' Roy is down at Chili Thomas' place. Henry, don't you have any sense at all?"

Henry looked downcast and nodded. "I guess I don't have any sense, Sheriff."

Sheriff Nelson said, "I heard that Kiowa Bob had been spouting off about Russell going after John."

Henry nodded glumly. "I need to shut him up, I reckon."

Sheriff Nelson shook his head 'no' and whispered. "Too late for that Henry, the cat's out of the bag."

"What am I going to do?"

The sheriff looked both ways down the darkened alley and then leaned in closer. "Look, send Kiowa Bob to me and I'll arrest him for something. After you hear I have arrested him, you hide a horse in that arroyo that is behind the jailhouse. Put some money in a saddlebag and a rifle. We'll save his life and send him to warn John and make up for his big mouth."

His hands tightened on Henry's shirt. "Now go to your room, and don't get yourself and Chili killed. Hell, don't you know they are watching you?"

The sheriff slithered down the alley and Henry caught his breath. His eyes moved to the right and left and he moved cautiously out and back toward the saloon and toward his boarding room.

Meanwhile, Kiowa Bob was making himself ready for bed. He removed his boots and was leaning toward the candle to blow it out in his crude-adobe hovel. As his lips pursed to direct his breath, he heard a boot scrape on the rocks he had placed around his peach tree.

His eyes narrowed and he grabbed his knife and then he blew out the light and moved to the wall and waited for further noises.

Kiowa Bob's attention was then placed on the backdoor as he heard someone try the latch. He lifted his knife by the tip and was ready to throw it when he heard his name being called. He swallowed and then lowered the knife and went to the door.

"Who is it?"

"It's me, Harley Rawlins."

Kiowa Bob's face changed into a puzzled look but he opened the latch and allowed the burly Harley and Slade into his place. Kiowa Bob relit his candle and he indicated for them to sit on the boxes he had around the room for chairs.

He looked at them suspiciously in the yellow candlelight. "Why are you here?"

Harley pushed his hat brim up revealing a sweat-beaded forehead. "I think we're supposed to watch you or kill you whatever suits us."

Kiowa Bob's hand immediately dropped to his knife now in his belt.

"Now hold on, Kiowa Bob." Harley held up the palms of his hands. "If I wanted to kill you, I could have when you went to the privy ten-minutes ago."

Kiowa Bob's hand moved from the knife. His eyes went from Slade to Harley. "You're Ned Rawlins' boys."

Harley nodded. "Look, you shot off your mouth about Russell going to get John Johnson and all hell has broke loose."

Kiowa Bob dropped his eyes in a shame. "I did do that." But his eyes moved back up in alacrity as he asked, "But why would you care?"

Harley leaned in closer and he indicated for Slade to go back outside and make sure no one else was around to eavesdrop. When Slade eased out the door and could be heard out the window, Harley began to speak. "Ed Johnson paid payments on our ranch for us when my dad was snake bit. He made three-payments that my dad was never able to pay back. I ain't worth a damn, but I ain't an ingrate either."

Kiowa Bob nodded, "Your dad was a good man. He was

honest, and if he couldn't pay Ed Johnson back, I'm sure he told him why."

"That's neither here nor there with me and Slade. I ain't gonna kill you and I ain't goin' to beat you up."

"The Purvis brothers want me dead?"

"They don't at the moment but that might change."

"Kiowa Bob nodded and asked, "Why do they want to beat me up?"

"Because you are friends with the Johnson's."

Kiowa Bob nodded solemnly. "Bill Purvis is a bad man."

"Michael ain't good." Harley rejoined.

"What are you goin' to tell Bill Purvis?"

"I'm goin' to have to hit you and leave a bruise on you, Kiowa Bob." He sighed and continued, "I'll tell him I beat the hell out of you."

Kiowa Bob shrugged, "That ain't so bad."

"It'll buy you some time and keep him off my back about killing you maybe."

Kiowa Bob leaned forward and said, "Hit me on the cheekbone and it'll leave a bad bruise and won't hurt my vision."

Harley socked Kiowa Bob and sent him sprawling. Kiowa Bob grabbed his cheekbone. "I'm glad you weren't really sore at me that hurt like hell."

Harley nodded and grinned. "You spread the word that we worked you over. Like I said it might buy you some time to live."

Harley bade him goodnight and he and Slade mounted up and left.

# CHAPTER TWO

━━━━◆●◆━━━━

It was near sundown when John and Russell made it to the St. Francis River. They crossed the wooden bridge that led to Gainesville, Arkansas.

Russell looked at the flat cotton land and the green water of the river. "Looks like Texas except there ain't any mesquite trees."

John smiled, "We have a long ways to go before we get to Texas, Russell."

Russell nodded, "Yeah, that is a fact, a pure gospel fact." He looked over at his cousin and asked, "I reckon we got a good reason for stopping in Gainesville, Arkansas."

John nodded grimly. "I got to deliver some bad news, Russell."

Russell did not reply to that. He figured it was a death notification but that was something that he did not want to dwell on. He thought he would try a small hand at jocularity. "That LukeyDean and that mulberry tree. Lands, no one will ever believe me."

John smiled, "Yeah, he was a sight all right."

"It is amazing how much ignorance a man can amass in a

lifetime." Russell quipped. "You think we should've stopped at Mavis Jackson's and had a decent meal?"

John gave him a sidelong smile but kept his eyes ahead. He saw a man riding a mule down the road in the growing shadows. When they got within hailing distance, John waved at the man and inquired where he might find the father of Billy Taylor.

The man on the mule had on a slouch hat and homemade overalls. He had a trusting face and was free with his information. He turned in his saddle and pointed toward several lighted buildings in a grove of trees. "Jeremiah Taylor lives in a small house right next to the mercantile store. You can see the lights from here."

John thanked him and they rode wordlessly down the road and made a left down a well-traveled road. They rode up to the mercantile store hitching rack, but did not immediately dismount.

The store itself was larger than most he had seen in his travels. The windows were lighted and it had a long and broad porch that ran the length of the building replete with cane bottom chairs and even a porch swing. It appeared to have living quarters in the back.

Bulky feed sacks and barrels lined the ends of the porch. They reached to the porch ceiling. People were in the store and voices were coming from the doorway. It was obviously thriving.

John and Russell dismounted and tied their horses and left the mule attached to Russell's dun. They walked up the sizable steps to the porch and entered.

Canned good and fruit jars lined the shelves. There were mounds of shirts, pants, boots and gloves piled on counters, and behind the main counter were boxes of cigars, snuff and twists of chewing tobacco. Everywhere they looked, they saw well-stocked merchandise.

John panned the room and took in boots, saddles and bridles and saddle blankets and every form and shape of tack. Horse collars and reins and traces and cotter pins and wheels were in abundance.

As he marveled at the profusion of goods, his head swiveled around and there he saw the most beautiful woman he had ever seen in his twenty-four years on earth. She was busy talking to a customer and stacking his order of coffee, beans and bacon on the counter.

He tried not to stare but it was difficult. She had oceans of dark hair pinned up with a ribbon. Her eyes were shockingly blue with such a kind spirit projected in them. She was shapely and he could not help but notice she was very buxom. She definitely filled out the black dress she had on.

Russell saw her too and his eyes widened. He looked at John and John looked back at him but they said nothing. John and Russell both were men who admired a woman but were not disposed to ogle.

Soon the farmer paid his bill and lifted his sack of supplies and departed. Martha Taylor then turned her attention to John and Russell.

She had a strong but pleasant voice. "What can I get for you, gentlemen?"

John nodded at the coffee beans. "I think we could stand about five-pounds of coffee."

She smiled and grabbed a dipper and scooped up the beans, weighed them and began to grind them. Her eyes took in John. He stood so tall in the store. He loomed over the other customers. Several gawked at him. He did not acknowledge that he was being stared at. She had never seen such a man who looked so powerful and huge. But it was a controlled power. He appeared to be a man who could wrack great mayhem if he were so inclined, but she liked the air of kindness in his eyes. She sensed a certain civility about him. She took her eyes off him and back to the coffee grinder.

She decided to break the ice and asked, "Are you a soldier?"

He smiled at her and nodded, "I was one."

His answer piqued her interest. "You were one?"

"I served my time and am headed back to Texas."

She kept grinding and adjusted the sack. She poured some coffee into it. She looked back up at him and smiled a white-even smile. "Why in the world are you in Gainesville?"

He dipped his eyes and his smile vanished. "I'm here to see a Mister Taylor."

Her smile became more compressed, "He is my father-in-law." Her eyes searched his and took in his body language. "Is there anything wrong?"

He nodded and averted her eyes. "There's been a great wrong and I'm unfortunately the one to deliver the news."

She began to grind the coffee much slower with deliberate circles of the wheel. She licked her lips in thought and her eyes moved up to his. "Billy?"

He looked at her eyes, which were now filled with concern. He inhaled and nodded.

She swallowed and straightened herself. She left the task of grinding the beans and walked up to the counter and looked at John. "What happened to him?"

He did not want to tell her. He felt that he should tell the father but it was hard to deny her information. He had never seen such innocent and kind eyes. He inhaled and removed his hat and ran his hands through his tawny hair. "He was killed near Lexington, Tennessee. There was a skirmish, and he was killed trying to draw fire from me."

Tears flooded her eyes and she raised a dainty apron to her mouth and then dabbed the corners of her eyes. She called over her shoulder and called for her daughter, 'Sally.'

The daughter came through a curtain leading to the back and she looked to be nine-years old. Like her mom she was a strikingly beautiful. She had expressive eyes and the same piled lustrous hair.

She dutifully received her mother's instructions and began grinding the coffee.

John hated admitting to himself that he regretted the fact

that she was married. He tried dismissing the thought but it did linger. He nodded at Sally and tipped his hat. He had been around many women in camps and in cities and towns. None had ever affected him like this woman. She had a certain regality that he was drawn to.

Martha Taylor took off her apron and walked around the corner of the counter and extended her hand. "I don't think we have been formally introduced. My name is Martha Taylor."

He accepted her hand and it felt warm in his grasp. He lingered more than he should have and he ended the handshake by saying, "My name is John Lee Johnson." He inclined his head toward Russell and continued, "And this in my cousin, Russell Johnson."

She looked at each one with approval and then dabbed at her eyes to catch the incipient tears. "My father-in-law is next door." She pedaled her hands as if she were trying to prime courage. "He's been through a lot. My own husband was reportedly killed at Pea Ridge."

John caught the words 'reportedly killed' and that stayed with him as they all started walking out the front door and down the steps and making a hard right.

They heard fiddle music through the open window that emitted a thick, oily light. She led John and Russell past the window and around the house and up the wooden steps to the small house. Martha stood in the doorway and caught the attention of Jeremiah Taylor.

He laid his fiddle and bow to one-side and gave her a smile, "Howdy, Martha, you closing up early?"

She shook her head 'no' and stepped aside for John and Russell to enter. John looked at the tired old man. His hair was solid white and his eyes red and his face florid. Jeremiah tilted his head as to process the situation.

Martha stepped in front of John and Russell and said, "Dad Taylor, these men want a minute of your time."

Jeremiah pulled a pair of spectacles from his shirt pocket and put them on. He looked from person to person and then indicated by his head for them to sit down.

It was obvious by the awkward silence that Jeremiah Taylor knew that it was an ominous visit. He looked at John and asked. "It's about Billy isn't it?"

John compressed his lips and sighed, "Yes, Mister Taylor it is."

Jeremiah removed his spectacles and laid them aside and sighed deeply. "When did it happen and where did it happen?"

"He was killed in combat near Lexington, Tennessee and not that many days ago."

Jeremiah nodded and inhaled a lung of air. "It's hell getting old." He fumbled with his hands and fingers and looked up at John. "It's also hell to outlive one of your kids too."

John noticed he said 'one of his kids' and not 'two of his kids." But he certainly was not going to point out any contradiction. His eyes moved to Martha and she caught the hint of an intercession.

"Dad Taylor, this is John Lee Johnson and this is his cousin, Russell. John is done with the War and is headed back to Texas."

"My son wrote of you. He admired you greatly."

John looked up at the sad eyes and back to the floor. "Well, that works two-ways, Mister Taylor."

Jeremiah turned his vision to Martha. "Martha, why don't you prepare a meal for these men and see that they get lodging for the night."

John remonstrated by holding up his hands palms toward Jeremiah. "There's no need for that. I didn't come to be a burden or a bother."

"Nonsense. If you're riding to Texas, you rode out of your way to see me." He paused as his voice broke emotionally. "And that means a lot to me."

Martha broke in. "Come with me, Gentlemen." She walked over and kissed her father-in-law on the cheek.

They filed out after her and they dared not to look back at the forlorn father in his private grief.

Martha had them stand in front of the store and she went up the steps and soon came back with a lantern. She had them get their horses and the mule and she led them to a drainage ditch so they could water their livestock.

She went with them to a large barn nearby and she showed them where the corn and oats were and she stayed with them while they attended the animals.

Next she took them to a well-kept cottage not far from the barn and led them inside. There were two-beds with sheets and blankets and a kitchen. She showed them the pump on the porch and informed them that there was soap and a razor in the wooden stand in the kitchen.

She then asked them to meet her at the store in about thirty-minutes and she would have food for them. She left the lantern for them to see by and she left in the dark to return to her work.

John looked at Russell and Russell looked at John. "Well, if she is kind enough to do all of this, Russell, let's go down to that ditch and take a bath and shave up."

They found the soap and a towel and they made their way down to the ditch. There in the moonlight, they bathed in the cool water. Russell whooped some, "Man, this feels good. I hate putting back on those stinky clothes.

After soaping down and rinsing off and swimming for a while, they trudged back up to the cabin buck-naked. They had left the lantern still burning in the kitchen. They made their way to the small room in the back that served as the bedroom. There to their surprise were two-pairs of pants and two-new shirts and two-pairs of clean underwear.

John's face registered surprise. "What a heart."

Russell nodded and said, "What a woman."

They both shaved and slicked down their hair and put on their new clothes and made their way to the store.

As soon as they made their way up the steps to the porch, they could smell beef stew and it smelled like it was Texas style too.

Sally, the pretty daughter, dressed in a severe black dress like her mother met them and grabbed Russell's hand and led them through the curtain behind the counter to the kitchen area.

She showed them their places around the table. And bade them to sit down. John noticed the back of Martha Taylor as she worked around the stove. She had taken no mind of them, but she did turn around and her eyes brightened. "It's such a pleasure to have such handsome men around my table."

John smiled and said, "I doubt the handsome part but we're sure glad to be around your table."

Sally was smitten by Russell and talked to him almost exclusively. He liked the attention and soon they had a friendship going.

Martha, who still had her back to them as she prepared the cornbread, was smiling to herself. She liked these two-men and the way they conducted themselves. She enjoyed hearing her daughter laugh and joke and she also found John Lee Johnson most appealing.

Later Martha said the Blessing, and she started passing around the beef stew and cornbread and sliced vegetables. She poured lemonade into the large glasses and they commenced to eat.

John looked at Martha and said, "If we eat like we're starved wolves, I hope you'll overlook it."

She flashed a beautiful smile at him and replied, "Eat all you want I like that."

John started to take a big bite but let the fork linger in the air. "Before we go any further, we want to thank-you for the clothes and coffee and we'll gladly pay you for them."

"You'll do no such thing."

He knew he had no reply so he just started eating again. He had no idea of how much he and Russell had eaten but he knew they had put a big dent in the large pot of stew she had.

Later as the eating subsided, and the talk was more casual, Martha placed a hand on John's briefly and asked. "Is there some reason you're headed to Texas in such urgency?"

John had felt her hand on his and he only wished it had stayed there a whole lot more. He heard her question and hesitated before answering.

Her eyebrows moved up realizing that she perhaps had been indiscreet in asking the question. "If I have asked something I shouldn't, I apologize."

John sighed and looked at Russell and back at the breathtaking face of Martha Taylor. "Our fathers were killed by land swindlers. They were unjustly murdered for land." John nodded at Russell. "We have no choice but to go back and make things right."

Martha's face registered sadness. "I'm truly sorry, John." She paused her fork in the air and let it droop toward the table. "Especially since you've been through so much in the War."

John did not reply. He just looked down at his empty bowl that he had emptied three-times. "I appreciate your great hospitality. You have been so kind to me and Russell."

She smiled but it was a sad smile. "You know it is a privilege to do good things for good people."

She stood abruptly and started picking up the dishes. While Russell and Sally were talking about her horse, Martha leaned down to John and said, "There's one thing you can do for me."

He smiled and nodded, "You name it."

She said, "After I wash the dishes, I want you to go sit in the porch swing with me and talk."

He nodded, "That would be an honor, Martha."

Later while Russell and Sally sat on the steps and watched fireflies and talked, John and Martha shared the porch swing.

They sat for a moment without speaking. John looked over at Martha and said, "It's been a long time since I've sat in a porch swing, and I sure in the world have never been in a porch swing with someone as pretty as you." He paused and continued. "If I say something stupid, I hope you'll forgive my awkwardness."

She laughed a pretty laugh. "Not awkward nor stupid. I think you're a gentleman."

She looked over at him and smiled and he felt a great compulsion to reach over and kiss her but he restrained himself. She touched him on the shoulder. "Do you have a girl back in Texas?"

"No, Martha, there is no girl nor girls." He looked over at her and looked into her eyes. "The War came and I joined up and I went to Virginia and there just wasn't no time to get to know anyone." He paused and turned his eyes back to the silvery road illuminated by the moon.

He turned again toward her and looked at the beautiful profile in the darkness. He felt good just inhaling her nearness. He liked her comeliness, and he knew that she was the woman he wanted to spend his life with. It was more than spur of the moment feeling. It was life-changing awareness. She had such a depth of character that he yearned for and admired. He fought the instinct to reach over and pepper her face with kisses. He knew he could not do that. He wanted this woman, but he would not alarm her. He swallowed and let that impulse pass over. He asked, "Tell me about you."

"Okay, I'll tell you." She laughed that musical laugh that he was beginning to love. "I was the daughter of a Campbellite minister. My father and mother started a church here, and I met Robert Taylor when I was fourteen-years old. I got married at fifteen and had Sally when I was sixteen.

"Dad Taylor owned about a thousand-acres of ground, so, we had it better than most folks. But Robert wasn't much of a worker. But we set up this store and it has been very successful."

John nodded and asked, "Did Robert and Billy get along?"

Martha shook her head 'no.' Dad Taylor had two-wives. The first-one died giving birth to Robert. He later on married a much younger woman and he had Billy by her. She died a year before the War started."

She looked up at the stars and sighed. "But to answer your question, did Robert and Billy get along? Robert always resented Billy. So, no, they did not get along at all."

"So, your husband is dead?"

Martha's face tightened. "John, he has been reported as being killed, but...." She tossed up her hands. "I don't know."

John nodded and let his hand fall on hers. She did not move her hand and soon he felt her fingers intertwine with his. He liked the feeling and he felt better than he had in a long time.

Martha looked at him and gave him enigmatic smile. She turned from him and looked straight ahead but her hand tightened around his even more so.

They made small talk and laughed and enjoyed each other's wit and intelligence until it was obvious to John that he had kept her up way past her bedtime.

He looked at Martha before rising and taking Russell with him. "I would like to spend one-more day here, if that is okay with you?"

She looked relieved and nodded her head vigorously to such a degree that he knew she was definitely interested in him. He was pleased with that, and he and Russell made their way to the cottage.

When John and Russell entered the cabin, they immediately went to bed. John lay awake for a while thinking of Martha. He felt consumed by her.

Although it was pitch black, Russell strained to see his cousin. He turned his head toward John from his bunk. He had never seen his cousin so enthralled by a female. "You asleep, John?"

"Are you kiddin'?"

"You like her a lot don't you?"

"Yeah, Russell I do."

"She likes you too, John, can tell."

John sighed and ran his hands over his face. "You know you don't have to be a ladies' man to know quality when you see it."

Russell did not respond. He either was considering his words or sleeping.

John rolled and tossed and decided he would go outside and smoke a cigar. He got up and placed on his boots. He bare-chestedly walked outside. He stood on the small porch where the pump was and looked at the multitude of stars.

He walked a few feet off the porch and thumb-struck a match and lit his smoke. He sighed and tried to name all the constellations like he did as a kid. He walked over to a small copse of trees and just leaned against one and puffed contentedly.

He was just enjoying the peace and quiet of the night and a full stomach. He then saw a light come on in the building behind the store. He did not mean to look but he had a hard time turning away when he saw Martha enter the room. She walked to the mirror and with her back to him began to comb down her hair.

John dreamily watched her. She pulled off her top and he could see her bare shoulders and her shoulder blades. She languidly brushed down her hair. John was fascinated although he felt a tad uneasy. He started to turn and go back inside when she turned around. He saw her breasts as she walked to the window and peered out. She disappeared from sight and the light went out.

He stood with a fever. If she had meant him to see her was one thing, but just looking at her without her knowledge was another. He felt guilt. He did not like that feeling. He backed up and then turned and stealthily returned to the porch. He tossed the cigar and walked inside the kitchen and into the bedroom. He shucked off his boots and pants and quickly got under the cover.

Russell heard him come in and remove his boots. Where did you go?"

John choked on his words, "Just out for a smoke."

Russell raised his torso up and looked over at his cousin. "Are you all right?"

John sighed, "Yes, Russell, I'm all right."

Russell smiled, "Your voice sounds funny."

"Shut-up, Russell, we got a busy day tomorrow."

Russell grinned to himself and lay back down.

The next day was busy. They got up at dawn and went swimming in the sand bottom ditch. They shaved again and went over to the mercantile store and had breakfast with Martha and Sally.

John noticed during breakfast that Martha touched his shoulder and arms a lot. Her smile was radiant and her face registered happiness. She laughed a great deal. He had never felt such a force of attraction.

Later Jeremiah Taylor helped them shoe the horses and the mule and they spent the morning oiling and cleaning their weapons.

John found a stack of wood that had not been cut and he cut enough wood for two-winters. Jeremiah Taylor stood in amazement seeing how he swung an axe. "He turned to Russell and said, "I have never seen a man that strong before. He never lets up and he even cuts wood without a wood maul."

Russell smiled and said, "Yeah, well, he's amazing at a lot of things."

They went to the mercantile store for the noon meal and Jeremiah Taylor sat at the head of the table and gave the Blessing. John sat at the other end with Martha to his left. She sat smiling and she made him feel special by her kind looks and quick smiles.

They devoured a platter of fried chicken and boiled potatoes and gravy. The cathead biscuits disappeared quickly too. They consumed a gallon of lemonade.

John and Russell went to the barn and rubbed down the horses and the mule and watered them. They double grained them for the long trip on the morrow.

Russell spent the shank of the afternoon carving out Sally's name in wood and did a good job of it. John slept and replenished his strength.

That night they went back to the mercantile store and had supper with Martha and Sally. Jeremiah was not there but could be heard playing his mournful fiddle music.

After the meal, John asked Martha if she would go walking with him and she accepted with quick smile. She laughed, "I'm glad you asked because I was going to."

When they walked past Jeremiah's lodging, the sad fiddle music filled the air. It set a mood of sorts. They walked wordlessly down the road bordered by full cottonwood trees. John cleared his throat and Martha looked at him in the gathering moonlight and smiled. "You want to say something?"

"Yes," He licked his lips and turned his eyes to her. "I want to say that being here with you is one of the great joys of my life. I just do not want to say something dumb and regret it. On the other hand, I do not want something to go unsaid either and live to regret it." He sighed as he finished his thought by saying, "But I do want to say that you are a beautiful person in so many ways."

She did not respond immediately but smiled. "What a tender thing to say." She gave him a wistful smile and said, "I also do not want to say something dumb, but you are a most impressive man, John Lee Johnson." She looked up at him, contemplated her words adding, "I think a woman could fall in love with you."

She caught him off-guard. He tried to measure his words. "I don't want just any woman falling in love with me." His words caused them to stop and he turned to her and placed his hands on her shoulders. "But I would be honored if you fell in love with me." He sighed and licked his lips and continued, "This may sound strange to you and maybe tomorrow I will wish that I had not been so bold, but I love you."

Her eyes widened and she turned her head to look at the black silhouettes of the bordering cottonwood trees. He had begun to think he had spoken too boldly, but she moved in closer and placed her head on his chest. He thought he felt wet tears through his shirt, but he made no mention of it. He moved his large hand down and gently stroked the back of her head. He did not know how it happened, but in an instant, they shared a soft kiss. But it did not stay tender long. They melted into each other hungrily. The kiss seared both of them and left him breathless.

He pulled back and took a deep breath. He figured if he loved her, he would come back to her if she would have him. He did not want to do anything foolish that would endanger his future with her. He used all his discipline, but he put his passion on hold.

They began walking again. He, no longer, felt he had been foolish in admitting his feelings. She may not have said she loved him, but she sure in the world acted like it.

She sensed his thoughts and suddenly stopped. "I have no idea if I am a widow or an abandoned woman. But let me say that I will never forget you, John." She melted into his arms. He kissed the top of her head and felt her tightly against him.

Her muffled voice came up to him. "You will be leaving in the morning for Texas and you may square accounts there or you may be killed."

He nodded at her statement but she could not see his nod. She kept talking. "I know that with some people promises made in moonlight are not made of very substantial material, but if you survive the ordeal, I will wait for you."

John inhaled deeply and she could feel his large chest expand. "If I survive, Martha, I will return."

She raised her head from his chest and looked up at him. "I am going to live on that promise."

He kissed her tenderly. "I meant what I said. It may be a long time by your standards and mine about making it back here, but I want to come back."

John and Martha walked about a mile and then turned around and walked back. Just as he walked her the front steps of the mercantile store, she gently lifted his hand and kissed the back of it. She turned and walked up the steps, and just before opening the door, she turned and said, "I love you, John."

He knew by instinct that she did say that lightly. He was a good judge of character. He knew that she not only was a rare woman, but one you could love a lifetime and it still not be enough time. He was not thunderstruck by her declaration; he just wanted to remain in the moment longer.

He stood and watched her disappear into the shadows of the darkened store. He exhaled and walked toward the cottage. He knew of a certainty that it was a night of mixed blessings.

The next morning as the rooster was crowing, they pulled out and John gave a fleeting look to the window where he had seen Martha. But he compressed his lips and turned his head. He set his mind and they cantered off.

Unbeknownst to him, Martha stood in the morning shadows and watched his broad back as he moved finally out of view. She took a deep breath and made her way to the edge of the bed. She felt like she had not been wrong about him. He was a special man. She clutched her hands to her throat. She knew he would come back, if he could come back.

John and Russell made forty-miles that day and camped in the rolling hills covered in hickory and oak. They spoke little and kept to the task at hand.

For the next two-days they kept up a steady pace. John noticed that Russell each day had become more and more taciturn. Each day he talked less and seemed bothered.

Camped by a rolling stream, John passed Russell a cigar as he tended the fire. John lit Russell's cigar and his own and leaned back against an oak tree. "Russell, something on your mind?"

Russell inhaled air and exhaled it loudly and nodded. "Yep."

"Mind sharing what's on your mind."

Russell took a drag off his smoke and turned to John. "What I'm about to tell, I ain't proud of. But since you asked, I'll tell you." He looked around a bit at the surroundings and started talking. "When I left Texas, I was riding ole Sugar. Best damn horse I ever owned. I had thirty-dollars in gold coin that Uncle Henry gave me. I made it through the Nations okay and made it through Fort Smith okay, but when I got to a place called Gilbert's Crossin,' I had some problems."

John repeated, "Gilbert's Crossing?"

"Yeah, Gilbert's Crossin," Russell smoked some more and continued, "It's about two-days ride from here or maybe less." He sighed and looked sheepishly at the ground. "I stopped at a place called Bullner's Store. I was needin' some salt pork and beans."

John could see the pain in his cousin's face and he did not rush the story. He watched Russell's features tighten.

"When I went in and stood at the counter, there was a lot of men in there and bad lookin' hombres too. I could feel 'em eyeballin' me, and so, I bought my supplies and walked out the store and mounted up.

"They followed me out on the porch and watched me ride away. I could feel their eyes on me, and so, I just trotted ole Sugar till I was out of sight and then I hightailed it for all its worth. I guess I rode that afternoon and way into the night. I was afraid with all the rocks I was goin' over that I would stone bruise ole Sugar, so, I made a smokeless camp and went to sleep.

"That night about one-o'clock in the morning I felt something cold on my nose and I woke up and saw a gun barrel sticking in it. Those men were all around me. One of them named, 'Corn' made me take off all my clothes. He robbed me of my money and clothes and gun belt.

"He made me lie face down and him and all his men peed on me. They did a whole lot of whoopin' and carryin' on and I just had to take it. One of them named, 'Frog' hit me over the head with a gun barrel and I woke the next morning as naked as a jaybird and cold." He paused and grimaced as he continued. "No horse, no money, and no clothes.

"I walked in the woods and came up on an old-timer and he was working at a sawmill. He loaned me a pair of pants and shirt and I worked for him a week and he sold me a mule you see back there. He gave me a dollar and I left when I felt like I had worked it all out and headed for Memphis."

John's jaw worked as he listened in anger. "Well, Cousin, we're going to take the long way to Fort Smith. In the morning when we get up and eat our beans and jerky, just point the way to Gilbert's Crossing."

Russell sighed and frowned. "I'd just as soon forget the whole thing."

"Yeah, you would like to forget, but you can't forget. That's the problem."

Russell nodded, "That may be true, John, but they might not be there by the time we get there."

John looked at Russell evenly. "They'll be there. That's their domain. Thieves are like that."

They got up early and Russell pointed in the general direction and they started off. They rode hard that day and skipped the noon meal. That night they made camp and Russell did his usual job of tethering the horses. John made a pan of beans and they ate heartily. Their talk that night was terse and Russell still remained jittery.

"Are we getting close, Russell?"

"Russell nodded and answered, "It is still a day's ride or so but yeah, we are getting real close."

The next day they were making their way deeper into the hills and saw less and less trappings of civilization. They were surprised when they rounded a bend and saw a farmer hoeing weeds around a large gate that led to a pasture.

The farmer looked shocked when he saw them and reached for his shotgun he had leaning against a post. He brought it up across his chest and looked suspiciously back and forth at John and Russell.

John raised his hand. "We ain't thieves nor are we lookin' for trouble."

The farmer replete with a long black-beard, droopy slouch-hat, and homemade overalls asked in a raspy and wary voice, "Who might you be then?"

"I'm a soldier going back home to Texas."

The farmers' eyes piqued and he relaxed his shotgun. "Yankee or ours?"

"I served with Abraham Buford and Nathan Bedford Forrest."

"Forrest, you say?"

John nodded, "Yes, Forrest."

The farmer nodded and spat a goodly amount of tobacco juice to one side and squinted his eyes in renewed suspicion. "What in tarnation are you doin' around here?"

"I'm wanting proper directions to Gilbert's Crossing."

The farmer chewed some more and shook his head. "That ain't a proper place to be, Soldier." He placed his shotgun at his side and leaned on it. "There's some bad men there and they ain't worth a tinker to anyone. They're rapists and outlaws."

"Would one of them be named, 'Corn,' by any chance?"

The farmer nodded with squinted eyes. "Yes, and he's the worst of the lot."

"Well, he ain't a friend of ours."

The farmer almost smiled. "He ain't a friend of nobody I know but them cutthroats he runs with." He paused and spat again. "He rides by here sometimes and I just bar the door and stick my shotgun out the window. He leaves me and my family alone but otherwise he wouldn't."

John just nodded in agreement.

The farmer raised his free hand and pointed westerly. It's about thirty or thirty-five miles that away."

John said, "Much obliged and he and Russell rode away.

The farmer watched their backs until they disappeared around the bend. He shook his head in puzzlement and went back to hoeing weeds.

They rode slowly through the small, rocky paths that were afforded them. It as about four o'clock as they were riding up a rise that Russell spotted what looked like to him was a rag doll lying off to their left.

He yelled for John who was riding lead. John turned his head to see what was the matter and he also saw the bundle of rags that looked like a doll lying in an open space.

John sighed and looked at Russell, "That's a body."

Russell's face blanched and he swallowed.

John turned his big bay off the road and he rode down the gradual incline through the weeds. They came upon a clearing and rode up to the dead campfire. Both of their eyes were on the dead body of the small girl.

John dismounted, followed by his reluctant cousin. John walked up the small form and knelt down. He looked at the innocent face in death and he sighed. His eyes caught the small blue hole in the temple and realized the child had been shot.

Russell looked over his shoulder and shuddered. "Who would do such a thing?"

John shook his head but did not answer. He looked further along the clearing and saw a man's body twisted up. He stood up and walked slowly to the dead man. He had been shot several times.

John took off his hat and scratched his head. He observed a lot of hoof marks and horse droppings. He walked around the campsite and noticed several cigar butts.

He inhaled air and was preparing to bury the dead bodies when he heard a faint cry in the weeds. His eyes moved to a tree just beyond a stand of Johnson grass and milkweeds. He moved toward the noise.

When he stepped through the weeds, he saw a woman sitting and leaning against a tree. Her dress was ripped open and her breasts were hanging out. Her face was badly bruised. John knew she had been raped.

He stepped back and headed for his horse and got his old shirt and pants out and his canteen. He went back to the woman and leaned down and placed his shirt around her and forced her arms through the openings and buttoned it up.

He gave her some water and her eyes fluttered. She accepted the water and then began crying. He patted her shoulders and dabbed some water on a handkerchief and ran it over the bruises and cuts.

"Ma'am, you got to put these britches on, your dress is ruined."

He gave her some more water and helped her to her feet. "Go behind this tree and put these britches on and place your dress on the outside."

She staggered behind the tree and soon she reappeared with the pants on. She sank back down at the base of the tree and John rolled up the pant legs so she would not trample on the excess material and fall down. He straightened her dress the best he could and then called over his shoulder to Russell.

Russell soon looked through the weeds and down at the woman. He shook his head at the horror of it and went to his mule and pulled out some horse liniment and some beef jerky.

John accepted the liniment from Russell and dabbed it on the cuts and bruises. She winced but did not complain.

Her eyes opened with some clarity and she inhaled, "Mister, it's not that I'm not grateful, but if it's all the same to you, I just wished you would hand me your pistol and let me blow my brains out."

John shook his head 'no.' "I can't do that, Miss."

She looked at him and at Russell. "Who are you?"

"My name is John Lee Johnson." He tilted his head toward his cousin, "And that is Russell."

She made no expression. Her face broke into a frown and then into sadness. She began heaving and crying. "I just want to die."

John rose up and compressed his lips. He looked at Russell. You stay with her and I'll go dig the graves."

"What're you goin' to use?"

John held up his two-big hands. "You just take care of her and don't let her hurt herself."

John worked for two-hours and finally had the graves dug out enough to hide the bodies. He built a substantial cairn of rocks over the graves and placed two-crudely made crosses at the west end of the rock mound.

He later built a fire and place a skillet of beans over the fire and pot of coffee. He fixed a place against the tree for the woman. Russell had let her cry herself out and he carried her to the spot John had indicated for her.

She slept and did not accept food. John and Russell smoked. "You think she's gonna be all right, John?

John shook his head in indecision. "I don't know, Russell, apparently that man was her husband and the little girl was her daughter. I would guess that anyway. That's got to be a shock to her system."

"What're we gonna do?"

"I tell you what we're going to do, Russell, we're going to treat her kindly. We're going to show her that not all men are animals." He paused and shook his head again. "After that I don't know."

"This has been one hell of a trip, John, it's all I can say."

John nodded and sighed, "Would you rather be here or living in a small house in Honersville, Missouri?"

Russell shrugged. "I guess here."

John looked over at the sleeping woman. "Keep your eye on her through the night. She is out of her head and she's existing on raw emotion."

They let the fire burn out and they rolled up in their blankets and went to sleep.

The next morning, the woman awoke from her fitful sleep and rolled out of the blanket and her eyes went to the cairns and crosses. She stood on wobbly legs and went to the rocky mounds and sat on her haunches and lifted her arms up to the sky as to reach for mercy. She heaved in pain and made guttural noises that made the two-Texans wince.

John and Russell were making breakfast. They watched her with sympathetic eyes. John allowed her to cry. He felt she needed some time to purge herself. After a measure of time, John walked over and lifted her up and led her to resting place against a large oak tree. He nodded at Russell who handed her a cup of coffee and a small plate of beans.

"I don't want anything to eat." She sobbed.

"Miss, you have to eat. You got to live."

"I have nothing to live for." Her gaze went to the rock graves. Her eyes were wide and empty.

John followed her eyes to the graves and then to his face. She had no tears in her eyes. It was a forlorn look of no hope.

"They're dead and gone. I wished it was not so but it is." He handed her the metal cup. "Now, Miss, there's somebody out there who loves you and would miss you a whole heap if you was to die." He knelt down and looked her in the eye. "Don't be selfish and make someone else unhappy by your death."

She looked into his eyes for a long time. Apparently his words caused her to think. A tear began to brim. She looked at the metal coffee cup in her hand. She drank it and she accepted a spoon from Russell and began to eat from the plate of beans.

She looked up at John with tear-laced laced eyes. "I am most grateful for all you've done."

He gave her a smile. "You just tell me when you're up to traveling."

John could tell she was not up to traveling. He figured she was still bleeding but he was not going to be indelicate. He just gave her kindness and she began to eat on her own volition. They stayed there the whole day.

That night around the fire, she felt strong enough to tell them what happened.

"I guess I should tell you my name." She drank her coffee and looked into the eyes of both men. "My name is Bonnie Harper. My husband was Ned Harper and my baby was named 'Nellie.'

"We lived in Ashland, Kentucky and we were on our way to Texas to buy a house and lot next to my brother, 'Hughey'. He's a Baptist preacher. We had almost 500 dollars saved up and we had no problem crossing Tennessee even if the War is going on. We had some axle problems in Eastern Arkansas but we got that fixed and we were headed to Fort Smith. We were dreading going across the Nations but we had no fears from the hill folk around here or that's what we thought.

"We camped here off that rocky trail you were on and had a fire going and I was going to make biscuits and beans. I was down at the creek just behind that tree where you found me. I heard some horses ride up and as I was walking toward the campsite, I heard my husband arguing with someone. When I walked through the weeds carrying water, those men began to make comments that were uncalled for.

"My husband became angrier and a man called 'Corn' shot him in the chest. My daughter went crazy and attacked Corn with a hand full of gravel. He shot her in the head. I dropped my water and ran to my child and just before I got to her, a man called 'Frog' scooped me up and he and Corn and a man called 'Toehold' raped me.

"They beat me and took the money from wagon and then drove off the wagon and mules leaving me for dead."

John's jaw muscles worked as he listened. He did not say anything but his eyes were slits of intense gray. He stood and went walking into the woods.

Bonnie turned to Russell. "Is he thinking of taking on those men?"

Russell drank his coffee and nodded. "He is for a fact."

"There's a whole lot of them." She looked evenly at Russell. "He'll be killed."

"Maybe and maybe not."

She lowered her cup and her eyes squinted in thought. "You have a high regard for your cousin, don't you?"

"Yes, ma'am, I do. He ain't ordinary in any thing he does."

Bonnie sighed, "Well, maybe so but he ain't so unordinary that he can't be killed."

Russell nodded and then added, "Did you see all those pistols he has?"

"Yes, I saw them."

"He knows how to use them, ma'am, real good."

She smiled for the first time in days. "I hope so. I really hope so. I was raised a Christian but those men are animals."

Russell sighed, "That's a fact. I know."

Bonnie, who had no knowledge of Russell's problems with Corn, sat and stared at him for a moment. She finished her cup and gathered Russell's. "Let me go clean these up."

"No, ma'am, John would have my head. You sit and rest. Maybe you can travel tomorrow."

The next day she indicated she wanted to leave this tragic place. They put Bonnie on Russell's dun so she could use the saddle and Russell mounted his mule. They rode most of the day and John could tell Bonnie was hurting. He stopped several times and repeatedly asked her if she wanted to rest. Each time she shook her head, 'no,' and they kept riding.

Bullner's Store was in a clearing. There was a crossroad that ran catty-cornered in front of the store. The building itself was sizeable for the sparsely populated area. The open area, in front of the store had a lot of horseflesh tethered to the hitching posts. Cottonwood trees bordered the scene.

It was about four o'clock when they came in sight of it. John looked up at the sky. The clouds were roiling and the smell of rain caught his nostrils. He dropped his eyes back to the store. He saw a group of men standing on the porch smoking.

He led his entourage into the clearing and headed for the

porch. Out of the corner of his eyes, he viewed a wagon he guessed was Bonnie's.

Standing on the porch, watching them come forward, were Frog and Toehold and several unshaved-rough looking customers. Frog, who was a large man with buggy eyes and thick lips, smiled when he recognized Bonnie.

"Well, looky here, boys, we got us that woman coming back for some more."

The surrounding laughter was coarse and ugly. Frog continued. "I reckon she knows real men after all. I think it's me she wants."

Toehold laughed. "I was last and she remembers who was the best."

Again the Greek chorus laughter made its ugly rumble. Frog caught sight of Russell, "Well, hell, look at this. We got pee boy back."

Toehold laughed, "I guess he wants another bath."

Frog's eyes went to the large man with all the pistols. His eyebrows moved up and he smiled. "I think we got us a gent who thinks he's pretty damn salty."

John pulled up in front of the porch positioned in front of Frog. He said over his shoulder. "Bonnie, is that your wagon?"

She pulled her horse closer to the wagon and said, "Yes."

Frog grossly grabbed his groin and shouted to her. "That's my wagon I got your bill of sale right here."

The coarse laughter again ran the length of the porch. Frog's eyes settled on the big Texan. "Who in the hell are you and what's your damn problem."

John slowly dismounted and looked up at Frog. "You're my problem, but you won't be for long."

Frog was momentarily startled. He never had anyone talk to him in that manner. He straightened and the greasy smile on his face disappeared.

Before he could respond, Corn came out the batwings and stood facing John and Russell. He was tall and had straw-blonde hair hanging down from his black-brimmed hat. He had a black leather vest with large matches protruding from the pocket. His twin Colts were crisscrossed by two-matching gun belts.

He had an evil smile and he let his sky-blue eyes pan the whole area. "What do we have here?"

Frog pointed to John. "I think this gent is on the prod."

Corn's eyes moved to John and locked in to his. "Are you on the prod, Big Man?"

John smirked. Somehow this scorn disconcerted Corn. His eyes suddenly darkened and the smile dissipated. "What do you think is so damned funny, Stranger?"

John's expression changed. His face became angry. His gray eyes looked unnaturally fiery. "I am not here to talk or explain. I am here because you raped that woman like a bunch of dogs. I am here because you stole my cousin's horse and took his dignity. And I am here to kill you."

Corn's smile returned. "Oh, we got us a live one here, boys." His evil grin spread across his face, "I like that. You got brass, stranger, but I'm not sure about brains."

"Just fill your hand or I will kill you where you stand."

Corn's eyes narrowed and he licked his lips. This man was pushing him. He usually was the man bracing people not the other way around. He knew the time for talking was over. He moved to his left and let his hands hover over his twin-Colts. He decided to kill the big man, and then finish off Russell and take possession of the woman once again.

He made a fast move for his weapons but the two-Navy Colts appeared in John's hands with telegraphic speed. John's two revolvers spat orange flames. One shot hit Corn in the stomach and one creased his head. He fell against the wall but not before he fired a shot into the porch. His eyes held disbelief as he slid down the wall. He settled on his haunches and keeled over to his side in an awkward posture. He knew he had been gut-shot. The pain shot through him like liquid hell.

Frog licked his lips in shock as he looked at the bleeding and moaning Corn. His buggy eyes turned to the big Texan. He thrust out his chest and his eyes glinted. "You ain't heard the last of this, Stranger."

John moved over to his left and stood in front of Frog. "Would you mind repeating that, so, I'll know that I got it straight."

Frog's voice grated against the air. "You'll pay for this."

John's head nodded exaggeratedly up and down. "I thought that was what you said." He quickly lifted his left-Colt and fired a roaring round. A blue hole appeared in Frog's forehead and part of his skull was shattered. Blood and brain matter ran down the store wall. He collapsed face forward and landed with a sickening 'kaplop' face down on the crude wooden steps.

John moved down the line of outlaws. They stood transfixed. There was no noise. He looked them all in the face and each face registered fear. "Which of you turds is Toehold?"

The outlaws did not respond. They acted as though they did not hear him. John smiled and said. "Well, hell, I'll just kill all you son-of-a-bitches and I'll eventually get Toehold."

One of the more seedy ones stepped forward. "I ain't going to die for that bastard." He pointed to a slender, ugly man with a broad brimmed hat.

"Are you Toehold?"

Toehold swallowed and nodded. His eyes were filled with fear. John said, "Before I kill you, I want you to know how that woman felt before you killed her husband and child." He paused and grinned a mirthless smile. "And raped a Christian lady who never did you no harm."

Toehold's eyes went to the dead Frog who was face down on the steps and toward the gagging Corn to his left. He tried to talk but his mouth could form no words.

John shrugged and said, "Oh, hell, I'm tired of talking. He raised his left-Colt and put a hole in Toehold's right-eye. He fell backwards and then forwards off the porch into the dirt.

John moved up and down the line. He called to Bonnie who stood by her wagon. "Is there another rapist up here?"

"No, John, you got them all."

John then turned to Bonnie and said, "Turn your head."

John turned and faced the quaking outlaws. "I want you to take off your clothes and pile them on the porch."

"Can we keep our drawers on mister?" The seedy one who fingered Toehold asked.

John nodded and raised his Colt. They disrobed in record time for outlaws undressing. John called for Russell to dismount, and go through their clothes for money. He went through Corn's clothes first and then Frog's on down the pecking order until he collected 400 dollars.

John told him to give it all to Bonnie as soon as he had the men get dressed. "Leave your gun belts and pistols on the porch. We're going to keep them and sell them for this woman you all have wronged. You can keep your horses except for the two-men who are dead and your wounded compadre, Corn."

John walked up and down the line and with scorn told them. "If there is anyone of you who's really sore at me, and you have the courage, I'll give you a fightin' chance. I'll let you strap on your holster and we'll have at it."

The seedy one spoke up. "Mister, I think I can speak for everyone here today, we want to get the hell as far from you as possible."

John nodded, "Well, get your duds on and get out of here fast."

The outlaws were equally deft at dressing as undressing and they mounted up and rode away in a fury.

Russell tapped John on the shoulder. "Corn is still alive."

John turned his attention to the gagging Corn who clutched his stomach. He went up the steps, sidestepping Frog, and removed Corn's gun belts and tossed them to Russell. He hoisted the thin body of Corn over his shoulder and walked back down the steps. He motioned for Russell to follow him.

They walked around the building and John deposited Corn's body with a loud thud to the ground. Corn groaned and his mouth was filled with blood. His eyes looked up at John in complete agony.

John turned to Russell. "I want you to piss all over him."

Russell swallowed and looked John in the eye. "I can't do it with you watching."

John made a wry face and said, "Hurry it up, too."

John was waiting on the other side of the store when Russell came around the building buttoning up his pants. He nodded at John and made his way to Bonnie and the wagon.

John whirled around and went back to where Corn was lying. It was obvious by looking at him that Russell had been holding it for a good while.

Corn's hair was soaked and plastered to his head. He looked up at John and asked, "Who are you, Mister?"

John leaned down and said, "I'm John Lee Johnson from Texas."

He made Corn open his mouth. He pushed the barrel of his Navy Colt between his lips. Corn's eyes were as big as saucers. His pupils focused fervently on the pistol barrel. John pulled the trigger and Corn's head shattered. John looked down at the body and holstered his weapon.

He went around the store and had Russell collect the three-horses of the outlaws. He told him to tether them behind Bonnie's wagon. "Drag the saddles off and we maybe can sell them later on."

Theo Bullner came out and stood on the front porch and inspected the carnage. Theo was a large man. He was in his fifties: big mane of hair and rheumy eyes, purple nose and large stomach.

He looked at John and pointed at the two-sprawling dead

bodies. "Mister, you took a wide swath through the criminal population of this area."

John looked up at him and nodded. "That's what I intended to do."

Theo looked again at Toehold and over at Frog. "Where's Corn?"

"He's around back."

"Dead?"

"Dead."

Theo looked at Russell leading Corn's horse to the back of Bonnie's wagon. "I'll tell you what I'll do." He swept his hand dramatically back and forth panning the death scene. "I'll give you and your friends a 100 dollars of free merchandise, and I'll give you 100 in gold for Corn's horse, saddle, bridle, and gun belt and guns."

John smiled and said to Russell who had been listening. "Get all he requested."

He turned back to Bullner. "You got yourself a deal."

Theo looked again at the dead bodies. "What am I going to do with all these dead carcasses?"

John shrugged, "I ain't got the foggiest. I imagine you can bury them or feed them to the hogs."

Theo made a thoughtful face. "I hadn't thought of feeding them to hogs."

John answered, "Hogs eat garbage you know." He turned and signaled for Bonnie and Russell to enter the store with him. They side stepped Frog's body and eased up on the porch.

The inside was as liberally stocked as Taylor's mercantile in Gainesville but was gloomy and dark. John walked up to the counter and looked at all the supplies. He dropped his eyes noticing an open can of beans with a pocketknife lying beside it.

Theo Bullner caught his eyes and he glanced down at the can of beans. "Corn was eating that before you shot him." He added, "He didn't pay for it neither."

John ignored the remark and told Bonnie to pick out a hundred-dollars worth of merchandise.

She looked at the dresses and hats but she dragged her eyes off because she felt like she was being selfish. John, who caught her eyes, picked up on her mood. "Bonnie, pick out some dresses and a hat or two and get yourself some shoes."

She looked at him with a bit of frustration. "But we need so many things for the trip."

John caught the word 'we' and nodded to himself. She was healing some.

Bullner excused himself and went into a back room and returned with a leather pouch and counted out one hundred dollars in gold.

Bonnie looked at the stack of money and then at John's approving face. "Here's our supply money. Now go get those dresses and shoes."

She smiled and he had not noticed how pleasant she could look until that moment. She bought all the supplies first that they could utilize on the trip and later she allowed herself the luxury of four new dresses and a pair of shoes.

As they were leaving, Theo Bullner came out of the store and stood on the porch and waved 'goodbye' to them as they pulled out. He sighed and then dropped his eyes to the dead bodies and shook his head in consternation. His eyes brightened some when he remembered his hog lot in back.

The threatening rain clouds finally let go. Heavy drops peppered them for an hour before giving way to bright-orange sun.

They had enough daylight to make it five-miles down the road and made camp. The equipment from Bonnie's wagon made cooking easier. She set up a metal tripod with hooks and stands that facilitated cooking.

Russell took care of the livestock and after a solid meal of beans and biscuits and coffee, they sat around the fire in a small circle and just stared at the fire. Bonnie was her normal taciturn self.

Russell looked at some of the confiscated weapons and John just sat stolidly saying little.

Bonnie broke the silence. "What're you thinking, John?"

He gave her a half-smile and said, "Not much." But he was thinking much. He gave her a long look and then added, "You both know those thieves are not done with us."

Bonnie gave a start and brought her hand up to her throat. "After what you did to them?"

John nodded. "That don't matter, Bonnie, they're probably at this time sitting around a fire just like we are and getting liquored up and getting some Dutch courage."

Russell laid aside his Navy six, and gave John a searching look. "What makes you think so?"

"They're too used to making money without labor. They've gotten a habit of easy money and that's not easy to give up." He paused and looked at each one of them. "They know that Bonnie has some money. They'll probably hit us some time tomorrow early."

Russell, who had been with John too long to doubt him, took off his hat and ran his hand through his red hair. "What's the plan?"

John laid out the plan for them and asked them to go to bed and be ready to get up early.

They got up before daylight and started off. Bonnie was driving her mules and Russell was hidden under a tarp in the bed of the wagon. Even though the wagon had a canvas top, he did not want to leave a silhouette that could be noticed.

John rode ahead and stayed off the main road as much as possible. He saw several places he thought might make good ambush sites and he just kept to the shadows of the bordering trees and watched and listened.

Sure enough within an hour's time, he heard the sound of horses. He saw two-men dismount. They tethered their horses behind a thicket. They pulled their pistols out and gathered themselves behind a large rock and hunkered down. John tied his horse and soundlessly made his way behind them.

He stealthily moved from one bare place to the next so as not to crack a branch or stumble on a rock. He was upon them in no time as they sat staring down the trail.

They whirled around when they heard the hard metallic click of his Navy Colt. He nodded at them and with his eyes and features noted their weapons. "Drop 'em or use 'em."

They dropped them like hot potatoes. John looked at the chubby one with the green teeth who stood trembling and then he looked at the thin, short one with the sad eyes. "You boys need to take up a new trade." He sighed, "Cause you're sorry-ass thieves."

The one with the sad eyes nodded, "Yeah, we ain't much as bad men." He looked at the ground. "We ain't much of nothin'."

The chubby one asked in a tremulous voice. "Are you goin' to kill us like you did Corn?"

"That depends." John remarked, "Take off your gun belts and pants and let's see how much money you boys have."

John placed their guns and holsters over his shoulder and went through their britches. He found five-dollars.

John told them to put on their pants. "You start walking. I'm keeping your money and horses and guns."

The two-forlorn thieves began making their way through the woods. The one with the sad eyes looked back with a pitiful look. His wretched expression for some reason touched John. He looked like a dog that had beaten too many times.

He shook it off and made his way to their horses and soon he was pulling them behind him as he made his way back toward Bonnie and Russell.

Bonnie was driving along with her eyes moving to the left and right. She could handle a team very well and she was making good time and hoping that John was wrong about the bandits.

She was wrong. Two-men who had scouted and established

that John and Russell were not with her, were waiting for her just around the bend.

She saw them as she rounded the curve and pulled up her mules. They were brandishing pistols. One of the thieves was tall and had a mouth filled with bad teeth. The other was short and had a mouth filled with bad teeth.

"Hold up, lady."

She looked at them from face to face. "Why don't you leave me alone?"

The tall one smiled exposing a dentist's nightmare. "Cause you got money, Missy."

The short one added in, "Just fork it over."

She shook her head. "I'm not gonna do it."

The short one's mouth opened in exclamation. "The hell you say. We got guns, Missy. We got guns that'll kill you dead."

Russell poked his Navy Colt through an opening where the wagon top was tied. "Drop your guns, gents."

The two-thieves looked at each other, not sure if it were John in the back of the wagon or not. They swallowed and first the tall one dropped his weapon and then the short one. Bonnie reached down under the seat and pulled up a loaded .44. "Now get off your horses."

Russell's quick appearance with his cocked revolver caused them to dismount with greater celerity. He told Bonnie to hide her eyes. "Now get those duds off and let's see what kind of money you boys are carrying."

He went through their clothes and found four-dollars. He had them redress and Bonnie reopened her eyes. She reminded Russell to take their horses and guns.

After he tethered the horses and placed their guns and holsters with all the others, he joined Bonnie in the wagon box and she slapped the reins and the mules again began their trek.

Russell gave a mock salute to the two-thieves who sat dejectedly on nearby rocks. As the wagon passed from view, the short one sighed. He started to say something when he was quickly silenced by the taller one's "Shut up, just shut up."

They met John down the trail bringing in two-horses and with gun belts drooped over his saddle horn. They met and exchanged stories and Bonnie surprised them all by laughing. She exclaimed, "I hope we meet some more bandits down the road. We'll be rich by the time we get to Fort Smith."

In Fort Smith, Arkansas, the town sheriff, Kenesaw Buchanan, was working at his desk. He was a tall, raw-boned man, with a gray mustache that trailed down his granite like features. He had a resonant voice that came deep within his chest. He liked black hats and black coats, and he always displayed his badge so there would be no misunderstanding.

His four deputies were present and he was addressing them. He looked at Fat Phil, the wiry Frankie Jenkins, the cowhand attired Roscoe Taylor, and the nondescript William Green. "I want you boys to keep your eyes peeled for strangers in town that look a little shady. I have got word that Jack Filson has been seen in this area and I don't want him taking advantage of the Big Willard fights over at Ace's saloon."

He pointed at Frankie and Fat Phil. "Every time there is a fight, everyone and his mother goes to it and that leaves the town vulnerable. I'll tell you how the fight turns out. So, don't fret. I want you two-birds to go along the river and just take a look see."

He looked at the other two-deputies. "Big Willard is fighting this afternoon and I want you two patrolling the streets. And separate yourselves and make sure your presence is known."

Fat Phil cleared his voice. Sheriff Buchanan looked at him. "What is it, Fat Phil?"

"Who's Big Willard fightin'?"

Sheriff Buchanan shrugged, "Some yahoo from the Nations. Some guy who calls himself, Battling Bob Sykes."

Down at Ace's saloon, Ace Gilmore was leaning against the bar talking to Battling Bob Sykes. Ace was nattily dressed in a black suit. He was a handsome man with jaded eyes and a pencil-thin mustache. He had a disinterested look that belied his intense knowledge of what was transpiring. He ran a hand over his slick black hair and was turning his attention to Bob Sykes.

"For your edification and those of your pals, here are the rules. The bet is a fifty-dollar minimum and a thousand-dollar maximum. You can make all the side bets you want. The ring is back of the building and you fight till one of you just flat-out quits or one of you gets knocked out."

Battling Bob, an angular rough-looking man, turned to his friends. "I got fifty-dollars here. Anyone else want to chip in?"

His buddies coughed up another thirty five-dollars. Battling Bob turned to Ace, "Who holds the money?"

"Sheriff Buchanan." Ace looked at his watch and then down at the eighty five-dollars in Battling Bob Sykes' hand. "He holds the money, not me."

Bob Sykes ugly features broke into a smile. "When am I goin' to meet Big Willard?"

Ace's eyes moved across the room and settled on the man eating boiled eggs down at the end of the bar. Ace pointed his finger toward him.

Bob Sykes looked toward a man who was about thirty years old. He was thick in the shoulders and had a massive chest. His derby hat was slightly tilted to one side and wore a suit coat. Sykes guessed he might be six-feet or six-one. He turned to Ace and said, "Do you mind if I go meet him?"

Ace admonished him. "Don't go down there and spoil the fight. But if you are all fired up about meeting him," he paused as he extended his hands outward, "Then have at it."

Big Willard watched Battling Bob Sykes amble toward him. He inwardly smiled as he saw the screwed up-tough looking face. He popped in another boiled egg and sucked his lips. He took a heavy drink from his schooner and picked at a piece of lint on his coat.

Bob Sykes sidled up to him and grinned a malicious smile. "I just want you to meet the man who is goin' to knock your ass off in about an hour."

Big Willard looked over the room and raised himself on his tiptoes to see over Bob's head. "Well, send him over here and let me meet him."

Bob scowled and gritted his teeth. "I've heard a lot about you but you don't look all that tall to me."

Big Willard eased Bob's hand aside, which was blocking his route to the boiled eggs. "I'll look a lot taller to you when you're lying on the floor."

Some of Bob's comrades snickered and that infuriated Bob even more. He whirled and traipsed off followed by his admiring minions.

Smitty, the officious bartender, came over to Big Willard and tilted his head toward the retreating back of Battling Bob Sykes. "He looks pretty damn tough to me, Big Willard."

Big Willard shrugged and took a sip of his beer. "Yeah, I guess that's why he's fighting me."

"You ever get nervous fighting all those guys coming in off the plains?"

Big Willard smiled, "You know, Smitty, I get nervous when they don't have at least fifty-dollars."

Smitty sat looking at him and toweled out a mug. "We got some pickled pigs feet. You might like them better than those boiled eggs."

Big Willard made a face. "I hate pickled pigs feet. I hated them when I was a kid and now that I'm older I still hate them."

Smitty looked down at the diminishing eggs. "You like those boiled eggs. Don't you?"

Big Willard picked up an egg and looked at Smitty. "Why are you working here when you could've been at Harvard?"

Smitty, who did not understand the sarcasm about Harvard, was smart enough to realize that he was being gouged. He sharply walked away to greet a patron.

At four-sharp, Sheriff Buchanan entered the saloon. There was a shout from all the patrons. Ace could almost hear the metallic clatter of gold coins reverberating in his mind. They exited the back door to the ring area. The bleachers were filled, and beers were being bought as fast as they could be drawn.

Ace pulled a thin cigar from his pocket and lit it. He looked over at Sheriff Buchanan who was holding his usual cigar box. Ace pulled a roll from his pocket and counted out eighty five-dollars and tossed it in the box.

Battling Bob Sykes who was standing near the sheriff saw Ace's eighty five-dollars in the cigar box. He let out a 'whoop.' "Hot damn, boys, we're gonna be rich."

The sheriff looked at him levelly and Battling Bob suddenly realized his betting money was in his pocket. He pulled it out and tossed in his eighty five-dollars.

Ace began walking around the ring holding up his dollars and asking anyone if they wanted to bet on Battling Bob Sykes. When he got no takers, he dejectedly took his place at ringside beside the sheriff.

Battling Bob entered the ring and took off his shirt. He was a muscular individual with many battle scars on his body. Ace estimated that he was six-two and weighed about two-hundred and fifteen pounds.

Big Willard took his time getting to the ring among the catcalls of his friends and admirers who were riling him intentionally. He climbed into the ring and took off his coat and shirt. He had a massive chest and large arms. His usual bored look was plastered on his face.

Battling Bob's friends were both shouting and taunting Big Willard. Ace took advantage of their emotion and quickly took two-extra bets at ten-dollars.

When Ace had made all the bets he could make, he signaled Smitty to ring the bell.

Battling Bob came out swinging. He threw jabs and wild

roundhouses and uppercuts. He was moving in on Big Willard and peppering him with a lot of shots. Big Willard took most of the shots on the arms and shoulders. But he was retreating.

Battling Bob emboldened by the early success let out a war whoop. His friends were going crazy in their excitement.

Ace was looking out of the corner of his eyes hoping for some more bets on Battling Bob. He made one more bet for forty-dollars from Bob's foreman as Big Willard kept retreating and Bob hot on his trail.

Ace, seeing that the bets were all made and no more would be made, cupped his hands around his mouth and said, "I'm bored, Big Willard."

That was their signal. Big Willard nodded and began moving forward, he deftly turned aside the jabs and even more easily avoided the wild haymakers. Big Willard saw an opening and his heavy left hand looped over Bob's jabs and caught Battling Bob squarely in the forehead.

Battling Bob shook his head like a stunned bull and raised his hands again to continue the fight, but something strange happened. His eyes lost focus. His legs became wobbly and he collapsed where he stood.

His friends and his foreman looked thunderstruck. The noise was sucked out of the arena. Big Willard walked over to where Battling Bob's body was convulsing. He noticed that the cowhand's boots were vibrating.

Big Willard shrugged and walked to his corner and put on his shirt and coat. He looked at Ace who gave him a sly smile.

Ace handed the sheriff his usual ten-dollars for his trouble and he pocketed the rest.

Later Big Willard, while standing and smoking at the end of the bar, saw Battling Bob's friends drag the unconscious body out the door. He pulled up a boiled egg, salted it and gulped it in one easy motion. He hoped Battling Bob would be back someday with another fifty-dollars.

# CHAPTER THREE

Back in Texas, Kiowa Bob was exiting his rickety back door. He was headed for his leaning toilet. As he opened the toilet door, he heard a pebble hit the backside of the outhouse. When he looked around the structure, he saw Chili Thomas' head looking over the edge of an arroyo.

Kiowa Bob looked both ways and made his way swiftly to the arroyo and went down the soft escarpment to join his friend. "What're you doing here?"

Chili grabbed Kiowa Bob by his shirt and pulled him close. "Now listen to me and listen good." He inhaled and said, "Henry wants you to go to the sheriff and turn yourself in."

"For what?"

"For your own protection, you knot head."

Kiowa Bob pried the fingers from his shirt and gave Chili a curious look. "Chili, what're you talking about."

"Henry thanks that the Purvis brothers are going to kill you and him. He believes it's just a matter of time. They're too upset about Russell leaving town and going to get John. He thinks they will kill you two because they don't want John having anyplace to go or find any allies when he gets back here."

Kiowa Bob nodded his head. "I believe that but why should I turn myself in?"

Chili inhaled, "Because Sheriff Nelson is your friend and a friend of John's."

Kiowa Bob shook his head. "Let me see if I got this straight. I turn myself because he is my friend and a friend of John's." Kiowa Bob made a face and scornfully gazed at Chili.

"He'll keep them from killing you and figure a way for you to escape with a horse and money. You'll ride across the Nations and try and intercept John in Fort Smith and tell him they know he's coming."

Kiowa Bob nodded with enlightened eyes. "Now that makes sense. Why didn't you say that in the first place?"

Chili ignored the remark. "I got to get back to town. You have to do this, Kiowa Bob."

Kiowa Bob nodded. He knew he was responsible for the hornet's nest that was buzzing in Bailey County.

Chili gave him one serious look and asked, "What happened to your face?"

Kiowa Bob shook his head as to disregard the question. "You go get your horse and get out of here before you're seen. I'm going to go to the toilet and I hope in peace." He paused and added, "And I'll head to town."

Chili shook his head affirmatively. "All right, see that you do." He then scurried down the arroyo and found his horse and galloped away.

When Kiowa Bob rode into town on his old pinto, there were several interested bystanders. 'All-Night' Roy was standing on the street with Michael Purvis. 'All-Night' Roy was of medium height. He wore a black ten-gallon hat cocked to one-side and leather slick black-leather chaps. He had gathered his nickname by chasing women all hours of the night. He had a shock of black hair hanging down over his forehead. His youthful face broke into a caustic smile. He had never expected to see the half-breed again much less ride boldly into town.

He looked over at Michael Purvis to catch his reaction.

Michael Purvis, who usually had the plastered smile, let the smile morph into a look of concern. He had figured that Kiowa Bob would be hiding out or avoiding any contact with him and his men.

He, along, with 'All-Night' Roy wordlessly watched Kiowa Bob tether his horse in front of the sheriff's office. They took note of his heavily bruised face.

'All-Night' Roy snorted, "Harley worked him over."

Michael begrudgingly smiled. "Harley's a good man." His grin evaporated as he turned to 'All-Night' Roy. "You keep your eye on the sheriff and Kiowa Bob."

'All-Night' Roy nodded. His eyes moved to Kiowa Bob opening the door to the sheriff's office. "I'll sit on that bench over there in front of the mercantile store and keep tabs on them."

Michael tilted his head in thought. He was wondering why Kiowa Bob was going into the sheriff's office. So, he stopped walking to his horse and made an about face. He walked to the sheriff's office and opened the door.

He saw Sheriff Nelson escorting Kiowa Bob to a cell. "What's he in here for, Sheriff?"

Sheriff Nelson turned his head and flashed a weak smile to Michael. "He was seen breaking and entering Chili Thomas' livery stable."

Michael frowned, "And he turned himself in?"

"Well, it's that way or I come for him and kill him."

Michael did not like this. He felt uneasy with the whole setup. The story sounded fishy and unbelievable. He nodded on it as if he believed him, but as he waved a tentative goodbye, the wheels in his brain were spinning. He decided to double-check all this with his brother. He shut the door behind him and stood on the boardwalk beneath the short-shelf roof.

He walked across the street toward the seated 'All-Night' Roy. He looked both ways and leaned in close to 'All-Night' Roy. "Listen, we might have to kill Henry Johnson and Kiowa Bob. I want to make sure the sheriff is not figuring on someway to save him."

'All-Night' Roy nodded in understanding. "Sheriff Nelson is afraid of you and Bill, but he's still an independent man."

Sheriff Nelson was watching them from his window. He stood far enough back that they could not see him but he could see them. He figured 'All-Night' Roy was going to birddog him. He rubbed his hand up and down on his chin. His eyes moved up in thought.

Michael walked away from 'All-Night' Roy and mounted up his big sorrel and galloped out of town.

The sheriff watched his trail dust and then went and got his keys off his peg. He turned the tumblers with a clatter and threw back the door. He indicated with his head for Kiowa Bob to follow him.

He took him to the backdoor and opened it. "There's a horse about a quarter of a mile from here in an arroyo." He pointed to a solitary mesquite tree that bordered the gully in the distance. "It has a rifle and a gun and thirty-dollars in gold hung over the cantle. Now you scat to it and get your ass to Fort Smith and warn John."

Kiowa Bob shook the sheriff's hand firmly but quickly and wordlessly began to trot to the mesquite tree.

The sheriff watched his back as he ran. He swiftly shut the back door and hurried to the jail cell and closed the door. He went to the window and looked at 'All-Night' Roy who was sleepily looking up and down the street.

The sheriff honestly did not know if he had signed his own death warrant but he knew he had done right. He decided to take Kiowa Bob's pinto to Chili Thomas' livery and refresh their stories.

"All-Night' Roy eased up from his seat and made his way to the sheriff. "You impounding his horse?"

Sheriff Nelson nodded and said, "You damn right I am. There's nothing I hate worse than a thief."

'All-Night' Roy smiled and stopped walking but asked as the sheriff kept walking. "How's old Kiowa Bob doing?"

"He's sleeping it off."

'All-Night' Roy smiled. He fell for the sheriff's words hook line and sinker. He decided he would go to the Texas State Saloon and have a cold one. He gave a second look at the jail but kept walking.

The sheriff handed the reins to the old pinto to Chili. "Now this is how we give ole Kiowa Bob some extra time. You close up at noon and take your horse and pull that pinto behind you and hitch him up in front of Kiowa Bob's shack."

Chili nodded, "They'll think he's at his house."

The sheriff nodded and added. "Now, you go out there at night and move the horse around some and make sure he's fed and watered." He raised an index finger for emphasis. "You'd better keep your own horse in that gully behind his house so you won't leave any tracks."

Chili sighed, "Now when you tell Bill Purvis that I dropped charges on him breakin' and enterin' what should I say?"

"You tell him that he paid for the damages and the stolen saddle."

Chili shook his head, "That'll be a stretch. Kiowa Bob don't have a pot to pee in."

The sheriff nodded. "Yeah, but as suspicious as Bill is, he might think he's got some hidden Indian treasure."

They both chuckled, but as the sheriff departed both men lost their smiles, replaced quickly with sober and thoughtful faces.

When Michael pulled into the ranch yard, he saw his brother untying his horse at the hitch. Michael threw up a gloved hand to halt him.

Bill looked at him curiously and stood waiting. Michael rode up to him and said, "Sheriff Nelson arrested Kiowa Bob for supposedly breaking and entering Chili Thomas livery stable."

A sarcastic smile edged across Bill's face. He snorted and turned his head and shook his head in disgust. "He's trying to protect him from us."

Michael grinned that creepy grin. "Why don't we just kill him and Henry Johnson and Kiowa Bob and stop all this pussy-footing around?"

Bill shook his head 'no.' "Michael, let me explain some things to you. When our uncle was here with all those Federal troops, we were protected when we evicted Ed and Roy Johnson." He smiled when he said the word 'evicted.' Bill dusted off his black vest and narrowed his eyes as he formulated his words. "We were not only cautious but smart when we bought out Henry Johnson and kept him alive."

He pointed his glove finger up at Michael to make his point. "That legitimized us to a degree. The people around here hate us because we are outsiders and if we had killed all the Johnson's and Sheriff Nelson, they would have revolted." He dropped his finger and curled it up into a fist.

"We're a whole lot stronger now than we were; we got some folks around here in our financial grip. But we still have to be careful. Sheriff Nelson needs to stay alive but watched." He inhaled and looked toward the horizon. "Since we both know that Sheriff Nelson will concoct a story of why Kiowa Bob won't be in jail, let's not kick up a fuss. We'll just send some boys after the half-breed and kill him."

Michael asked, "What about Henry Johnson?"

Bill shrugged and answered, "I want him dead just like you do but we'll hold off until we hear how the Kiowa Bob thing turns out."

Michael showed his chagrin and shook his head. "You're the boss, Big Brother, but if we are going to send men after Kiowa Bob why not send them after John Johnson too." He raised his hands palms up. "Two-birds with one-stone."

Bill nodded and said, "All right, Michael, you pick out the men and send them to get two-birds."

Michael pleased with that turned his horse and headed toward the bunkhouse.

Bill stood there thoughtfully and then mounted up and began cantering to town.

Later that night, Bill met with Michael in his study. Bill was sitting stolidly with his hands folded tightly across his large desk. "It was like we thought. He let Kiowa Bob go."

Michael looked at his brother with a puzzled mien. "Harley said his pinto was at his place."

Bill snorted. "He ain't there, count on it."

Michael smiled, "If he's not there then it is a ruse to make us think he's there. 'All-Night' Roy said the sheriff never left town."

Bill grimly smiled. "Look he and Chili Thomas are in this with Henry Johnson. They're not fooling me."

Michael smiled, "well, let's get after Kiowa Bob then this John Johnson."

Bill nodded, "Have you picked the boys who can do the job?"

Michael nodded, "The Rawlins brothers, Delford Dolittle, and Sanchez."

"When can they start?"

Michael answered, "I was waiting on you."

Bill slammed his fist on his desk. "Well, wait no longer, Little Brother. "Get this thing going." He paused as Michael stood up to execute the action. "Always have a backup plan."

Michael smiled, "I got the backup plan." He dryly added, "If the Rawlins brothers, Delford and Sanchez don't kill 'em, I'll just send four more."

Bill smiled and relaxed, "I like that."

Michael exited and made his way to the bunkhouse. He met his four-men waiting. He gave them all pouches of gold coins for expenses and gave them his explicit orders. "You kill Kiowa Bob and John Johnson both and you'll receive a thousand-dollar bonus each. If you kill just one of them you'll get a five-hundred dollar each." He paused and gave each man a hard look. "But if you come up empty on both of them, don't come back here."

They looked at each other and nodded that they understood. They mounted up and left galloping pulling a packhorse with them.

John Lee Johnson and his crew were having a hard time keeping up the pace that they had initially set since leaving Gilbert's Crossing. Hard and narrow trails had cut down on speed.

John always rode ahead and scouted and had picked the best trails but even the best roads or paths proved to be difficult for wagon travel. Heavy red rocks and cumbersome tree limbs made the small trail even more demanding.

Russell was commandeering the wagon as they rocked along a narrow rocky path that was bordered by trees that scraped against the wagon bed and canvas. Russell felt like cussing but he held his tongue for Bonnie's sake.

Russell and Bonnie were constantly jounced by the hard pits and odd-shaped rocks in the road. Bonnie looked at Russell as he concentrated on driving. "I'm not sure my husband could've done this. Bless his heart, he was a good man but he would have been discouraged I'm sure."

Russell just nodded not knowing how to answer that. "John will see us through. He always does."

Bonnie's eyebrows lowered as she concentrated on Russell's comment. "John is an unusual man."

Russell nodded his head 'yes' and slapped the reins. "I'm related to him and guess I'm prejudiced but he is one of a kind."

Bonnie sighed and looked at Russell's profile as he concentrated on the tough navigation. "How can a man be that gentle to me," she paused and pointed with her finger to Russell, "And to you and even the horses and mules and yet be so violent to some men?"

Russell answered, "We talked more than once about shooting people and he told me that when he shot a man who deserved it, that it didn't bother him too much. He said it was like shooting an intelligent squirrel."

Bonnie placed a hand over her mouth to keep from laughing. "I guess that's one way of looking at it."

"John would really grieve if he shot someone who was innocent or some bystander who had no quarrel with him. But, I tell you, Bonnie, he's yet to shoot someone who didn't need it."

They traveled a bit longer and they saw John headed their way. He had a smile on his face. He swiveled in his saddle and pointed down the road. "We get a break. The road gets wider and more traveled."

Russell pulled up and wiped his brow with his handkerchief. "Man, that's good to know. These last fifteen-miles or so have been hell."

John smiled and nodded, "It's been tough on horseback much less a wagon. "You did well, Cousin."

They made it a few miles further and they made camp by a gurgling brook. Russell unhitched the mules and took care of the animals and John started the fire. Bonnie got her cooking gear from the wagon and began making their dinner.

They ate hungrily and John and Russell sat with their backs to the trees and smoked cigars. Bonnie gathered up the utensils and headed to the creek.

John looked at her form as she disappeared into the tree line and walked to the brook. He made sure she was out of listening distance and he turned to Russell. "How's she doing today?"

Russell shrugged his shoulders. "She had some bad spots today, John." He looked into John's eyes and continued. "She'll cry some and then she'll cheer up but she keeps going back and forth."

John sighed and took a drag off his smoke. "I guess that's to be expected. She lost a lot. We just got to make her feel that she's important, and that she has something to live for. If we work on saying the right things maybe it will keep her spirits up."

When Bonnie returned, she carried the utensils to her wagon and just sat down apart from them with her back against her front wagon hub.

John noticed she was slumped over and she looked like a forlorn rag doll. He could see the worn soles of her little shoes emerging from her dress. He reasoned she wanted to save her new shoes.

He took another draw off his smoke and sat helpless. If a man needed his ass kicked, he could sure accommodate him. If a hard case needed shooting, he could sure send him to the Promise Land. But in a case of a broken hearted woman who had lost her family, he had no answers.

John was thinking about turning in, when Bonnie started humming 'Amazing Grace'. The way she hummed it sent eerie feelings down his spine. He could almost feel his arm hairs stand up.

Russell was watching her and was affected also. He tossed his cigar aside and stood and walked to her. He sat down on her right side and reached for her hand. He stroked it gently. She then began to sing the words.

To John's surprise Russell began singing it too. He had a good voice and it was a touching duet. John got a lump in his throat and tossed his cigar aside and walked over and sat on her left side and grabbed her other hand and he began singing the bass part.

While they were singing, John thought he heard another voice singing. He first discounted it as to his emotional state, but he kept hearing a voice that sounded like it was coming from the dense woods behind them.

He softly laid Bonnie's hand down and stood and walked a few feet from the wagon and inclined his head. He knew for certain someone else was singing.

He began to tip toe through the weeds and made his way tree by tree to find the source of the voice. The voice would sing and then he would hear what sounded like a sob. He was watching his feet as he stepped stealthily from a grass sward to another grass patch.

He reckoned that the voice was coming behind a large pin oak tree. He raised his revolver and eased to the thick bole of the tree. His head eased around the tree and there sitting on the ground was young man wearing a shaggy hat. He observed him for a good while and it seemed to him the young man was singing and crying both.

When John clicked back on the hammer of his Colt, the head swerved around, and the shaggy hat brim went up and two-sad eyes peered at him. It was one of the robbers from back on the trail. The one who had the hard down lonely eyes. He remembered the kid walking away in the woods and how pitifully forlorn he had looked. John reached down and hauled him up roughly. He started to talk loudly to him but he could still hear both Bonnie and Russell singing back at their camp, so he tempered his anger and said in a low voice. "What in the hell are you doing here?"

The young man swallowed and looked at John with the saddest eyes he had ever seen on a man. "I was following ya'll."

John's head tilted as to understand. "You've been following us?"

He nodded his head quickly, "Look, mister, I ain't worth much and if you need to shoot me, I don't guess I'd blame you."

John seemed puzzled by his remark. "Why are you here besides singing off key that is?"

He shrugged and tears began streaming down his smudged face. "I want to make amends to that woman."

John's eyes narrowed but he eased back on the hammer of his pistol and holstered it. He released his shirt and looked the young man up and down. "What's your name?"

"Seth Ragsdale."

John nodded and repeated the name idly, "Seth Ragsdale."

He nodded humbly.

"How long has it been since you've ate?"

Seth reached into his grimy pants and pulled out some peanuts. "I've been eatin' these but they ain't too fillin.'"

"How did you keep up?"

"I got a ride with a drummer who gave me those peanuts. When he turned off the road about ten-miles back, I just kept walking and running and tryin' to keep up."

John sighed. He was not sure how to read this situation. The poor young man was touching his heart, but he decided he would lead him to Bonnie and Russell and see how they felt about him.

He pointed to the flickering campfire that coruscated through the night branches and weeds. "Head that way."

Russell and Bonnie were standing by the campfire talking when John and Seth Ragsdale walked into view. Bonnie stood silently and Russell started to reach for his pistol but catching the sad face of the ragamuffin, he stopped himself.

John walked Seth up to the fire and presented him to Bonnie and Russell. "Tell them who you are."

Seth looked at the soft look on Bonnie's face and the stern appraisal of Russell's. "My name is Seth Ragsdale. I'm a thief." He paused and looked down humbly. "I was a thief."

He sighed and put his hands in his pockets. "I've been going down the wrong road for a long time. I decided I don't want to be a outlaw no more." He paused and looked up at Bonnie. "I want to rectify things with you. I'm hopin' ya'll will take me with you and I'll work hard to earn your confidence."

Bonnie looked him up and down and asked, "When's the last time you had a meal?"

He looked at John and Russell and back to her. "It don't matter, ma'am. I don't want to be no bother."

Bonnie at first seemed troubled but then she broke into a soft smile. "Seth Ragsdale is it?"

He nodded, and said, "Yes, that's my name."

"Go over by the fire, Seth, and let me fix you something to eat."

John and Russell looked at each other with a certain apprehension, but acquiesced upon seeing the frail form sit so meekly with his eyes straight ahead.

John decided to give him the benefit of the doubt so he sat down with him. Russell saw that John was offering a form of mercy. He decided to sit down too. John pulled a cigar out and handed one to Russell and then offered one to Seth.

Seth looked with wonder at the cigar being proffered. He tentatively reached out and took it and accepted the burning match from John's hand that torched his smoke.

They made small talk while Bonnie made more beans, coffee and biscuits. After Seth had eaten like a starved wolf, he went to sleep with the cigar still in his mouth. John removed the dead cigar and covered him with a blanket.

Bonnie looked at John and then at Russell. "He "asked for mercy and we gave it to him."

Russell shook his head indecisively. "That mercy might come back on us and bite us in the ass."

Bonnie shook her head. "I'm a pretty good judge of character. Anyone that would trail after us on foot has to be a good person. If he came to rob us, where's his weapon or his horse?" She looked over at John. "Anyone trying to rob us would have to be touched in the head."

John said, "Let's don't jump to any conclusions yet. In a few days will know his colors."

They accepted that judgment and they all went to their separate bedrolls.

The next morning after breakfast, Seth proved to be a better hostler than Russell. He tended to the horses and mules and hitched the wagon up both quickly and skillfully.

John and Russell, at first looked around to see if anything had been stolen, but seeing everything looked okay, they sheepishly looked at each other and mounted up.

Seth offered to drive the wagon and Bonnie agreed, and they took off. Seth handled the team skillfully and they made good time.

After they stopped to eat at noon, Russell approached John in private and said, "You know I like that little scamp." He gave John an awkward smile and said, "You know what I think?"

John shook his head, 'no.'

"I think if he steals anything," he paused and said, "What the hell!"

John gave back a quick, "What the hell!"

They both chuckled and went to their horses.

Harley Rawlins and his crew were making a fast trek across the Nations. They figured if they went double-time eventually they would come upon Kiowa Bob. They traveled well into the night because Delford Dolittle was well acquainted with the area. They had about exhausted their mounts when Delford suggested that they spend the night in the Indian town of Duty. They pulled into the livery stable and checked their mounts and sauntered down to large cantina that was owned and operated by one of the most notorious figures of the Nations.

The large adobe cantina had a large frescoed sign over the large rounded doorway that read 'Indian Melvin's.' Delford stopped them from entering with the back of his hand. Delford's appearance was deceiving. He was tall and lanky with two-large buckteeth. His eyes looked dull and unintelligent, but in truth he was very alert and had antennae that picked up things that others missed. His dull eyes fell on Julio Sanchez and he said, "Injun Melvin has a very pretty wife."

He addressed Julio with his eyes arched. Julio had a reputation of being a 'womanizer' and had a problem with women in general. He had difficulty controlling his language and his goat like appetite.

Delford placed a finger on Julio's chest. "So, watch what you say and do."

Julio looked down at the offending finger on his chest and then his dark brooding eyes moved up to Delford's. Delford nodded that he had made his point and dropped the finger and he looked cursorily at Harley and Slade.

Harley halted Delford with his own hand. "What's the word on Indian Melvin?"

Delford looked over his shoulder as to check on any eavesdropper. He leaned in and said, "He ain't no Injun. He runs this part of the Nations. He can have you killed with the snap of his fingers."

Harley cocked his head to one-side. "He ain't no Indian?"

Delford shook his head, 'no,' rapidly.

"Why do they call him 'Indian Melvin,' then?"

Delford shrugged. "I reckon because he married an Osage princess." He shook his head side-to-side as to indecision. "But I don't know why he's called. 'Injun Melvin.'"

Delford turned and led them into the cantina. It was well lit and had many round tables. The adobe walls were covered in frescoes of Indian life. Rough-hewn logs ran just under the ceiling and red peppers hang in decorative clusters from them. Oil lanterns were bracketed with thick bolts to the walls.

A giant of a man with blond features was behind the bar. He stood almost seven-feet tall. He greeted them cordially and told them to take any table.

There were a number of patrons near the far wall. They were rough looking hombres. But they hardly took notice of their entrance. It was obvious the outlaws drinking and playing cards were on their best behavior. The singular presence of Indian Melvin had that effect on them.

Harley sat first and soon all his companions took their seats. They all swiveled their heads to and fro taking in the colorful eating and drinking site.

Soon, a beautiful raven-haired woman came from behind the bar through a beaded curtain. All eyes went to her. She was like some pagan goddess that had descended to earth. She smiled evenly at them all and asked, "Beers?"

Harley nodded and she left to go draft the beers. Julio's eyes widened. "Delford, amigo, you should've talked to me. What a woman!"

Delford let his wary eyes move to Indian Melvin who was still behind the bar and seemed to be preoccupied. Delford turned his eyes back to Julio and cautioned him about the loudness of his voice.

Soon the beautiful woman returned with four-large schooners of beer. She looked around at all four-faces. "Steaks and potatoes?"

Harley nodded and she excused herself and left to the kitchen.

Julio leaned in and whispered too loudly. "I think she's looking at me."

Delford looked down and cussed Julio to himself. Harley and Slade gave him stern disapproving looks.

He was not deterred however by their reproachful looks. He laughed a lusty graveled laugh.

When she returned she placed a platter of steak and boiled potatoes and green beans for both the Rawlins brothers. She left to get the other two-platters.

Julio looked at the good food and then gleamed. "She's saving me for last."

Delford kept making nervous looks toward Indian Melvin. He looked pleadingly to Julio to control his emotions and words.

When she returned, she placed a platter in front of Delford and walked around to place Julio's plater down. He reached up and ran his fingers up her flank and settled on her butt.

She stood still and looked at Delford and then the Rawlins brothers. She made a hissing sound and she whirled quickly wielding a knife. Where the knife came from was a mystery. She placed it at the throat of Julio Sanchez. "You filthy greaser."

She grabbed him by his hair and looked down at his shocked whisker stubble visage. "You dog." She pressed the blade taut across his Adam's apple. A thin-line of blood trickled down from the sharp edge.

There was an instant rumbling of outraged masculine voices from the other side of the room. Several of those rough customers rose, making grating sounds by chairs being pulled-back, and were making threatening moves to their weapons.

Indian Melvin held up a hand and they settled back down. His attention went to Julio. He gave a neutral look to the Rawlins brothers and Delford. But a hard edge appeared in his eyes when he saw the oily face of Julio and the blade held at his throat.

His voice seemed almost gentle coming from such a giant but all he said was. "Marilla."

She looked at Indian Melvin and back at the gasping Julio. She shoved his face down with her hands roughly grasping his hair. She removed her knife and it went back to its mysterious hiding place.

She gave the other three a biting look and then disappeared around the bar and through the beaded curtain.

Indian Melvin walked slowly toward them. He looked at Harley, Slade and then Delford. "You gentlemen enjoy your steaks and beer. I want your stay to be pleasant."

He tendered them a tight smile. He asked if the beer was good and made small talk. Julio was touching his throat and was looking both embarrassed and uncomfortable.

Suddenly Indian Melvin spun his huge body around. The big man moved like a panther and as if by magic a machete was held his big paw. He made a wide sweep and Julio's head was dismembered from his body and the head landed like a cabbage and rolled through the cigar butts and trail dust that was settled on the floor.

Indian Melvin placed his boot on the convulsing body spurting blood into the air. He gave it a shove and it fell to the floor jerking in spasms.

He held up his hand and signaled with his finger. Two-Indian workers came and picked up the head and the body. Another came and picked up the chair and cleaned it out.

Harley's eyes were wide. He looked at the bad men who sat across the way. They looked at him and his two-comrades with humorous curiosity. They were well controlled, however. They made no threatening moves. They quickly turned away and began talking among themselves again.

Delford swallowed and said, "Damn, that almost made me lose my appetite." He took a bite of steak and nodded his head in approval. He looked at both Harley and Slade who seemed green about the gills. Delford sighed, "Well, since we're going to have to pay for it anyways, I want Julio's steak." He reached across and pronged the steak that was in Julio's platter.

Delford looked at the shell-shocked faces of his two-compatriots. "If you let those steaks go, you'll hate yourselves later."

Indian Melvin smiled and cleaned off his machete with a large handkerchief. "You boys eat up. I want your business again."

After eating, they walked listlessly to the livery stable. Harley was hardly in a talkative mood. They moved along the small boardwalk with silvery spurs. They had no idea that they were being watched. But they were.

Kiowa Bob's features moved from the shadows and his eyes zoomed in on Delford Dolittle. He knew him to be a cold-bloodied killer. He was undecided on the Rawlins brothers even though Harley appeared to be ingenuous about his loyalty to Ed Johnson.

Kiowa Bob pulled his face back from the twinkling town lights and the pale moon into the darker alley shadows. His eyes moved to edge of their sockets as he pondered his next move. He chose to follow the killers discreetly.

As Harley, Slade and Delford were walking along the boardwalk, Delford asked, "What's the plan, Harley?"

Harley looked past Slade directly at Delford. "We'll ruin some good horses if go on tonight. But I sure in the world don't want to stay here." He walked a bit farther and said, "But we don't have no choice."

Delford nodded and replied, "Hey, Injun Melvin runs a clean town, Julio asked for it and he got it."

When the two-Rawlins brothers did not respond, Delford stated, "We ain't going to find Kiowa Bob on the trail."

Harley agreed. "I don't think he's too far ahead of us, he couldn't be but we might as well plan on finding him in Fort Smith."

Delford inclined his head when he heard the words, 'finding him.' He thought that it was unusual for a man sent on a mission to use that expression instead of 'killing him.' He dismissed it for the moment as they sought shelter in the livery stable.

John decided to camp early the next day. The trail was becoming arduous again. He did not want to risk either a wheel or axle becoming damaged. So, while the sun was still up, Russell and Seth went looking for some firewood.

John was setting the stones for the cooking fire when he heard a loud shout and someone cussing. He heard a solitary gunshot. He stood with a concerned look on his face but from all indications it sounded like someone ran upon a timber snake. He was right. He saw Russell leaning heavily on the slender Seth.

John could see by the exasperation on Russell's face and the way he hopped on one-leg that he had indeed been bitten. He raced toward him and by looking down could see that the snake had nailed in the high- calf muscle just above his boot line.

John had him sit down with his back against Bonnie's wagon hub and he pulled his boot off and cut his pants right below his knee. He hollered for Bonnie who was in the wagon. She came out and looked at the wound. She went back into her wagon and brought back a bottle of pure white Kentucky shine and took a two-bandages and tied one above the wound and one below it.

She heaped copious splashes on the wound and Russell winced but did not cry out.

John, who had seen multiple snake bites in Texas and the wilds of Virginia and Tennessee, sent Seth to fetch a pail of the coldest water he could find.

Bonnie looked at Russell and said, "You're going to be sick at your stomach. We've got to get some broth or bean soup in you."

She handed a sheet for John to cut and she told him. "Up in Ashland when someone gets bitten, we change the bandages every four hours and pour lots of pure whiskey on it."

John nodded and reassured Russell. "You ain't going to die but you can't move either and that means even by wagon."

Russell began to sweat and he turned pale. "I can feel that damn poison in my system. "

John told him, "You just keep your upper body higher than your leg." John decided not to tell him that if he did not follow that advice he could lose his leg.

John gathered more firewood and started a big fire and Bonnie made some potato soup and some beans. They sat around Russell and took turns wiping his brow with cold water and feeding him sips of the soup.

After Bonnie removed his bandage and doused the wound with more white whiskey, and replaced the bandage, she sat for a long time and just twiddled her thumbs. She looked back and forth at the concerned face of John and the sad face of Seth.

"I tell you what we do."

John looked at her with a puzzled look.

She smiled at him and said, "Have you ever heard of Geoffrey Chaucer and the 'Canterbury Tales'? "

John nodded. "I read part of it in school. I don't remember too much about it now."

She looked at Seth. She knew he probably had never heard of Chaucer but she certainly did not want to leave him out.

Seth presaged she was going to ask him--so, he beat her to the punch. "No, I ain't ever heard of him."

"Well, it was about some travelers making a journey and they told about themselves on the trip." She looked back and forth to John and Seth. "While Russell sleeps, it'll be a good thing to do and pass the time.'"

John pushed his hat brim up and started to give her an 'oh please' look, but he did not. Seeing her smile and seeing her strive to enjoy life, he sighed and smiled back at her. "Sounds like a good thing."

She picked up on his insincerity and poked him on the arm. "Well, you do it, anyway, John."

Seth, who was so afraid he would say something wrong, sat there confused.

Bonnie looked at one then the other and said, "Okay, I'll begin." Her eyes twinkled and John caught note of that. He had never seen her eyes so full of life. "I was raised in Northern Kentucky close to Ashland. More near what used to be called Virginia before they decided to call it West Virginia. My father was a Baptist minister and he sent my brother Hughey, to Cincinnati to a famous seminary."

Seth inclined his head at the word 'seminary' so she stopped and looked at him. "A seminary, Seth, is where preachers go to study the Bible and become public speakers."

He nodded that he understood, so she continued, "My brother while he was there met Ned Harper. He was from Louisville and his father had sent him to be a minister but all he wanted to do was be a carpenter."

A moment of sadness passed her eyes, but she moved on. "Hughey brought Ned to visit our family. I liked him instantly." She sighed and looked back and forth at the two-members of her audience. "Make that I loved him immediately."

CONN HAMLETT

John gave her a sympathetic smile but dropped his eyes afraid that the emotions would overwhelm her. But her voice remained strong. "The first night he was at our place. I kept following him around and my mother got all over me telling me I was not acting very ladylike."

She laughed out loud. "But hey, I didn't care." She looked back and forth at each of them. "And you know what, he was in love with me."

John smiled and looked over at Seth. Seth hearing the lilt in Bonnie's voice and seeing the glint in her eyes, also smiled.

Bonnie's eyes narrowed mischievously and her voice dropped in register as though she did not want to be overheard. "The next two-days, I didn't let him out of my sight. I remember once, Hughey had to go to town for supplies and Ned and I got behind the barn and we started kissing. We were running a fever, when I heard my father calling for me and Ned for supper. I smoothed my dress the best I could and headed to the house. I don't mind telling you, my father looked at me with a strong disapproving look." She almost giggled when she said, "Ned had the good sense to come in from another direction and later."

She looked down at the ground and continued. "That night I was thinking of him and decided to sneak down the hallway and give him a 'goodnight' kiss. But when I gave him that 'goodnight' kiss it turned out to be a whole bunch of 'goodnight' kisses and soon I was in bed with him and well, you know the rest. I was still in bed with him when my father came to wake Ned up."

John gave her a smiling but understanding look. Seth looked sheepish. But neither interrupted her story.

"Oh, he threw a fit and a half. Soon my mother was there and Hughey. Ned took the blame, bless his heart, when it was all my fault."

John looked at her with an amused look. "What did you do?"

"We got married that morning before breakfast." She giggled

and shook her head. "It was a good thing too, because little Nellie was born about nine-months later."

John shook his head in wonderment and pulled out a cigar and handed one to Seth. John lit both cigars and leaned back against the tree. "The wonders of human nature."

Bonnie looked at Seth. "Well, , Seth, it's your turn."

He looked alarmed but gathering strength from the prodding of Bonnie he began. "My father was named Levi and my mother was named Eudora. I remember that my father drank a lot and would yell at my mother and would sometimes beat her. I had a little brother named, 'Ben,' and we would huddle together on the bed when he was on a rampage.

"I remember once that they got into an argument and he hit mom really hard several times. She passed out on the floor and me and Ben started cryin.' My dad told us to shut up or he'd beat the hell out of us for bein' big babies.

"He left shortly afterwards and took up with a neighbor's wife and they ran off to California. My mom suffered from that beatin' and she never really recovered.

"I was nine and Ben was five and we tried to chop wood and keep the house warm but we was both small and we didn't do a very good job of it.

I remember mom stayed in bed most of the time and tried to feed us cornmeal when she did get up, but she was just so sick. Me and Ben tried to make rabbit traps but they weren't no good and we never caught nothing.'

"Then one morning we found my mom cold in the bed and her mouth was moving but there weren't no breath. I took Ben and we walked down to the preacher's house and he and his wife came and looked at my mom and the preacher's wife hugged us. My mother was dead.

"The preacher buried her in the backyard and the preacher's wife left us a jar of stew and she said that she and others would check in on us. I guess they couldn't take us in because they had a passel of kids and could barely feed them.

"My grandpap came to see us in a buggy but when he drove up in the yard and took a look at us, he turned around and said, 'you look too much like your damned momma.' He left and I felt like cryin' but I knew Ben needed me to stay strong.

"That winter I chopped wood and tried to keep the stove goin' but it was cold most of the time and Ben got sick. He started coughin' and runnin' a high fever. I would give him all the blankets and sit by the stove. I would give him my portions of food that the preacher's wife brought but it weren't near enough.

"One morning I woke up and went to check on him and he felt cold and would not answer me---so, I went down to the preacher's house, and he came down and I remember his prayin' and cryin' some.

"He buried Ben by my mother in the backyard beside the smokehouse.

"One day I just started walkin' and I ended up down the road a fur piece and saw a house and just walked up to it and told the man I was hungry. Him and his wife took me in and gave me food and chores to do and they let me stay in the storm cellar.

"When the man's wife died the following spring, he began drinkin' and started yellin' at me and I left and started walkin' again and I ended up with some bad companions and later on I when I was older I met Corn and Frog. They didn't treat me very good but at least they gave me a horse and gun and introduced me to the world."

Seth, who had his head down, suddenly realized he might have talked more than he should have looked up to see two-sets of eyes fixed on him.

He inhaled and looked back down. "Did I say something wrong?"

Bonnie sighed and shook her head and said, "No, Seth you said it right."

John, who sat with a cigar stolidly in his lips, turned to Bonnie and said, "I've had all the Chaucer I need for tonight."

Russell, who had been enervated from the snakebite, had listened also and a tear trickled down his cheek. Bonnie as she turned saw the tear and used her apron to wipe it away. She gave a kind but sad smile to both Seth and Russell and retired to her wagon.

# CHAPTER FOUR

SEVERAL DAYS LATER IN FORT Smith, Sheriff Buchanan had no way of knowing that he was in for a busy day. He sat at his desk and was filling out reports for the mayor and the provost marshal at the Federal post. He was about to finish when the door opened and Colonel Daugherty entered.

Colonel Daugherty was a large, plump man with an engaging face. He was in his mid-thirties and had come up through the ranks fast. He and Sheriff Buchanan had become good friends and they had an amicable relationship.

The colonel pulled up a chair and grated it across the floor. He beamed at the sheriff and leaned forward and placed a telegram on the surface of his desk.

Sheriff Buchanan picked it up and started reading aloud: "Corn Dawson, Frog Turner and Toehold Jensen all killed by a man known as John Johnson. He is reportedly headed for Fort Smith and is due one thousand five hundred-dollars reward from the provisional government of Arkansas. Signed General Winfield Beasley."

Fat Phil, who had been sweeping the long corridor between

the cells, heard the reading and came forward with his broom and a surprised look. "That hombre wiped out a nest of vipers."

Sheriff Buchanan looked up at the Colonel and over at Fat Phil. "I ain't ever heard of a John Johnson."

The colonel nodded his head and leaned back. "Well, you have now."

The sheriff dropped his head to reread the telegram wordlessly simply said, "I reckon so."

The colonel looked at Fat Phil and back to the sheriff. "Fat Phil, you care if I talk to the sheriff in private."

Fat Phil, obviously displeased, placed the broom against the wall and grabbed his hat and trenchantly walked out the door into the street.

The sheriff looked at Fat Phil's leaving and then back at the steady eyes of the colonel. The sheriff was puzzled by the colonel's actions.

"The provisional governor of Arkansas wants to know if you would like to lead a group of deputies into the Nations and round up Indian Melvin?"

The sheriff inhaled and sighed. "Colonel, that is a tall request. He's got the meanest and baddest men on his payroll, and a whole lot of them too. Besides that, he's got Jack Filson working for him and I got a good idea that our bank is on his list. We got a thriving town, and with all that Federal payroll lodged in the bank---sooner or later Filson's going to try and rob it."

Colonel Daugherty shrugged and pursed his lips. "Since the War is still on, I am handcuffed about sending Federal troops into the Nations. I've been told that if I sent troops and the Rebs raided this area, I would be court-martialed."

The sheriff nodded and said, "I'm not saying that I will go after Indian Melvin, you understand, but if I was to, what's the monetary incentive?"

The colonel smiled and then tossed an envelope on the sheriff's desk.

Sheriff Buchanan noisily opened it and read the contents. It offered a ten thousand-dollar reward for Indian Melvin dead or alive.

His eyes moved back up to meet the twinkling eyes of the colonel. The sheriff's eyes moved back to the wording again. He placed the letter in his drawer and locked it with a key. "If I can find a really good man to help me on this, I might just take you up on this offer."

The colonel stood and said in parting. "You might want to check on this John Johnson."

The sheriff nodded, "Yeah, but I don't know a thing about him and moreover, have never heard of him until now."

When the colonel exited, Sheriff Buchanan walked to the dusty-panned window and looked out to the busy street. His eyes squinted in thought when he saw two-most unusual looking individuals riding in a buggy.

One was swarthy and had the look of someone from New Orleans. He had on a derby hat and was dressed very well. He did manage to see a gun belt around his waist.

The other one was dressed in a dark suit, which hardly concealed his impressive physique. He obviously was an athlete of some sort. He watched them go by and leaned as far as he could to see from the vista of his window.

Wanting to see them more he grabbed his hat from a peg and opened the door and saw them go down to Red Putnam's Saloon, which was cattycornered across the street from Ace's Saloon.

The sheriff's eyes narrowed and he decided to go see what Red was up to. He had known for a long time that Red was exceedingly envious of the thriving business that Ace conducted. When Big Willard fought in the back of Ace's saloon, Red's saloon could have been used for the morgue. He knew that Red harbored a real grudge against Ace.

The sheriff sauntered down the street and nodded at several citizens. He then centered his attention on the two-buggy patrons who had stopped and had stepped from the vehicle. He noticed that one of Red's bartenders had come out to greet them and was acting in a most obsequious manner.

He watched the two-men enter the saloon. He picked up his walking speed and entered through the batwings in time to see Red lead them to his backroom behind the bar.

The sheriff stood there for a minute and looked at the closed door. He ran his hand up and down his chin in thought.

When he exited the saloon, he noticed the bartender was driving the buggy toward Red's house on the outskirts of town. He watched all of that and then decided to amble over to Ace's Saloon.

When he entered Ace's place, he noticed that Ace was idly reading a newspaper at the corner of his bar. Ace gave him a quick look and said, "What brings the high-sheriff to my humble abode this morning?"

Sheriff Buchanan bellied up the bar and nixed with his hand that he did not want anything to drink from the ubiquitous bartender. He looked at Ace who was intently reading. "I didn't come as the sheriff. I came as a friend."

Ace's dark eyes moved from the newspaper up at the sheriff. "What the hell does that mean?"

Sheriff Buchanan gave a rare smile. "I don't want to sound like a gossipy old woman but Red Putnam, I think, has pulled in a prize fighter from New Orleans."

Ace's face sobered some and he moved his lips around to one side as he thought. "Yeah, that sounds like that bastard all right."

Sheriff Buchanan nodded and said, "I'd hate to see you lose a lot of money to a ringer."

Ace smiled and sighed, "Hey, if he's going to fight Big Willard, he'd damned better be a ringer."

The sheriff looked at him evenly. "You got that much faith in Big Willard?"

Ace pushed the paper to one-side and looked evenly at the

sheriff. "Sheriff Buchanan, there isn't a man alive, Texan, Negro or Jew that can whip Big Willard."

The sheriff raised his eyebrows. "Well, let me put it this way, Ace, if Red has brought in a ringer, he's going to put up some big money."

"I like big money."

The sheriff turned his back to the bar and looked at the batwings. "Red has to be operating mighty close. He spent a lot of money to buy the place and you've beaten him over the head for customers for every month he's been in business."

Ace nodded, "It won't take him long to get over here. He's wanted to get one over me for a long time."

The sheriff dismissed himself with a wave of a hand and departed.

Red Putnam sat behind his desk and looked over the top at the two-men from New Orleans. One was the manager, Philippe Pettibeau, and the other the heavyweight champion of New Orleans, Caron Beaumarchais. Red had enough education to know that the name was taken from a Revolutionary Frenchman, but it mattered little to him as long as he could kick Big Willard's ass.

Red tossed a hundred in gold in a leather pouch to Philippe. Philippe nodded and said, "I'll take your word that this is the right amount."

Red ignored Philippe and then looked at Caron. Caron seemed impressive. He had a handsome face with dark features and wide shoulders. He had the best musculature that Red had ever seen. Red leaned in closer. "Do you think you can beat Big Willard?"

Caron gave him a condescending smile. "In Louisiana, he would be a stiff. I don't underrate opponents and if my confidence is perceived as arrogance, I apologize, but if he were any good why would he be fighting in a saloon for pickup money?"

Red leaned back. "He's made a fortune here. Ace gets sixty per cent of the upfront bet, and he gets half of the ringside bets, but Big Willard gets the rest."

Philippe looked at Caron with raised eyebrows. "That does sound like a good profit for both."

Red nodded, "Big Willard fights all the time. There is always someone who thinks he can be whipped."

Red stopped himself as he thought about his last statement. "I'm hoping you can whip him."

Philippe leaned forward, "Red, you paid us one-hundred dollars to come here." Philippe jiggled the coins in the pouch. "I'm personally going to put up one-thousand dollars. Caron will put up 1000 dollars. None of this is your money."

Red sighed and nodded, "Yeah, but I am putting up my deed for this place against the deed of his place." He raised his hands palms up. "I am on the ropes."

Caron smiled his handsome smile. "You are going to be the owner of two-saloons if the man goes for it."

Red said, "I will go over and see him and set the fight up. I will try and get it for tomorrow at six o'clock."

Red stood, "Would you two-gentlemen like to accompany me over to see Mister Ace Gilmore?"

Caron looked at Philippe. "Sure, I would like to get a look at this so-called Big Willard."

About fifteen-minutes later, they entered Ace's place. Ace was behind the bar and he gave them a knowing smile. "I was expecting you, Red."

Red smirked, "Good ole Sheriff Buchanan, the unbiased sheriff of Fort Smith."

Ace ignored his remark and looked at the two-Creoles. He introduced himself and they reciprocated.

Red interrupted and said, "Since you talked to the sheriff, I gather you know why we are here."

Ace smiled and nodded. He looked over at Caron and said, "You look different than in the drawings I have seen of you. You're bigger." He then moved his eyes back to Red. "I know why you're here."

Red leaned in close. "They want to bet a thousand-each."

Ace shrugged, "It's a thousand maximum."

Red said, "You've got the money, and this is an opportunity for both of us."

Ace tilted his head and said sarcastically, "Both of us?" He smiled, "Frankly, Red, I don't give a damn about your opportunity."

Philippe insinuated himself into the conversation. "How about you bet your thousand and Big Willard puts up a thousand?"

Ace smiled and leaned back on his heels. He looked at Smitty, his bartender, "Go get Big Willard."

While Smitty went into the storage area, Ace looked at Red. "I understand their bets but what is your bet?"

Red swallowed and raised himself up to full height to put some steam into his courage. He pulled the deed to his saloon from his pocket and slammed it on the bar.

By this time a growing number of patrons surrounded them. When Red slammed his deed onto the bar, wild shouts and whoops filled the saloon. Ace, who was not one to be caught up in wild emotion, knew that Red Putnam's saloon was even larger and better stocked than his own. Just more empty.

Ace, who had lived by his wits and skill a long time, decided to go for broke. An uneven smile slithered along his handsome features. He dismissed himself and came back and slapped his deed on top of Red's.

There was a wild din in the saloon. Beer was being sold and wild and hoarse shouts were being made. In all this confusion and excitement, Big Willard made his way from the back and stood beside Ace behind the bar.

He merely looked over the riotous mob and then at Ace. "What's all this?"

Ace nodded toward the New Orleans' champion, Caron Beaumarchais. "Meet your new opponent."

Big Willard gave Caron a cursory look over and back to the frenzied crowd. He smiled and shook his head. He looked briefly at Caron and said, "I'd like to sit and jaw with you but I'm going to get me some boiled eggs before they're all gone."

Caron gave him a sneering smile. "Not before you bet me a thousand-dollars."

Big Willard stopped abruptly and looked at him evenly. "Okay, I'll bet you a thousand-dollars. Now if you'll excuse me." He zipped around the bar and joined the festivities down at his end of the bar.

Caron looked at Philippe curiously. "Well, that was quick."

Philippe looked at Ace, "Does your fighter know that Caron is undefeated?"

Ace smiled, "Hell no, he doesn't care one way or another."

Philippe looked through the mob at Big Willard eating boiled eggs and seeing people slap him on the back. "He's a fool, Ace. You both will lose everything."

Ace put out a hand and touched Philippe on the shoulder. "I haven't seen the color of your gold yet, either."

Philippe looked at Ace with a pompous sneer. "I'll have my gold and will soon have yours too."

Ace ignored his remark and turned his gaze on Red. "Let's set this up for tomorrow."

Red countered, "At six o'clock?"

Ace nodded and replied, "Perfect."

Some of the crowd followed Red and the champion of New Orleans over to his saloon. Ace had an enigmatic smile on his face as he watched them leave.

He looked over his saloon and looked at the still burgeoning crowd of drinkers and celebrants. He looked down the bar to the nonchalant Big Willard as he was downing a schooner of beer. He gave a resigned smile to himself and his foolish bet. He then glanced down at his new shoes. He simply said, "What the hell."

It did not take long for the news to filter down the street. Sheriff Buchanan was standing outside his office on the boardwalk when Lieutenant Gardner rode up and hailed him. The lieutenant was a young man who looked too young to be an officer but had a reputation as being tougher than he looked.

He looked down from his horse and gave a big smile. "I guess you heard that Caron Beaumarchais is in town and is going to fight Big Willard."

The sheriff smiled more to himself than to the lieutenant. "I figured that fight was going to take shape."

Lieutenant Gardner at first seemed puzzled that the sheriff would even have knowledge of Beaumarchais but continued, "When I was serving in New Orleans, I saw him fight some awfully tough men. He's never been whipped. I'm afraid that Big Willard may have bitten off more than he can chew."

The sheriff shrugged his shoulders. "There's been a whole heap of men who have thought they could put an end to Big Willard's rein, Lieutenant."

The lieutenant smiled that boyish grin. "I tell you what I'll do with you, Sheriff, I got a ten-dollar gold piece in my pocket that says Caron Beaumarchais will take him."

The sheriff nodded and said, "Okay, you're on." He paused and looked mocked-stern. "I don't reckon we have to shake on it do we?"

The lieutenant turned his horse's head to ride off and waved, "Nope, your word is good."

The sheriff watched him ride off and then opened the door to his office. His eyes widened some when he saw a half-breed Indian stolidly sitting in a chair facing his desk.

Sheriff Buchanan shut the door and Kiowa Bob turned and wordlessly looked at him. The sheriff walked behind him taking the long route to his desk.

He sat down and looked Kiowa Bob in the face. "What can I do for you?"

Kiowa Bob seemed ill at ease and squirmed in his chair. He sat gauging what type of response he would get from the severe looking lawman. "There's some men in town who are here to kill a friend of mine and are here to kill me."

The sheriff reached for his pipe and began packing it down with tobacco. He looked at Kiowa Bob levelly and then torched his pipe. He languidly tossed his match in a primitive tomato can on his desk. "Who in the hell are you?"

"They call me 'Kiowa Bob.'"

"You speak pretty good English for a breed."

Kiowa Bob nodded. He did not take exception to the word 'breed.' He responded, "My father was an Englishman." He paused and pushed out his chest proudly "But my mother was a "Kiowa,"

The sheriff leaned back in his chair. "Who's your friend that these men want to kill."

Kiowa Bob answered, "John Lee Johnson."

The sheriff's eyes narrowed and he sat up straighter. "John Johnson?" His voice showed some surprise that Kiowa Bob noted.

Kiowa Bob nodded but could see an unusual interest in John's name by the sheriff and he did not know how to perceive it. He decided to wait on the sheriff's response.

The sheriff could sense what was bothering Kiowa Bob so he allayed those fears by saying, "Your friend killed some criminals over in the central part of the state and is due a reward."

Kiowa Bob looked relieved. "He's a good man."

The sheriff nodded and drummed his fingers on his desk. "Why are these men wanting to kill John?"

Kiowa Bob asked if he could tell the whole story so he began telling about the Purvis brothers and the slippery, underhanded methods they used to bilk the Johnson's out of their ranches. He admitted in getting drunk and blabbing about Russell going to get John and bring him home from the War. He related how they wanted to shut him up before he reached John.

The sheriff puffed placidly and then asked, "What are the names of these men in town after you and John?"

Kiowa Bob responded, "Delford Dolittle and the Rawlins brothers."

The sheriff took down the first names of the Rawlins brothers and a good description of all three-men.

The sheriff asked, "Have they seen you yet in town?"

Kiowa Bob shook his head 'no.'

The sheriff used his pipe as an illustrator and pointed west. "There's a hotel that takes Indians just by the river and it is run by an Osage couple."

Kiowa Bob nodded that he understood.

The sheriff cut his eyes at him. "You got enough money to stay there?"

"I have thirty-dollars that I've not spent."

The sheriff assured him, "That's enough to keep you off the street for a spell."

The sheriff looked at the pad in his hand and back up at Kiowa Bob. "What does John Lee Johnson look like?"

Kiowa Bob gave a rare smile. "When you see him, you'll know it."

He watched Kiowa Bob exit the door and he sat smoking thoughtfully. He repeated the words aloud of Kiowa Bob. " 'When you see him, you'll know it.' " He shook his head in amusement.

The next day was the day of the fight. Even at breakfast time the whole town was talking and the streets were filled with soldiers, farmers, and cowhands. People were coming in from the countryside.

Sheriff Buchanan was holding court in his office. He gave greeners to Frankie and Fat Phil. He told them to watch the bank and all the businesses close to it for any suspicious characters. He also read off the description of Delford Dolittle and the Rawlins brothers. "These men are suspected killers."

He paused and pointed to main-street through the window. "Look, don't concern yourselves with public women plying their trade. Give them a hard look but don't be bringing any women to jail. We don't have time for that. Look for pickpockets and look for jaspers that look like they belong on a 'wanted poster.'"

He gave them all a business look and dismissed them. He took his hat off the peg and went out the door. He could see every hitch rack was filled and the livery stable down the street was doing a 'bang up' business.

The whole day was filled with drunks and fights. He had his jail almost packed by three o'clock. He knew that the ones incarcerated were losers and morons but not hard cases, and he did not concern himself with them.

At five forty-five, he began making his way to Ace's Saloon and a queue of people were already lined up trying to edge their way in. They recognized him immediately and they parted for him when he gave them that beetle browed look and moved through the masses to the back door and ringside.

Ace was sitting at his usual ringside chair and motioned to him and he took his seat and received his cigar box for bets. He looked down and saw four thousand-dollars and two-deeds. His eyebrows shot up as he looked up at the unflappable Ace.

"You going to take any more bets?"

Ace shrugged and said, "If I'm going to sleep in the streets, I might as well make a clean sweep of it."

The sheriff shook his head and replied, "I wouldn't want it no other way."

The bleachers were already filled and Ace's bartenders and his hostess, Judy, were selling beers like it was the end of the world.

The sheriff turned his head to give a perusal of the crowd. He thought he picked up on Delford Dolittle but he chose to let it go at the moment.

Ace stood up and held up a fist full of dollars and began making side bets. The thick roll was reduced in size considerably as the time ran toward six. The Federal soldiers were betting heavily on Caron. The townsmen were evenly divided. They had seen Big Willard wade through a heap of tough bumpkins, but they were beginning to waver whether he could handle a professional prizefighter.

Soon the cigar box was overflowing in cash and gold coins. Ace sat down and he still held 400 dollars. He sat and took more bets till he had nothing left.

Smitty rang the crude bell and that brought several hoots from the audience.

Red Putnam entered followed by Philippe Pettibeau and Caron Beaumarchais. Caron was wearing white tights and he looked a very formidable opponent. His muscles were delineated and tanned. Red and Philippe came over and sat by Ace and the sheriff. They both had the 'cat that had eaten the canary' look.

Caron climbed through the crude ropes and began shooting lizard-fast jabs into the air and dancing up and down loosening up.

Big Willard entered the arena last and made his way in his leisurely manner through the throng. He had on his derby hat and his usual ill-fitting frock coat. He climbed in the ring amidst a lot of catcalls and boos. He smiled and waved to the mob and took off his outer garments. Although he did not have the hard musculature of his opponent, he was massive and thick.

Caron stared at Big Willard and kept shooting those rapid-fire jabs into the air. Big Willard pulled on the ropes to loosen up and he stepped to his usual corner. While Caron was all business and his brows all dipped low in brewing anger, Big Willard looked his usual bored self.

The crowd was indeed tense for there were a number of them that had bet very heavily on the champion of New Orleans. There were no referee and no judges. You just fought till you dropped or you dropped your opponent.

Smitty clanged the bell and the crowd went berserk. Caron came straight across and began throwing blurred fast jabs at Big Willard. Big Willard shed most of the jabs with his arms and shoulders,

Caron was moderately surprised by his foe's deft defenses and he decided he would fight lefty and confuse Big Willard. However when he went southpaw, so did Big Willard.

Caron smiled to himself and reverted to his usual style using the left jab to keep Big Willard at bay and setting him up.

Big Willard kept coming toward him bobbing and weaving. Caron shot several jabs that connected to the top of Willard's head and he received a roaring ovation from the crowd.

Caron dipped down and shot a hard hook to Willard's midsection that sounded like a boat paddle hitting a side of beef.

Red Putnam and Philippe Pettibeau shared a grin and a sidelong knowing look.

The sheriff looked over at Ace and noticed a trace of perspiration under his hairline.

If that jab hurt Big Willard, he did not let on. He kept his inexorable pace always forward. Caron was backpedaling and jabbing.

Big Willard received a hard shot to the side of his head, but landed a hard punch beneath the looping right of Caron and it caught the Creole in the stomach.

The sheriff, who had seen his measure of fights, knew 'that the punch hurt the Frenchman.

Caron, like Big Willard, did not show any fear or pain. He countered with more rapid-fire blows that landed on the shoulders and arms of his adversary.

Big Willard then shot out a jab that connected in Caron's midsection again and this time the Creole winced.

Caron then began moving in circles with the indomitable Big Willard dogging him each step Caron then feinted a blow at Big Willard's head and shot a hard clout that landed in Big Willard's stomach. But when he did he left himself open and Willard countered with a wallop that landed on the side of Caron's head.

Red and Philippe's collective smiles went into the hold mode.

The sheriff always looking at Ace's expression noticed a sigh of relief through his nose.

Caron knew this bull of a man was an uncommon foe. Most outlanders just threw a lot of punches to excite the crowd but this man was not only ring wise but exceptionally tough.

Caron faked another shot at Big Willard's head in order to get in his body shot, however this time it did not work. Big Willard looped over another blow that hit the Creole like a small hammer on the temple.

Caron shook his head and flashed a smile to show it had no effect but Big Willard knew it did.

Caron then began to throw a barrage of punches and jabs. He wanted to confuse his antagonist, and keep him at bay. He unleashed his own heavy artillery with straight jabs and hooks, but again, Big Willard either dodged them or avoided them with his uncanny defense.

Ace looked up at Big Willard and cupped his hand around his mouth. "I'm getting bored."

Big Willard gave him a subtle smile and began moving in. He no longer was pussyfooting around. He meant to clean the Frenchy's clock. He landed several hard blows that landed on the arms of Caron. Caron was trying to block Big Willard's shots but he unknowingly played into the scheme that Big Willard had formulated.

The punches were so hard that they broke blood vessels in the Creole's arms. He caught Caron on the side of the head with one hard right hook. The stinging blow and the sheen of sweat momentarily blinded Caron and he did not see Big Willard 'wind up' deliver a haymaker from hell.

The blow actually distorted the Frenchman's face when it landed. Sweat went flying and he staggered. Big Willard then measured him and sent a sledgehammer straight jab that exploded into his face.

Caron's front teeth were sheared at the gum line. He staggered bloodily and collapsed.

Big Willard leaned over to see if he were alive. Caron's body was convulsing and shaking. Big Willard then abruptly went to his corner and began putting on his garments.

Red Putnam sat with all the blood drained from his face. Philippe Pettibeau sat stunned. His mouth was working but no words came out.

The sheriff handed over the overflowing cigar box to Ace. Ace gave a rare smile and handed a hundred-dollar bill to the sheriff.

Ace leaned over to Philippe's ear. "If you got any more Frenchies, bring them on over."

Philippe smoldered and glowered but he had no response. He got up and crawled through the ropes to pick up his fighter.

The sheriff, who had been caught up in the excitement, turned his head to scour the crowd for Delford Dolittle. He did not see the bucktooth man. But he had an inclination that he had seen him earlier. He made his way through the sodden crowd to the street. He peered both ways and did not catch sight of him.

He saw Red Putnam stagger by followed by the catcalls of the crowd. He saw Caron Beaumarchais hanging on to Philippe Pettibeau for dear life. Caron's glassy eyes were walling around unable to focus in on anything.

The sheriff began walking toward his office with his eyes ever moving.

Thirty-miles across the river, three men sat in a military style tent. The thick yellow light of the lamp globe sitting on the table threw dark-milky edged silhouettes against the sides. Indian Melvin sat overlooking a map. On each side of him sat the Filson's. Jack sat to his right and Buster, Jack's nephew, sat on the left.

Jack Filson was a large man with a black patch over his left-eye. He had grizzled and dark features. His one-good eye shadowed beneath a broad, dark hat brim was focused on the map of Fort Smith.

His nephew, Buster, was large like his uncle and his hat was cocked to one-side of his head. He had the same foreboding dark features of his uncle. He was listening intently to Indian Melvin whose size seemed to dwarf the large Filsons.

Indian Melvin was pointing to the bank and the alleyways around it. "It probably would take ten-men to take the damn thing properly, Jack." He paused and leaned back, "But you only have eight-men."

Jack Filson inhaled and kept staring at the map. "If you have the ferry boat waiting at the river, we can pull this thing off."

Buster, who had considerable experience robbing banks along side his uncle, was ill at ease. "I'm not sure, Uncle Jack. The bank is centrally located and the sheriff's office is just a block away. Look how long the streets are." He straightened his hat in his anxiety and put a gloved finger on the Federal encampment which was only five or six-miles away. "The Union cavalry is something to be considered too."

Jack, who was undecided, looked over at Indian Melvin for his opinion. Indian Melvin shrugged and said, "Well, hey, there's problems with any bank holdup. Besides, Buster, how many banks have fifty-thousand dollars in them."

Buster sighed and nodded, "Yeah, that is a lot of money, all right."

Jack straightened and pursed his lips in thought. "If you have the ferryboat there at the river and we can make it clean, I think it might just work."

Indian Melvin replied, "The ferryboat will be there with the gates down and ready to haul you away. The bank opens at nine. I will have the boat there at nine. If you're not there at nine-forty, I will have them pull out." He paused and looked back and forth toward each man. So, you'd better make it clean."

Buster nodded, "It seems like each time we rob a bank, there's always something that messes up the timing." He looked at

Indian Melvin and his uncle. "I reckon this time, we'd better be air tight."

Indian Melvin leaned back in his chair. "Is it set then?"

Jack nodded and held up his gloved hand. "You'll get your ten-percent commission. I think we can make this work."

John and his group had been sitting for two-days when Russell's color came back and he was no longer nauseous. John decided to put him in the back of Bonnie's wagon and they decided to leave at first light. John was satisfied that they had saved his leg.

The next morning as they were up and eating their breakfast, John pulled Seth aside. He placed his hands on Seth's shoulders and said, "Look, you've done your share around here and I think it's time for me to show you my appreciation."

Seth looked up with a puzzled look. "I wish I could've done more."

John smiled at him. He ignored Seth's modesty. Seth had waited on Russell hand-and-foot, cleaned his snakebite, changed his bandages, taken care of the livestock, hunted for game and brought in armloads of firewood. He treated Bonnie like she was the Madonna.

John pointed at the string of horses. "When we get to Fort Smith, I aim to sell all those horses and saddles. I'm going to sell every dang pistol and belt too. "We'll need the money." He looked down at Seth. "So, before we start off today, I want you to go over and pick out the horse and saddle and gun you want to have." He paused and continued, "If you're going to ride with me, you got to have a horse, and you need to protect yourself."

Seth stood stark still. His eyes were wide and he attempted a smile. "Can I tell you something."

John nodded.

"I sure plan on ridin' with you."

John slapped him on the arm. He looked toward the horses behind Bonnie's wagon. "Well, get to it."

Seth picked out Frog's pinto, and he put Frog's saddle and

bridle on it. He placed Toehold's twin .44's around his waist. He cinched them tightly and he climbed aboard. The gun belts were too large but he did not give a damn. He had a big grin on his face.

John smiled at him and he nodded over at Bonnie, who was grinning too. She slapped the reins. They were off again.

The road was good and they made thirty-miles that day. They went beyond sundown to do it but John knew he was very close to Fort Smith.

They got up before daylight and headed off again. They entered the town about eight o'clock.

They reined in at Andrew's Livery Stable and John dismounted upon seeing several men standing in the barn's maw looking at them.

A well-dressed and angular older man with snow-white hair appeared. His black hat was wide-brimmed and the shadow of it barely concealed his twinkling eyes.

He stuck out his hand and they shook. "My name is Bart Andrews." He looked at the string of horses behind the wagon. "What do you have there?"

John looked Bart up and down and liking the man said, "Well, Bart, I've got some horses for sale." He paused and continued, "And saddles and bridles and guns and belts."

Bart gave him a curious look but said nothing. He said over his shoulder, "Snuffy, come here."

A one-armed man still dressed in the butternut colors of a Confederate uniform came out stood by Bart. His eyes fastened onto the horses. Bart pointed to the horses and said, "Go take a look."

Snuffy walked around the horses and lifted hooves and looked at teeth and haunches. He stood mulling over the horses a good while and he turned and said, "Four good ones and one that's not so good."

Bart shouted back at him. "How about that mule?"

Snuffy shrugged and said, "He's old and not serviceable for more than a year."

Bart turned and looked at John and then up at Seth who was still mounted. "He knows his animals."

John nodded and replied, "I see he does."

Bart grinned. "But you don't care about that; you want to know what I'll give you."

John nodded. "Yeah, I reckon I do."

Bart sighed and said, "I don't cheat anyone. Horses and mules are a valuable commodity in this area. The Nations is right across the river and they're always buying horses." His eyes narrowed and he said, "I'll give you twenty dollars apiece for the good ones." He paused and rocked back and forth on his heels. "I'll give you five for the bad horse. I'll give you five for the mule."

John said, "Follow me and they walked to the back of the wagon. Bart's eyes widened when he saw the guns and holsters and saddles. His eyes widened further when he saw Russell lying there with his leg bandaged.

Bart rummaged through it all and he nodded at Russell, who watched him like a hawk.

Bart pulled back and looked up at John. "What happened to that fellow in there?"

"Snakebite."

Bart ruminated a good while and said, "I can always sell saddles and bridles. He thought a bit longer and said, "I could sell those guns too but they're a little out of my line." He looked over at Snuffy and back at John. "What'll you take for them?"

"I'll take sixty-dollars and two-free nights of lodging for the wagon and mules and horses."

Snuffy's eyes grew larger and he nodded at Bart.

Bart stuck out his hand and they shook on it. He looked at Bonnie and said, "Have that young lady pull the horses into the entrance and let Snuffy do the rest."

Later John and Bonnie followed Bart into the shadows of the

barn and he led them to his office. He opened his safe and counted out one hundred and fifty-dollars in gold coin.

Bonnie gasped when she saw the gold coins stacked on the crude counter. John smiled at her reaction. He slid ninety-dollars to one side and asked Bart for a pouch. Upon receiving it, he placed the gold coins in it and handed it to the remonstrating Bonnie.

He shushed her with a caring nod and he slid the three-twenty dollar gold pieces into his pocket.

Bart looked at Bonnie and at John. He could sense they were not married. He said to Bonnie. "Looks like you got a guardian angel."

Bonnie looked down at the rough floor and then back up at Bart Andrews. She gave him a sad smile and nodded and exited dabbing at her eyes.

John looked at the inquiring eyes of Bart and simply said, "She's had it rough."

Bart walked with John to the barn maw. When they were in the sunlight, Bart pointed to the bank. "If you're going to be here two-days, I would put the young lady's money in the bank." He pulled out his pocket watch and looked at the time. He pointed out that it was eight-twenty five and that the bank did not open till nine. He recommended a café that was three-buildings down.

John knew that Bonnie had considerably more money than ninety-dollars, so he agreed that it would be far safer for her to deposit her money in the bank than in some unsafe mattress or insecure hiding place. He also liked the idea of breakfast. It had been a long time since he had steak and eggs.

Bart shook his hand 'goodbye' and disappeared into the shadows of the barn entrance. As John stood peering down the street, Russell, Bonnie and Seth walked up and stood by him.

Bonnie stood now smiling and was excited to be in town after the rigors of the trail.

Russell was gimpy but was beaming also. Russell felt like they had made a big leap on their way to Texas. He stood looking at

John and Seth, and feeling frisky after being confined, reached over and play-wrestled with Seth.

Seth seemed in a good mood. He had a horse, pistols and a measure of self worth. He now was smiling and it looked good on him.

John reached into his pocket and handed Russell a twenty-dollar gold piece and Russell yelped for joy. His started to jig but winced and stopped when he felt the sting of the snakebite.

Seth was grinning at Russell and Russell's good fortune. He laughed out loud when his jig ended up short.

When Seth saw John's hand extend to him with a twenty-dollar gold piece, he looked both shocked and meek. His eyes went to the three-sets of eyes looking at him. He swallowed as if he did not deserve the kindness.

John nodded at him forcefully. He said, "Don't worry. This afternoon, you're buying the first-round of beers."

That broke the spell, he eagerly accepted the gold coin and said, "You doggone right I will and glad to do it."

John then announced to them all. "We're going to eat breakfast first and then we're headed to the bank. Missus Harper's going to make a deposit on her future."

They made their way to the café. They were talking and in good spirits.

On the other side of town, in another café called the 'River Café' sat Delford Dolittle, Harley Rawlins, Slade Rawlins and Judy Treffery.

The small eatery was semi-filled. Delford's eyes moved over the premises and thoughts were going through his mind.

He looked at the owner of the place behind the serving counter. The man had a horseshoe hairstyle with sweat beads on his forehead. He held a steady flyswatter in his hand and he occasionally zapped a fly and slid the dead offender adroitly off the counter and readied himself for the next victim.

Delford noticed the man's wife, who was the cook, when she

walked from the back to the front did not stand too close to her husband. She looked tired and depressed. Delford imagined her husband was a tyrant at work and in the home place.

He also observed their overweight daughter, who was the waitress. She would flash a phony smile at the clients but she seemed bored and shallow. He thought to himself that he would hate to be her husband, if she ever got one. The poor dope would be obliged to sleep with her. Delford almost shuddered when he imagined her doughy body and that bored, fat face.

Delford sat with his unlit cigar in the corner of his mouth. He occasionally sipped his coffee. His eyes then moved to his own table. He took in Slade Rawlins. Delford was skillful at observing and acting as though he were not. He noticed Slade looked very similar to his brother. But he was not as smart and he seemed dull and unimaginative. He watched him shake his head in agreement and smile at things that were not all that funny. He would laugh out loud with more volume than the humorous occasion called for. He hardly knew how to initiate a conversation unless it dealt with weather, saddle cinches or why his gun shot to the right.

Delford analyzed Judy Treffery. She had beautiful green eyes that hardly left Harley. She had oceans of auburn hair piled up and some of it down that framed her pretty face. They all had met her at Ace's Saloon. She was a hostess but not a working girl. She had become enamored with Harley when he treated her with respect. He was always the gentleman and never made sexual comments or made reference to her anatomy, which was splendid.

Delford could tell she was one well-built woman. She had large cantaloupe-sized breasts that were hard to ignore. Her blouse hardly concealed that fact. He noticed a faint circle on her left-hand and felt she had been once married. He could see the sadness in her eyes and the hope she had in Harley.

Delford's thoughts then moved to Harley. He was stolid and stubborn and was an enigma. He could be a fierce man but was for the most part gentle especially with Judy. He could get a read on him. He felt he might be more intelligent than he first surmised.

Delford sipped his coffee and let his mind move to the mission at hand. He had been the only one who had been actively looking for Kiowa Bob. Harley spent most of his days mooning over Judy. He never planned for or mentioned John Johnson and that seemed most peculiar to Delford. Slade was a boring clod, who did nothing unless Harley told him to.

Delford's gaze took in two-men who were seated next to them and close to the door. He looked at their boots, which were caked in orange clay. He knew that clay was indigenous to the Nations and he wondered why they would be in Fort Smith so early.

He had listened to their conversation covertly enough to know their names. Catfish was the more assertive and the dominant one. He was a tall and gray man with grey-blue eyes. He kept pulling his pocket watch out and looking at the time, as though he had an appointment. His face was impassive and shadowed by the stained-gray hat brim.

His partner was Arkansas Bob and Catfish called him that. Not Arky not Bob but Arkansas Bob. That was important to Delford. It told him Catfish did not hold Arkansas Bob as a familiar friend. Catfish's body language indicated that he seemed offended that he had to share time and space with Arkansas Bob.

He noticed that Catfish kept the repetitive procedure of checking his watch--when there was a perfectly good Regulator on the discolored wall.

He watched them stand up and throw some change on the table and then stridently walked to the open door and exit. Delford's eyes moved to his three-companions and they seemed in a world of their own. He laid a nickel on the table and rose up. He excused himself and the other three hardly paid him notice. He sarcastically smiled to himself as he left his three-friends. He felt alone. He realized quickly that 'four' was a crowd.

He left and kept Catfish and Arkansas Bob in sight. He walked nonchalantly. He managed to avoid eye contract with Catfish, when he occasionally looked back. He looked like any cowhand from the Nations. Hell, he had just proved he was anonymous even with his so-called friends. He would stop and look at his reflection in store windows and would cross the street and re-cross the street. Curiosity kept him going down the street following his suspicions.

Jack Filson was seated almost across the street from the bank. He held a newspaper close to his face. He was afraid his eye patch would alert some nosy citizen or deputy.

He would lower the paper when he felt safe and look. He watched as a dray wagon passed by nosily. He heard the chirping of birds in a sycamore tree and the desultory barking of a dog in the distance.

His vision panned the street and he saw Three-Finger Louie down the street. He was whittling wood and trying to blend in. He watched Buster and Luke Dooley walking along the boardwalk carrying a dummy sack of feed.

He knew that Cecil Tate was in an alley holding most of the horses but not his and Three-Finger Louie's. They had theirs hidden in a special place. He had learned that keeping all the horses in one-place could be dangerous.

Just beyond his sight but down the street in a pecan grove by Andrew's Livery Stable, John Ferris had ridden up and pulled his Sharps from the boot and quickly disappeared into the dapple shadows of the trees.

He saw Catfish Link and Arkansas Bob moving along at the right pace.

He pulled his watch out and looked at it. It was nearing opening time. He pulled the paper close to his face again, but out of his peripheral vision he caught sight of four-people moving toward the bank.

One in particular caught his interest. He was tall and broad-shouldered-- a most singular individual. Jack took a lingering gaze and noticed the twin-military gun belts and the ivory-handled Navy Colts. He also took in the other two-pistols stuck in his belt.

The one walking beside him was short and slim but had .44's in his holsters. He did not look all that threatening but Jack knew looks could be deceiving.

The tall one limping behind them was also heeled with a weapon. He took little notice of the woman.

Jack went back quickly to his paper, but his eye was keeping the threat in sight and in mind.

John's thoughts were on Martha Taylor. He loved daydreaming about her. He relived the moment she told him she loved him. He was reminiscing about their walk. He could just see her white teeth and red lips. His wistful reverie ended by Seth nudging him on the arm.

John looked at Seth curiously and asked, "What?"

Seth kept his face forward and his words came out of the corner of his mouth. "John, you can call me crazy, but that looks some men are settin' up for a bank robbery."

John's eyes moved from Seth, and he took in the man, behind the bank, in the alley holding horses. His vision went quickly to the man reading the paper, who was trying too hard to look unobtrusive. He observed two-men carrying a feed sack that one-man could carry easily.

The bank employees were walking across the street. The Two-men and one-woman were walking as though they had no problems in the world. They were animated and an occasional laugh erupted. They seemed oblivious of the danger.

John then spotted two other men behind the two-men carrying the ridiculous feed sack. His eyes narrowed when he saw one slink into an alley.

John said over his shoulder to Russell. "Keep your eyes peeled."

Russell, who had been unaware of any danger, suddenly became alert. He knew not to answer John. He pulled Bonnie in closer. She also had heard John's admonition and her eyes began oscillating to both sides of the street

Several merchants and a few citizens also were moving toward the bank. It all seemed like a normal day but John and his crew thought differently.

Buster and Luke Dooley dropped the seed bag and hang back some and let the merchants follow the employees in when they opened the door.

The two-male employees went immediately behind the metal grilled frame and took up their work positions. The bulky female made her way to a backroom through a door.

John noticed that Buster and Luke let them enter first. He fixed his eyes on them. They were not shy in looking back and giving menacing looks. The two would be outlaws walked to one-side and allowed Bonnie and her bulging reticule to go stand in line behind a fat merchant.

Seth remained with Bonnie. He had become almost obsessively protective of her. Russell made his way to the opposite side of the bank and kept the edges of his eyes on Buster and Luke.

Buster and Luke sauntered in. Their predatory eyes moving wolfishly beneath shadowed hat brims. Buster did not waste time. He pulled his .44 out and said, "Folks, this is a robbery."

John, who been expecting this, kept his silence. He had no desire to see innocent bystanders get killed.

Buster turned the ominous black bore of his .44 on John. Luke, who had pulled his pistol out, stood by the door.

Both John and Russell watched them with wary eyes. Buster looked squarely at John. "I would be obliged if you would drop those gun belts, Big man."

John, who had never taken his eyes off Buster, began slowly unbuckling his holsters.

Luke, who had been standing by the door, noticed the heavy reticule of Bonnie. He could see the bulges of coins. Overcome by a sudden urge of greed, he suddenly bolted toward her and seized the cloth purse. When he did, Seth hit him solidly on the jaw.

Luke, having been knocked backwards, shook his addled head. He recovered his senses and growled in anger. He raced forward cursing. He lifted his Colt and clubbed Seth on the side of the head sending him to his knees.

Buster, who was watching all of this, shouted in an emotionally ragged voice, "No, Luke!" He made a serious mistake by taking his eyes off the big Texan. He was shifting his .44 back and forth trying to cover all the customers, and trying to calm Luke, who stood over Seth cussing a blue streak.

Seeing that Buster was distracted, Russell reached for his revolver.

Russell's impulsive action and the quick motion of his rising Colt caused Buster to turn his attention to him. Buster took his eyes off Luke and Seth. He whipped around with his Colt leveled ready to take Russell out.

John grabbed Buster's wrist and wrenched the Colt from his hand. He seized the outlaw's shirt and cuffed him with hard fleshy slaps. He busted Buster's mouth and sent his hat flying across the lobby like it was caught in a whirlwind.

Buster, enraged, jerked back and took a wild swing at John. John grabbed the fist in mid-air and twisted it into an unnatural shape and snapped Buster's arm. It sounded like a tree limb snapping in an ice storm. He then reached down and grabbed Buster in the straddle of his pants and lifted the large bandit over his head as though he weighed nothing. Buster's mouth was open in both disbelief and pain. John sailed him through the bank window like a mail sack.

Glass shards were raining everywhere and Buster broke his hip when he hit the boardwalk. He rolled to his side up against a horse trough and looked up at the shattered window in shock.

Luke, who was stunned by all of this, was swinging his weapon around to kill John or anyone else he damned please.

Seth, who had recovered from the pistol whipping, suddenly pulled his .44 and fired up. An orange jet erupted from his pistol bore. The ball went through the back of Luke's skull and exited his right-eye. He fell forward and he reflexively fired a round into the front wall of the bank near the doorway.

John jumped over Luke's convulsing body and raced to the front door.

He saw Catfish standing over Buster with his Colt extended looking for a target. Catfish's eyes widened when he saw the big Texan leap through the doorway. He momentarily froze, shocked by all the hell that had broken loose.

When he hesitated, John shot him two-times in the chest. Catfish twisted in agony. He gurgled and wobbled drunkenly. He fell into the powdery street dust.

Arkansas Bob, seeing Catfish stagger and fall in the dusty street, suddenly bolted and ran down the alley between the bank and a hardware store.

Jack Filson and Three-Finger Louie both were stunned when the gunfire started. They were equally thunderstruck when Buster came flying through the window in a spray of glass.

Filson was reaching for his pistol when he caught sight of Catfish being pounded by the Navy Colts of the stranger. His vision shifted to the sight of Arkansas Bob turning tail and running. His Colt was shifting to one direction and then another.

John, who now had been joined by Russell, shot across the way and nailed Jack Filson in the hip. Jack dropped his pistol and hollered for Louie to open up. Jack gritted his teeth and glared at John with his one-good eye.

Seth, who now had exited the bank, joined Russell in a barrage at Three-Finger Louie.

Louie took a shot in the shoulder and the shots that missed ate big holes in the wall behind him. Louie did manage one-shot and it missed and went through the shattered window and ricocheted off the iron grill cage and shattered the glass facing of the wall-braced Regulator clock.

Louie looked over at Jack Filson and knew the jig was up. He raced toward his boss and slipped an arm around him. They were saved by the loud report of the Sharps rife in the grove. The rifle ball whizzed over John's head like an angry hornet.

The two-bandits alerted to the fact that John and his men were distracted by Ferris' rifle fire, limped down the alley toward their horses.

John told Russell to run around the bank building and get the man holding the horse and Russell gimped around the building with all he had and surprised the startled Cecil Tate. Cecil threw up his hands, and Russell quickly disarmed him and marched him out of the alley and around to the front of the bank.

At that very moment, John Ferris fired a second-round at John and it zinged into the dirt but it was enough to draw John and Seth's attention from Three-Fingered Louie and Jack Filson who had escaped the alley and were at the back of the building where their horses were tethered.

Another report of Ferris' Sharps sent John into the bank with only his pistol looming out. John had seen the escaping bandits but was powerless to do anything about it. He cussed to himself but knew it was useless to fire his Navy.

The sheriff and his deputies were running down the street and Sheriff Buchanan noticed the rifleman firing from the pecan grove. He yelled at Frankie and Fat Phil to get mounted up and pursue the bushwhacker.

John walked out the door and pointed to the alley. He told the sheriff that two-men, both wounded, had run down it when they saw the robbery had gone bad.

The sheriff yelled over his shoulder to his two-remaining deputies to bring horses. He looked up at the tall Texan. His eyes narrowed. "Would you be John Johnson by any chance?"

When John nodded at him at him strangely, the sheriff

remembered the words of Kiowa Bob that when you saw him you'd know him. He smiled to break the tension and said, "Proud to see you and hope to know you better later."

The sheriff looked at the scene and told one of the two-deputies who had brought horses to arrest Buster and Cecil. He and the one-remaining deputy mounted up and headed for the river in a gallop.

Delford stood on the corner two-blocks away and witnessed the gun battle at the bank. He had seen Arkansas Bob desert his comrades to save his own skin. He had seen the body come crashing out the window like a cannon ball, and had seen the big man blast Catfish to kingdom come.

He looked more closely at the large man standing in front of the bank. Suddenly it hit him like an epiphany. That was John Lee Johnson! He knew it had to be. The military gun belts and the daunting appearance. He reached for his cigar and removed it from his mouth and exhaled. For a moment he felt breathless. He studied the situation and then retraced his steps back down the street.

Harley was standing on the boardwalk with his brother and Judy. The seedy restaurant owner stood gawking with his arms folded and the flyswatter jutting out. His depressed wife and fat daughter stood nearby and were half-heartedly peering down the street. The whole motley crowd of restaurant patrons was murmuring and looking through dullard eyes supposing what happened.

Delford caught Harley's vision and Delford signaled him with his index finger for a private parley away from the ears of the diners. Harley squeezed Judy affectionately and left her standing with his brother. He walked toward Delford and they walked into the alley between the café and a feed and seed store.

Delford's usual dull eyes were now animated. He started to talk, but Harley interrupted him by holding up his hand. "You saw John Lee Johnson didn't you?

Delford looked surprised. He nodded at Harley. "How did you know?"

Harley exhaled and looked at the ground. "He has that effect on people and you're no exception."

Delford's eyes narrowed and his features grew hard. His voice became accusatory, "Well, it's going to take a lot more than me to kill him."

Harley gave him an irritated smile. "Well, let me put it to you this way, Delford. It'll have to be you."

Delford gave him a knowing smile. "So, that's how it is, huh?"

Harley gave him a freezing smile in return. "Yes, I ain't killing John Lee Johnson and I doubt seriously if you are either." He paused and said, "You might try, but it'll be the last thing you ever do."

Delford nodded knowingly with the sarcastic smile still on his face. "Why did you take the damn job then if you knew you were not going to kill him?"

"To get away from the Purvis brothers."

Delford's eyes widened and a creepy smile etched its way across his features. "So, it was supposed to have been me and Sanchez all along and all alone."

Harley nodded. He started to turn but suddenly stopped. "He touched his hat brim and said, "Adios, amigo."

Delford watched him walk away and he cussed and spat out a tobacco fleck. He checked his revolver and then moved deeper into the recesses of the alley.

# CHAPTER FIVE

———◆·◆·◆———

THE SHERIFF AND HIS DEPUTY William Green reached the river and saw tracks and blood on the ground at the landing dock. Sheriff Buchanan dismounted and he could see the smoke still lingering in the air from the ferry. He knew he couldn't catch it and he stood frustrated and cussed

William dismounted and joined him looking at the wispy smoke. "Indian Melvin?"

"Indian Melvin."

The sheriff stood for a while and then looked over his shoulder as if he were both forgetting something and remembering something.

William gave him a sidelong look but said nothing. He knew the sheriff was uncanny and wise and had something up his sleeve. "What you gonna do?"

"William, I have a plan." He rubbed his jaw in thought. He suddenly conjured up the image of John Johnson. "I think."

After all the commotion at the bank, Bonnie still managed to deposit her money. John and his crew walked to the hotel and found out their stay was 'on the house.'

They all had their own private room and bath. John took the

opportunity to shave and bathe. They left Bonnie, who decided to sleep.

The three-men made their way to Ace's Saloon. They noticed that the other saloon was boarded up with a sign that read 'Under Construction New Management.'

They entered into the saloon with the rinky-dink piano playing 'those golden slippers.' They took a table near the door and John leaned back and sighed, "What a day."

Judy Treffery, who now was on duty, stood at the bar and her eyes immediately picked up on the big Texan who had saved the day at the bank. Her eyes stayed focused on him through the cigar smoke. Harley had spoken of him and Harley had been correct. He was a remarkable looking man. His shoulders were wider than she had ever seen. His neck was thick and muscled. He had an arresting face.

Ace was standing behind the bar and close to the corner, where Big Willard was. He edged closer to Big Willard. "See that jasper sitting at the table by the door?"

Big Willard turned and looked. "He's a big one all right. Hope he ain't got fifty-dollars."

Ace chuckled. "That's the guy who blew the Filson gang to hell today at the bank."

Big Willard gave a second-look. "He sure saved your hide and mine then."

Ace agreed. "Yeah, those bank holdups can reduce your bankroll sizeable."

Ace noticed Judy, the hostess, walking toward John. He looked down the bar to Smitty and hailed him. Ace nodded toward the table that Judy was moving to. "Don't charge anything for the first two-rounds on those three men."

Smitty peered through the smoke and got his bearings and then nodded affirmatively.

Judy walked toward John who was half asleep with his back to the wall.

John's eyes opened when he saw the curvaceous woman with the lush auburn hair. He tilted his chair forward and ran his hands over his face.

Judy perused the three and liked their looks. They appeared decent men who just wanted a drink. .

"Gentlemen, we have beer and we have whiskey. What is your pleasure?"

Seth held up three-fingers and said, "Beers."

They watched her hips as she walked away. Russell sighed. "Damn, it's good to get back in civilization."

John and Seth grinned and soon they began a pedestrian conversation about mules and horses.

When she returned with a tray and three-beers, John noticed she was quiet and thoughtful, and that she kept her eyes on him even when she placed the beers in front of each person. Before Seth could pull his twenty-dollar gold piece out of his pocket, she shook her head and turned and pointed her finger toward Ace. "The first two-rounds on the house."

They all acknowledged Ace by holding their hands up and waving. Ace waved back.

Instead of leaving, she stood there indecisively, and John picked up on that. He looked up at her and asked, "Would you like to sit down?"

She wordlessly sat down and looked around the table. "Is there any chance, I could speak to you alone?"

Although he was sleepy, his eyebrows moved up and he straightened. He peered at her with a look of askance.

She caught his look and then threw up her palms. "Oh, no, I'm not a working girl. I just have something important to tell you and then ask you."

John was puzzled. He had never laid eyes on this woman before and could not think of anything possible she would have to say that would be of interest. She was a looker; he had to admit. He did not like to be rude to women especially pretty ones. He sighed and gave

157

Russell and Seth a 'see you later look.' They picked up their beers and headed toward the bar.

He looked at her while she collected her thoughts with a 'well what is it look.'

She leaned in closer and her green eyes locked with his gray ones. "Have you ever heard of Harley and Slade Rawlins?"

He broke the gaze and looked away. "Yeah, Russell has told me they're working for the Purvis brothers."

"They were working for the Purvis brothers."

He looked at her with interest. "Why are you telling me this?"

She wet her lips and inhaled. The sound of the rinky-dink piano moved over and around them. "Harley and I are engaged."

He said a 'quick congratulations' that lacked warmth.

She ignored that and continued. "He was sent to kill you. The Purvis brothers want you dead. They don't want you coming back to Texas to make trouble."

When he did not respond, she continued, "Harley says he owes you and your father a debt. He left Texas with Delford Dolittle, who's a cold-blooded killer, and they've had words. Delford is still in town and Harley figures he'll try and dry gulch you."

John looked at her with level eyes. "Miss?"

"Judy," she quickly replied.

"I don't mean to be rude. But maybe I have to be. What is your point?"

"Harley and Slade are on your side. The Purvis brothers took their ranch too, you know."

"No, I didn't know."

"You asked me my point earlier, well, here it is. Harley and Slade want to ride with you. They don't know that I'm even talking to you, but I wanted you to get my point of view."

John inhaled and gave a thoughtful look to nowhere in particular. "You're asking me a tall order. I haven't been around Harley and Slade in years. I have no way to know if they're secretly still involved with the Purvis brothers. I have to watch my back and I have to know who else is watching my back."

She nodded gravely. "I just wished you'd give him a chance. He wants to talk with you." Tears welled in her green eyes. "Everyone needs a second-chance."

John turned his head from hers and studied on her words. He looked at Russell and Seth at the bar. He noticed how Russell was filling out and seemed larger and healthier than when he rode into the encampment along the Tennessee River.

His eyes moved to Seth who was animatedly talking to Russell.

Seth had evolved. He no longer had the hang-dog look of a starveling. He had weapons on and he had some spirit. He looked happy and that he belonged and that he was important.

John turned to the tearful Judy. "All right, have Harley meet me at the livery stable about nine-o'clock tomorrow morning."

She sighed and said, "Thanks, John, you won't be sorry."

He started to say 'he hoped not,' but he refrained.

She stood up and kept standing there awkwardly. She hastily kissed him on the cheek and hurried off with her tray. He felt the kiss was totally unnecessary. He reserved judgment on the Rawlins brothers.

Sheriff Buchanan and William Green rode into the Federal military encampment and were greeted by two-sentinels who waved him them through.

Colonel Daugherty was outside his office on the boardwalk talking with Major Ambrose, an officer that Sheriff Buchanan deeply disliked. He felt he was just one-step up on a skunk and that might be giving him the edge.

The sheriff warmly hailed the colonel with a friendly wave and frostily nodded to the Major who gave a curt nod of acknowledgement.

The colonel turned to the sheriff and gave him a searching look.

"Anything wrong, Sheriff, we usually do not get a visit from the sheriff of Fort Smith unless there is a problem."

The sheriff looked at the colonel and over at the beady eyes of Major Ambrose. "Is there anyway I can talk to you in private?"

The major gave the sheriff a condescending smile and abruptly saluted the colonel and slowly walked away with a backward look at the sheriff.

The sheriff watched him slink away. Sheriff Buchanan's jaw was clinching as he very well caught the look of Major Ambrose's contempt.

His eyes slowly backed to the colonel. "The bank in Fort Smith,"

The colonel blanched and interrupted. "Don't tell me it was robbed?"

Before he answered the colonel, he glanced again at the major who had slowed his steps. He sat there until the major could sense he was not going to answer until he was out of ear sight.

The colonel looked at his directed face and then he turned and looked at the major was now walking faster and getting out of hearing range.

Their heads turned at the same time and squarely looked into the other's eyes. "No, it was foiled."

The colonel exhaled deeply and almost looked faint. "Well. congratulations, sheriff, on a job well done,"

"No, congratulations to me. It was done by a customer."

" A customer?"

The sheriff nodded. "A customer named John Johnson,"

The colonel straightened. "The hell you say?"

"The hell I do say."

The colonel looked at the ground and then let his eyes move to the far figure of Major Ambrose who was crossing the parade area. His eyes moved back to the sheriff and William Green's.

This time the colonel gave the request. "Is there any chance we could talk in private?"

The sheriff gave a quick look to William Green. William caught the implied look and pulled his reins and waved 'goodbye,' and turned his horse and started a slow trot through the military compound.

The colonel went to his horse and mounted up. "Let's ride and talk." He pointed to his block-building office. "Sometimes offices have ears."

The sheriff gave a quick cursory look at the doorway and caught sight of Lieutenant Gardner writing at a desk. The lieutenant, feeling his gaze, rose and walked to the doorway. He glumly reached into his pocket and tossed a spinning gold piece to the sheriff. The sheriff deftly caught it and pocketed it while the colonel was mounting up.

The colonel looked at the lieutenant and back at the sheriff. "Big Willard?"

"Big Willard."

The colonel did not smile. He shook his head and they cantered the horses out of the compound and down the trail. The colonel, when he felt that they were away from eyes and ears, said, "What I'm about to tell you has to remain confidential." He looked warmly at the sheriff. "And I have the satisfaction of knowing it will be."

"It goes two-ways, Colonel."

The colonel exhaled in exasperation and spoke. "For the last three-months whenever we have a scheduled shipment of things monetary, medical or even good horse flesh, we have had some problems."

The sheriff gave him a sidelong look. "Exactly what kind of problems?"

"Well, it isn't the Rebels that is for sure. They have broken into small groups of irregulars and are operating far-east of here." He looked troubled when he turned and caught the eye of the sheriff. "The trouble is Indian Melvin. He knows things he should not know. He has robbed overland medical supplies and hit money headed for Little Rock for the troops there. He stole three-hundred prime horses headed for General Beasley."

The sheriff rubbed his jaw. "I gather, although you've not come out and said it, that it's someone tipping him off."

The colonel nodded. "It's someone from my office."

"The general and I have talked about it and we are certain and we are certain of whom it is."

The sheriff's eyes narrowed. "How many men are privy to what you and the general know."

"Four." The colonel enumerated holding up gloved fingers. "Me, of course, Major Ambrose, Captain Woodward and Lieutenant Gardner." The colonel rode and ruminated some more. "Captain Woodward has been sick the last three-months. He has been ailing with a problem akin to dysentery. He is informed about certain things but not enough to be a primary source. Lieutenant Gardner is not really included enough to get all the facts."

The sheriff inhaled and nodded in understanding. "Major Ambrose."

The colonel gave him a stiff smile. "You have had your problems with him."

The sheriff gave him a sobering look. "He chases anything with a skirt on or off. He used to gamble hard at Ace's place until you told Ace to cut him off. He married and I guess divorced Judy, the girl who works for Ace. He was married to her and seeing about three-other women at the same time." The sheriff paused and added, "I've got no use for him."

The colonel shook his head. "Neither do I."

The sheriff looked over at the troubled profile. "I know he's had some sizeable gambling debts and I know he likes the ladies and that's motive enough for money." He paused and shook his head but how would he get the information to Indian Melvin?"

"Telegraph."

"Telegraph?"

"Telegraph."

The sheriff's eyes widened considerably. "Damn, I hadn't thought of that."

"He sends someone and I'm not exactly sure but someone to the telegraph station we have south of Fort Smith. This person sends a coded message to someone at Fort Till. We are not skilled enough in cryptography to break the code but somehow Indian Melvin taps into the line and gets the information he needs."

Sheriff Buchanan sighed, "I'm sure a lot of messages are sent back and forth. The message must be titled a certain way."

The colonel nodded. "It always starts out. 'The weather here.'"

The sheriff gave him a beady look. "Colonel, , if you know that, you know who's sending that damn telegram."

The colonel gave a half-laugh. "That's what I get for giving out half-truths." He grimly grinned. "It's that woman named 'Judy.'"

The sheriff hardly ever surprised was surprised. "She hardly would be my candidate for such a chore since she hates him."

The colonel snorted, "I've long given up on the dilemma of love-hate relationships."

The sheriff said, "The vagaries of love or not--she is either being blackmailed or forced someway. Maybe I should bring her in?"

The colonel shook his head. "No, not at this time. I don't like to pull jurisdiction on you but it is my affair,"

The sheriff looked back at him with a dark look. "But robbing the bank in Fort Smith is in my jurisdiction."

"True enough, Sheriff, and it had the army payroll in it." He turned his eyes evenly on the sheriff. "That is why I got so upset when I thought the bank had been robbed."

The sheriff shrugged. "I don't want to be nosy with the occupational army commander, but what are you going to do about it."

The colonel laughed and repeated the words, "occupational commander." He turned to the sheriff. "Let's forget the War and concentrate on this problem."

The sheriff did not reply. He rode and looked ahead.

The colonel, sensing the sheriff's frustration, said, "Let's do this." He paused and in and spoke in a conciliatory voice, "And do it together as men who want justice." The colonel pulled his horse up and the sheriff catching his cue did the same. "The general and I have a plan and want you in on it."

The sheriff looked at him inquiringly and asked, "What sort of plan?"

The colonel paused and looked the sheriff in the eye. "I need your services, Sheriff, whether as the 'occupational commander' or your friend, but take note I need your aid."

The sheriff sighed. "I'm your friend and you know that." He held up his index finger for emphasis. "But I do need to know your plan."

"The plan is this. We are going to send an armed-coach to West Texas. The soldiers there have not been paid in three-months. It will hold a lot of cash. Lieutenant Gardner will escort it. We will send eight-men enough to guard it but not enough to scare off Indian Melvin.

"We want you to shadow the coach from a distance and that is the part we will keep from Major Ambrose. If Indian Melvin attacks and we bag him, we also get Major Ambrose and we can court-martial the bastard and hang him.

"If you arrest Judy, you'll jeopardize the whole set-up."

The sheriff was mollified. He relaxed his tense face. "I think it's a good plan, but I don't have the deputies to pull that off."

The colonel smiled, "Yes, you do."

Sheriff Buchanan tilted his head as though he did not hear him correctly.

"Since we are restricted from sending in uniformed and armed troops into the Nations while this rebellion is going on. We have decided to circumvent this technicality by sending in non-uniformed troops as your deputies."

The sheriff rubbed his jaw in thought. "Will they do what I tell them to do?"

The colonel threw up his hands and said, "You damn right or they will or be court-martialed."

The sheriff's eyes narrowed and a rare smile etched across his granite like features.

The colonel catching this look asked, "What is on your mind, Sheriff?"

"Colonel, I'll do this for you under one condition."

The colonel frowned in puzzlement. "What "condition?"

"I want John Johnson to go along."

The colonel seemed nonplussed. "Why would he do that?"

The sheriff told him about his plight in Texas and the bogus land takeover."

The colonel listened intently. "I will do this. I will meet with John Johnson and if I like him and what he has to say, you can take him."

The sheriff reached across and shook hands with the colonel. "How about at seven o'clock tonight at my office?"

The colonel wheeled his horse around facing the military camp. "I'll be there."

John and his two-comrades had drunk their two-beers and were contemplating going down to the livery stable and getting some of their gear and returning to the hotel and eat and turn in.

John was in position to slide back his chair when Harley and Slade Rawlins entered. Harley glanced to his right as he came in and was somewhat startled to see John. John looked up and saw him.

Harley swallowed and motioned for Slade to keep walking and he looked at the open-chair to John's right and asked if he could sit down. John inclined his head and Harley walked around the steely-eyed Russell and the other gent and slid back the chair.

Harley looked at Russell's suspicious eyes and back to John's noncommittal eyes. "Would you give me a chance to talk with you?"

John did not mention that Judy had already talked to him. He gave the 'dismissal' look to Russell and Seth and they stood up and departed for the livery stable.

Harley sank slowly in the chair and scooted it up to the table. "I guess Russell told you I was working for the Purvis brothers."

John pulled a matchstick from his pocket and stuck it in the side of his mouth. "Before we go any further, your fiancée and I have already talked."

Harley looked momentarily baffled. He had not known that she had taken that initiative. He drummed his fingers nervously on the tabletop. He, by force of habit, turned his head this way and that looking for eavesdroppers. Seeing no one, he nodded.

"Well, this is something she didn't say I'm sure. I'm willing to give a deposition to the sheriff here that I'm a witness to the murder of Ed and Roy Johnson." He paused and wet his lips and continued, "I know he don't have jurisdiction there, but he might know someone who does." He paused and added, "Maybe Sheriff Nelson."

John straightened and pulled the matchstick from his mouth. "You're willing to do that?"

Harley grimly nodded. "Me and Slade have done a lot things that I'm ashamed of--some criminal even. But you have to understand that since the Purvis brothers have took over that the only law there is their law." He paused. "The Purvis brothers took over the bank and foreclosed on our ranch. They paid the ranch off and paid the overdue taxes. They offered us a job that paid us three-times we could make anywhere else."

John thoughtfully replaced his match and said, "But they didn't give back your ranch?"

Harley shook his head 'no.'

John nodded slowly. "What about this Delford Dolittle in town?"

Harley sighed and clasped his meaty hands together. He leaned forward and said, "He's here and he's going to try and kill you." He looked John in the eyes. "But it won't be eye-to-eye. He's scared of you."

John talked to Harley for about two-hours. The conversation entailed about what was going on in Bailey County and some shared memories of their fathers. He told John about his meeting Judy and how he wanted to marry her and get back his ranch.

John liked Harley. He naturally had reservations, and some lingering doubts, but many of them had been put aside.

He told him to meet him at the livery stable at nine the next day. He would go over his plans with him. He did not tell Harley that his plans were not clear to himself yet.

John stood and asked Harley if he would go over to the sheriff's office with him and give him that deposition.

Harley agreed and signaled for Slade to join them. All three-men walked out the batwings.

Judy, who had been standing at the bar and watching all this transpire with Ace, turned and smiled. Ace, who cared for her in a brotherly way, looked at her with some concern. "I remember when you were in love with Major Ambrose."

She snapped her head around. Her eyes were sharp. She looked into Ace's kind eyes and she softened. "Yes, I suppose you do."

She sighed and snatched up two-beers on her tray. She looked up at Ace. "I know many women have said this and maybe I'm no different, but I know this is real."

When she walked away, Big Willard who had been eavesdropping said, "Don't take away her dream. It may be all she's got."

Ace looked over at him and dryly answered, "You don't have to pick up the pieces."

Sheriff Buchanan, who had just recently returned, watched John and the Rawlins brothers enter his office. He greeted John and warily took notice of the two-men that Kiowa Bob had warned him about.

He sat and listened as John introduced the brothers and Harley began talking. The sheriff listened to the story and then reached into his drawer and pulled out deposition papers.

He wrote the story in his own legible handwriting and had Harley sign it. It was witnessed by two of his deputies and dated.

He then pulled out another written deposition that had been signed earlier by Kiowa Bob. He placed both documents in an envelope and locked them in a drawer.

The sheriff looked evenly at Harley and Slade. "I gather you two are planning on riding to Texas with John."

Harley looked nervously at John. He had not yet been granted that privilege. He looked back at the sheriff and shrugged, "We are hoping to."

Harley then told his story of having his ranch foreclosed and how he wanted it back. He told his intentions to marry Judy Treffery.

Sheriff Buchanan sat stolidly and inwardly groaned. He looked at all three-men. "I want all of you to wait about going back to Texas for a few days." His voice held a hint of mystery.

John's expression moved from calm to puzzled.

The sheriff caught the baffled look on John's face. He did not want to say too much in front of Harley and Slade. He regretted mentioning a delay, but had no choice. He quickly shifted his mental gears and brought up the reward money.

The sheriff looked at John and said, "You have a lot of reward money due you. Since it is from the provisional governor of Arkansas, it has to be countersigned by Colonel Daugherty." The sheriff hoped this development would hold John a few days, while he could work out what to do with Judy Treffery.

John canted his head. "Reward money?"

The sheriff nodded and answered, "You have money already approved for the deaths of Corn, Frog, and Toehold. You will have more money to take with you for the capture of Buster Filson and Cecil Tate. The two-men killed are wanted men and you will receive compensation on them as well." He stretched the truth some by stating, "That will entail a few days for it to be processed."

John said nothing. He was thoroughly surprised by the news. He really wanted to be on his way to Texas and settle matters but he knew he would need money.

As John rose up from his chair, the sheriff added, "John, I might have other news for you soon. I want you here at eight o'clock. The colonel is coming here at seven, and he and I need to talk before you come over."

John pulled his pocket watch out and checked the time with the Regulator clock on the wall. He nodded that he would. He and the Rawlins brothers wordlessly exited the office.

As they stood under the wooden roof that shadowed the porch, they discussed the events that led to his reward money. Delford Dolittle was standing in the alley that was cattycornered from the jail.

Although it was twilight, he could plainly see John Johnson and the Rawlins brothers. He eased slowly to the corner of the building that served as his aegis. He pulled his .44 slowly from his holster and sighted down the barrel at John.

His finger tightened in the trigger guard. And when he fired his shot, Slade who was moving toward the street, took the slug meant for John. The bullet tore into his temple and he toppled headfirst to the dirt street.

Harley, who stood transfixed in horror, watched his brother fall. John, seeing the muzzle flash, quickly drew and snapped off two-rounds. The first round landed in the wall opposite of Delford and tore a thick hole in the wood siding. Splintered wood showered the alley. The second-shot caught Delford high in the shoulder and tore a bloody groove in it.

Delford cussed his luck and began running to his horse.

Deputy William Green, who had been on patrol, was walking the back of the store buildings when he noticed a rider-less horse tethered to a back lot pump handle. When he heard the first pistol shot, he ran to the alley. He saw Delford running toward him.

William, pulling his Colt and leveling it, ordered Delford to stop and throw down his weapon. Delford fired immediately and hit the deputy in the throat. His second-shot caught him in the chest, and he fell awkwardly backwards and dying.

Delford made the turn and was headed for his horse, when a silvery knife sliced through the air and nailed him in the back. He dropped to his knees in agony. He was trying desperately to reach back and remove the offending object, when a grim form appeared in front of him.

His tormented eyes moved up to see an unsmiling Kiowa Bob. Delford groaned, "You!"

Kiowa Bob wordless walked behind him and pulled the knife wetly out of his back. Delford, who still was paralyzed in pain, sat on his knees looking up Kiowa Bob wielding the blooded knife.

Kiowa Bob then placed the blade at his hairline and began scalping him. Delford's agonizing cries of pain pierced through the gloaming shadows and caught the ears of both John and the sheriff as they ran down the darkened alley.

The sheriff, who had briefly stopped to check the status of William Green, made the turn with John and saw the bloody Delford Dolittle. The mutilated outlaw's shrieking cries of terror seemed to reach to the emerging stars.

Before the sheriff shouted, 'No," Kiowa Bob slit Delford's throat and he fell forward in the dust.

The sheriff, who stood breathless, shook his head in dismay and backtracked to William Green.

John looked at Kiowa Bob and then at the bloodied carcass on the ground. He wordlessly turned and walked down the alley. He saw the sheriff holding the body and the sheriff's apparent grief.

John looked down and knowing he could not console him walked on and when he reached the end of the alley, he could see Harley cradling his dead brother's body.

He stood there for a moment and looked at the incongruous scene. The thick, oily light of the saloon was splayed on the ruts of the street and its afterglow showed the lamenting face of Harley.

The happy rinky-dink music spilled over the batwings and serenaded the street that was filled with sadness.

John noticed the growing crowd on the boardwalk in front of the saloon. He watched as Judy made her way through and ran holding her dress across the dirt street. She threw her arms around the back of Harley and shared in his loss.

The sheriff soon arrived and ordered Fat Phil to go get the coroner. They all stood for fifteen-minutes and the coroner arrived and pronounced three-men dead.

The sheriff commandeered the men of the saloon to carry the bodies of William Green and Slade Rawlins to the mortuary. He ordered Frankie, another deputy, to go to the river and dispose of the corpse of Delford Dolittle.

John watched Harley and Judy walk holding each other following the men carrying his dead brother's body. He stood and watched this sad scene and sighed.

He was about to turn and walk away when he saw the sheriff sputtering at Kiowa Bob. When he walked closer, he could hear the sheriff say, "Don't you ever scalp anyone in this town again." The sheriff raised his finger and waggled it at Kiowa Bob. "And don't tell me it's a Kiowa thing either. I've known many Kiowa that don't scalp." He paused and thought and reworded it. "I know some Kiowa that don't scalp." He looked into the impassive eyes of Kiowa Bob. "All right, all the Kiowa I know scalp, but you don't in this town."

He whirled and went muttering into his office.

Kiowa Bob stood watching the back of the sheriff. A slow smile moved across his coppery features. He felt John's hand on his shoulder and he turned. "Hello, John."

John moved them to the shadows away from the yellow light. "What are you doing here?"

"Looking for you."

John looked at him with a tilted head. "Me?" He paused a bit and said, "Why, is Uncle Henry dead?"

Kiowa Bob shook his head 'no.' The sheriff sent me to warn you the Purvis brothers know that you're coming and are sending men to kill you." He grinned again. "But there's one less."

"How about Uncle Henry?"

"He's still alive."

John sighed a sigh of relief. John looked both ways. "You've got to go back and tell Uncle Henry that I'm headed that way." John sighed again and took off his hat. "I know they'll be there to kill you and you've got to be careful."

Kiowa Bob nodded, "I don't like Fort Smith. I want to go back and you're right, if they see me, they'll kill me." He paused and grinned broadly, "But to know you're alive and coming back is a great feeling." He paused and added cunningly, "And I ain't so easy to kill."

John slapped him on both shoulders. "You need any supplies or money?"

"No, I started off with thirty-dollars and still have thirty-dollars."

John, who normally would have grinned at his penurious friend, just nodded soberly. "Same ole Kiowa Bob." He then looked over at the sheriff's office. "If I was you I would ride away as soon as possible."

Kiowa Bob glanced at the sheriff's office. "Yes, me and the sheriff have a difference of opinion on handing out justice."

He saluted with his finger Indian style and disappeared in the shadows of the alley.

John drifted down to the livery stable and whiled away the hours with Snuffy.

The colonel arrived promptly at seven. He had several soldier escorts. He had one posted at the sheriff's door and told the others that they were dismissed. He reminded them of a 'two-beer limit.

He entered and saw the sheriff writing a report in the lantern light. He pulled up a chair and looked across at the weary sheriff. "Rough day, Sheriff?"

Sheriff Buchanan nodded and said, "I just hope the missus ain't expecting any romance tonight."

The colonel suppressed a smile. "Okay, what is on your mind?"

The sheriff tossed his pencil aside and straightened. "You remember when you said you would let me take John as a deputy."

The colonel cocked his head to one-side. "Sheriff, no need for a long and sonorous preamble. We both are busy men."

"Colonel, I had a long talk with Kiowa Bob. He's a breed that's very intelligent and I have his deposition and one from a white man that claimed that Ed Johnson and Roy Johnson, the former being the father and the latter the uncle of one-John Johnson, were killed in cold blood by the Purvis brothers when they resisted being evicted."

Colonel Daugherty inclined his head. "How could they do that when it is a state and local matter?"

"That's the point, Colonel, they can't, but they did." The sheriff held up his finger to make the point. Their uncle is Colonel Purvis who is now chasing General Kirby-Smith all over Texas. He had been fighting Sibley over in the territory when he came across all this cattle country in West Texas. He hatched up the idea of punishing the secessionist by taking their land and naturally his kinfolks were the recipients of it all."

The colonel smiled gently. "I think I see where all this is headed."

The sheriff leaned back and reached for his pipe. "If he's going to stick out his neck to catch Indian Melvin, I got to help him. He ain't no average man. I can guarantee you. I need him but if you were to aid in this, it sure in the hell would help."

The colonel slapped his knees with his leather gauntlets. "Well, it is like this, sheriff. I want Indian Melvin and you say that John is vital in taking him down."

"I do."

"All right. I will write a letter stating he is of worthy character. I will also state that he has been working for the United States government in fighting crime in the Nations."

The sheriff leaned forward. "He will need that and maybe more help." His eyes met the colonel's, "We have to assure him we will give him justice."

The colonel gave a cautious smile and nodded. "If you go to West Texas with him and aid in his fight for justice, just make sure it is fast. I would have a hard time explaining that to General Beasley that we have troops fighting to get back land that belonged to a Rebel soldier."

The sheriff lit his pipe. "If I bag Indian Melvin, that'll look mighty good on your report."

The colonel sighed. "Yes, I would like that being a career military man." He looked up with twinkling eyes. "What else are you going to do to convince him to go along on this trip?"

"Give him five-thousand dollars of the reward money."

The colonel smiled. "He'd better be good."

The sheriff nodded. He is."

The sheriff and the colonel continued talking about Indian Melvin and plans on bringing him in. The colonel laughed out loud when the sheriff told him he was having a special wagon being built to haul him back in.

They spent the remaining time discussing John Lee Johnson's leaving home to join John Bell Hood's Texas Brigade as recounted by Kiowa Bob.

When John walked in, he filled the doorway and the colonel's eyes kept moving up and up till they landed on the face. He stood and extended his hand. "Damn, you Rebels are big. Must be all those good Yankee supplies you take."

John shook his hand and smiled, "I've never seen a Yankee colonel up close either. You fellas are usually behind the lines giving orders and keeping out of harm's way."

They both laughed and John sat down and looked at both at the sheriff and the colonel.

The colonel was obviously impressed. He had intended to let the sheriff do the talking but he had instantly liked John.

The colonel began speaking. "John, may I be very candid with you and you not take offense."

John looked at him strangely and answered. "I can't promise something like that. I just might take offense."

The colonel and the sheriff both smiled. The colonel responded, "Well, just hear me out."

John nodded, "I can do that."

"You know and I know that the South is going to lose the War. Robert E. Lee and the Army of Northern Virginia is the only viable army left in the field and it is on the ropes.

"General Johnston, down in Georgia, is retreating daily and Atlanta is going to fall soon.

"Nathan Bedford Forrest is in Mississippi and General Sturgis is tracking him down."

John gave him a dry smile and said, "Lots of luck."

The colonel smiled back, "Well, if Forrest is successful and beats Sturgis and that could happen, what has he attained, 'Mississippi'?" The colonel gave him an arch look and leaned back to await the reply.

But John did not reply. He pursed his lips and leaned back and took in the colonel's words.

Colonel Daugherty did wait for John's reply. "Look, John, Forrest is in Mississippi and he should be in Georgia fighting the rearguard of Sherman.

"Tennessee is in Federal hands. Arkansas is in our hands.

Texas has General Edmund Kirby-Smith and he's running scared, and the state for all purposes is under Union control."

Colonel Daugherty leaned forward with his eyes fixed on John. "If you go back and kill those two-men who took your father and uncle's ranches, you could end up a fugitive and running for your life." He did not wait for John to reply. "The Union government will just see you as a Rebel who killed two-upstanding citizens. They will not investigate your side of the story."

John looked curiously at the colonel. "No, disrespect, but you are saying a whole lot to get to something, just say it."

The colonel licked his lips and looked at the sheriff, for bolstering, and back at John. "We want you to help us to capture Indian Melvin over in the Nations.

"If you help us, we'll do all in our power to help you get your ranches back and bring the men whole stole them and who are guilty of murder to justice."

John sat pondering his words. "I don't want to be a fugitive and live on the run, but those two-jaspers will pay."

The colonel turned his attention to the sheriff and said, "Sheriff, give me some help here."

Sheriff Buchanan, who had been holding his unlit pipe, lit it and the match sizzled in the silence. He tossed the match in a misshapen tin can on his desk and took a thoughtful puff.

"John, if you go with me, and help me capture this thief, I will pay you five-thousand dollars. You will also get the backing of the colonel and myself." He held up his pipe to make a point. "I'll go with you to West Texas and take some deputies and make some inquiries.

"With the depositions I have and the letter of commendation by the colonel and the manpower, we might just settle this thing. I ask that you allow the law to work and not embarrass us by brutal killings of these two-varmints." The sheriff raised his eyebrows to aid in making his point. "Let the law work. With Texas in Union hands, it is your only wise choice."

John looked back and forth at the two-faces. John was not sure of how much help the colonel and sheriff could truly give him, but it was a step up from where he currently was. But another niggling matter was on his mind. "I have another obligation to consider."

The sheriff looked at the colonel in surprise and back at John. He had been unaware of any obligation. "What is that?"

"The woman that we found on the trail is trying to get to West Texas also. I need to get her there. I promised her. I aim to keep my promise."

The sheriff's expression relaxed some. "This woman that you found was she assaulted by those men you shot at Gilbert's Crossing?"

John nodded. "I like what you're saying, Sheriff, and I don't mind bringing someone to justice." He looked at the colonel and back at the sheriff. "Just give me justice."

The sheriff took another thoughtful puff. "If I can guarantee you that I can get this lady to where she wants to be, do we have a deal?" The sheriff puffed his pipe thoughtfully and added, "And we make an honest effort to bring in the Purvis brothers for murder." He puffed and even said, "And I mean an honest effort."

John sat for a moment and nodded, "You got a deal. I've heard of Indian Melvin even before the War and none of it good."

The colonel looked at the Regulator clock on the wall and slapped both thighs. "Well, this has been a most enlightening meeting, but I must go."

He stood and shook John's hand again. "I just wished I had a man like you in my command." He gave a quick but genuine smile to the sheriff and John and exited.

The sheriff looked at the door thoughtfully and back at John. "I want you to hang around town for a few more days till I get everything planned." He looked at his pipe stem pensively and continued. "You plan on taking Harley with you and your cousin and that young fella?"

John nodded. He still had not made up his mind on Harley at the moment but chances were he might need him.

The sheriff narrowed his eyes. "Harley seems like a good sort but don't tell him a thing about going after Indian Melvin."

John looked surprised. "You must have a reason?"

The sheriff looked perplexed, "I'm going to have to trust you, John. I have good faith that that trust is justified." He puffed for a few seconds and exhaled. "His girlfriend, Judy, the pretty one over at Ace's saloon is somehow mixed up with Indian Melvin."

John was surprised but not shocked. He frowned. "But Harley don't know?"

"No, Harley don't know. He is in love or thinks he is." The sheriff shrugged. "I think Harley is a lot like you. He's a good man and he's been dealt a bad hand of cards. He has no idea of what she has been doing lately or that she has been married before."

John tilted his head. "You know a lot more don't you?"

The sheriff nodded. "Some things I can't tell you."

John inhaled deeply. "Damn, poor Harley's luck."

The sheriff ignored that and continued. "Let's get back to you. Besides working within the law and getting a measure of revenge on the Purvis brothers your reward money is going to be two thousand five-hundred-dollars. You'll get the five-thousand deposited in your name when Indian Melvin is captured. You will receive a five-dollar a day 'per diem' that starts today."

John stood. There was so much to process and he was exhausted. He looked at the sheriff through the haze of the pipe smoke. "I did not plan for this long of stay, Sheriff."

The sheriff answered by canting his head toward the hotel. "Your stay at the hotel will be free and your livery stable fees will be picked up by the county also. We should be ready in two-days, three at the most. So, stand by."

John turned to walk away when he slowly turned in after thought. "Who's going to tell Bonnie?"

The sheriff sighed. "I reckon I will when the time is right. I just don't want anything to get back to Harley who will tell his girlfriend."

John sighed and walked out the door. Although he had lots on his mind and felt like he could go to sleep right on porch of the county jail, he decided to go to Ace's Saloon for one-beer. He rubbed his face. He knew the colonel and the sheriff had plans for him, but he wanted to digest those plans more fully.

The sheriff pensively watched him go and then as he was rising from his desk looked at something he had jotted down earlier that day. "Arkansas Bob." He decided to seek further information on the bandit who had gotten away.

His eyes moved down the sizeable corridor of jail cells. He stood and walked down the long walkway to the last cell.

Buster Filson was fidgety and trying to make himself comfortable on his cot. The sheriff looked at him through the bars.

Buster looked up and caught the stare of the sheriff. Buster's arm was wrapped up in a splint and he was instructed to lie on his right side to alleviate the pain of his broken hip.

"What in hell do you want, Sheriff?"

The sheriff looked at his pipe as though he were contemplating. "Arkansas Bob."

Buster snorted. "The bastard." He inhaled and continued, "The yellow bastard."

"Exactly. He ran out on you."

Buster looked at him through pain-racked eyes. "Uncle Jack will take care of him."

"He didn't take care of you."

Buster gave him a baleful look. "That big man messed everything up."

The sheriff took a puff and leaned close to the bars. "You don't owe any allegiance to Arkansas Bob do you?"

"Hell no. I hope you get him."

"You have any idea of where he might hide?"

Buster grimaced and moved his broken arm. "Anywhere there's no danger, Sheriff."

The sheriff wheeled around knowing he could get nothing further from Buster.

Buster called after him. "Who was that big guy?"

The sheriff couldn't resist. "The one who's going to get your uncle."

Judy had been watching the sheriff's office covertly while she waited on tables. She made it a point to go over and peer over the batwings. She saw the soldier posted at the door and she knew the colonel was there. She had been tormented for months about the possibility of being exposed.

When the colonel came out, and the soldiers rose up from their beers, she knew John would be exiting soon, but he did not. She knew the sheriff might be telling him things about her. She anxiously looked at the clock on the wall and tried to maintain her poise.

Ace, who always appeared as bored and jaded, was far from it. He observed Judy's erratic and harried behavior. He watched her under his brows and his eyes narrowed.

Judy went by the batwings and looked over the top. She peered at John as he exited the sheriff's office. He appeared to be making up his mind on where to go. She saw him glance at the saloon. He hitched his gun belts up and proceeded toward the yellow lights splashing over the batwings.

She did not want him to know that she was observing him. She hastened to the bar and stroke a bored pose.

John pushed back the batwings and he caught her eyes. He gave a polite nod but one without feeling.

The fear she felt at being discovered and the guilt she bore caused her to swallow and feel nauseous.

Ace, catching John's eyes, waved him over to the corner where he and Big Willard were. They shook hands and Ace introduced him to Big Willard formally.

John shook Big Willard's hand vigorously and said, "I've heard a whole lot about you."

Big Willard smiled and said, "And I have heard a whole lot about you."

They instantly liked each other and began a comfortable conversation.

A swarthy man with deep socket eyes was seated nearby. He had been watching Judy. His creepy, uneven smile gave her the 'willies.' She was nervous and upset about Slade's death and the possibility of losing Harley. The spooky man turned her stomach. He signaled with one-finger and since he had just downed a shot of whiskey, she took a bottle from Smitty and headed his way.

She poured a 'tinkling' shot of whiskey into his glass and purposely avoided his lecherous eyes. When she turned to leave, he roughly grabbed her hand and hauled her onto his lap. His gravelly voice grated in her brain. "I could stand some loving to go along with that drink."

When she twisted away, she made a desperate whimpering noise. He reached for her again and grabbed her hand and was in the process of pulling her back to his lap.

John, who had just received a beer from Smitty, placed the schooner down and turned and delivered a bone crunching shot that knocked the offender off his chair and scooted him across the floor ramming into chair legs.

John turned and began drinking his beer again. He expressed no more emotion as if he had swatted a gnat. Big Willard's eyebrows shot up. "That was a hell of a punch, John."

Judy looked at the back of John and then moved to the knocked out lecher. She did not feel sorry for the sleeping bastard but she had never seen a man hit so hard.

John looked down and saw a pocket watch on the floor. It had fallen from the pocket of the man he had just knocked the hell out of. He reached down for it and turned it over it read: 'Robert Taylor.'

John looked at it for a long time with thoughts running through his mind. He had a 'could it be' look on his face.

Big Willard leaned back from the bar and then over to the pocket watch in John's hand. "You recognize the name?"

John paused as if he wanted to share his suspicions but decided that might be a bad idea. He handed the watch to Big Willard. "No, guess not." John sighed and said, "Seems like I run into a lot of pocket watches these days." John added, "Must be thousand 'Robert Taylor's."

Big Willard gave him a curious look. He knew there must be more to the Big Texan's words that met the ear, but turned his attention to the unconscious form on the floor. He went over to the snoozing lovebird and placed the watch in unconscious man's pocket. Then he hoisted him up to his shoulders as though he were nothing and walked to the other end of the bar. He exited to the area where the ring was and then through another exit and tossed him into the weeds close to the outhouse.

Judy moved closer to John. "Thanks, John, Thank goodness most of them don't act like that."

He gave her a halfway smile and nodded. "I don't like men who mistreat women." He then turned face forward leaving her staring at him.

His polite but cool demeanor caused her alarm. She swallowed and looked at Ace. Before she could even ask, He said, "Go on, home."

Ace watched her exit. His eyes moved to John's. "She's been jittery for the last hour of so."

John tilted his schooner and said, "That so?"

Ace's eyes slid to John. He did not make any comment on John's remark but he knew that it held more than two-words.

Fat Phil entered about fifteen-minutes later and joined the group gathered around Big Willard's corner. Big Willard informed him about the incident and told him he might have a customer out back by the toilet. When he heard the description of the man, Fat Phil's eyebrows shot up.

Fat Phil hurried around the bar and when he got there the body was gone. He saw a shadow on a horse riding behind the buildings but the man was too far distant for a shout or a gunshot. When the man passed a bull's-eye lantern on the back porch of the hotel, he recognized his features. He knew he was one of the missing bank robbers.

He went back in and informed them that Arkansas Bob was still on the loose. John's eyebrows knitted when he heard that. His suspicions were growing. Robert Taylor, reportedly killed at Pea Ridge, now could be possibly classified as a deserter and bank robber.

# CHAPTER SIX

In Gainesville, Arkansas Martha Taylor was standing on the front porch. It was late and usually her father-in-law was asleep, but his light was on bright and as she stepped down from the steps, she heard voices.

She recognized Jeremiah's voice but the other voice was unknown to her. She felt guilty about eavesdropping but curiosity got the better of her and she padded herself to his window. She eased her eye around the window frame and saw a Confederate soldier sitting in a chair across the room talking to her father-in-law.

The soldier looked like he was in his fifties. He had on a forage cap and the butternut of the Arkansas army. He seemed solemn and she heard him say. "Jeremiah, I saw him purposely fall in the weeds and crawl and then play 'dead.'"

Jeremiah Taylor's voice was even and not wavering when he responded, "He was selfish as a boy and he never grew out of it." He paused and cleared his throat and continued, "Robert wanted the glory of war but he didn't have the stomach for it."

The old soldier sighed resignedly. "I hated to have to come and tell you all this, but I think your son knew that some of us knew he was pretending to be shot so he wouldn't have to go in to battle."

Martha could hear Jeremiah sighing. She heard his sad voice when he asked, "Have you got any idea of where in the world he might be?"

The soldier said, "It's just a guess but I think he ran off to the Nations. He met some Indian allies at the Battle of Pea Ridge and befriended some of them. I ain't for sure but I would guess that."

The soldier seemed uneasy in his task. "I hated to come and see you but I hated not coming to see you."

Jeremiah answered, "You did right. Maybe someday he'll come slinking back and pretend he was addled or lost his memory or some other cock and bull story."

The soldier just nodded. "I reckon, but for sure, he wasn't killed at Pea Ridge."

Jeremiah responded, "I had a feeling that was the case. He left a wife and daughter and never cared a thing about them or me." He said with finality. "He just cared about himself."

The soldier stood and said, "I'll take my leave."

Jeremiah mumbled 'goodbye' to him and Martha could hear the sound of the soldier's boots on the steps and later she could hear him ride away.

She flattened herself with her arms spread against the side of her father-in-law's house and wept silently. Her eyes opened in the dark and she realized she was crying because he was still alive.

At the same time, Judy Treffery was moving along the boardwalk briskly. She was headed to her small rented house on the outskirts of town. She would walk and look back anxiously. She blamed it on nerves. As she stepped off the boardwalk and walked by an alley, she saw Major Ambrose waiting in the shadows.

She gave an involuntary start and put her hands to her throat. He materialized from the shadows with that evil smile etched in his face. "Hello, Missus Ambrose."

She glanced around him to make sure no one heard that

remark. She looked back into his handsome face. It was strange in the mirror of her mind how someone could look so handsome but appear so ugly. She glared at him. "I don't intend sending any more telegrams to your phony aunt."

"Oh, but you will."

"Frank, listen, the colonel and the sheriff have been talking and."

He interrupted her by holding up his gloved hand. "They don't know jack beans. The colonel is a dumb ass from back when."

She looked around nervously. "I've no idea of what you are up to exactly but I know it is illegal. Sending nonsensical weather reports to your 'Aunt Doody.' You're still paying off gambling debts and you're in a bind."

His face tightened. "Look, you send one more telegram for me and it's over."

"Why me, why don't you do it?"

"Because it appears innocuous if you do it."

"What does that mean?"

"It means harmless, my dear."

"And if I don't."

"Then I'll be forced to confess to that Texas cowboy staying with you that I'm your legal husband and that you're committing polyandry by marrying him."

She felt a flow of panic move through her chest. Losing Harley would be the same as dying. There would be no hope for her.

She glanced behind her and around Frank Ambrose. "All right. Hand it over."

He handed her a long letter and a ten-dollar gold piece. Nonmilitary personnel paid more for telegrams. He handed her another twenty-dollar gold piece. "For your trouble."

She hesitated but caved in and reached for the money. She asked when he started backing up and edging into the darker shadows of the alley. "Is it the Filson gang or Indian Melvin?" When she asked the question, she knew it was a mistake,

He reappeared with rage in his eyes. "Don't ever ask me a question like that again if you want to live." With almost acid-white eyes he backed into the alley and trotted to his horse.

She walked more fully to the mouth of the alley and watched him ride away. Her hand went to her throat. She felt the nightmare would never end.

The next day, she took a rented buggy from Andrew's Livery and trotted her rig out to the station. The telegraph office was located south of town because of the river.

It was a block cinder building with yellow lettering that announced: Telegraph.

She noticed the two-soldiers there were more vigilant than usual and that caught her eye immediately. It was though they knew she was coming. She took a deep breath and tried to allay her fears. The previous six-times she had been there the soldiers had been more relaxed with bored and slouching postures.

A soldier came off the rough-plank porch and tied her horse to the hitch rack. He nodded at her courteously and she smiled back. She felt more at ease by his smile. She sighed to herself that she was just on edge. He helped her down.

She walked up the steps and stood on the porch and looked around. She inhaled and tried to shake her anxiety. She then bowed her neck and entered the office.

The officious telegrapher named 'Jake' was receiving a call and writing down a message. He was a tall, skinny man with bad breath.

He finished and looked up at her with his eyebrows raised. "You sending another telegram to your aunt?"

She quickly nodded still flushed with angst. She let her eyes peruse the place: the cheap desk, the off-centered calendar on the wall, the small uncomfortable bench for patrons and the loud ticking clock, the smell of dead cigars wafting in the air. She was attempting to act bored and that her sending a telegram was merely pedestrian.

He accepted her message sheet quickly and glanced at it. He shook his head as though bewildered, "This is one queer letter."

He counted the words and said, "Six-dollars, please. This is one long weather report." He looked at it again as at her as though it was a ridiculous thing for her to send such useless but costly message. He did not bother to tell her that the Latin and French words were nonsensical. He just raised his eyebrows and exhaled his bad breath.

She handed him the ten-dollar gold piece and he counted out four dollars change and she quickly placed it in her reticule.

He looked up at the time. It was ten-fourteen. He turned and sat down and hammered out her message and then signed off.

He nodded at her and handed her lengthy paper back.

She abruptly turned and walked out and down the steps and the soldier handed her the reins when she got into the buggy and she trotted the horses back to town. She had to take deep breaths to keep from fainting.

Colonel Daugherty came in from the backdoor and held out his hand. Jake handed over a copy of the message. The colonel shook his head. "All those French phrases and Latin words. That is one smart saloon girl."

Jake gave him an amused look. The colonel stopped before exiting the door. "Jake, do not say a word about this."

Jake held his hands before him in a prayerful clasp. "I don't want to lose my job, Colonel.

The colonel gave him one searching look and then departed.

John had been in the back of Andrew's Livery stable at eight o'clock using saddle soap on his gear. Russell and Seth were oiling their weapons both pistols and rifles.

They were busy, when John heard a female's voice, he wondered if it were Bonnie's. He stood and walked and looked around the ponderous bales of hay. He was surprised to see Judy standing talking to Snuffy. She rented a horse and buggy. John watched for a minute and took note of her nervousness.

He pulled his head back and his eyes narrowed in thought. He wondered to himself, 'why would she be renting a buggy without Harley?'

He mused on that as he slowly rubbed the soap in with small thoughtful circles. The sheriff's opinion of Judy had caused a nagging suspicion. He reasoned the girl had a right to go buggy riding, but she did not appear to be one who just took off for a joy ride.

At nine o'clock, Harley arrived and made his way back to where they were taking care of the tack and weapons. He nodded at everyone and was relieved when Russell smiled at him. He knew Russell might have harbored some hard feelings against him. He wanted to allay those fears. He smiled back at Russell and threw up his hand in greeting.

He sat on a bale of hay opposite John and made small talk for a while and then his eyes moved up to John's. "John, I'm going to ask a favor of you and if you say 'no' there'll be no hard feelings." He knew his own father had once owed money to John's father.

John knew it was about money. But he was not going to interrupt and be rude. He looked up and caught Harley's eyes. "Ask, Harley, if you're going to ride with me, you got to talk to me."

"Well, that's part of my hesitation because I haven't rode with you yet." Harley sighed and slapped his thighs. "I want to marry Judy. And with the money on me and the money I got from." He paused and stifled his breaking voice. "You know the blood money." He then composed himself and admitted in a low voice "I reckon I got twenty-four dollars and some odd cents."

John looked down and nodded. "You want to buy her a ring and a wedding dress?"

John felt a sense of dread. It as like seeing someone walk into quicksand and would heed no warning. He knew he could refuse him the money, but he knew he needed Harley. John realized that there were two-sides of the coin. It was possible that the sheriff was wrong. He doubted it. But he reasoned it would be better to lend the money and have Harley wronged than not lend him the money and have Harley wronged.

Harley sighed and nodded, "That's about the size of it."

John gave him a smile and he tried to make it genuine. "Well, hey, how much are we talking for a marriage in Fort Smith?" "Fifty-dollars should cover it all and the preacher." Harley searched John's face for his reaction. He felt that the big man might reject such an amount.

John without hesitation and without taking Harley's self-worth reached into his pocket and handed him fifty-five dollars. "The five is a wedding present."

Harley accepted the money meekly. "I ain't one to forget."

John sighed. "I know, Harley, that's why you're here with me and not with the Purvis brothers."

Harley stood and pocketed the money and looked down at John as he returned to his task. "I got one more favor."

John looked up at him. "All you got to do is ask?"

"I want you for my best man."

John swallowed and all sorts of feelings coursed through his large frame. He wanted to be rid of the Harley-Judy matter. But he stifled his words and just sighed and nodded, "You damn right I'll do it."

It was about noon when Judy returned. Snuffy met her and helped her down. She paid him a dollar and then started walking toward the saloon.

John walked around the bale of hay and into the barn area and then out the maw and watched her walk. Snuffy, who was tossing the dollar up and down in his hand, looked over at John. "Wonder where she goes on them buggy rides?"

John licked his lips and shook his head negatively at Snuffy.

John and his crew sat on a bench close to the barn and whiled away the hours. Bonnie came down and got some things out of her wagon and sat with them and they made small talk and listened the birds singing in the sycamore tree up the street.

They spent their time yawning and stretching and cigar smoking and lots of talking. They kept trying to cheer up Bonnie and they kept their words decent.

John saw the sheriff walking his horse toward him. The sheriff looked tired and slumped. The last few days had been taxing.

He rode up to the bench and hailed everyone. He jokingly said he was enforcing the laws against loitering and vagrancy and he felt like he was at the right place. But, although he had made a joke, he seemed faraway and preoccupied.

They all laughed, and he motioned to John with his head that he needed to speak to him. John could tell the sheriff was in funk. John nodded up at the burdened face of the sheriff. He rose from his bench and left his puzzled companions.

The sheriff turned his horse around and headed more into the street. It was obvious that the sheriff wanted privacy. John sidled up close to the side of his horse.

The sheriff said, "Fork your horse and meet down in front of the River Café."

John nodded and quickly disappeared into the maw of the barn. His three-friends wondered what the sheriff had said to John that would spur him to get his horse, but did not make any comment.

John rode down the street and saw the sheriff impatiently waiting. The sheriff was flicking his reins over and back and had a faraway look. He nodded at the big Texan and took the lead. They slow-galloped about five-miles to a grove of crabapple trees. They pulled into the dappled shadows and waited.

They had not been there five-minutes until the colonel rode in with General Beasley. The General was a short man with a large head. He had a beard similar to the one worn by Ulysses S. Grant.

John noticed the general looking him up and down and then saying, "I'm damn glad you're on our side." The general turned to Colonel Daugherty and continued, "Look at those pistols. No wonder Forrest is such a bedeviling man with men like this."

His words disarmed John and he liked the general. He gave the general a genuine grin.

After all the levity, the general's face became more sober. "I have been assured by Colonel Daugherty that I can speak freely to you men. "We don't have the personnel to break the code of the telegram sent by the young lady today. But that is all right. Here is the plan. And Major Ambrose knows just part of it. The part he does not know will hang his worthless ass."

Major Ambrose's name stuck in John's mind as the talk continued.

"He knows that a coach carrying over two hundred thousand-dollars is going through the Nations. He knows that eight-soldiers headed by Lieutenant Gardner will guard that armored coach. What he doesn't know is that John Johnson and his men will ride near the skyline and watch for any sign of Indian Melvin." He paused and looked at John. "John, , you're a professional soldier and I expect you to protect those men. You've been around long enough to know if they kill the mules, they will strand Lieutenant Gardner and his men and they will be at the mercy of that sorry bastard, Indian Melvin."

John agreed with that.

He turned to Sheriff Buchanan. "Something else the major does not know is that you will have sixteen-deputies at your disposal and damn good men. They will take your commands and be under your direction. I'm sending two-teamsters to drive that infernal iron-bar cage you have that can accommodate twenty prisoners too."

They all grinned at that.

The general continued. "Sheriff, no matter how tough it gets for the lieutenant or for John and his men. Don't tip your hand until you bag that son-of-a-bitch." The general slapped his gloved hands together and made a leathery pop.

The sheriff said, "You want me to leave my own deputies in town?"

The general sighed and looked down. "I hate telling you what to do, but in this instance 'yes'. If we go to martial law that will definitely arouse the suspicion of that sorry ass, Major Ambrose."

The general cocked his head to one-side. "Now, if you find someone in town that is a good man on the order of," He pointed to John. "Well, take them but make sure they have a good excuse for leaving town."

The general turned his eyes on John once more. "When this is all done and we hope for an optimistic outcome, the sheriff is authorized to look into your personal affair. If it is as you say and the depositions say, and you don't go there and commit mayhem, I will see that you get your justice." He smiled and added, "Damn Rebel or not."

They all chuckled.

The General then added, "This has to be done piece meal. John, you ride out the day after tomorrow. I would say about six o'clock and cross the river and make your way to Dunbar's Landing about one hundred and twenty-miles away.

"I would imagine about twenty or twenty-five miles into the journey that Lieutenant Gardner will be spotted and scouted. I also would imagine that Indian Melvin will formulate his plans on that scouting report, and will marshal his forces for an attack somewhere past Dunbar's Landing.

"He's one tricky scoundrel and he has a whole lot of shiftless no accounts working for him." The general straightened his frame and looked at all three-faces. "John, you want justice, Sheriff you want justice and Colonel you want justice. And I am no exception. The War may have skewed proper thinking but right and wrong will never go out of style.

"I want men like Major Ambrose who would sell out his comrades for money and men like Indian Melvin who use the

Indians and whites for crimes to line his own pocket and men who seize ranches under false pretenses to be brought to justice."

The general nodded abruptly after speaking and turned his horse. He looked at Sheriff Buchanan. The colonel will be in touch."

He winked at John and said, "And I have to get back to the business of tracking down Rebels."

They all chuckled and the colonel and the general rode away. The sheriff and John turned their horses and galloped back into town.

When John got back to town, he saw his crew still sitting on the bench and talking. He rode into the livery stable and unsaddled his horse. Snuffy took the bridle and led his bay away. John watched him briefly and then turned and walked out the barn to his friends.

When he sat down, Bonnie, who was seated on the end, leaned out and said, "John, I like Fort Smith but I'd like to be on my way to Texas soon."

He nodded at her and sighed. "I know, Bonnie, I know." He knew if he said more it would open up a floodgate of questions. So he just remained mum.

She leaned back and looked at Russell questioningly and then decided to drop the subject. She knew John was hesitant about leaving but she could not fathom why.

Russell gave an "I don't know what's going on look' back to Bonnie. But all of them including Seth knew something was slightly awry.

But John was the boss and they did not question him. They knew he would do what was best for them.

Their silence bothered John and he was frustrated by not being able to divulge any information. He just sat stone faced and thought about his new assignment and getting back to Texas.

It took Indian Melvin a full day to get the telegram. He had Marilla, his beautiful wife, to crack the code. She knew both Latin and French fluently and she used a special code that she and Major Ambrose had worked out. The Latin was coded and the French mathematical. The English words that started with vowels had every other letter forming a word. The consonants had the first and third and every odd number forming a word.

After working an hour she brought the translation to her husband. She had written: the U.S army is sending an armed coach with eight-escorts not including the driver and the guard. The coach will be carrying 200,000 thousand dollars. It will be met by a cavalry patrol coming from the Union army from West Texas. It is the payroll for officers and men of the army fighting in Texas and the Territory. The weather is clear here. See you in three-days.

Indian Melvin's eyes narrowed. He felt it was odd that only eight-men would carry that much money. But then again, eight-good men could be a force. He sat mulling over the telegram.

Marilla climbed into his lap and caressed his face. "What is it, cara mia?"

"This could be a trap."

"Has Major Ambrose ever been wrong?"

Indian Melvin grunted and shook his head 'no.'

"What do you have in mind?"

He smiled broadly, "If it's a trap we'll spring it, if it is not a trap then we'll rob it."

The next morning at six o'clock sharp, Major Ambrose strolled into the officers' mess and heaped a plate of eggs, biscuits, gravy, and grabbed a cup of coffee. He sat down at the end of a bench and looked down at Lieutenant Gardner. The lieutenant's breakfast dish was laid aside, and he was working on a sheet of paper.

As the major took the first bite, he turned his head in mild alarm when he saw the lieutenant threw his pencil in obvious and dramatic frustration.

The major took a few more bites and his attention returned to the lieutenant as he watched the young officer retrieve his pencil and began writing again. He heard him growl once more in abject irritation.

The major placed his fork down and then placed his full concentration to the lieutenant. He was stumped what was causing this uncharacteristic frustration of the young officer. "What's eating you, Lieutenant?"

The lieutenant gestured to the sheet of paper that was before him. "Oh, it's these damned Latin phrases the colonel wants me to translate. "It's been years since I've had Latin and it's driving me insane."

The major turned back to his plate but his curiosity was growing. He had never mentioned to anyone that he was an honor Latin student in Boston. He had money matters on his mind and was momentarily content to let the lieutenant stew in his own problems. But his ego began to surface and the idea of showing the lieutenant a thing of two about Latin seemed fitting.

Seeing the annoyance on the junior officer's face caused him to place his plate aside and stand and walk over and peer over his shoulder. He saw the words 'De mortuis nil nisi bonum' and beneath that line were the words, 'Finis coronat opus.' His eyes widened when he got to the phrase, 'Fere libenter hominess id quod volunt credunt.' When he saw the purposely, misspelled word in Latin, his heart landed in his throat. He knew these were the same phrases he had used in his telegram. There were several phrases in French too that he had used and it was all in front of the lieutenant. It was obvious that the lieutenant was trying to break the code and not just translating Latin.

The Major, panic stricken, backed to his original spot at the table. He drained his coffee and pushed the almost full plate aside and walked apprehensively out the door. The mess sergeant looked quizzically at the plate and at the back of the exiting major. His eyes then slid toward the lieutenant who sat with a mysterious smile plastered on his face.

The major hoofed it across the parade ground and into the

stable. He quickly signed out and ordered a private to saddle his horse.

He galloped out of the stable and headed toward Fort Smith. He rode up to Judy's cottage on a chuffing horse covered in lather. He dropped from the saddle and bounded up the steps and opened the door with a great deal of force.

Judy, who was sitting in front of her dressing mirror, was combing her hair. Her face registered great shock at his sudden appearance. She dropped her brush and looked at him with widened eyes.

"Frank." Her voice was tremulous.

He took a nervous look outside the door and then slammed it fiercely.

She stood and swallowed. "What's come over you?"

Frank Ambrose did not have time to tell her that men who crossed Indian Melvin died horrible deaths. He knew of two-men, who had given false information. One of those fools had his skull cleaved by an axe and the other was gutted but left alive so he could tell others before his agonizing death.

He raced toward her and grabbed her by the shoulders in imploring fear. "Judy, you have to go back to the telegraph station and send another telegram."

She wiggled from his grip and shook her head 'no' violently. "I told you, Frank, no more telegrams. You're doing something illegal and you're going to get caught and you're going to drag me down with you."

His eyes narrowed as he looked around the room. "Where's the groom-to-be, Judy? I just might have to tell him that you are still legally married."

She folded her arms defiantly and answered. "Go ahead and tell him and get it over with. I am divorced from you. I told the pastor about your infidelities. He said I was absolved from the marriage."

The major growing more frustrated shouted, "I don't give a

damn what that puissant pastor said, "You're still my wife. Now get your shoes on and let's get to the telegraph station."

She stood back and defiantly re-crossed her arms. "Tell me why and I must send it. Otherwise go send it yourself."

He hissed. "It's about money and money I could use."

"Whose money?"

He grabbed her and shoved her hard against the wall. "Now get those damned shoes on and let's go."

She fell to the floor. She looked up at him through her tousled hair and asked, "Is it Indian Melvin?"

"You tramp." He agitatedly pointed his finger at her. His voice choked in mixed anger and desperation. "You're the one in danger. You sent the telegrams, remember?"

She looked up at him and said, "I'm not moving until you tell me who the telegrams were really sent to."

He shouted, "Indian Melvin, you Idiot."

He stood over her with clinched fists. The way she smiled up at him with a triumphant smile caused him to step back and look both ways. In his panic state he had forgotten his senses but now that he had said what he did, his sensibilities returned and his eyes once filled in anger suddenly turned fearful. He swiveled his head left and right. Her smile, the damned smile said it all. He had been exposed.

He heard the sound of boots on the porch and he saw the door to the bedroom open. Colonel Daugherty stepped out. He had the look of a curious man who just had his suspicions confirmed. Behind the determined officer stood Sheriff Buchanan and Harley Rawlins

Major Ambrose instinctively turned to run out the front door, but before he could bolt, five-troopers, armed with Army Colts, entered and every barrel was aimed at him. As soon as he had made his rash admission, the colonel had the sheriff signal them from a bedroom window, and they had immediately cut off his path of escape.

The colonel walked up to him and relieved him of his side arm. The colonel let a smile cross his face. "Not bad for a 'dumb ass colonel from back when,' wouldn't you say, Frank?" Major Ambrose's face was drained of blood. He looked accusingly at Judy who only smiled back.

The colonel motioned with his own pistol barrel and the major glumly walked to the back door. The colonel momentarily halted him and a sergeant walked forward with a pillowcase and shoved it roughly down the major's head--hat and all.

The major heard the clattering of a wagon. He was guided quickly out the door and tossed unceremoniously into the back of a wagon where more soldiers had been concealed. He was trussed up tightly and the major said to the driver. "Head him to the railroad spur and send him to Little Rock. If he has a bowel movement, let him soil his pants. Just don't stop till you get the railroad station. The general is expecting him. He does not like to be kept waiting."

The colonel walked back into the cottage. He smiled at Judy. "What you did was courageous. But I'm afraid you and Harley's wedding will have to wait. I have to take you back to camp and let you give your testimony to a military tribunal."

Judy turned to Harley with anxious eyes. "Do you hate me, Harley?"

"What kind of man would hate you for a shortcoming when he's got so many of his own.

They hugged and kissed him passionately. Harley breathlessly released her and nodded to the colonel.

She turned as she was being led away. "Wait for me, Harley." She started walking again. She turned once more with a bit of trepidation, "You will won't you?"

Harley unashamedly had tears running down his face. "You damn right I will."

The colonel turned to the sheriff who stood watching her head descend the steps. "Whatever you do, keep this quiet."

The sheriff nodded solemnly. He looked at Harley and said, "You come with me."

The sheriff and Harley marched along toward his office with Harley casting suspicious eyes on the sheriff all the way and with good reason.

Once the door was shut, the sheriff pointed at gun rack beside the hat pegs on the door. "Put the gun belt on the rack and come with me."

"Why."

The sheriff tilted his head this way and that and said, "Loitering."

Harley made a wry face, "You want to shut me up about Indian Melvin don't you?"

The sheriff gave him a mock open-eyed look of surprise. "Harley, you win the prize."

Harley grunted in displeasure. "You don't have to lock me up to keep my mouth shut."

The sheriff stopped and turned back to look at Harley, "Yeah, maybe so but this way I'll know for sure."

Harley hang his gun belt on the rack and followed the sheriff dutifully down the corridor and walked into a cell that had been pointed to.

"I know you're mad now, Harley, but in a few days after you think it over you'll see the wisdom of it."

Harley said nothing but dolefully walked to his cot and lay down and listened to the metallic sound of the door shutting.

The sheriff later walked across to Ace's Saloon. He had to settle the matter of Judy's forthcoming absence. He walked through the batwings and noticed a sparse morning crowd and made his way to the bar. He looked for both Ace and Big Willard and not seeing them looked at Smitty.

Smitty, while talking animatedly with a customer, caught the eyes of the sheriff and tilted both his eyes and head to Ace's office which was located six-feet from the end of the bar.

The sheriff rapped with his knuckles and got a quick "come in" and he opened the door to see Ace smoking with his boots on his desk and Big Willard half asleep in a soft, cushioned chair to Ace's left.

Ace swept his hand to a comfortable chair by the door and the sheriff dropped in it and nodded at both men. "Ace, we got to talk."

Ace slightly raised his eyebrows and puffed his smoke. "Oh?"

The sheriff got to the point. "I got to ask your confidentiality in the matter."

Ace shrugged and answered with a gleaming smile. "We've shared secrets before."

"Yeah, well, this one ain't about widow women."

Ace leaned forward. "Sheriff, I'm not in any hurry and you can see that Big Willard isn't either but just say what is on your mind and I think you know that it's not going anywhere but up these four walls and then settle on the floor."

"It's about Judy. She's been mixed with Major Ambrose for quite a spell. She's been sending coded telegrams to her aunt that didn't exist. They were a bunch of Latin and French phrases and words and idle weather comments." He paused. "Now Judy is a smart girl and all of that but she don't know any Latin or French except for maybe 'oui' or 'madame.'

"Major Ambrose was blackmailing her to send them by threatening to reveal that they were still man and wife. He would pay her twenty-dollars to send them and that's a lot of money for a single gal.

"She was probably nervous doing it, but she did. She could live with it until she met Harley awhile back and they got serious and she wanted to quit."

Ace dipped his cigar into his ashtray. He shook his head negatively and sighed. "Major Ambrose was married to her and sleeping with her best friend at the time. I knew it, Big Willard knew it and the whole universe knew it, but her."

Ace looked at Big Willard and shook his head dejectedly. Ace turned to the sheriff and spoke again. "He was a snake in the grass and he never did anything good for that girl. He had a gambling debt to me you wouldn't believe."

"Did he ever pay you off?"

Ace nodded and said, "I knew it had to be illegal. He might be a major and all but he didn't have that kind of money, but to answer your question he paid me off in cash."

Big Willard straightened his sleepiness had vanished. "Who was getting those telegrams that she sent?"

The sheriff gave a sarcastic grin. "Oh, some hombre back at Fort Till, and the army's checking on him." The sheriff shrugged with his palms up, "But he don't matter, it's Indian Melvin who's really receiving them. He's got a tap between here and the fort and he's got someone who can receive them messages."

Big Willard's eyes narrowed. "So, the major has been sending that bandit messages through Judy and he's selling army secrets of sorts."

The sheriff nodded, "You got it in a nutshell, Big Willard."

Ace thoughtfully placed his cigar in the ashtray and leaned forward with both hands clasped. "What's happened to Judy and the major?"

The sheriff told about trapping the major and Judy being taken to the camp to be grilled by a military board of investigation.

Ace sighed and grimaced. "Are you going after Indian Melvin?"

"Yes, and it's a secret mission. I've already told my deputies that I'm going to Little Rock to meet the provisional governor. which is a damned lie, but the lid has to be tight."

Ace grimly smiled. "If you're going to be successful it is. That damned Indian Melvin has agents everywhere."

The sheriff smiled back. "Well, I got a few agents of my own."

Big Willard sighed and said, "Back when the War first started my cousin was in Galveston and was working for a teamster that hauled furniture and products from England. They had a five-wagon caravan going across the Nations and they were all slaughtered and all five-wagons vanished into thin air."

Sheriff Buchanan nodded solemnly. "I could tell you a whole lot of tragic stories about that bastard."

Big Willard leaned forward. His eyes were serious. "I bet you could and I got something I'd like to ask you."

"Fire way."

"I'd like to go as one of your deputies."

The sheriff looked at Ace who sat nonplussed. He looked back at Big Willard. "Can you ride and shoot?" He paused and added, "I already know you can fight."

"I can ride and I can shoot good enough. "I've wanted a chance at that bastard for almost three-years."

The sheriff looked at Ace and asked, "How can you explain his absence?"

Ace steepled his fingers and mused. "I can always say he went to New Orleans to fight for a big purse or I can say he's visiting his Aunt Tillie who has dyspepsia."

The sheriff said, "I doubt anyone but the town doctor would know what dyspepsia meant. I think you'd better go with going to New Orleans."

Ace nodded and quipped, "And not to damned sure about the doctor either knowing dyspepsia either."

The sheriff sighed and said, "You're hired, Big Willard. Meet me behind that pecan grove on the other side of Andrew's Livery at six, tomorrow morning. Wear your outdoor clothes and bring a pistol and canteen. I'll give you one of the best horses of them we impounded during the attempted bank holdup."

He concluded the conversation speculating on what was probably going to happen to Judy and Harley and then he abruptly stood and nodded 'goodbye' and departed.

The sheriff hated each step of his next duty and it was a duty.

He walked to the hotel and went into the lobby and by chance he saw Bonnie coming down the steps with Russell and Seth.

He attempted a weak smile and took off his hat. She looked blankly at him and then her eyes turned curious. "You wanting to see me, Sheriff?"

He licked his lips and nodded weakly. "I wonder if we could go for a walk?" He put back on his hat and sighed.

Russell and Seth looked at each other and then at the sheriff. They gave him an edgy look, bordering on suspicion, and then walked past him and out the door.

He watched their backs and then turned to the innocent eyes looking up at him. He swallowed and tilted his head to the door. They began walking slowly and when they exited the doorway. The sheriff took the lead and they began walking across the street. "Let's go down to my office and maybe you can have a nice glass of well water."

She looked up quickly. "I already had some water."

He looked down at her and her naïve face as she looked up at him with searching eyes.

"Well, maybe you might like a nice oatmeal cookie."

Her eyebrows arched. "Look, sheriff, I may be young but I'm not that young. What's on your mind? And I don't need water and oatmeal cookies to talk."

He sighed and took off his hat and replaced it. "Bonnie, I hate like the dickens telling you this, but I'm counting on you understanding."

She reached out and grabbed his shirtsleeve. "You're not sending John away or something?"

"It's something like that."

Her eyes immediately welled up in silvery tears. "Please, Sheriff, No."

Sheriff Buchanan looked at her sad face and the extreme despondency mirrored in it. He had rather have had an abscess tooth or a bunion that would not heal than keep talking but he did.

"Bonnie, there are some bad men who are just as mean and shiftless as the ones you met over at Gilbert's Crossing. They're causing a whole lot of problems and it may be that by John going with me, that I can put a stop to it."

She put her hand to her mouth and tears were streaming down her cheeks. She was not enjoying this talk at all.

The sheriff inhaled and asked, "You sure you wouldn't want a nice oatmeal cookie?"

She shook her head side-to-side. She swallowed and in a choking voice she said, "Sheriff, you don't understand. Russell and Seth and me," she paused as she tried to get enough voice, "We need him and depend on him. When bad things or bad men come along, he just blows them to Hell." He always knows what to do and it's always right."

The sheriff sighed, "well, I'm sure beginning to see the truth in that." He placed his hands on her shoulders and looked into her eyes. "Miss, I wished I was good with words but all I can say is that we need him badly. You're going to have to learn to share him."

They continued walking. He looked down at her. "He's not abandoning you. And I am not abandoning you either. I've got plans to send you to Texas and with protection."

"He's not abandoning me?"

He smiled warmly and stopped her and took her by her hand. "No, Bonnie, you got a whole lot friends now and no one is abandoning you. I'll have my deputies take you to the fort and you will stay there in safe lodging. When Judy is set free and she marries Harley, there will be an escort to take you up to Missouri along with her and then you will go with a whole lot of Baptists across the Nations and with some armed men to take care of you."

"Judy is she Harley's betrothed?"

The sheriff nodded, "Yeah, I guess that's a nice way to say it."

She stopped crying. She gave him a brave smile. "I like you, sheriff."

He looked down and tilted his head to one-side. He gave a breathless sigh, "Well, there's a heap that don't feel that way, Bonnie."

He looked up the street and saw Frankie and Fat Phil waiting on them. He caught her attention. "See them nice men up there?" He continued, "One is fat and the other is ugly but they are good men and they're going to go with you and get your wagon and take you to the army camp."

She pulled on his shirtsleeve again as they started walking. "I think I'd like an oatmeal cookie if you'll eat one with me."

He nodded. He hated oatmeal cookies, but he said, "I would be most proud to. "

The next morning, at five o'clock, John and Russell and Seth mounted up and pulling a pack horse covered in supplies, they rode down the street. They could hear roosters crowing and dogs barking as they rode along. It was near dawn and soon the dull shadows gave way to a light-blue.

When they arrived at the Arkansas River they saw the ferry waiting on them as Sheriff Buchanan had promised. They crossed wordlessly and began their steady pace across the Nation. John could sense the groused state of mind of both Russell and Seth and he divined it to be the absence of Bonnie.

He pulled them up about five miles into the journey and turned to them both. He began telling them about the mission at hand and what the positive consequences could be. He gave them all the information he could on the plight of Harley and Judy. He told them about the colonel and the major and what the sheriff had in mind. When he got through, he could see that they were still both upset and not fully persuaded.

"All right you two. Judy is safe at the fort. I went to see her last night and she told me to tell you both that she loved you like brothers and that she would see you in Texas for a glorious reunion." John pointed to rolling countryside. "You wouldn't want her on a mission like this with some of the sorriest pieces of humanity laying in wait for us, now would you?"

"Listen, good friends never forget. And she's our good friend. Now a good friend would want the best for the other and this is best for her."

Russell looked at Seth and he looked back. They both nodded and gave a happier face to John.

He smiled and whirled his horse around. "Now let's get going."

As John wheeled his horse around, and they rode off, another set of eyes were observing him. Arkansas Bob, who had watched them leave town, had gotten a late start with the ferry, but he had ridden double-time to catch up.

He knew he could not go home and he knew that if he wanted back in the good graces of Indian Melvin and Jack Filson, he had to kill John Johnson.

From hillside to hillside and from one grove of trees to another one, he followed diligently.

This journey took four-days. They sighted Dunbar Landing extending out into the river and they camped near a grove of mixed willow trees and cottonwoods. Russell and Seth took care of the animals and John started a small fire.

After eating, they sat back and smoked cigars and looked at the emerging stars. The flame of the fire licked up and cast scintillating shadows of orange and black.

John shoved his saddle against a tree and laid down his saddle blanket and pulled another one over him. He was sleeping while Russell and Seth talked.

Russell asked Seth about women. "Have you ever met one that you really liked, Seth?"

Seth shrugged and placed his cigar in the corner of his mouth. "Yeah, I met some gals that I liked. But I am always tongue-tied around them. I know some of them can be high-toned and loud, but for the most part, they seem more gentle than men. I just don't know how to talk to women, I reckon." He gave a long sigh and added, "But I sure in hell like 'em"

Russell sighed, "Yeah, well, I like women too. I'm not sure about getting married though."

Seth shrugged, "you think ole Harley tied the knot?"

Russell looked into the fire. "Yeah, bet he did at that."

"Wonder when he'll join up with us?"

Russell laughed and lowered his voice, "I bet he'll be later than normal. I know I sure would be."

Seth smiled. "I think I'd be real late."

They looked over at John. He was snoozing.

Seth nodded at John, "Do you think he'll ever get married?"

Russell shrugged, "He met this lady up in Gainesville, Arkansas and he sure in the world liked her.'

Seth nodded, "He'd be good to a woman. But he sure in the world can be bad to men."

Russell laughed, "When he was young and back at home…."

John interrupted them both. "Go to bed both of you."

They sniggered and laid out their bedrolls.

Arkansas Bob was on a distant hillside looking into the trees where John had camped. He saw the campfire get dimmer until there was only a slight glow of embers. He was undecided as whether he should sneak down and take a shot or just bide his time or catch him in his sights when the sun was up.

He chose the latter and he made camp for the night. He made no fire and ate beans from a can with his knife and pondered if this killing of John would truly grant him clemency with Indian Melvin. He was fearful of Jack Filson but he was deathly afraid of Indian Melvin.

At that same moment, Indian Melvin was talking to Jack Filson. Indian Melvin had a map out on a table and was tracing the line from Fort Smith toward Texas. The thick overhead light was casting large blobby shadows on the delicate lines of the map.

Indian Melvin asked Jack how he was healing and Jack gave a positive grunt. "That damn big guy, he took a chunk of flesh out of me but yeah, I could ride now if I had to."

Jack's good eye zeroed in on the spot where Indian Melvin had his finger. He looked back up at Indian Melvin who was giving him a steady stare. "What you got in mind, Indian Melvin?"

"They will come along this road."

Jack looked down and quickly up. "What's there to shield you from eyesight?"

"There's a thick patch of woods off to one-side. If you came out slinging a lot of lead and got their attention, I would send about dozen men from the other side from the draw and catch them in a crossfire."

Jack grunted and sighed.

Indian Melvin looked at him. "Don't you like the plan?"

Jack nodded he liked it. "I just got my mind on that damn big guy and my nephew Buster."

Indian Melvin gave a disapproving face. "Jack, you could lose your life and a lot of other men's lives trying to spring him. You need to forget that."

Jack knew better than to say too much back. He just nodded and looked back at the map. "You told me earlier that they have eight men escorting and a driver and guard in the box."

"That's correct."

"How many men would it take for me to make a good jump at them and spook 'em good?"

"Well, I would let you take your two-remaining gang members and I would throw in about ten." Indian Melvin extended his palms out as in thought. "I would hit them from the other side once the shooting started and would probably use about a dozen good men."

Jack sighed and agreed. "That ought to do it. If they have four troopers to a side, we should bang 'em pretty good."

Indian Melvin stood erect. His head almost touched the ceiling lantern. His eyes leveled on Jack's one eye. "We got a deal?"

Jack extended his gloved hand. "We got a deal."

Indian Melvin, as he was about to walk away asked, "What ever happened to that new guy?"

Jack looked at him in thought and then his eyebrows bent. "You mean Arkansas Bob?"

Indian Melvin nodded, "Yeah, Arkansas Bob."

"He turned yellow and ran when Catfish got nailed. He ran down an alley and hung us all out to dry."

Indian Melvin grunted in thought. "I'll put the word out." He said over his shoulder to Jack Filson as he was walking out the door. "He's as good as dead."

Jack watched the huge frame move into the shadows. He shuddered some. You did not want to cross Indian Melvin. He looked once more at the map and then reached up and turned off the light.

As Indian Melvin made his way back to his own house, he stopped suddenly and looked back at Jack's cottage. The green shadows of the full moon revealed a malevolent gleam in his eyes. He ambled onward to his house where Salty Phillips, his second-in-command was waiting.

The tall and angular Salty was talking to the shorter and stockier Junior Grease. They both were entrusted with the boss's more difficult jobs. Indian Melvin entered and nodded at them both.

Salty's eyes darkened by the shadow of his hat brim raised his eyes and smiled. "Well, boss, did he go for it?"

Indian Melvin inclined his head for them to follow him and they entered his study and they took seats opposite his desk. When Indian Melvin moved his vast bulk into the seat, he began talking.

"Jack isn't any use to us anymore. He's lost his gang and he's lost his edge. Here's what I want you to do."

They listened intently to his instructions way into the night. He dismissed them only when he thought they could say what he told them by rote.

John and his crew waited patiently for the armored coach to arrive. It was two-days late and John began to wonder if something had happened to the coach even before they had anticipated trouble.

He was sitting with his men beneath a tarp early in the morning and listening as the rain pelted the trees and countryside.

He heard the unmistakable sound of hooves on the wet road and heard the clink and chink of harness.

They all stood and watched the coach come to a lumbering stop. It was pulled by six-mules and was surrounded by eight-troopers all dressed in military slickers. He could see a string of reserve mules being pulled by two of the troopers bringing up the rear.

The lieutenant, wearing his usual forage hat, pulled away from the others and rode to the grove of trees. He raised his right hand and greeted John.

He introduced himself and explained, "We're late and sorry about that but we started off with small wheels and then decided we needed big wheels."

John nodded and said, "Big wheels or not it's going to be long trip regardless."

John could tell the lieutenant was trying to be courteous but he also could tell he was impatient. John and his crew fished out their slickers and dismantled their camp in five-minutes and joined the group around the coach.

The troopers were not overly friendly and through hooded eyes viewed them as outsiders. John could see the apprehension in their looks. He knew it might take a while for the two-groups to meld.

He signaled the lieutenant that they were ready and they began lumbering down the road.

John and his group peeled off from them and he gave assignments to his crew. "Seth, you stay back apiece and look after our backside. I'm going ahead and see what I can see." He looked at Russell and pointed to some nearby hills. "Ride the hills so you can be elevated but don't go to the skyline."

They rode the whole day and the entire day was rainy and slick and the mules labored on the muddy road. They made camp after they had made about twenty miles.

The coach was placed in the middle of some trees and the mules were taken care of by the driver and guard and placed in a secure place. They placed the spare mules apart so they could be used the following day.

The soldiers kept to themselves and there was little interaction between them and John's crew. The lieutenant called John aside and they started walking to nowhere in particular. "The colonel said you would be the one to seek advice from and so I'm asking advice."

John stopped and looked up at the blue and black clouds. Rain was dripping from his hat brim. "All right, Lieutenant, ask."

"I frankly have had no experience dealing with outlaws and leading a coach through this sort of terrain. I am not adverse to your telling me when you think that there is danger or when we need to stop."

John again cast his eyes upward at the sky and back at the lieutenant. "Let's go somewhere dry and let's take a gander at your map."

A group of soldiers were in the process of setting up large tarps. The lieutenant and John waited until they were finished and they walked under the one designated for the officer. He pulled out his map and spread it between his hands.

It was a topographical map and it showed rivers, hills and trees. When John's eyes moved along the map's trail, his eyes immediately caught the heavy tree line, which was up the road about thirty-miles or so. "If I was setting up an ambush, this would be one very likely spot." He punctuated his thought by placing a finger on the drawing of the trees.

The lieutenant sent his eyes down the road and back at the map. The lieutenant pursed his lips and looked back at John and said, "I would imagine the way we're traveling that it will be probably noon the day after tomorrow before we get there."

John looked down the road and saw the heavy puddles and the mud. "I'm not sure, but whenever we get there, we need to be ready."

The lieutenant rolled the map up and placed it in the leather cylinder he had under his arm. He looked around and said, "This wet wood is going to be difficult to start a fire."

John said he had dry wood kindling and he could do it. He went to his packhorse and retrieved several sticks of dry wood and began a fire beneath one of the military tarps.

The soldiers gathered around him and he began making coffee. Soon Russell and Seth walked under the tarp and the soldiers became quieter and more reserved.

The lieutenant was still under his tarp some distance away and his lack of proximity caused one of the men named 'Harp' to become emboldened. He grabbed Seth by the seat of his britches and said aloud to a few laughs that he was going to see how far he could toss a midget.

John reached out and grabbed him by the shoulder. "Keep your hands to yourself."

Private Ray Harp, also a large man, let go of Seth and turned his attention to John. "I've heard about how you rode with Forrest and how you stopped that bank robbery but that don't cut no ice with me."

John pole axed him with a straight jab and Harp went wind milling from under the tarp and landed in a pool of muddy water.

John walked to the edge of the tarp and looked at the private. "Does that cut any ice with you?"

Private Harp got up rubbing his jaw and caught the embarrassed look of his peers. Harp looked over at the lieutenant who seemed busy searching for something. "It's a good thing the lieutenant was here is all I can say."

John gave him a hard look and went back to the fire. He asked Russell if he would go get some more wood.

Another soldier named 'Jackson' said, "There's no need for you all to do all the work. I'll go get it."

There were no more 'incidents' that night. The next morning, they all had coffee and a plate of beans. The rain had gone away and they began their trek again.

As John began to turn his horse's head and start scouting down the road, he caught the sly grin of the lieutenant who waved at him. John smiled to himself. The lieutenant was more man than he had initially given him credit. He waved back and cantered down the road.

John rode and searched the surroundings for any place of ambush or place where a number of men could be concealed but he was satisfied that there was nothing of danger for the present.

They made twenty-five miles that day and the mules were spent when they called it a day. The fresh mules were keeping them on schedule.

The next morning, John rode miles ahead and was distant from the coach. When he topped a hill he saw the trees. The trees were off to the right. They had brambles and bushes beneath them but they were spaced as such where horsemen could gallop through the openings. He knew by experience that this was a danger spot.

He turned around and galloped back to the coach and hailed the lieutenant. John told him of his concerns. The lieutenant nodded and stopped the coach.

He ordered his men to gather around. They rode their horses as to encircle him and the lieutenant asked John to address them.

John nodded his head in the direction in which he had ridden. "I'm not saying there is anyone there, but up ahead, on the right, is a large grove of trees and it has all the earmarks of a good spot for an ambush.

"If I was you, I'd make sure you have no tie-downs and keep them pistols handy" He paused and pointed with his hand as though he were describing the place. "On the other side of the trees is a low ridge but it's tall enough to hide riders." He looked at each of them and all eyes were on him. "Me and Seth will ride in the coach. We will try and cover both sides till we get past the trees."

He dismounted and Adrian Jackson, the private from Illinois took his horse. Seth, who had seen the coach stop and ridden ahead, was told to dismount and he hopped to the ground and was bidden by John to enter the coach.

Their horses were tied to the back of the coach and the guard checked his scattergun. The coach began its lumbering pace once more. John urged Seth to check his .44 and make sure he had the proper rounds.

Up ahead was Jack Filson. He had Three-Finger Louie on his left and John Ferris to his right. He had all new men behind him including Salty and Junior. He told them to check their weapons. He caught sight of Indian Melvin on the other side of the road. Indian Melvin waved at him and Jack gave a wave back.

They sat on their horses and there was no noise except the occasional blowing of a horse or a droning of a fly.

Jack was fidgety and his hip was hurting him badly. John Ferris looked down and saw the blood seeping through Jack's pants. His eyes moved up and saw the pain in his boss's good eye.

The coach could be heard plodding along over the rise. The noise of the lumbering coach masked the metallic sounds of pistols being cocked.

When the coach was square in their sights, Jack gave a growl and he spurred his big, truculent black horse forward with his gun pointed at the troopers. They poured out of the woods with guns blazing orange flumes.

The troopers, forewarned or not, were momentarily stunned by the abrupt charge, and two took a hard hit. The hard zing of pistol balls and the sparks bouncing off the armored coach spooked them momentarily but they answered with a barrage of their own.

Private Ray Harp was one of the first that had been hit by the air furrowing balls. The shot hit him in the shoulder and he fell heavily from his horse. He dropped his Colt and was desperately scrambling for it. He felt a presence above him and looked up to see Seth blasting away with a foot on each side of him.

John, who had leaped from the coach, stood side to side with Seth and had both Navy Colts barking. Three-Finger Louie took one of those shots in the chest and he fell flip-flopping over his horse's rump stunting the charge of the others.

John Ferris turned his horse to aim at John. Seth, seeing this deliberate movement, aimed across and fired twice, hitting Ferris in the neck and head and sent him reeling sideways to the earth.

Jack Filson's good eye bulged when he noticed that Indian Melvin's attack from the other side was not materializing. He looked down and saw Three-Finger Louie dead and then his eye went to John Ferris who was balled up in a knot.

He looked behind him and saw Salty and Junior pulling away and headed back into the woods with the majority of his men.

Jack cussed Indian Melvin and he cussed the big Texan. He recognized him from the attempted robbery in Fort Smith. He looked back at the tempting woods and safety and he looked at his tormentors. He realized with deathly finality that Indian Melvin had set him up. He cussed himself for not divining this duplicity and his own run of bad luck.

He placed his reins in his mouth and began charging toward John. The troopers all aimed and fired blasts from hell and sent him reeling from his saddle.

Indian Melvin peered over the ridge and nodded to himself, when he saw Jack Filson take six or seven shots. The outlaw kingpin slid down the hill and walked to his mounted men who patiently waited for him. He was handed the reins to his big sorrel and he mounted up and with a nestled finger ordered his men to follow him. He rode away with a smile on his face.

When the gunfire ended, there was one-dead trooper. Some of his associates gathered around the dead body and there were both tears and cussing.

John saw the group around the dead soldier but his eyes moved to the wounded Ray Harp. He went to him and knelt down and lifted him up by his good shoulder and unbuttoned his tunic and tossed the lapel aside.

The gaping hole was clean through and that relieved John. He asked the Lieutenant for some whiskey or alcohol and the lieutenant passed that on to some of his men around the coach.

Soon a bottle of alcohol was given to him and he poured a copious amount into the wound and Ray Harp gasped and gritted his teeth. One of the soldiers came over with some bandages and John did the best field dress of it that he could.

John and Seth lifted his body up from the ground and carried him to the coach. The soldiers improvised him a bed and laid him down.

As Seth was about to close the door and let him rest, Harp reached up and grabbed him by the shirt. "Your cousin may be bigger than you, but you stand mighty big in my eyes." He released his Seth's shirt and continued, "I just wanted you to know that."

Before Seth could tell him that he was not John's cousin, the lieutenant shut the door.

The lieutenant nodded for John to go with him and they walked a goodly distance. The lieutenant nodded toward the woods. "What are we going to do with those dead bodies?"

John looked over the carnage and saw Jack Filson's beautiful horse standing there. "Well, I'll tell you, Lieutenant, let Seth go through the pockets and see what he can find and share it with the men."

The Lieutenant looked at him strangely. "You mean rob the dead?"

"They ain't going to need it any more."

The lieutenant looked evenly at John and shrugged. "That makes sense to me." He looked at John peering at the beautiful black horse. "Why don't you take that horse?"

"With your permission that is exactly what I'd like to do."

"Should I get a burial detail and bury those outlaws?"

John shook his head 'no.' "They wouldn't have you." He looked at Seth and nodded to the four outlaws that lay dead. He told him to gather all the money he could and to strip them of guns and any valuables.

John turned to the lieutenant. "If I was you, I'd impound their horses and sell them when we reach a settlement."

The lieutenant nodded, "I'll let you handle that, John, I am not sure army regulations permit me to do that."

Seth found eighty-dollars and ninety cents among the corpses. He tethered the outlaws' horses to the back of the coach and gave the money to John.

John with the Lieutenant's permission handed out money to all the troopers.

The lieutenant had to admit that was a morale booster.

John tied on his bay to the back of the coach and mounted up on the spirited but beautiful horse that once belonged to Jack Filson. Many of the troopers admired the spirited horse, but none begrudged the big Texan for taking him

Russell rode up as the Lieutenant was assigning a burial detail for his dead soldier.

He looked at the dead bodies of the outlaws and then at the soldiers carrying the body of the trooper. He then looked at John and the horse he was mounted on. "Where did you get that horse?"

John nodded to the near body of Jack Filson. "It once belonged to Jack Filson, but it's mine now."

Russell leaned over and ran his hands over the satiny neck of John's new horse. He looked back over at the dead outlaws. "I heard all the commotion but I was too far away. I rode down as hard as I could."

John sighed and shook his head. "It was one-poorly planned attack is all I can say."

"Poorly-planned?" Russell asked.

John turned his horse and pointed at the trees. "They came at us hard, but only three were really charging. The rest just laid back some and fired from a distance as though it was token attack. Jack Filson and his two-cronies were killed and one-outlaw back at the tree line. I think several were winged." He paused and ruminated and looked back at Russell. "It don't make any sense to me."

Russell straightened and pointed to the rise across the road. "Well, if you want to know something else that is strange, there was a dozen men on the other side of the rise."

John looked at him in surprise. "When did you see 'em?"

"I saw them when I was comin' down them hills you see over yonder. He pointed to some distant hills. "But they high tailed it when the gunfire started."

John's brow furrowed in interest. He asked Russell to follow him and they galloped across the road and up the rise. When they crested the long hillock, John could see the tracks of many horses and the piles of horse manure. His eyes moved to the marred dirt where someone had apparently been looking and then scurried down the rise in haste.

John and Russell rode down together and looked around. John continued to be puzzled.

Russell looked at his cousin and asked, "How come they didn't fire?"

John shook his head as in bewilderment. "They would've done us in if they had." He pointed at the tracks. "I'd say there was twelve at least here and Jack Filson had twelve I would guess."

John turned his horse's head and said over his shoulder. "I'm going to think on it."

They rode up over the rise and saw the lieutenant mounted

waiting for John. Russell, catching the cue, pealed off, and headed back to the hills.

The lieutenant watched the men finish the grave and set a marker. He turned to John who was riding up. "What do you think we should do?"

John tilted his head as though saying 'get going again.'

So the lieutenant gave the orders when everyone was saddled and they started their measured journey again.

The lieutenant seemed pale and distressed. "I have to confess to you, John, that I have never been in a skirmish before."

John looked over at him and gave him a playful hit on the shoulder. "You handled yourself good, Lieutenant."

John thought he heard the lieutenant mutter, "I hope so."

They rode together for several miles and John began to tell him his concerns and about what troubled him about the attack.

The lieutenant listened and asked, "Why do you think they held back?"

John's eyes squinted. "I think Indian Melvin was checking to see if there was more cavalry than was evident here."

The lieutenant widened his eyes. "We could not have survived an attack from both side." He rode, along further, silently ruminating. He nodded his head as if the outlaw's plan had come to him. He then offered his mind. "You think Indian Melvin was thinking this was a trap on our part and he was testing the waters?"

John nodded thoughtfully. "I do."

He rode and reflected on John's opinion. "You think he'll try again, don't you?"

John nodded gravely. "Most assuredly and the cut of his haul is much greater." They both pulled up their horses and John looked evenly at the lieutenant. "He saw our number and he saw that there is no more cavalry. You can bank on it that he'll try again and soon."

John bid 'goodbye' to the lieutenant and galloped away. He had to find where the next attempt was going to be made.

Indian Melvin led his men to a nearby hollow. He watched them dismount and pull cigars from their pockets and start talking idly. His blue eyes looked up and he saw Salty and Junior ride in with the men who had made the half-hearted attack.

The men, following Salty, turned off and joined their comrades. Salty and Junior remained saddled and rode up to the chief.

Salty seemed thoughtful. "Boss, we could've taken that coach."

Indian Melvin nodded affirmatively. "I know that now." He looked at his two-lieutenants. "But I didn't before hand."

Junior inclined his head in the direction of the attack. "Who was that big jasper with them?"

Indian Melvin shook his head as to say 'he didn't know.' His eyes narrowed in thought. "But two-men hidden in a coach sure in hell isn't going to stop twenty-four men."

Salty pulled a cigar out of his pocket and lit it and tossed the match aside. "When are we goin' to nail 'em for good?"

Indian Melvin nodded his head toward 'Canebrake.' "Salty, you and Junior gather up some of the men here. Get some of the boys at Duty and divide your men into two-groups of twelve." He looked at Junior. "You meet me in Canebrake tomorrow at noon."

He looked at Salty. "You have your men down by the red rocks just beyond the bend of Sylvester Creek. When I send for you start riding toward the coach head on."

They both nodded and both rode away quickly to do the boss's bidding.

That night when the cavalry made camp in a cove of rocks, they gathered around a fire and eating. The troopers were now animatedly talking to Seth and Russell,

As they sat with their pan of beans, one of the troopers named Harris, leaned forward and looked at Seth. "Seth Johnson, all I've heard about is your cousin since he rode into town. But what you did today with all those lead balls flying around is something I'll never forget."

Russell, who was sitting next to Seth, knew Seth was embarrassed and did not know the proper reply so he answered for him. "He's one of my two-favorite cousins. I'm damned proud of him." Russell took no note of the misunderstanding. He figured that he and Seth would have a laugh about it later.

The line of conversation went on for an hour with soldiers slapping Seth affectionately on the back and calling him 'Seth Johnson.' They looked at his .44's and he was the object of 'hero worship.' When they asked him personal questions, he avoided talking about himself, which they interpreted as modesty, but was in reality embarrassment.

Seth ate meekly with his head down and occasionally would glance up at Russell. Seth was irritated at himself for not correcting those calling him, 'Seth Johnson.'

When they had eaten, the corporal came and handed out the duty roster, they dispersed and went their way and stacking their tin plates on the ground, which was picked up dutifully by the one-man kitchen patrol.

Seth and Russell were walking to their bedrolls, when Seth sighed and said, "Russell, I hope I haven't brought you any shame by them callin' me 'Seth Johnson.'

Russell was moved by his humility. He had no idea that Seth was feeling guilty. He suddenly stopped and placed a hand on Seth's shoulder. He peered into his friend's eyes and said, "You've made me proud, Seth, not ashamed."

John and the lieutenant were looking at the map by the glow of their private campfire. John was tracing his finger along the topographical map and it stopped when it reached the bend of Sylvester Creek. The lieutenant watched John's finger stop and then jab at the spot on the map.

The lieutenant looked over at John. "What makes you think it will be there?" He was not questioning John, he was in fact in awe of him, but wondered how he could predict with such confidence.

"The rocks will conceal any men and the bend in the river

leaves you blind around it. If they strike us there, we'll have little wiggling room."

The lieutenant added glumly, "If we do escape, I imagine they will resort to shooting the mules."

John nodded toward the horses in the remuda "If matters get that rough, we can always use horses."

The lieutenant sighed, "That would be tough using saddle horses for pulling a coach." He paused and added, "A heavy one at that."

John pulled the pocket watch out that had been given to him to deliver. He sighed twice over when he saw the time and was reminded of his obligation.

He nodded silently at the lieutenant and took his leave. As he walked toward his campsite, Adrian Jackson, one of the two-guards on duty, tentatively approached him. Jackson, a pleasant looking young man, asked, "May I have a moment of your time?"

John nodded.

"All the men are so disgusted the way Ray handled your cousin the other day and all of us want to apologize for his behavior."

John was taken-aback by that. He started to tell Adrian that Seth was not his cousin but stopped when Adrian kept talking. "We all knew you were something special by the way the colonel and the lieutenant talked about you before we left. But we had no idea that your two-cousins would be so effective."

John smiled at him and nodded. "Yeah they're something all right."

Adrian's eyebrows moved downward in thought. "How come you and Russell are so tall but Seth is so short?"

John thought for a moment and decided he would not disappoint Adrian by telling him Seth was not related. "I guess it's just one of those things of nature, Private."

Adrian laughed, "Yeah, I reckon so."

John walked on to his bedroll and reached down and plopped his saddle against the tree. He noticed that Russell and Seth were still awake.

Seth looked up at him as he sat down around the small fire. "John," he timidly began. "Folks have been calling me Seth Johnson and I want to tell you that I'm sorry about that."

John smiled and sat down. He felt puzzled that the matter would mean so much to Seth. "No need to be sorry about a thing like that. In fact I'm sort of glad they think you're kin, it might give us a better reputation."

Seth tossed a twig into the fire. "Are you mad that I didn't tell them any different?"

John looked across at Russell and back at Seth. "Why would I be mad at a thing like that?" He smiled and pointed his finger across toward Seth. "What you did today would have made any person proud including me. The way you saved Harp's skin after he made a fool out of himself." John pulled back his finger into a fist. "I'm proud that they think you are a cousin."

A tear began streaming down Seth's cheek. He tried to stifle a sob.

John looked at Russell and back at Seth. He asked gently, "Seth, what is it?"

Seth looked directly at him with his eyes filled with tears. "I don't want to be Seth Ragsdale anymore, I want to be Seth Johnson."

John sat looking at the ground and then over at Russell who had tears also in his eyes.

John stood and reached down and pulled Seth up. He fought tears himself as he looked into the lonely eyes. "I pronounce you Seth Johnson. Not only are you our cousin, but you'll be part owner of a ranch. From this day forth, you are our kin."

Seth dropped to his seat on the ground and never looked up but he held up his hand and John took it and squeezed it.

John walked thoughtfully and with a full chest to his bedroll. He smiled to himself when he thought back to Arkansas and the frail little guy who had now emerged as a hombre to be reckoned with.

# CHAPTER SEVEN

———◆———

The following day Indian Melvin rode into Canebrake by himself. Canebreak was a misnomer. There were no canes and no bamboo. It consisted of a large, unpainted saloon and general store combined. The large rain-splattered gray building stood alone on the prairie. A solitary sentinel set in windswept and lonesome looking tableau.

It was eleven o'clock and there was one horse hitched to the hitching post. Indian Melvin looked at the horse as he rode up. His eyes then moved to the man sitting on the far end of the porch. It was Arkansas Bob.

His eyes tightened. He saw Arkansas Bob uncoil from his relaxed state and stand and walk toward him and position himself at the top of the steps. Indian Melvin marched his horse up to the steps and looked up at the frightened features of the man he vowed to kill.

Indian Melvin cocked his head to one side and said, "You got a hell of a lot of nerve is all I can say."

Arkansas Bob held out his hands plaintively. "Just hear me out."

"Start talking."

"I've been following John Johnson since he left Fort Smith."

"Who is John Johnson?"

"He's the man who killed Catfish and captured Buster and the rest."

Indian Melvin sneered, "Yeah, and you turned and ran."

"I couldn't do nothing. He had the drop on Jack and Three-Finger Louie. I just decided to bide my time and kill him."

Indian Melvin shook his head as to clear it. "You better get to the good part before I shoot you in the head, you yellow bastard."

"John Johnson is the man who shot Jack and the others."

Indian Melvin nodded thoughtfully. "He's the one with the twin Navy Colts?"

"That's him and I aim on killing him."

Indian Melvin ran his several fingers under his chin in deliberation. "How do you plan on doing this, Arkansas Bob?" The way he said, 'Arkansas Bob' was dripped in sarcasm.

This was not lost on Arkansas Bob. "I plan on using my Sharps on him. I aim to ride ahead of that slow as molasses coach and get me a spot and nail him."

Indian Melvin mused this over still rubbing his chin. "All right, you'll live but if you mess this up. I'll cut your throat and leave you flopping in the dirt like a chicken."

"I won't mess this up."

Indian Melvin nodded knowingly. "You damn right you won't. I'm going to lead you to the spot where I want you to take him."

Arkansas Bob exhaled and agreed to it.

Indian Melvin turned in his saddle and pointed to a small copse of trees. "You go over to those trees and wait for me. I've got to talk to some real men."

Arkansas Bob slunk off the porch with the insult still in his ears. He mounted up and rode to the trees.

Later that afternoon John was riding point again and scouting the road far ahead. He was about to pull up and head back a few miles and wait for the coach when he caught the sight of an overt mirror reflection. He pulled up and turned his mount and looked at the ridge of tall craggy hills. He knew it was someone who definitely wanted his attention.

The mirror kept flashing. When he headed toward the source, the mirror stopped winking at him. He made his way, tree by tree, and thicket by thicket, until he reached the scree at the bottom of a rocky hill. He rode his way through a constricted path until he reached a point where he had to dismount.

He drew his right Colt out and made his way by feeling his way with his left-hand along the hard rock surface of the craggy hill. When he turned the bend, he saw Big Willard sitting atop a rounded boulder and eating an apple.

John holstered up and gave him a smile. "I don't mind telling you, Deputy, that I'm not only surprised to see you here but eating an apple."

Big Willard chomped down and smiled back. "Well, it's good for your breath and keeps you regular." He turned his large upper body and pointed up the trail. "Someone wants to talk to you real bad."

John trudged up the narrow path through two-sentinel boulders and came to a flat place atop the incline. Resting against a flat-faced large rock was Sheriff Buchanan peacefully smoking his pipe.

He stuck up his hand for John to shake. They shook and John sat down opposite him with his back against a rock.

The sheriff's granite features eased into a slow smile. "I reckon you tasted a small sample of Indian Melvin's wares."

John nodded. "Jack Filson made a show of it but got killed for his efforts."

The sheriff shrugged. "I was keeping watch and if it had gotten real bad, I was going to jump but saw you and that kid handle the situation." He shrugged when he said, "If I had jumped, we might have lost Indian Melvin."

John did not reply. He grabbed some pebbles and began tossing them one by one idly.

The sheriff continued, "I want to give you some information. Indian Melvin was at Canebrake this morning and he had Arkansas Bob there. Arkansas Bob's been tailing you to kill you I would imagine. I guess he figures if he kills you he's back on the payroll."

John's face registered no surprise. "He's probably been following way behind. But I haven't seen him."

"No, but we have."

The sheriff placidly puffed on his pipe. "Indian Melvin will probably have him try and ambush you. So, I'm sending Harley with you when you scout up ahead tomorrow."

They talked briefly about Harley and his marriage. The sheriff told how Judy had been exonerated by the military tribunal and had been released the following day. He went on to say that Harley married her as soon as she was released and Judy was riding with Bonnie up to Missouri and then cutting across to the Nations with a group of missionaries. He smiled when he said Harley was with the deputies but maybe in body only.

John smiled and then changed the subject to Indian Melvin again. "I think he'll hit us just above Sylvester Creek."

The sheriff nodded, "Yeah, , that would be just around the bend."

John was surprised he knew. "You do have good information. I always thought Forrest had good spies but not sure he was as informed as much as you are."

The sheriff almost laughed. "Well, I've thought of Indian Melvin for a long time and we have people in the Nations and they know things and do not care for him. He's ruled as a tyrant for so long and many have been hurt by him."

The sheriff sat for a spell and puffed his pipe and his eyes moved toward John. "I'm not sure of where he'll attack you, but am sure that he'll do it soon." The sheriff removed his pipe and used the stem as a pointer. "I know that Salty Phillips has got a group and I know that Junior Grease has got some men. Wherever they hit you it will be from two-sides."

John agreed, "If they fail in this next attack, I'll imagine they'll shoot the mules."

The sheriff nodded, "I imagine the only reason that they've not already done that is that Indian Melvin thinks he might need the mules just to carry the infernal armored coach off."

John looked up at the sheriff with a sly grin on his face, "How do you know that Indian Melvin was at Canebrake today with Arkansas Bob?" He knew the information was too quick for any of the conventional ways he knew.

"John, the man who owns the saloon there and the general store has been a friend of mine for over twenty-years. He feeds me information and I've got a deputy disguised as a slow-witted handy man."

John said, "Well, he got you that information fast." He knew the sheriff was holding out on him.

"I have to be quick and have to be a step ahead."

John added, "I think you've done a hell of job staying concealed and knowing what you do." He paused and added, "I'd begun to think that you had got lost."

The sheriff nodded back and answered. "If I can fool you, maybe I have fooled him."

John rose up and dusted off his pants. "I think you have." He turned to leave.

The sheriff's voice rose up to him. "Harley will meet you at the bottom of the hill." He paused and added, "You'll sure in the world need him."

John gave him a backward wave and made his way down. He nodded up at Big Willard still eating his apple. John said, "Maybe you can get back to them boiled eggs soon."

Big Willard took a big audible bite and answered, "I'm counting on it, John, so don't let me down."

John gave him a farewell wave and moved on. When he made the bend and reached bottom, he met Harley. They shook hands and gave greetings to the other and mounted up. They rode cautiously out around the hill and avoided the tumbled scree and went from one grove of trees to the next.

Feeling secure they were not seen, they rode along the main road. Harley brought John up-to-date on his marriage, and John brought Harley up-to-date on all the sequences since they had left Fort Smith. He informed him of Seth's name change. Harley smiled and said, "He's a good kid make that man. I'll call him Seth Johnson."

They met the rumbling coach and John informed the lieutenant that Harley would be joining them for the remainder of the journey.

The rest of the day was uneventful and they made camp. The lieutenant and John made plans for the next day. They wanted to deploy all the able bodied men they could and make sure the coach was protected from the front and back.

At sunrise, John arose and gathered his men around him. "After you've had your coffee and breakfast, I want you to make sure you've got all the pistols you can carry. The lieutenant informed me we have dozens of Spencer's in the coach and they are fully loaded. So carry a rifle."

Russell asked, "John, you think this is the day?"

John grimly nodded. "I would be greatly surprised if it is not." He went on to say, "Seth, you take the drag and follow but not too far today. If the shooting starts, you'll sure in the world be needed."

Harley slapped Seth on the shoulder and winked. "I know I'd want you on my side, Seth Johnson."

Seth gave a shy grin and stood straighter.

Russell, you take the right flank. Be careful not to be seen but if you see any dust or sign of men moving, you can fire a shot in the air. It'll warn us and not spook Indian Melvin's men. Hell, they have all the intent of wiping us out today,"

He turned to Harley. "I want you on the left-side and be careful. I'll be riding point, but if I suddenly stop and just sit there, it's because I've bird-dogged something." He had no idea at the time, those words would materialize so fast.

Harley spoke, "If you stop, I'll just keep riding just below skyline and try and get behind them."

John nodded, "Exactly."

They ate a quick breakfast and gathered weapons.

The lieutenant gave his men a similar speech about vigilance. His men seemed tense but confident. They all felt better when they saw the big Texan ride by.

The heavily bandaged Ray Harp mounted up and as he turned his horse he rode toward Seth who was sliding in another .44 into his belt. "Seth," Ray extended his hand. "Watch out for us."

Seth accepted his hand. "You can count on it, Ray."

Each man turned his mount and the day was started.

John rode easily down the road. His eyes working attentively to hillocks and trees. When he rounded a small bend, he caught sight of tall craggy hill that had tumbled boulders.

He slowed his pace and rode toward a stunted tree beside the road. He wanted the tree to shield him while his eyes searched the crest of the hill. He felt uneasy and having ridden with Forrest, he had learned how to avoid ambushes and to set up ambushes. All that had given him an edge. This had 'dry gulch' written all over it.

He stopped and looked around the bole of the tree and started visually inching across the top.

Arkansas Bob was there and had his Sharps clutched in his hand. He had removed his hat and was peeking through a small aperture between the boulders. He could see the vigilant Texan.

Sweat was drooling from Arkansas Bob's forehead. He would

wipe at it with his soiled handkerchief and then send his eyes back to the small opening. "C'mon damn you," he hissed.

Arkansas Bob's tension mounted when John did not move. He was incensed that the Texan could have presaged this. It was uncanny and that unnerved him. His slippery finger moved into the trigger guard.

And they waited the hunter and the hunted. The sound of meadowlark's singing resounded between the tree and the hill. The meadowlark's call seemed unusually magnified in the space formed by the rocks.

Arkansas Bob sighed and wiped more sweat beads. A fly stridulated by him several annoying times. His eyes went to the buzzing fly and he murmured several silent cuss words. He tried to block out the noises. Annoyed by both the meadowlark's trilling and the damn fly's buzzing, he shut his eyes and gritted his teeth. Both noises seemed to echo and reecho in Arkansas Bob's brain. It was though the hand of nature had turned up the volume.

John was convinced that the hill held a bushwhacker. He moved his horse closer to the trunk of the tree and pulled his Sharps from the scabbard. He eased down slowly. His boot raised a hint of dust. Then he carefully placed his other foot to the earth. He tied the horse to a branch and carefully eased his eyes around the tree.

Harley had been watching John and he nodded to himself. He realized that John suspected a bushwhacker. He spurred his horse and he quickly made his way around the jutting rocks and stones of the hillside.

His sight moved from John to the rocky hill. He spotted a sandy trail and began riding harder. He rounded the hill and dismounted sending a cloud of dust. He ground reined his horse and moved up the slope boulder by boulder.

John, who could see Harley riding along the hillside, grunted to himself in thought. He waited till he thought Harley had gone behind the hill and he sighted his rifle and fired a roaring shot between the twin-boulders at the precipice.

Arkansas Bob was completely shocked by the shot and it ricocheted wildly among the rocks sending shards of splintered rocks splaying his cheeks and shoulders. The damn metallic 'whang' of the shot seemed to go on forever in his brain.

He cussed his luck and in swift anger fired back. The report of his rifle reverberated among the surrounding hills. The ball hit the tree and shattered the bark straight on.

John reloaded and bade his time. He peeked around the tree and seeing the rifle smoke wafting above the boulders knew his instincts had saved his life.

He slid the muzzle again around the tree and cut loose again. The shot whizzed over the head of Arkansas Bob. The slug hit the top of a rock and made a whining noise that furrowed the air.

When Arkansas Bob heard the eerie sound of the shot ricocheting, he sat with his back to the wall and inhaled deeply. He knew he was in trouble. He sat there trying to summon his courage. He was in the process of standing and turning his attention to his tormentor when he caught sight of the crown of Harley's hat bobbing far below among the rocks.

His eyes widened and he aimed the rifle at the hat. He fired a roaring shot that barely missed. Harley had just moved or the slug would have eaten into his skull.

Harley hugged the ground and inched himself to a large boulder and pulled his Colt out. His back to the rock and his weapon held across his chest, he inched out and fired two-quick bursts up the hillside.

The shots were off target but it caught the attention of Arkansas Bob. He now had one man behind the tree who was a danger and he had one moving up the rocks.

Arkansas Bob was drenched in sweat. His face had slithering droplets of salt coursing down his coarse features. His teeth were clinched and his eyes were wide and burning.

John, hearing the second shot of Arkansas Bob, and knowing the shot was intended for Harley, quickly booted his rifle and untied his horse from the limb. Upon hearing the sound of Harley's Colt, he mounted quickly and urged his big black down the caramel-colored road.

Arkansas Bob was reloading when he glanced through the twin rocks and saw John galloping down the road. He hastily shouldered his weapon and fired a quick shot.

John felt the slug go by his face and he gigged the big horse, and he accelerated into another speed his bay did not have.

Harley, hearing the shot, knew the man had to reload the single-shot Sharps. He began to move faster up the hill to a closer boulder. He moved up rock by rock, his Colt held out in front of him ready to fire.

Arkansas Bob turned and tried to sight Harley. He moved his pistol jerkily right and left and, until at last saw Harley's hat brim. He recklessly sent two-wild shot to warn him.

John circled the hill, and as he did so saw two-things: the couch passing by with its troopers, and he saw Arkansas Bob's horse.

The lieutenant was about to pull up and help him when he caught John's warning wave to move on. The lieutenant turned to the driver and exhorted him. The driver slapped the reins and the mules broke into run.

John moved to Arkansas Bob's horse and undid his saddle cinch. He then moved to a large boulder and waited.

Arkansas Bob was panicking. He heard the coach go by and the sound of many horses. He knew unless he escaped now it would be too late for him. He grabbed his Sharps and snaked his way down the hill and out of Harley's sight.

When he reached the bottom of the hill, he was relieved to find horse was still there. He ran and stuck his foot in the stirrup and he fell saddle and all. As he was lying on his back and struggling to regain his feet, he heard the portentous sound of a hammer clicking.

His deep socket eyes moved to the large man moving around

the boulder leading a black horse. The big Texan held a Navy Colt and the bore of it looked as big as a rain barrel to his perspective.

"Howdy, Arkansas Bob or do you prefer Robert Taylor?"

Arkansas Bob, as he lie there, let his eyes move to his weapons, which were tantalizingly close.

John moved closer and kicked them away. His eyes bored in on Arkansas Bob.

Arkansas Bob exhaled dispiritedly. His eyes moved up to the Texan. Suddenly the words of John echoed in his brain. "How do you know my name?"

"I know that Jeremiah Taylor is your father and I know that Billy Taylor was your brother."

"Half-brother," Arkansas Bob quickly retorted.

"I know you got a wife named 'Martha' that is too good for you."

Harley was moving down the rocks and he heard John talking to Arkansas Bob. He was moving quickly until he heard the personal tone of their conversation and he slowed.

"How do you know all of this?"

"Because I'm in love with her."

Arkansas Bob's mouth opened but he had trouble framing his words. "You bastard." He finally expelled.

John continued, "You're a liar, a thief, and a coward."

Arkansas Bob's eyes moved under his hooded lids. He was eyeing the Colt that was off to his right.

John continued, "I'd like to know how you live with yourself trapped in your own skin?"

Arkansas Bob rose, using the ruse to dust himself off, dived for his .44.

Harley stepped out from a nearby boulder and shot him in the head.

John looked at the dead body and back at Harley.

Harley moved forward and holstered his weapon. He looked

at the dead Arkansas Bob and back at John. "I kind of figured you didn't want this man on your conscience."

"You figured right, Harley."

Harley slapped him on the shoulder. Harley's actions caused John to look at him oddly. He said to Harley, "You heard?"

Harley nodded, "I heard." He paused and put his hand on John's shoulder. "But I sure in hell ain't telling."

John walked over and went through Arkansas Bob's pockets and found one-dollar and his pocket watch. As he nodded to Harley to collect the outlaw's horse, they heard a barrage of gunshots.

John ran to his horse and bounded into the saddle and raced to the road. He watched Seth ride by and Seth was brandishing his .44.

Harley forgot getting Taylor's horse and bolted into his saddle and followed John's trail dust to the road.

Junior Grease's riders had ridden over the low rise with their pistols already leveled. They fired a barrage of gunfire and the first trooper casualty was Adrian Jackson. He had been riding even with the doorway of the coach and he caught the brunt of their gunfire. He fell with several bullet holes in him to the earth.

The troopers, prepared for such an attack, fired back accurately and several of the outlaws were hit and pulled their horses up yanking their mounts' heads to one side and sending a sheet of dust and dirt flying.

The lieutenant yelled for the coach to pull over into a nearby cove among the hills. He was yelling and firing as the coach bumpily made the turn.

The guard leveled his scattergun and shot both barrels. Outlaws yelled as one horse was slaughtered and its rider went tumbling head over heels.

Seth went through the outlaws before they could catch on that he was not of their number. He shot one in the face and then turned in his saddle and emptied his .44 as he zigzagged into the hastily made fortress of the soldiers.

He was wildly cheered and he made a running dismount and ran to a nearby rock to join two-troopers who were returning fire into the milling outlaws.

John saw the remaining outlaws look his and Harley's way. He and Harley pulled up short and sought the shelter of large rocks by the roadside.

Junior Grease could see that his men were in a fix so he ordered them dismounted and the siege began. His men ran to cover and laid down a heavy volley toward the troopers.

The angle the outlaws were in was difficult because of the position that John and Harley had. The steady fire from the big Texan and his comrade were whizzing by and unnervingly close. As the fight continued, the outlaws' position looked like a parenthesis.

Indian Melvin who was watching through a collapsible telescope cursed Arkansas Bob. He turned to his nondescript aide and hissed, "How could that idiot have missed?" He slammed his telescope together and put it in a case hanging from his saddle. He shook his head and said, "That big guy's messing us up for now." He turned his horse's head violently and galloped away followed by his aide toward Salty Phillips' position.

Salty heard the gunfire from the red rocks he and his men had hidden in. He knew he should take the initiative, and just ride down the road and give support to Junior but he waited on Indian Melvin's orders.

He did not have to wait for long. Indian Melvin galloped into the road and gave a violent swipe with his arm and pointed down the road.

The outlaws rode out with pistols drawn and the thunder of the hoof beats sounded like a dozen drums in the hollow of the rocks.

They hit the road and made a violent left-turn and Indian Melvin led the way on his blazed-face sorrel.

John could see Indian Melvin and Salty Phillips' group coming down the road and their bullets were zipping and zinging all around his protection. Their bullets chipped the boulders and made copious plumes in the sand.

Junior Grease, who had been hugging the sand, gave a heartfelt sigh. He nodded at his remaining men and they laid an enthusiastic sheet of gunfire upon the troopers.

Lieutenant Gardner was unaware of the advent of Indian Melvin and Salty's reinforcements. He was not blinded long as the outlaws now had laid a semicircle battle line.

The lieutenant made adjustments and troopers took their lives into their own hands as they shifted from the threat to their right. They ran firing as they moved to their left trying to form their own semicircle.

Seth laid both barrels over his rock and emptied them with shots that were dangerously close. Junior who was trying to shift his men to link up with Salty's group was prevented by this burst of deadly gunfire.

Butterball Beasley, one of Junior's men, asked Junior as lead was flying precariously near. "Who is that bird that doing all that shootin'?" He was referring to Seth.

Junior shook his head and hugged the sand belly down. "I got no idea, but this is going to take longer than we imagined."

John kept firing too. He winged two-men from Salty's group as they shifted to keep the pressure on the lieutenant's right flank.

Indian Melvin, situated behind a rock that was being pelted by John and Harley, peered up at the high steep rock face that was behind the lieutenant and his men.

Indian Melvin called to Salty who was across the road and both firing and hugging his boulder too. Salty looked at his boss and caught the upward tilt of his boss's eyes and he turned and looked at the sheer cliff behind the lieutenant's position.

He nodded knowingly and he sent five-men in a long and roundabout way to scale the hill from the other side and pour gunfire down at the troopers.

Salty nodded back at his boss and Indian Melvin nodded satisfactorily back. He knew it was only a matter of time. He looked up at the hot sun and back at John and Harley. He wanted to get the lieutenant and the coach, but he wanted John most of all.

John could see Salty's five-men peel off and steal their way around the hill. His heart sank. He knew if something drastic did not happen, it was over. He had almost resigned himself to kill as many of Indian Melvin's men as possible and accept the inevitable.

He turned his head and watched as Russell rode up and dismounted down the road and began his arduous zigzagging from rock to rock to give support to him and Harley.

John looked at Harley across the road. Harley was shooting for all his worth and he looked sweaty and exhausted. He felt gratified that he had taken a chance on him. He had proved his worth.

John's eyes moved back down the road and he saw one of Salty's men try and move to his right to link up with Junior's men. John drew a bead with both his Navy Colts and fired. The man got both slugs and he tossed his gun into the air and fell in a tight ball.

Indian Melvin saw his man fall. He kept looking at the cliffs and at the Big Texan who kept a steady pace of fire. He muttered curses on John. He looked at Salty who looked weary. He looked at two of his men who were winged. He looked at the dead body to his right. His eyes lifted to the sun; he then swung his eyes back to the cliffs and waited.

The sun crept higher and the orange rays were torturing the combatants. Heat began rising from the ground. Men were reaching for canteens and running weary hands over greasy-whiskered stubbly features--both troopers and outlaws.

The shots now were calculated and they grew fewer. Indian Melvin stood stooped over by his boulder and looked up at the cliffs. He knew the sand incline that Junior's men were lying on had to be tortuous. He gritted his teeth and through slits he watched the edge of the sheer wall behind the troopers. He thought that anytime now, his men would fire down and catch the vulnerable soldiers and that would conclude a tough day.

The lieutenant also kept looking behind him and up. He had his heart in his throat. His men who caught his quick glances began to realize what he was thinking even without it being verbalized.

Melvin's eyes caught the sight of five-figures on the edge of the cliff. His anxious look moved into one of smug satisfaction. Salty looked up and saw them and he nodded back agreeably to his boss.

The five-figures fired simultaneously military style with Spencer rifles. But they were not aiming at the lieutenant's men, they were leveling an enfilading fire at Junior Grease's men.

At first, Indian Melvin thought it was just an egregious error and he held up his hand as to stop this onslaught, but the sudden knowledge that he was in a trap slid quickly into his mind.

Both his eyes and mouth widened. He looked at Salty and Salty looked back with this same realization. They both holstered and yelled to the men to get to their horses.

Seth heard the Spencers barking from the edge of the cliff and he knew they were not aimed at him. He stared up at the edge of the cliff and then back at the outlaws who were flopping and scrambling in the hot sand trying to crawfish back to their mounts hidden in a draw.

He took Ray Harp's .44 from him and aimed it with his own and leveled a continuous blast at the departing outlaws. One shot creased Butterball's Beasley's ass and he yelped and rose up. He then caught two-slugs in his chest.

Junior Grease's eyes bulged when he saw Butterball topple over. He gave a quick glance at Seth with his twin .44's firing orange flames and at the cliff and then slithered backwards through the hot sand and out of sight.

As he and his remaining four-men reached the sandy draw

where the horses were, they looked up and saw eight deputies riding down the hill all in a horizontal line.

He looked desperately at his men and they looked back frantically. He knew it was over and he dropped his Colt and threw up his hands in surrender.

The deputies rode around them and quickly dismounted. The ordered him and his men to hit the sand belly-down. He was quickly handcuffed and shackled.

He was snatched up roughly and ordered to hobble up the hot sandy inclined he had just slid down.

Several deputies led them into the encampment, but the rest galloped after Indian Melvin, Salty, and the other group of bandits.

Sheriff Buchanan was standing near the road and halted the detail of prisoners. He ordered them to halt on the opposite side of the road and the captured outlaws became the curiosity of the troopers.

In thirty minutes, a large-caged wagon pulled up and the last vestige of Junior's group and a sizeable amount of Salty's group were herded up the steps and took their benches aligned on each side of the wagon.

The sheriff ordered the driver and guard to pull the prison wagon over to the shade. John, Harley, and Russell led their horses up as the caged-wagon rolled by.

Deputies, troopers and John's group intermingled and traded stories of what had transpired. They stood in disbelief considering they had lost hope in the situation and could scarcely believe their luck.

The lieutenant was shaking his head in astonishment as he held out his hand to shake with Sheriff Buchanan. "That was a close shave, Sheriff. I honestly thought we were goners."

The sheriff gave them all a quick smile but he pulled the lieutenant and John aside. "We caught those yahoos as they made their bend around the hill. I figured it was time to throw the lasso."

His face sobered some as he squinted at the road that Indian Melvin had escaped on. John caught his look and he turned and looked at the hot sandy road. "It looks like we got some more work to do."

Sheriff Buchanan made a wry face. "The deputies are chasing him but they ain't going to catch him."

John gave him an inquiring look. "What makes you say that?"

"He's like a rabbit. He'll give them the slip and return to his hole."

John asked, "And the hole being?"

The sheriff inhaled and said, "John, go get your bay and get another hat and shirt."

John looked down at the sheriff to see if he were serious. When he saw he was, he started walking away leading his horse to the back of the coach.

The sheriff turned to the lieutenant. "I ain't telling you what to do, Lieutenant, but if I was you, I'd make camp here."

The lieutenant looked searchingly into the eyes of the sheriff and stated, "Since you're taking John with you, I guarantee you I am."

The sheriff looked evenly at the lieutenant and answered, "Yeah, and I wouldn't go where I am going without him."

That being said, the lieutenant broke away and returned to his men. Several of his charges had received flesh wounds and there had only been one-mortality.

John rode up on his bay with his old butternut shirt on. He had borrowed Harley's hat.

The sheriff smiled up at him. "Looks like you got here fresh from Forrest."

John nodded and checked his pistols. "Let's go to the rabbit hole, Sheriff."

They rode the rest of the daylight and up into the night. The moonlight was shining bright as they crested a hill and caught sight of the mercantile store and saloon. The bright, oily yellow light was thick coming out the windows and over the batwings. It looked like a tableau painted by a romantic artist. But the sinister reality of it was far from being ideal.

The sheriff pointed toward the building. "That's Canebrake." He paused as he sighed wearily. "That's where the rabbit stops."

John looked at the store and back at the sheriff. He leaned forward crossing his large forearms across his saddle horn. "What's the plan?"

The sheriff nodded to the lights. "You go on down and take you a seat in a corner. Take a snooze if you like. But just be on guard." The sheriff looked up at the moon and back at the store. "He'll probably come around in about two-hours or so, I would imagine."

The sheriff sighed and held his hands out palms up and quietly brought them together in a quiet slap. "I'm going to be watching."

John nodded and walked his horse calmly down the gradual incline. He heard several noises of nature as he walked his horse: an owl hooting in the distance, the sound of crickets.

There was no rinky-dink piano music and no women laughing shallowly over the batwings--only a silence.

He walked his horse up to the hitch rack and dismounted softly and tied his bay and walked up the creaking steps. He pushed the creaking batwing back and saw a man sitting at table near the door. He looked at John and gave a soft smile. The man put a finger in a whiskey glass and dabbed at his neck and collar and then placed his head sideways on the table and covered his head and face with a slouch hat.

John looked at the owner behind the bar. He had a gray handlebar mustache and eyebrows. He seemed tense as he stacked beer mugs on the counter.

John swung his vision down to the end of the bar and was

surprised to see Big Willard there. Big Willard gave him a blank look and he gave one back to the brawler. John could see that Big Willard was all business. He was acting as though he did not know him.

John caught the cue and he walked up to the bar and tossed a nickel on the bar.

"It'll take two of 'em out here." The bartender softly said.

John tossed another nickel on the bar and received his schooner of beer. He walked across the floor dodging the tables and sat in the far corner on the same side of the room where the batwings were.

He drank quietly and observed the man faking sleep. His eyes moved over the store-saloon. He noticed on the wall behind Big Willard that the shelves were stocked in blankets, coal oil, lanterns and matches. Coming toward him were canned goods and fruit jars and bowls and dishes and horse supplies and tack.

He looked out the window but saw little in the blackness but the oily splay of light the lanterns bracketed on the wall provided.

He pulled up another chair and put his legs on it and pulled his hat brim down and tried to doze.

It was near ten o'clock when he heard something other than crickets and the distant owl. He heard the unmistakable sound of horse hooves tiredly thudding the ground. He pulled his legs back from the chair and straightened some with his hat brim still shielding his face.

He listened as the horses stopped--followed by a long period of silence. The sound of the creaking steps ensued with the harsh jangle of spurs.

The batwings slowly opened and in came Big Melvin, Salty and a tall man named 'Lester.'

Big Melvin as he entered looked down at the sleeping cowhand and reached down and lifted the hat off the cowhand. Catching the smell of whiskey he gave a knowing smile and plopped the hat back carelessly on the sleeping man's head.

He glanced John's way but did not let his gaze linger long there. John had the hat pulled down as far as he could get it without totally obscuring his vision.

When Indian Melvin walked up to the bar with his two-henchman, Bob, the owner, hurriedly placed three-beers in front of them. Indian Melvin drained half of it the first drink and slammed the mug hard on the bar. He picked up his mug again and was turning his back to the bar when he caught sight of Big Willard with his cocked derby hat on.

He watched as Big Willard was eating a boiled egg and tossing salt and pepper on it. He observed Big Willard chug-a-lugged his beer noisily. Indian Melvin frowned. He instantly did not like the looks of the barrel-chested man with the off-centered derby hat.

Indian Melvin turned around belly up to the bar and drained his mug. He inclined his head toward Big Willard and asked the bartender Bob who the stranger was.

Bob answered that he was a drummer out of Saint Louis. Indian Melvin ordered another beer and sent several coins rattling along the bar. He would drink and then would send a baleful stare down the bar toward Big Willard. He did this over and over.

Big Willard knew he was being watched and he enjoyed it. He noisily popped in another egg into his mouth and licked his lips and made 'smacking' noises.

Indian Melvin placed his beer mug down gently with both hands on the bar. He turned and looked down the length of it and called out. "Hey mister, can't you keep the noise down. You sound like a pig down there."

Big Willard looked up and had this 'mock' surprise look on his face. "Am I disturbing you?"

Indian Melvin caught the sarcasm in Big Willard's voice. He worked his jaws in anger and then with the back of his hand slid his schooner to one side. He walked toward Big Willard with furrowed brows and anger in his eyes.

Big Willard was reaching for another egg when he heard Indian Melvin say, "If you're going to eat another egg, go outside and eat it."

Big Willard pushed up his derby hat with his left-hand and sighed. "It's dark out there and I might get a gnat in it."

"I don't give a damn what you get in it. I've had a trying day and I'd like to drink in peace. I don't need a drummer eating like a damn hog and messing up the peace and quiet."

Big Willard took off his derby hat and placed it on the bar. Indian Melvin eyed him as he did that. It looked provocative to him. Indian Melvin let a sarcastic smile run the width of his face. "Oh, you take exception to those words, drummer?"

Big Willard pushed his beer to one-side close to his hat. "Yeah, I do. I like to eat alone myself and you're getting on my nerves."

Indian Melvin was incredulous. No one in years had talked to him in that tone. He turned his body and grinned to Salty and Lester. He forked a thumb over his shoulder to Big Willard. "Boys, have you ever seen a drummer get his ass kicked?"

Salty took a heavy drink and shook his head. "No, boss, but I always wanted to."

Indian Melvin turned back around and caught the hard-eyes of Big Willard. Indian Melvin said over his shoulder as he moved menacingly along the bar, "Well, Salty, your wish is going to come true."

"Drummer, you asked for it and now you're going to get it."

Big Willard took off his coat and held up one finger. "Do you mind if I have one more egg before I beat the holy hell out of you?"

Indian Melvin cocked his head to one side and said, "You're not a drummer are you?"

Big Willard folded his coat and ate another egg and hastily drank another swig of beer. "Nope."

Indian Melvin's curiosity got the better of him. "Who are you?"

Big Willard tired of playing a role said evenly. "I'm the cousin of a man you brutally murdered."

Indian Melvin grinned. "And you're here for revenge?"

Big Willard returned a mirthless grin. "You got it, you bastard."

Indian Melvin shook his head in chagrin. "You may not know this whoever you are, but you're going to get the same treatment as your cousin."

Big Willard moved to his left. His eyes glued to the sneering face of Indian Melvin. "I don't want to waste any more breath with you."

Indian Melvin looked down to the sides of Big Willard. "I see you're not armed; drummer, pilgrim or whoever the hell you are."

"No, I'm not armed."

Before Indian Melvin could reply he heard the sound of Navy Colts clicking and he sent his eyes to the corner where John sat. His eyes went to the face and down to the two-menacing bores that were leveled at him.

John said firmly, "You and your boys drop your gun belts." He paused and he said louder, "Now."

Indian Melvin snickered out of the corner of his mouth. "No problem." He unbuckled his holster and his men also did the same when the Colts moved to them.

Indian Melvin placed his hardware on the bar and his eyes narrowed as he began to recollect John's face. "When I get through beating this man," he paused as he pointed at Big Willard, "To a pulp, I'm coming for you and do the same for you."

John stood and walked to the bar with his Colts still out. He collected the holsters and weapons and pushed them off the bar so they fell heavily on the other side where Bob the bartender stood. He turned and holstered his own weapons. He walked slowly backwards to his chair and then said, "Let's get it on." He sat down and crossed his arms.

Indian Melvin looked at John with veiled eyes and then slowly turned his attention to Big Willard. Indian Melvin rolled his shoulders to loosen up and then brought up his ham-sized fists. He began to move forward.

Big Willard placed on his derby hat and gave an enigmatic smile to the bandit king. He did not have the usual bored look on his face that he had reserved for the ring fights at the saloon. He moved slowly toward his opponent. His fists were up and his eyes were glinting beneath his eyebrows. He had the look of a man on a mission. He lashed out with a hard left jab that caught Indian Melvin in the chest with a hard thud.

Indian Melvin countered a right over the top of the left jab with a looping right-hand that crashed against the side of Big Willard's face. The force of the blow smacked 'fleshy' in the silence of the saloon.

John noticed that Indian Melvin was beguilingly fast for a big man and that he had fighting skills. He had no knowledge of Big Willard's ability other than what he had been told. He did notice that, if the blow hurt Big Willard, he certainly did not indicate it.

In truth, the blow made Big Willard smile embarrassingly. He had not anticipated Indian Melvin's fighting skills. He would catalog that move in his mind and not allow that again.

Big Willard moved in again, this time bobbing and wind milling his fists. He faked another left jab and sent a right haymaker that caught Indian Melvin on the temple and sent his hat spinning off his head and over a table.

Indian Melvin staggered and his eyes widened in surprise. He smiled unexpectedly and nodded, "You are pretty tough for a drummer. He said sarcastically as he put up his fists. "What do you sell, women's underwear?"

Big Willard nodded as he moved forward. "Yeah, and I got a pair that would fit you well."

"Damn, a tough drummer with a sense of humor."

Big Willard warded off several hard jabs and kept the pressure on Indian Melvin. He lashed out his own jabs and Indian Melvin avoided them by either moving or blocking them.

Salty and Lester watched sipping their beer. Bob the bartender was wiping out a mug in record speed. John's attention was rapt. The sleepy cowhand was sitting up straight and now had his hat on.

The two combatants moved closer and Indian Melvin threw an overhand punch that hit Big Willard squarely in the forehead and sent him flying backwards into the wall near John. A horse collar fell from its peg and several cans fell thudding to the floor. The force sent dust puffing out the wood seams of the plank wall.

John's eyes broaden at the force of the blow and the fact that Big Willard was still standing.

Big Willard was still standing and smiling. Indian Melvin stood perplexed. He shook his head in admiration. He simply stated, "I got some more of them, drummer."

Big Willard said, "Use them. You're going to need them."

Big Willard came forward again. He avoided a similar straight-jab and countered with a right hook that hit Indian Melvin in the left-cheek and sent him wheeling toward the once-sleeping cowboy.

The punch enraged the composed Indian Melvin. He straightened and came in throwing a lot of hard jolting punches that rained on Big Willard's arms and shoulders.

Big Willard survived the rain of blows and countered with several precise shots to the mid-section of his large foe. Big Willard's heavy blows sounded like someone tossing a bulky feed sack to the ground from a tall wagon.

Indian Melvin backed up and appraised the situation. He was no longer jocular or happy. He began peppering Big Willard long-distance to keep him away from his body.

Big Willard inexorably kept up the pace taking two-blows to land one. Once he got inside Indian Melvin's defense, he threw an uppercut that caught the big bandit under his chin and lifted him up to his toes.

Big Willard then threw a punch that sounded like a ponderous limb that had fallen from a tall tree when it landed. His fist struck along the side of Indian Melvin's nose, splitting it and loosening some of his teeth.

Indian Melvin astonishingly was still upright. He dabbed at the blood coming from his nose. He looked at it and then growled in rage as he charge like a wounded rhinoceros.

Big Willard avoided his desperate blows and measured his next shot. He sent a straight right hand that connected between Indian Melvin's eyes and sent him wind milling backwards and he collapsed on the floor supinely.

Salty stood dumbfounded and he and Lester made moves to jump the bar and retrieve their weapons. But they heard the ominous words of John. "Stop or die."

They stopped and looked at the unconscious Indian Melvin and then back at John with wary eyes.

The sleeping cowboy rose from his table and pinned on his badge. He pulled a smoke-blue .44 from his boot. He asked John to help cover them and he went around the bar and pulled out a burlap bag. He removed some handcuffs. He ordered the bandits to drop to their knees and he cuffed them.

Big Willard went to the end of the bar and put on his coat and cuffed out the sweat from the band of his derby hat. He resumed drinking his beer and reached for a boiled egg.

John watched the incredible aplomb of the fighting machine. He walked toward him and said, "Big Willard, if I was to ever get drunk enough to want to fight you, please talk me out of it."

Big Willard smiled and said, "John, we two are always going to be on the same side. That's one fight no one will ever see or ever be."

Sheriff Buchanan entered the batwings and pulled up a grating chair next to the sleeping Indian Melvin. He looked over at Big Willard. "I see you introduced yourself to Indian Melvin."

Big Willard nodded and added more salt to his egg.

The two-outlaws looked at Big Willard out of the corner of their eyes. Salty said, "I've heard of you but I thought you was just a legend or something."

The sheriff answered them brightly, "He is a legend, Salty." He then pointed at Indian Melvin. "And he's not."

The sheriff was careful not to talk to Bob the bartender. He did not want any secondary issues to come back to haunt the owner.

They sat silently for five-minutes. Indian Melvin stirred and sat up drowsily. He shook his head and through glassy eyes looked around the room. His eyes focused when he saw Salty and Lester sitting against the bar. His eyes moved up to the unsmiling sheriff. He panned the room and saw Big Willard nonchalantly eating boiled eggs and sipping beer. His view moved to the sleeping cowboy and then to the strapping Texan standing close by.

He shook his large head and said, "What a damn day."

The sheriff answered, "And it ain't over yet."

Indian Melvin sighed and nodded as he wiped blood from his nose. He inclined his head toward Big Willard. "That was one tough son-of-a-bitch."

The sleeping deputy lifted Indian Melvin's torso forward and fastened on the cuffs with a harsh ratcheting sound.

The sheriff ordered the deputy to stand him up. John catching the cue leveled his gun on the two-sitting thieves and ordered them up.

They all walked out the batwings and stood on the porch. The sheriff looked at Big Willard who had just exited the store and stood looking out into the night.

"Well, Big Willard, are you headed back to Fort Smith now?"

He shook his head and straightened his coat. "Nope, I'm going with you and John. I'm getting real fond of 'deputying'. 'Sides. I kind of like this adventure."

They helped the three outlaws onto their horses and began the long trek back to the encampment.

They topped the rise where Junior had positioned his men the day before. It was not quite ten o'clock. When they crested the hill the first thing they saw was the prison wagon filled with outlaws.

Indian Melvin through weary eyes caught sight of it and blinked thoughtfully as the horses slogged down the hillock in the sand.

Someone shouted from the camp and deputies and soldiers ran to line the road and greet them. There was a murmur of gladness when they saw the infamous bandit himself astride his tired horse.

The sheriff rode his group up to the deputies and dismounted wearily. John, Big Willard, and the other deputy followed suit. Russell and Seth took their horses and walked them into the makeshift compound.

The sheriff's tacit look was all that was needed.

The deputies and troopers pulled the three-outlaws roughly from their horses and quickly shackled them.

Indian Melvin recognized Harley as he came forward and went through the pockets of Salty and Lester. When he reached Indian Melvin, he received a menacing look. Harley had collected over 200 dollars among the three of them.

Indian Melvin turned his malevolent eyes on the sheriff. "You going to let him rob me? That's my money and I want it back."

The sheriff snorted, "I imagine that is what a lot of people have said to you before."

Indian Melvin exhaled in anger as his eyes went to the prison wagon. He turned once again to the sheriff. "You got me now but that don't mean you are keeping me."

The sheriff answered, "I agree with the first part and will have to wait and see on the second part."

Indian Melvin grinned wickedly. "I ain't been hanged yet, sheriff."

The sheriff walked closer and with tired eyes looked up at the glaring eyes of the bandit. "That can be arranged, I was just told to bring you in dead or alive." He paused and added, "I ain't got a qualm that's preventing me from hanging your sorry ass right here."

Indian Melvin broke his stare and turned his eyes to the prison coach. He watched soberly as Salty and Lester made their way up the steps to the cage and took their seats with their comrades.

Indian Melvin shrugged his huge shoulders and began shuffling toward the steps and up into the cage. His men watched him with both disappointment and sullen anger.

The door slammed with metal finality and the sheriff walked up to the deputies who were mounting up. He looked up into the cage as four-deputies rode up on each side. His eyes went to the driver and the guard who were heavily protected from the inmates by good spacing from the bars.

Satisfied he turned to the head-deputy. "If they have to urinate let them do it through the bars, if they have to defecate let them do it in the slop jar." He pointed to a porcelain jar positioned on the back of the wagon. "If one of them throws his waste at you, shoot him on the spot." He paused as he looked at the surly outlaw leader. "If he does it, just shoot him in the knee cap."

When John walked by leading the horse that once belonged to Jack Filson and having already changed back into his other shirt and wearing his usual slouch hat, Indian Melvin hailed him.

John stopped and looked at the head outlaw. Indian Melvin pointed his finger at him. "I promise you, Texan, you and I will meet again."

John gave him a strange look. He wanted to meet Indian Melvin again, but he doubted that would ever happen.

The sheriff interceded, "Well, the first introduction shore did not turn out so well for you, now did it, Melvin?"

The sheriff nodded at the driver and he slapped the reins and the mules began to trot away. The large metal water container in the back sloshed water and with jarring metallic sounds the wagon clattered down the hot, caramel-colored road.

They all watched the wagon become a smaller and darker figure moving over the horizon.

The sheriff sighed and turned to John and the lieutenant. "Lieutenant, we could stand some beans and bacon and a good cup of coffee."

The lieutenant excused himself and went to two of his soldiers. He gave them orders and they hastily went to the ashes of the breakfast campfire and rekindled it.

The sheriff called the lieutenant and John aside and said, "While it's cooking and while we can still stand, let's talk."

The lieutenant interrupted. "Sheriff, , you don't have to ask for my indulgence. You and John and a few other deputies need rest and if you're going to ask me to wait here until you have recuperated, don't bother because I want you to consider it already done." He grinned. "We are not going anywhere without you and John."

The sheriff nodded and said, "That saved me from a long tiring speech."

They both looked at John who looked back at both of them. John pursed his lips and shuffled his boots as he measured his words. "Those damned Purvis brothers will be laying for me. I know that both of you've been through a lot and I just want you to know that I don't hold either of you to any promises made to me."

The sheriff placed an avuncular arm on John's shoulder. "You ain't the only one who keeps promises." He looked John in the eyes and continued, "What I said back in the office is just as true as it is out here." He turned his body and made a quick motion with his fingers in the direction of the prison wagon. "We got Indian Melvin. Now let's get those damned Purvis brothers."

The lieutenant quickly interjected. "As far as I am concerned the Purvis brothers are my enemies too. General Beasley would give me hell if I did not see this through."

The sheriff gave a tired smile. "Now that is over let's get some grub and sleep."

The whole camp including tired horses and mules took a much-needed needed siesta that day.

# CHAPTER EIGHT

BACK IN TEXAS, SEVERAL DAYS later, Bill Purvis received two-pieces of bad news. His revered uncle, Colonel Purvis, was dead, killed by a Confederate sharpshooter. He had been pursuing the rear vanguard of the Southern General Edmund Kirby-Smith. He and his detail had been ambushed. No other details were given.

He sat in his study looking glumly at the telegram. He would drop it and ponder and pick it back up and read the words again. He was about to receive the second-piece of bad news.

His younger brother, Michael, had brought him the telegraph earlier and was waiting at the bunkhouse for Java Stevens, the new ramrod of the Purvis ranch. Java was a dark and morose individual who usually dressed in black and gray colors. A handsome man who liked the ladies but he was even better with his Colt revolver. He had thrown his lot with the Purvis brothers. He was loyal but at high cost.

Java had made the arduous journey across the Nations checking on the status of the Rawlins brothers and Dolittle and Sanchez. When he rode into the open yard with his two-companions, he caught sight of Michael standing in the shade of the cottonwoods opposite the bunkhouse.

Java dismissed one of his compatriots and dismounted wearily. He handed his horse to Jaybird Roberts, who had ridden with him, and walked to Michael dusting off the trail dust.

They talked about fifteen-minutes and Michael was taken aback by the news. He insisted that Java go with him to confer with Bill.

Bill was sitting still mulling over the telegram's message and the possible ramifications to him and his brother. He looked up and saw the unshaven and unkempt foreman take a seat next to his brother. Bill looked across the desk at them both and dropped the telegram again. "Well?" He asked.

Java ran a weary hand over his whisker stubble. He looked at Michael for moral support because he knew that Bill would go into a rage when he started talking.

"Boss, Harley is in with John Johnson. I have an idea he went there, knowing he was going to join up with him. Delford was killed while in Fort Smith and I don't have a clue about Julio Sanchez. Java reached into his pocket and handed over a folded Fort Smith newspaper.

Bill looked at the bold headlines, which extolled John Johnson from Texas. He read about the attempted bank robbery and how that John was headed to Baileysboro, Texas.

This second-piece of bad news raised Bill's eyebrows and his blood pressure. He leaned back and took in a lung of air. He asked in monotone denoting that he expected more negative news. "Anything else?"

Java nodded, "It seems that John Johnson is in cahoots with the sheriff there. Whether the sheriff is coming this way with him is unclear, but he ain't coming here by himself.

"I spent one-day and one-whole night there and everyone speaks favorably about him. I have no idea of where he is, but I heard from some people at Ace's Saloon that he's headed back here and he's got Russell, some new guy from Arkansas and Harley.

Bill quickly asked, "What happened to Slade?"

"Delford shot Slade in the head trying to take out John Johnson. Kiowa Bob, as rumor has it, then scalped and killed Delford. The town sheriff then tossed Delford's body into the Arkansas River."

Bill disregarded the death of Delford Doolittle with a casual shake of his finger. He shrugged and tossed the newspaper to one-side. He sighed, "Well, he's probably got more men than that." He sat silently for a while and shook his head disgustedly. He suddenly regretted his decision to allow Kiowa Bob to live. He asked in mild irritation, "What about Kiowa Bob?"

Java shook his head negatively. "He ain't in Fort Smith. He may be riding with John Johnson too."

Bill sat straighter and looked at Michael. Bill said almost accusatory, "Or here."

Michael took mild offense. "He may be here but he'd have to be hiding in a gopher hole."

Bill looked back at Java. "Anything else?"

Java shrugged and answered. "This is just based on hearsay but when I came across the Nations, people are saying that Indian Melvin was captured by a group of deputies and some military people."

Bill cocked his head sideways as to ascertain. "Why would that interest me?"

Java sighed and leaned forward and placed his elbows on his knees. "The same folks, whether true or not, are saying that a big Texan was involved. I am not sure if they were talking about John Johnson or not."

Bill leaned back in his chair. He nodded his head as if here putting pieces together and had solved the puzzle. He reached into his drawer and tossed Java one hundred-dollars in greenbacks. He said to him in a civil voice. "Go get some sleep and see me bright and early."

When he departed, Michael looked at his brother and asked, "What's on your mind?"

Bill leaned in to his brother and said, "With our uncle dead that leaves us without the Federal help with all these damned secessionist around us. It also necessitates that we send men to kill John Johnson, not three nor four but a whole lot of men who are killers."

Michael nodded his head. "I can pull Java and some of the other boys from the ranks and head that way."

Bill compressed his lips and thought. "I'm going to send Bushrod Elkins and his gang."

Michael was surprised. "It'll cost you plenty."

Bill retorted, "It'll cost us a lot more if we don't."

Michael sighed. "I can kill just as well as Bushrod Elkins. And cost us a whole lot less."

Bill nodded, "You are going Michael. If Bushrod fails, you take over, but let him try first."

"I'm not riding with Bushrod Elkins."

Bill sighed and said, "I'll hire him and let him take the lead. He won't go if you two are competing. 'I'll offer him five-thousand dollars for John Johnson's head."

Michael whistled in astonishment. "What will be my role in all this?"

Bill pulled out a map in his desk drawer. "There's a town called 'Ten Strike' just about forty-miles from the Texas line. I'll send Bushrod there with his men and you shadow him in the hills and keep tabs on him. If he fails, you take over the mission, you can have Java Stevens, 'All-Night' Roy and Freddie Taylor. Take whoever you want except Monk Danielson."

Michael inclined his head and asked, "Do you think John Johnson is that big Texan that Java mentioned?"

Bill turned his palms up. "I have no idea but I would rather be wrong and safe than be right and dead."

"How do you know that Bushrod will work for us?"

Bill smiled, "I've already hired him. He'll be here in the morning."

"You knew that John Johnson would not be killed in Fort Smith?"

"No, I had no way of knowing but I promised Bushrod a thousand-dollars to come here. If John Lee Johnson had been killed and I didn't need him, I would have paid him his thousand-dollars and he would've been on his way happy. But I hedged my bets and he'll be here."

Michael stood and asked, "How much longer are you going to allow Henry Johnson to live?"

Bill made a face and turned his palms up. "He's bait and we need him. When John Johnson is killed, we'll have Java kill him. It's that simple."

Michael leaned forward with his hands on Bill's desk. "Does Bushrod know who he is supposed to kill?"

Bill shook his head 'no.' It shouldn't matter. For five-thousand dollars, he'd kill his own grandmother."

The next morning at nine o'clock Bushrod Elkins and his eight men rode into the main yard of the Purvis ranch headquarters.

Bushrod was a singular looking individual. He was blond and had soft-blue eyes--eyes that belied his cold-blooded nature. He had a handsome face and he measured six-feet tall. He dressed in buckskin and wore dark-brown, stovepipe boots. He carried a Colt in a brown holster. The holster was bedecked with bright silver conchos.

His two-lieutenants were Garcia Avila, a thick Mexican, who wore an oversized sombrero. He carried his two-Army Colts in crisscrossed holsters. The other man was Burt Greenway. He was older gunman. He was no nonsense and cold as an adder. He wore the unassuming garb of cowhand.

Bill Purvis, who heard them ride up, came out and waved at the infamous Bushrod Elkins and beckoned for him to enter his house.

Bushrod dismounted and handed his reins to Burt Greenway. He looked to his left and caught sight of the Rocking P cowhands who were gathered in front of the bunkhouse observing him. He smiled to himself and walked briskly up the steps.

Bill Purvis took him into his office and bade him 'sit down.' Bill reached into his drawer and tossed a rawhide pouch that jingled in sound. "There's your one-thousand dollars."

Bushrod caught the leather pouch in his hand and tossed up and down as to weigh it and then placed it in his lap. He looked curiously at Bill and said, "I know you want me to kill someone and someone damn important, so, let's get down to it."

Bill nodded and leaned back. "I agree time is of the importance."

Bushrod canted his head to one side and let his blue eyes peruse the office. He noticed the antlers on the wall and the Regulator clock and the neat stacks of papers. He looked back at Bill Purvis who was arranging his thoughts as on how to begin the conversation.

Bill leaned forward with his hands clasped. "His name is John Johnson. His dad owned this very ranch house." Bill took one of his hands and moved it through the air. "I evicted his father by the order of the conquering Union army coming back from fighting Sibley. He was a secessionist and he had paid his taxes in Confederate money. I paid the taxes in Union money and drove him out and he was killed in the process."

Bushrod nodded, "So the cub is coming home for revenge and you want me to take care of the problem."

Bill shrugged and said, "That pretty much sums it up."

Bushrod's narrowed as he thought. "How much?"

"Five-thousand dollars upon completion."

Bushrod, who normally was unruffled, sat back and stared unbelievingly at Bill. He emitted a soft whistle in amazement.

"Where is this John Johnson?"

"I think over in the Nations and each day getting closer to the town called 'Ten Strike.'"

Bushrod nodded in recognition of the town and added, "That would be a straight shot to here most likely."

Bushrod pursed his lips and looked at the pouch of gold coins in his lap. "I will take the deal gladly, but I don't want your brother killing him and then claiming I don't deserve the five-thousand."

Bill leaned forward and said with level eyes. "Michael will go and will observe at a distance, but it's all your show." Bill leaned back and again spoke, "I would like to send a couple of my men to serve as messengers between you and Michael."

"You can send all the men you want, but only me and my gang will get the money."

Bill nodded at him and they spontaneously stood. Bill said to him as they walked down the hallway. "Before you leave, I'll send a couple of men to ride with you.

Bushrod exited the house and mounted up and placed the money pouch in his capacious saddlebag. His men sat with him patiently until Jaybird Roberts and Fuzzy Williams rode up. He curtly nodded at each of the Rocking P riders and then he turned his horse and the whole group galloped out of the yard.

Michael walked up to his brother. "My boys are ready. I've left you enough to handle the chores and watch the place in case he gets around us."

Bill nodded and answered, "Don't let him get around you." He added, "But, yes, I need some men here. I got cattle to move and I have some other plans here."

Michael grinned his annoying grin. "And you got the meanest man on the planet here, Monk Danielson."

It rained two-days in a row and the armored coach was moving slowly through the mud. Progress was limited and the coach became stuck several times in gumbo mud. Both soldiers and deputies cursed the mire and muck they had to travel through.

The third-day the sun broke through and they picked up the tempo and the fourth-day they were moving along at a reasonable speed. The fifth day they had made a good clip.

The sixth-day, Seth had been given the task of riding the hills along the flank of the coach. He was riding well ahead of the coach and it was nearing sundown. The cadence of the walking horse had almost lulled him into slumber. When he raised his head from a jolting nod. He caught the glint of silver refracted through the orange fingers of light from the dying sun. The flash of it had come from a nearby hill that was adjacent to the road.

He jerked to attention and his horse seemed to catch his mood. He looked again to see if his eyes had played tricks on him, and he caught the sparkle of silver again.

He stopped to get his bearings and looked down to see how he could stalk whomever it was on the hill. He saw a bare trail that led down through the stunted trees. He could see that the trees would block his view. He gently clucked his tongue and started down the incline.

He rode down the thin path until he reached an even lower level. He rode cautiously going from tall shrubs to boulders. He finally was able to make the turn and he came up behind the hill. He spotted a pinto behind a large rock and he stealthily walked to it and led it away to his horse which he had hidden a thicket.

He noticed boot marks in the dirt. The scruff of them led up through some jutting rocks. He pulled his .44 out and silently padded up the dirt between the boulders.

Garcia Avila was stretched out at the top of the hill. He was observing the trail through binoculars. He had been following the coach since noon. He had seen the big Texan briefly but he had to make sure. Jaybird Roberts had given him a good description earlier and he felt like he had seen such a man.

He reached down to his pocket and pulled out a cigar and was rolling to one side to find a match when he saw the shadow of Seth emerging from a large rock.

Garcia's eyes widened and he started to reach for his .44. He was halted by stern words. "You ain't the first man I've ever killed but you could be next."

Garcia's mind raced when the short but mean looking gent come around the rock with a leveled Colt. The Mexican decided to try a different tack. "Senor, I was hunting for antelope," he held up the binoculars and shrugged his shoulders. He smiled a grizzled grin and said again, "There must be some mistake."

"Yes, on your part." Seth remarked coldly. "Now just toss them pistolas over here and toss them gentle like."

Garcia smiled. "But senor."

He stopped grinning when he heard the hammer click. "You heard me." Seth said levelly.

Garcia decided to take his chances. He quickly made his move for his sidearm.

Seth fired and Garcia's holster and pistol were shattered.

Garcia looked down and saw the remnants of his weapon. His eyes narrowed and his grin dissipated into a livid snarl. Garcia raised himself up. He looked with contempt at the shorter Seth.

Garcia took his fingers and began to remove dirt from his pants. He cut up his eyes at Seth. He began to smile again.

Seth nodded knowingly. "Look, we both know you got a pig sticker in the back of your pants. You can drop it now or go for it, your call." He dipped his pistol toward Garcia's remaining pistol.

Garcia answered, "I am getting a real hate going for you, Chico." But he reached down and dropped his other .44.

"Name's Seth."

"Chico!" Garcia shouted and was reaching around quickly for his knife when Seth shot the bottom of his earlobe off. Garcia shouted in agony and grabbed his ear.

Seth cocked his revolver again. "I got some more shots left and another gun in my belt. Now reach behind and toss that knife in the dirt or my aim's going to the right a tad." He added, "And I ain't Chico. My name is Seth Johnson."

When he said 'Seth Johnson,' Garcia's demeanor changed. He reached behind tentatively and took the knife and tossed it in the dirt. Garcia's eyes were wary and he kept his hand on his bleeding ear.

Seth's gun barrel indicated that they take a walk. Seth knelt down quickly and retrieved the binoculars. They eased down the path and Seth pointed to a thicket.

When the lieutenant saw Seth headed his way with a Mexican, he halted the coach and waited.

Harley, who had been riding drag, saw the coach stop and he rode up quickly and saw the lieutenant staring down the road. Harley, seeing the lieutenant's intense gaze, also looked down the road.

When Seth and Garcia rode up to the lieutenant, Garcia recognized Harley and knew the game was up. He had envisioned getting off the hook but that seemed a slim chance now.

The lieutenant asked, "What have you bagged, Seth?"

"I caught this Mex lookin' down the road with binoculars."

Harley turned to the lieutenant. "His name is Garcia Avila. He's been riding with Bushrod Elkins for years."

The lieutenant looked puzzled.

Harley continued, "Bushrod is a hired killer. That means the Purvis brothers have employed him."

The lieutenant nodded his head in the revelation, and said, "We need to let John know about this, unfortunately, he's away with the sheriff."

The lieutenant's eyes swiftly turned to the Mexican. "Is this true, that you're working for the Purvis brothers?"

Garcia turned his head in scorn and spat sideways. "I was hunting antelope."

Harley smiled and said, "Give me a little time with this hombre, Lieutenant. I guarantee you I can make him talk."

The lieutenant took off his gloves and inspected his nails. "Since this is a civilian matter, Harley, I can hardly stop you."

Garcia's eyes bulged. "You cannot do this, Lieutenant, I'm your prisoner."

The lieutenant smiled at Garcia. "I gave you a chance to talk and you spit on the ground and lied." The lieutenant sighed and put his glove back on. "Let's try this again. Are you riding with this Bushrod--er?"

"Elkins," Harley quickly interjected.

The lieutenant nodded thanks to Harley and began again, "Are you riding with Bushrod Elkins for the Purvis brothers?"

Garcia shrugged and said nothing.

The lieutenant turned to Harley. "He's all yours."

Harley smiled at Seth. "Go get your cousin Russell, and meet me around those rocks." He pointed at a conical pile of rocks that stood above the tree line. "And tell him to bring some matches."

When Harley said the word 'matches' both the lieutenant and Garcia gave a start.

The lieutenant overlooked the remark and turned and commanded his men to make camp. Several of the troopers who had heard the comment grinned mischievously and chuckled as they eyed the nervous Mexican.

Twenty minutes later, Harley, Seth and Russell had Garcia tied up with a mule rope. Harley looked at Garcia and said, "Last chance, amigo."

Garcia gave a sneer and turned his head as to break away from the searching stare.

Harley nodded and walked to the circle of rocks he had arranged and struck a match and lit a fire with the dry wood he had placed.

Garcia looked nervously at the fire and at the three-men who sat calmly. Beads of perspiration drooled down his forehead and slithered through his whisker stubble. He licked his dry lips and breathed shallow breaths.

Harley went to his provision sack tied over his saddlebags and pulled out a branding iron. It was the Flying R. He walked back unconcernedly and placed the end of it in the fire. He fed the fire and turned the brand as though it were a piece of meat.

Garcia sat transfixed peering at the brand in Harley's hand. He swallowed. "What is it that you want to know?"

Harley kept tending the brand. "I want to know the truth. If you tell me one thing that sounds half-way like a lie, I'll personally brand your ass."

Garcia sighed and nodded, "Okay, but will you let me go when I finish?"

Harley craftily smiled, "You talk first and then we'll see."

John and the sheriff and several deputies rode in about nine o'clock. They had canvassed a whole lot of territory. They had seen riders but had not seen anything definitive.

John walked toward the campfire that revealed his men. He sat down wearily and looked around at his crew. They were fully clothed and they were looking at him. He knew something was up. It was late and that they should have been sleeping by now. He looked at each set of eyes and then asked, "All-right, what is it?"

Harley spoke, "Seth captured Garcia Avila today." Harley filled John in on the Bushrod Elkins' gang and their association with the Purvis brothers. He told him about Garcia's spying on him for Bushrod.

Harley took a breath and said, "They're waiting on you in Ten Strike. They figure the coach is going to pass through and you'll be there and Bushrod's going to call you out and shoot you."

John deliberated on his words. "Did he say how many men are there with Bushrod?"

Russell answered, "He's got eight-men of his own and two of the Purvis brothers. The two are the messengers. Michael Purvis is about a day's ride from Ten Strike. He's got more than a dozen riders."

John dwelt on their words. "How did you get Garcia to tell you all of that?"

Russell smirked and said, "We threatened him with a brandin' iron."

John looked again at each face. "He told you all of that just by threatening him?"

Russell sighed, "He told us all of it when Seth branded him on one of his ass cheeks."

John nodded and shook his head. "What did he say when you branded the other one?"

Russell chuckled. "He didn't do nothing except cry."

John looked around the camp and at the sentry, which was not too far away. "I gather you let him go."

Russell nodded 'yes.' "Where is a man goin' to go when he's been branded on the ass? We tied him to his horse and shot over the horse's rump and watched him bob up and down like a sinker line."

John smiled. "I want ya'll to bring that branding iron with you."

Russell looked at John amusingly. "You thinking about goin' somewhere tonight?"

John pulled a pocket watch out. He held it up to catch the glow of a nearby fire. He seemed satisfied with the time he had. "Boys, get your saddles out, and go for your horses. We got to be in Ten Strike when the saloon opens."

John went to see the sheriff and the lieutenant and informed them of his plan. They both offered assistance but he demurred. He informed both of them that he would like for them to head there as soon as possible. They both told him they would leave at first light.

As John and his crew mounted up, he told his plans to his crew. He seemed determined to challenge Bushrod face to face. They rode out quickly. No one spoke. They could tell by John's visage that his anger was mounting.

Bushrod Elkins woke up about ten-thirty the next morning in the dinky Ten Strike hotel. He rubbed his face and looked over at the naked brown rump of the Indian girl. He ran his hand over her contours and she stirred. She looked at him and then over her own shoulder to peer at her naked ass. She pulled a cover over it and gave him a sly look.

He tried to remember her name as he rose up on the bed and began putting on his buckskin clothing. He pulled his boots on and then went to the cheap dresser and poured water into a basin from a porcelain jar. He rubbed his face vigorously and made guttural noises.

His Indian consort rolled over on her back still clasping the cover. "Why are you up? Come back to bed and let's play some more."

"Sorry, Honey, but Bushrod's got some killing to do today."

She made a moue with her face. "Can't it wait?"

He bent down to look under the stained shade and made a cursory view of the sunlit buildings through the window. "Nope."

She watched him put on his gun belt. He reached for his hat and placed it cockily to one-side. As he reached for the doorknob, he momentarily paused as if where forgetting something. He turned to her with expressionless eyes and tossed a gold dollar on the end of the bed.

She watched him exit and then her eyes went to the gold dollar. She looked back up at the door and sadness filled her almond-shaped eyes. She was hoping that the night had meant something to him, but she could see clearly that it did not.

Bushrod made his way along the second-floor and saw a salesman with a bowler hat on. The salesman blanched when he saw the notorious gunfighter. The man edged close to the wall and Bushrod could see the fear registered in his face.

Bushrod smiled to himself. He liked to see fear in faces. It fed his enormous ego. He placed his hands on the balustrade when he reached it and ran his hands over the smooth finish and then turned and walked self-confidently down the steps.

The clerk in the lobby looked at him with apprehension as he passed by. Bushrod gave him a clipped head nod. He never liked to be too friendly to the help. He liked the emotional distance. He exited the lobby and stood under the ramada.

He stretched and looked over the town. There was not much to see but it was all his. He felt good. He felt powerful. He was going to kick some ass.

His men were up and moving down the boardwalk. Some were leaning on building fronts and enjoying the shade. He gave a favorable wave to some of his men headed toward the café across the street. He saw Burt Greenway walking toward him with a concerned look on his face. Bushrod paid little attention to his tight face. Burt found drama in a sundown.

Burt pulled him aside and looked up and down the street. "I ain't seen neither hide nor hair of Garcia last night or today."

Bushrod was ready to tell him to brighten up, but that news bothered him. He frowned and said, "That's strange all right. But he always turns up. Maybe he met a senorita last night."

Burt shook his head 'no.' "It ain't like him to disappear when we are on a job."

Bushrod looked down the street. He saw the open doors of the saloon and the batwings. "Well, when he wakes up wherever he is, tell him to meet me at the saloon." He gave a smile back toward the frowning Burt. "A man has to have his breakfast even if it is two-beers." He gave a nonchalant look over his shoulder at the vexed Burt Greenway. "I expect that cavalry unit to get in here about one or two o'clock today. I don't have time to worry about Garcia at this moment."

Burt watched him walk away and looked at his back. He sighed and walked to the hitch rack and leaned on it. His eyes went up and down the street. He did not like Garcia's absence. Something felt wrong.

Inside the saloon, the bartender was drying glasses frenetically. His eyes were on the batwings and back at the huge Texan who stood at the corner of the bar next to him.

John had awakened him early and had him open up the saloon.

The big Texan stood with a full schooner of beer at his elbow. He looked at the batwings and then at the cheap clock on the wall of the cheap saloon.

The fat bartender had oily sweat drooling down his jowls. The ticks of the clock were pronounced in the empty room. The sound of a fly droned by. The bartender swallowed and his gulp even was magnified.

One of Bushrod's men came in and ordered a beer and took a seat near to the bar. He was a seedy sort with a bad overbite and oversized hat. John paid him no mind. He figured he might have to kill him sooner or later, but he decided on later. He was waiting on bigger game.

The bartender was highly attuned to the noises: the ticking clock, the beer-slurping seedy outlaw, the distant barking of a dog, the wind creaking the batwings. He would have gladly given his day's receipts to be a hundred-miles from Ten-Strike.

Bushrod pushed the left-batwing open and entered. He had his head down thinking. When he raised his eyes, he was startled to see the big Texan standing there. It was a surrealistic moment for him. Whether it was John's imposing size or the twin Navy Colts on his hip, he was confounded. He could have planned for a decade and never have guessed this unusual development. He stood trying to grasp the situation.

John stepped aside from the bar. "I heard you were looking for me and I thought I would make it a hell of a lot easier."

Bushrod still did not say anything. He tried to make sense of this. He was not used to being the hunted. He pushed his hat up slowly and blankly stared. His mind could not process this reality.

John nodded at his .44. "You got two-choices, Bushrod, pull that iron and die or have me beat the hell out of you."

Bushrod shook his head as to clear away the irrational meaning of all this. He was stunned and stood groping for words that did not come. He began hovering his hands over his .44 more from habit than planned.

John stood patiently. John gave him a patronizing smile and that smile infuriated Bushrod.

Bushrod's hand snaked for his weapon, but the twin Navy Colts had already leapt into the hands of John Johnson. He fired two-shots. One creased the head of Bushrod and the other hit him in his gun shoulder. He fell and his gun scooted across the floor.

The seedy cowboy with the bad overbite rose from his table and was reaching for his gun when John quickly turned his left Colt on him and fired a roaring round that lifted the gunman off his feet. His hat went one way and he went another sliding along the floor as dead a two-day turd.

Burt Greenway heard the shots and was wondering whom Bushrod had shot. His spurs jangled as he ran down the boardwalk and bounded through the batwings. His eyebrows moved up when he saw Bushrod wounded on the floor and 'Brushfire' dead across the way.

When he lifted his eyes, he saw John Johnson staring at him. Burt growled in anger and went for his pistol. John cut loose with two-more shots and Burt went flying backwards propelled by the thudding impact of lead balls. This deadly momentum carried him out the batwings and over the boardwalk and into the street. A horse shied and nickered when the body fell into soft dust.

Harley entered from a backdoor and looked at the terrified bartender, whom had a towel clinched in his teeth. His eyes went to the groaning Bushrod Elkins and at the dead outlaw with the bad overbite.

Harley said, "I'm not sure but I think that last hombre you shot was Burt Greenway."

John took his beer and drank a gulp. He simply shrugged and calmly said, "He didn't introduce himself, Harley."

Harley knowingly nodded and said, "He was never a very friendly fellow."

Harley asked the bartender for a beer. The bartender looked back in abject fear. "At a time like this?"

John looked at the bartender and said, "Give the man a beer. He's been up nearly all night."

The bartender hurriedly drafted a beer and put the mug shakily on the bar.

Harley and John stood calmly drinking. Harley looked at Bushrod who was attempting to get to his feet. "What do you want me to do with him?"

"When you get through with your beer, brand the bastard and send him on his way."

The citizens passing by looked over the batwings and could see what had transpired. The word quickly spread up and down the short street. The man who had held the town captive was wounded and captured.

Bushrod's remaining men quickly mounted up and were galloping back to New Mexico Territory. They sensed something was 'all-wrong' with the situation. They did not want to hang around and contest John Johnson.

Russell and Seth soon appeared and had a beer while Bushrod moaned holding on to a table. Seth went over and picked up the gunfighter's silver-plated .44. While he was in the neighborhood, he searched the wounded gunman and found his pouch of gold coins.

Russell caught the pouch tossed by Seth and held it up for John to see. "Blood money."

After they had drunk their beers, Russell and Seth helped Bushrod out back. Harley went to retrieve Bushrod's horse tied behind the hotel in a shed. He also pulled his branding iron out of the mesquite fire he had blazing.

John was still at the bar having his second-beer when he heard the shrieking cries of Bushrod.

The bartender hesitantly asked, "What was that noise?"

John shrugged his large shoulders and said, "What does it

sound like?" He answered his own question as he looked at the bartender's frightened face. "It's Bushrod getting branded."

There was another frenzied cry. It was obvious to the bartender that Bushrod had been zapped again.

The bartender swallowed. His large Adam's apple bobbed up and down. "You are funning me, ain't you?"

John moved his head side-to-side in a negative way. He thoughtfully remarked, "Nope."

They waited awhile as John drank another gulp and he heard a gunshot. He turned to the bartender and said before he was asked, "That's the shot across the haunches of the horse. Bushrod is on his way to New Mexico Territory."

The bartender mopped his face. "I think I feel faint."

Jaybird Roberts had watched as they hauled Bushrod out of the back of the saloon. He stood with an open-mouth as they pulled down his leather britches and bent him over. He watched Harley brand him on one ass cheek. He heard the wounded Bushrod beg for mercy and scream like a woman.

But there was no mercy. Harley branded him on the other ass cheek. They trussed him over his saddle and Harley shot his pistol across the rump of the horse.

Bushrod rode bouncing and jouncing on the crazed horse. He was met with jeers as the horse raced through the alleyway and onto the street with his branded ass exposed to God and all creation. The citizens had no sympathy for him.

Jaybird crept deeper into the thin shadows of the alley. He pulled a handkerchief from his pocket and mopped his brow. His eyes squinted in thought. He swallowed and raced down the alley and found his horse.

He looked over his shoulder and then put the spurs to his mount and raced to Michael's campsite.

Jaybird rode all that day and through the night. He reached Michael as the sun was coming up. He dismounted his jaded horse and bent over holding onto his knees.

Java Stevens caught sight of him and the weary horse. He caught Michael's attention and then pointedly nodded his head in Jaybird's direction. "What in the hell is wrong with him?"

Michael, who had his back to Jaybird, caught the look in Java's eyes, and he turned and was alarmed to see Jaybird. He knew he was not supposed to report unless there was a disaster. Michael, in a hundred-years, would have never guessed that Bushrod would ever fail in this open and shut case of killing.

Michael accepted a cup of coffee and walked to the exhausted rider. He looked at his lathered horse, which was blowing. If he had been pushed any farther, the horse would have burst his heart.'

Jaybird held up a finger to ask for a 'rest-break' as he stayed bent over.

This seemed to unease Michael and Java all the more.

Jaybird finally got his breath and stood. He explained to them all that had happened. He informed them that all the men who had been on the mission had departed back to New Mexico Territory.

Michael stood frowning. He took a sip of coffee and turned and looked in the direction of Ten Strike. He turned back around and looked inquiringly at Jaybird. "John Johnson did this all by himself?"

"The shooting part, yes, but he didn't brand Bushrod. His men did that. He definitely is not alone."

Michael weighed his words through eye slits. "How many men does he have?"

Jaybird said, "I saw three-men brand Bushrod's ass. But Burt Greenway told me yesterday that he felt that John was traveling with some troopers and deputies."

Java, who stood nearby and who had been listening, tossed out the dregs from his coffee cup. For the first time, Java realized the enormity of the problem. He, like Michael, thought that Bushrod would make quick work of the Texan, and they would all go back to the ranch carefree. He now knew that they were facing a serious threat.

Michael asked again. "But how many men did you actually see that are part of his crew?"

"Three."

Michael nodded, "I can't get a handle on this. I can't imagine a Rebel soldier riding with deputies and Union troops."

Java sagely commented, "But he ain't a Rebel soldier anymore, Michael."

Michael glanced at Java and raised his eyebrows in thought. "I say let's go to Ten Strike and take him on."

Java looked at him oddly. "Michael, to go after John Johnson is one thing but to take on the U.S. cavalry is another--plus Federal deputies."

Michael tossed out his remaining coffee and whirled around. "Well, give me a better plan." His eyes were desperate.

Java reasoned, "If they drop that coach off somewhere, those cavalrymen and those deputies might drop off too."

Michael asked, "You think we should ride back to Baileysboro and let him come to us?"

Java looked at Michael evenly. "I haven't lived this long being foolish. If a man can beat Bushrod Elkins, and then brand his ass, he's got to be pretty damn tough."

Michael shook his head negatively. "Bill's not going to like this. He's not going to like this at all."

Java shrugged and said, "Listen, you're calling the shots. Not me. If you say go get him, we will."

Michael shook his head 'no.' "You may be right. I hate facing my brother, but I say let John Johnson come to us."

They broke camp and saddled up. Jaybird Roberts and Fuzzy Williams were left behind to keep tabs on John Johnson.

Michael and Java headed to the Purvis ranch headquarters to plan their next move.

# CHAPTER NINE

THE NEXT DAY JOHN WAS riding with the sheriff a few miles ahead of the coach. The sheriff informed him that in two-days they would be a full platoon of soldiers coming from the territory to take the coach off their hands.

John looked at him and asked, "I've got something to ask you?"

The sheriff simply said, "Ask."

"How do you know that a platoon of soldiers is coming and going to meet the coach and when?" John turned in his saddle and asked another question before the sheriff could answer. "Something else is troubling me, how did you know that Arkansas Bob was in Canebrake that morning back before we reached Sylvester Creek when it is one grueling ride from where you were?"

The sheriff stated, "The deputies that were assigned me have special skills. Many of them are officers who volunteered. They've spoiled the hell out of me. It'll be hard to go back to Phil, Roscoe and Frankie." He raised his finger to make a point. "You remember the deputy who was pretending to be asleep?"

John nodded.

The sheriff continued, "Well, he is Captain Levi Brown. Not

only is he good with a gun, but he and about four others used mirrors to send me messages. I think they call it heliography.

"They kept me informed about Indian Melvin and kept me up-to-date on who was doing what."

John sighed, "Mirrors, eh?"

"Good as Morse Code except when the sun is not shining."

John shrugged his shoulders. "It's a shame that such men have to go back to the War. They would be invaluable lawmen."

Sheriff Buchanan agreed, "I think when the War is over that the justice department will probably see that we need U.S. marshals and probably some of these men will be chosen."

John smiled to himself. "I'd think you'd be one great marshal, Sheriff. You've done well so far."

The sheriff looked back at John. "I'm getting too old for all of this but I think we both know who'd make a good marshal."

John did not respond. He could tell by sheriff's look and the register of his voice he meant him.

That night by an open fire, the sheriff, lieutenant and John were standing around with a plate of beans in their hands. Their meal was interrupted, when Levi Brown, brandishing an Army Colt, brought in two-men.

Levi pushed the two-men forward brusquely and looked at Sheriff Buchanan. "These two-gents have been following the coach for over twenty-miles and I thought they might want to explain why."

Jaybird looked over nervously at Fuzzy, and back at the compressed eyes of the men waiting for his response.

Harley standing about thirty-five feet away at another campfire recognized both men and ambled over. He could see that the deputy had his weapon drawn and that he was having trouble identifying them.

Harley said as he walked up, "That one is Jaybird Roberts." He paused as he tried to remember the other one. He snapped his fingers, trying to coax his memory, and pointed to Fuzzy. "He's Fuzzy Williams and they both work for the Purvis brothers."

Both Jaybird and Fuzzy gave Harley a menacing look. They had thought initially they could wiggle their way out of the predicament.

The sheriff cut them off by saying. "No need to frown and look tough. It won't do you no good." He also added, "And no reason to lie, either."

Jaybird, a tall and thin man, responded, "We ain't done nothing wrong. We can ride along this trail just like the next man."

The sheriff answered, "Not when it's an armored coach going down this trail you can't." The sheriff exhaled and said, "Let's not play games, you're following John."

When Jaybird and Fuzzy looked at John, their eyes expanded. He looked fierce by the reflected orange flames of the campfire. The hard eyes and the yard-wide shoulders and the two-Navy Colts made him appear like a bad dream that had escaped the bounds of sleep.

Jaybird audibly swallowed. Fuzzy looked panic-stricken.

John reached across and grabbed Jaybird by the shirt and pulled him inches from his face. "You've been following me?"

Jaybird tried to pull back but John yanked him back again. John's voice was hard as steel. "You better answer, you son-of-a-bitch."

Jaybird nodded frenetically. John shoved him back to his original place. Jaybird straightened his shirt to restore some lost dignity. "We was ordered to."

The sheriff said, "Who ordered you to?"

"Michael Purvis."

The sheriff had Captain Levi Brown take their deposition that they were following John Johnson on the instructions of Michael Purvis for the sole purpose of mayhem and obstruction of justice. The sheriff was not sure those were accurate charges, but it was good for starters. The two men signed the document hurriedly. They wanted to get the hell away from John Lee Johnson.

The sheriff said, "I'm letting you go and it's okay if you back and tell Bill and Michael what I made you do." He pointed his finger at each one of them. "When we get to Baileysboro, you had better not make any attempt to harm and hurt any of these troopers or deputies. I'll take you back to meet General Beasley and you'll be charged."

Jaybird, having regained some composure, said, "How can you charge us when you are out of your jurisdiction?"

The sheriff smiled and answered, "These are all Federal men that's how."

Jaybird looked soberly at the sheriff, the deputy, and the lieutenant. He felt a measure of trepidation. He knew he was swimming in deep water. But when he looked into the eyes of John Johnson, he felt like he might soil his long johns. He had never met a man who looked so fearsome.

Another deputy led their horses up and Jaybird and Fuzzy mounted up and rode away hurriedly into the night.

Five-days later in Bill Purvis' office, Michael and Java sit across from the surly leader. "You mean to tell me that Bushrod was beat in a gunfight and had his ass branded?"

Java nodded, "That's about the size of it, Boss."

Bill drummed his fingers on his desk. "Who's left to hire?"

Java answered quickly. "A man who is a heap better than Bushrod Elkins."

Bill whirled his index finger for him to keep talking.

"Latigo Wilson."

Bill leaned back. He repeated the name but drew it out, "Latigo Wilson."

Java nodded, "He usually works alone but he likes money just like the rest of us."

Bill snapped, "Well, hire him. Get him here."

Java and Michael stood but Bill indicated that he wanted

Michael to stay. Bill said to the departing Java, "I want him here fast."

Java nodded, stood-up, left, and his spurs could be heard going down the hallway.

Bill listened until he heard the door open and close. He fixed hard and accusatory eyes at Michael. "How could you just ride back here and not make a damn effort?"

Michael looked sheepish. "I've told you, Bill, that John Johnson is riding with troopers to take a armored coach through. And not only troopers but Federal deputies, too, and they just might be backing his play."

Bill sighed and said, "When they deliver that coach or whatever it is, do you think the troopers will come here with him?"

Michael shrugged with his palms ups. "Who knows? I don't."

Bill sat up straighter. "Do you know how many men was with him?"

Michael answered back. "No."

Bill slammed both fists on the table. "Damn it, Michael, that was not supposed to be a damned pleasure excursion."

Bill composed himself and inhaled deeply. "I want every road that leads to this county covered. I want men in town and I want Sheriff Nelson watched."

"What about Henry Johnson?"

"I want him watched too." He paused and said, "Not killed yet, but watched."

Michael, bothered by the scolding, stated, "Why are you so upset? We got more men than they do. Both Java and me can handle John Johnson."

Bill looked at him with questioning eyes. "If you have noticed, John Johnson is still alive. He was supposed to have been killed in Fort Smith and in Ten Strike."

Michael felt like telling him that Bushrod was his idea but he did not want to blow the lid off and make his volatile brother any angrier. He nodded, "I'll hand out the orders tonight and we'll be ready."

Bill dismissed him abruptly.

At sundown, Bill rode into town and had a beer at the Texas State Saloon. He sullenly watched Henry Johnson work the bar and talk energetically with his friends. He felt like going over to the bar and conking him over the head with a gun barrel.

He was sitting and drinking and stewing on his setbacks and disappointments when Jaybird and Fuzzy walked in. They spotted him and walked to him and took a seat without being asked which piqued him.

They told him about being captured by a deputy and being questioned by the sheriff. They left out the deposition part seeing their boss becoming angrier and redder.

He dismissed them unexpectedly and told them harshly to get back to the ranch and see Michael. He had work for them. He rose up and dourly looked at Henry Johnson and left. He did take note, however, that Henry Johnson looked too damned happy.

The next two-days were uneventful. There was no sign of John Johnson and his men. His men were watching the roads and trails that led to Bailey County and they saw no suspicious activity.

On the third-day Latigo Wilson rode into town, and he immediately caused a big stir. He was dressed in all black. He was tall and angular with deep, angry eyes. He wore a black hat with a wide brim that shadowed his eyes. The crown came to point, and he had a ornate silver band around the base of crown.

When he dismounted in front of the Texas Saloon, he stepped down from his black horse with stovepipe boots adorned in heavy, silver, Mexican spurs.

He wore black sleeve garters on each of his arms and wore black gloves that looked slick with use.

Each stride he took up the steps sang silvery with spur music. He pushed back the batwing and looked over the crowd. The cigar smoke seemed suspended in the air. All eyes were on him-even the rinky-dink piano quit playing.

Java Stevens, who was playing poker with 'All-Night' Roy, stood and walked to him and introduced himself. They walked to the bar and the smoke seemed to stir again and the piano started playing again.

After paying Latigo a goodly sum of money, Java watch the gunfighter exit to check into the hotel.

Java seemed in a jovial mood. He nodded his head at 'All-Night' Roy. All-Night' rose from his chair and grated it back and walked to his foreman.

Java grinned nastily and canted his head toward the sheriff's office, which was cattycornered from the saloon across the street. "It's time to baby sit."

Sheriff Nelson had watched Latigo Wilson ride in through his sun-blazed window. He backed to his desk and then went around and sat down heavily. He knew the Purvis brothers had brought in another heavyweight. He was sitting idly drumming his fingers in exasperation, when 'All-Night' Roy entered.

'All-Night' Roy sarcastically said, "I see you're doing what you do best---nothing."

Sheriff Nelson replied nothing. He leaned back and opened a drawer and pulled out some gun oil and a rag. He pulled his .44 out and began to wipe it down. He looked at 'All-Night' Roy as the irritatingly mean-spirited man sat down in a chair in front of him.

Sheriff Nelson said as he applied a droplet of gun oil, "Don't you have nothing better to do?"

'All-Night' Roy answered in an acerbic way, "I like hanging out with you and seeing how our tax money is spent." He raised his eyebrows mockingly, "And it ain't spent worth a damn."

The sheriff kept oiling and cleaning his gun and ignoring 'All-Night' Roy. The sheriff would look up occasionally and see the mocking eyes staring back. As the sheriff was putting up his oil and cloth, his eyes passed the near window directly to his left. He saw a familiar face. He tried not to give away his sudden jubilation.

The sheriff suddenly was infused with much needed hope. He looked up at 'All-Night' Roy and asked, "Want to do something useful?"

'All-Night' Roy shrugged. "That depends, sheriff. I stop at carrying toilet buckets."

The sheriff inclined his head to the door. "Go see who that is at the door?"

'All-Night' Roy's eyebrows shot up. "What in the hell are you talking about?"

The sheriff lied, "I just think I saw Java peek in." He knew that would get 'All-Night' Roy's attention.

'All-Night' Roy rose up from his chair and looked weirdly at the sheriff but walked to the door. As soon as he opened the door, a sledgehammer punch met his nose. He was propelled backwards clanging against the cell bars. He collapsed on his haunches.

John entered quickly and shut the door behind hastily.

Sheriff Nelson sighed and said, "Hallelujah."

John looked at the unconscious 'All-Night' Roy but taking no chances, he said, "Meet me in that dry wash just beyond the mesquite tree."

The sheriff did not have to tell him to leave by the back door. John took it on his own initiative and promptly exited it.

The sheriff looked at 'All-Night' Roy. He hurriedly took a gander out the window. He grabbed his hat off the peg and departed out the back door also. He found his horse tethered near the water trough by the lone peach tree. He mounted up and looked both ways and galloped toward the mesquite tree.

He pulled up two-times and whirled his horse around to check his back. He searched the backside of the store buildings but saw no one watching. He then turned around and spurred his horse and galloped to the mesquite tree.

His horse skidded down the sandy embankment and he

reached the bottom in a swirl of dust. John set astride his big black horse, seventeen-hands tall, smiling at the sheriff.

"John, how long have you been here?"

"You mean in this arroyo or in the county?"

Sheriff Nelson gave him a wry look, "Now c'mon."

John sighed and answered, "I'm a little head of the group. We've been moving at night. We spotted some of the Purvis brothers' watchdogs, but me and Russell know our way around here pretty doggone good."

The sheriff's haggard face showed his strain. "Listen, I've been counting down the hours when you would return."

"That bad around here, eh?"

Sheriff Nelson shook his head in disgust. "I'd "sooner die, if I knew that I had to keep on living with those damned Purvis brothers running the show."

John turned his head and looked to the north. "You know where the ole Fallon place used to be before the house was hit by lightning?"

The sheriff nodded.

John said, "Well, in the dry creek bed just south of where the house used to be, is several cottonwood trees. Be there tomorrow at six o'clock in the morning."

"That's good timing for me, John, there won't be so many nosy eyes."

John smiled at the sheriff and gave him a hand signal of 'goodbye' and he rode down the dry wash a quarter and then climbed the dirt incline and rode like thunder across the level terrain.

When Michael Purvis rode into town he saw "All-Night' Roy stagger coming out of the sheriff's office. He pulled up his sorrel and dismounted and hitched his horse speedily. He jumped up on the boardwalk and saw the blood caked around his swollen nose. "What in the hell happened to you?"

'All-Night' Roy shook his head and bent over and puked. "I opened the door and someone hit me in the face."

"Where's the sheriff?"

'All-Night' Roy shook his head as to say 'he did not know.'

Michael went to the door of the jail and opened it. He peered inside and then entered seeking the sheriff. He looked down the walkway where there were more cells. He went to back door and opened it. He saw the sheriff tying his horse to the peach tree next to the water trough. Michael barked at him strongly, "Where in the hell have you been?"

The sheriff dodged a low limb of the tree and thought quickly. "I was chasing the man who hit 'All-Night' Roy.

Michael momentarily mollified backed up and let the sheriff enter. The sheriff tried to look sympathetic. "Where is he?"

Michael thumbed toward the boardwalk. "He's out there puking his guts out." Michael looked searchingly at the sheriff, "You got any idea of who it was?"

The sheriff sighed and lied, "It's someone I've seen over at the Texas Saloon before." He shrugged, "Probably a sore loser."

Michael nodded slowly. It made sense to him. He turned thoughtfully and made his way back to his comrade.

The sheriff exhaled nervously and made his way to his desk and sat down heavily.

Michael had 'All-Night' Roy's arm around his shoulder as they hobbled together over to the saloon.

Java Stevens was at the bar lifting his glass when he saw them enter the batwings. He swiftly set his glass down and walked through the heavy cigar smoke toward them. "What happened to him?" He pointed to the groggy, 'All-Night' Roy.

Michael told him all that the sheriff had said. Java nodded as he talked. Java helped Michael sit the wobbly 'All-Night' Roy into a chair.

Java walked the short distance to the batwings and peered over the top and rubbed his chin in thought. "I know there's hard losers but the ones I know would most likely attack you in the dark and not in front of the sheriff's office."

Michael, who was bent over inspecting the smashed nose of his friend, cut his eyes up at Java. He straightened and went to the batwings and joined Java looking at the sheriff's office. "You think the sheriff lied?"

Java shrugged, "Well, I'm not sure but we need another watchdog over there." Java's eyes narrowed. "Who in the hell would hit, 'All-Night' Roy? It don't make no sense."

Michael sighed, "I will send Freddie Taylor over there after I have a beer." He peered over at Java and asked, "Has Latigo Wilson made it into town?"

Java turned and pointed through the wafting cigar smoke. His finger extended toward the saturnine man playing cards against the far wall. "That's him in the flesh. One of the meanest men to ever come out of Texas."

Michael grinned and said, "You know I like mean especially if he's on our side."

Java looked down at the woozy 'All-Night' Roy. "What do you want me to do with him?"

Michael shrugged, "Get him a beer and after he comes to his senses let him play cards with the one and only Latigo Wilson."

Michael and Java left 'All-Night' Roy and walked to the bar. Michael leaned in closer and said to Java, "Bill wants to talk to you and me at the ranch at seven. So, don't be late."

Michael signaled for Freddie Taylor and dispensed him to the sheriff's office. Michael finished his beer and departed giving a pensive look toward the jailhouse.

At seven o'clock, Bill Purvis leaned back and looked across at Michael and Java. "One of the boys found a lot of tracks near an arroyo close to the ranch road." He pointed at Java. "I want you to send back about six or seven good men and post them in that area."

Java nodded that it would be done.

Bill continued, "I think if he's really coming back, he'll most likely be prone to come straight here. "I don't see why he would want to come to town, but he might."

Michael tilted his head to one-side and said, "If he did come to town what would he want that is of importance?"

Bill thought for a minute and said, "I think he would want his Uncle Henry." He studied on that for a moment and then pointed at Java. I want you to make sure you pick up that bird and bring him here."

Java asked, "Why not pick up the sheriff and make a clean sweep of it?"

Bill shook his head 'no.' "Just keep someone close. He definitely would help the Johnson's if he could. But I don't want him brought here. There's too many secessionist around here and I don't want to give them fodder for joining forces with John Johnson. And bringing him in would make us look a lot worse." He paused, "No, let's maintain some proper propriety if we can."

Java asked, "If we get in a bind, do I have the okay to kill?"

Bill gave a quick answer, "You damn right. I don't care if it's troopers or deputies or whoever it is. We're fighting for survival here." He wavered his finger in the air, "But use good sense. I want John Johnson to be the outlaw not us."

The next morning, Sheriff Nelson cinched up Ole Nell and mounted up. He rode out his ramshackle barn with quick glances to the left and right. Seeing nothing but velvet, familiar shadows, he galloped north to the deserted Fallon ranch house.

He avoided roads and rode across the level plain. The sunrise was breaking when he came in view of the stand of cottonwoods and he rode down a low escarpment into the sandy bottom of the wash.

When he raised his eyes, he was startled but heartened at the number of men there. He rode up and dismounted and a deputy took his reins.

John introduced him to all the principals and they all took seats on flat rocks that were abundant. The sheriff was shocked when one of the deputies led Charley Danton, the trustee of Bailey County, to the assembled group. He obviously was not happy at being there and sat down with a disgruntled demeanor.

Charley looked from face to face and said, "Do you gentlemen know what you're doing?"

Sheriff Buchanan snapped back, "Do you know what you've done?"

Charley turned to him abruptly. "What have I done to be taken from bed at four in the morning at gunpoint?"

Sheriff Buchanan did not want this rapid-fire tempo of questions to continue so he started talking lower. He was a wily man who had engaged in many unpleasant talks. He stopped the interrogation to start introducing each person gathered around.

"Charley, this is Lieutenant Gardner. He is a representative of Colonel Daugherty in the Arkansas campaign." He pointed at Captain Levi Brown. "This man is hand-picked by General Beasley, the leading military figure in Arkansas and Northern Louisiana. He is serving as a special deputy in this injustice here.

"My name is Sheriff Kenesaw Buchanan. I am the lead sheriff of this group. We just captured Indian Melvin in the Nations and we are here to investigate and arrest the Purvis brothers for the unjust killing of Ed and Roy Johnson and for the unlawful takeover of their land."

The psychology of slowing down the pace the conversation and the introductions seemed not only to disarm Charley Danton, but to impress upon him that this was not just a mob, but men of substance.

Charley sighed and placed his hands on his knees. placed "Gentlemen, I'm not a crook, nor am I working hand-in-glove with Bill Purvis. Let me explain to you my problem. When Colonel Purvis was headed across this way from fighting General Sibley in New Mexico. He established martial law in Bailey County. He expelled from public office any Confederate loyalist. He forbade Confederate money as legal tender.

"He made me go through the files and find any rancher who had paid his taxes in Confederate money. He made those tax payments null and void. He sent his two-nephews to collect the taxes in Union money or gold. The two-Johnson brothers refused. They were put up for public eviction and they were killed unfortunately when they resisted the eviction notice.

"Bill Purvis and his brother paid the taxes and I was ordered by the Union authority here that if I did not comply in giving them the deeds, I would be arrested for treason.

"Now I see you Federal men telling me that I did wrong and that I could be aiding and abetting killers."

The sheriff held up a gloved hand and stopped him. "We are not here to arrest you nor hold you on any crime. You did what any reasonable man would have done."

Charley's countenance softened as he looked from man to man including the looming presence of John Johnson peering over the shoulder of Deputy Levi Brown.

Sheriff Buchanan continued. "I have eyewitnesses to the murder of Ed and Roy Johnson and have signed depositions stating to that effect. These depositions say that Bill and Michael Purvis are the killers. I wanted you here not to arrest you for complicity with these killers but to inform you of our intent and why.

"And they will be arrested for murder and the unlawful takeover of someone's else's property, and it was an illegal act. The colonel acted illegally and outside the pale of his command by using a pretense to takeover property and parcel out to his ranches to his nephews. It was a Bailey County affair and not a Colonel Travis affair.

"Charley, when this is all over I want you on a commission to mete out justice. I want the laws of Bailey County to be enforced. Not my laws, not the laws of the Confederate or Union governments."

Charley exhaled a breath of relief. "I would like that. I want justice and what is right to be just that. If you are able to bring them to justice, I will gladly serve on that commission. I am not a Bill Purvis minion and never have been, but let me inform all of you that he has a sizeable army and bringing him to heel will not be easy."

The sheriff said, "We never said it was going to be easy but we've got to do it and with your help we can."

"How can I help?"

"By allowing the troopers to guard your office so no files can be touched or doctored with."

Charley Danton arose. He studied each face and then relaxed his face. "Consider it done. I don't like the Purvis brothers and I hope you do bring them to justice."

He waved 'goodbye' to all of them and went to his horse in the wash and mounted up and rode away swiftly.

Sheriff Buchanan turned to Sheriff Nelson. "I'm hoping he can keep his mouth shut."

Sheriff Nelson replied, "He can keep his mouth shut. That is how he's stayed alive this long. He's like me in a sense. He just tried to survive and preserve his dignity the best he could."

Sheriff Buchanan stood and everyone else stood when he did. He looked at Sheriff Nelson. "This is your town and I'm not into interfering but here's my advice. Swear me and my deputies in to be your deputies. Let's head to town. Let's take back the sheriff's office and make it a working law agency."

He turned to Lieutenant Gardner. "Here's my advice to you and hope you take it. "You secure the Trustee's office both front and back. You and your men be civil to the citizens but defend those deeds with force if need be."

He turned to John. "Go find your Uncle Henry. Make sure he's safe."

John noticed his sage and diplomatic message. He was grateful that he did not lecture him on going foolhardily to the Purvis ranch and trying and kill every son-of-a-bitch there. He knew the respect that Sheriff Buchanan had for him and he knew this course of methodical and legal action was one that would be respected by General Beasley and Colonel Daugherty.

Sheriff Nelson had them raise their right hands and he duly swore them as Bailey County deputies.

Sheriff Nelson gave quick directions to Lieutenant Gardner to the location of the Trustee's office. He repeated it until the lieutenant nodded that he understood.

They all mounted up and thundered down the arroyo until it reached level ground. They galloped toward Baileysboro.

It was nine o'clock in the morning, when Java and his men rode into the town and hitched their horses. The saloon was open and they strode up the steps and entered the spacious room.

Otis Quigley stood behind his counter and was counting the cash in his moneybox. He nodded at them and let his eyes go up to the wall clock. "You boys are a mite early for beer."

Java cut him off by saying, "Just consider it a late start from last night and it's all right."

His men laughed coarsely and sat down.

Java walked to the bar. "Otis, where is Henry?"

Otis looked at him guardedly. He shrugged his shoulders and noncommittally stated, "You know he's not on duty until eleven."

Java half-turned and said to his men. "June Bug, you and High Pockets go down to the boarding house and see if you can find Henry, if he's not there go down to Chili Thomas' livery."

He turned his body to the bar as June Bug and High Pockets were pulling back their chairs. Java looked down the zinc counter toward Fuzzy Williams. Fuzzy, you go and be the messenger back and forth so I'll know what is going on."

Otis Quigley acted as though he were oblivious to this conversation. His eyes were squinted as he counted his money. Java knew better however. He moved down toward the owner and pushed his face irritatingly close until he had Otis' eyes. "Otis, bring us some beers and don't even dare try and get word to Henry."

Soon the rinky-dink piano was playing and the men were

drinking beer and several poker games were in earnest. The men raised a cheer when Latigo Wilson entered and carried his usual dark self back to the wall.

Latigo, soon, was joined by'All-Night' Roy, Sonny Stevens, Java's cousin, and Freddie Taylor in an intense poker game.

June Bug and High Pockets were exiting the boarding house after finding Henry's room empty. High Pockets seemed agitated until he thought he caught a glimpse of Henry's face peering around the back corner of the saloon. He pointed and got June Bug's attention. They walked toward the rear of the saloon and moved behind the store buildings till they reached Chili's livery. They entered the shadowed entrance and found Chili casually stitching a bridle.

June Bug immediately pulled his .44 and yelled at Chili. Chili laid aside the bridle and looked up at the two-men. "What in the world is wrong with you, June Bug?"

June Bug sneered. "Don't play coy with me, Chili." High Pockets saw Henry Johnson, and we think you're hiding him."

Chili's eyes widened. "You're joshing me."

June bug shook his head 'no.' He kept his weapon on Chili. He looked over at High Pockets and said, "Climb up that hay loft ladder and take that pitchfork."

Fuzzy Williams entered the barn and walked up beside June Bug. June Bug explained to him what he was doing.

Chili shook his head disgustedly and reached for his bridle to resume his stitching. June Bug whirled on him and said, "Don't you dare play games with me, Chili. I'm just liable to blow your damn head off just on the slightest excuse."

High Pockets climbed the ladder and soon his footsteps could be heard traipsing up and down the length. Dust puffed from the cracks between the planks. The sluicing sound of the fork slicing into hay could be heard.

June Bug's scrawny neck was craning upwards looking and

hoping for the slightest sound of discovery. He would periodically drop his head and glare at Chili.

High Pockets shouted down. "He ain't up here."

Fuzzy turned on his heels and started walking away. "Java says if ain't in the boarding house and the livery stable for you two to ride out to Kiowa Bob's adobe hut and check that out."

When Fuzzy walked away, June Bug walked over and slammed the barrel of his .44 across Chili's head. Chili went sprawling into the fine dust of the barn. "That's for lying and me knowing you're lying, Chili. There's nothing more than I hate than a damn liar."

Chili said nothing but put his hand up to his head. He thought sarcastically to himself that it was not so bad being pistol-whipped by such a paragon of justice like June Bug. He was derisively sure that June Bug spoke at churches and schools on morality and the virtues of truth. He was also sardonically certain that he visited hospitals and funeral parlors comforting the sick and heartsick.

June Bug stood with a calloused look on his face. He watched High Pockets climb down from the loft holding carefully the pitchfork.

June Bug was about blast Chili again verbally when he heard the sound of thundering horse hooves on the street. June Bug holstered his weapon and he and High Pockets went to the entrance to see a lot of men wearing metal stars on their chest ride by and rein up at the sheriff's office.

June Bug was trying to make sense of all this when another man reined up right beside the barn. This man was big. He had shoulders a yard wide and a thick neck. He noticed the twin-military gun belts around his waist. In fact, he had two-others poked in as well.

John tossed his reins around the hitch rack with practiced ease and walked toward June Bug. He ignored him and entered the shadows of the barn. He saw Chili lying in the dirt with a welt across the side of his head.

John asked, "What happened to you, Chili?"

Chili pointed to June Bug. "He pistol whipped me because he's looking for your Uncle Henry and can't find him."

John turned and this time he did not ignore June Bug. "You did that?"

June Bug, who was dwarfed in the presence of John, swallowed and started backing up. He did not back far enough. John reached over and snatched him and pulled his own Colt out and thudded him across the face.

June Bug fell holding his eye and nose. He looked up in fear and agony at the huge man. John without looking reached over and grabbed High Pockets by the shirt pulled him in close and pistol-whipped him across the forehead and nose. He went flying into the barn dust beside his partner. They both sat in fear rubbing their heads.

Harley walked around the corner and took a look at the two-men on the barn floor rubbing their bruised features. "Allow me to introduce you to John Lee Johnson."

Harley raised his eyebrows as though he had made a mistake and then he sarcastically said again, "Excuse me, but I think you've already met him."

John looked at Harley and back at the two-men. "Who are those two-birds?"

Harley smiled and said, "June bug usually shovels horse manure." He then pointed toward High pocket. Now he," he paused and acted as though he were reaching for words, "Well, he usually shovels horse manure too."

John reached down and took the two-men's weapons. He looked at Harley and asked, "Do you mind taking them down to the jail. I need to talk with Chili."

Harley fished out his .44 and inclined his head. "Come on, you two toughies."

John helped Chili up and they sat and talked for about fifteen-minutes about his Uncle Henry and his whereabouts.

The noisy entrance of the deputies caused the saloon patrons to run to the batwings and spill out onto the boardwalk. Java stood there with his mouth gaping as he watched the deputies rein in and the troopers roll by.

He had not anticipated this. He licked his lips and tried to think. He noticed both deputies and troopers rode with quickness and precision. It was damned obvious these men were professionals. The deputies reined in quickly and took key positions around the sheriff's office.

The troopers rode by in formation and stopped abruptly in front of the Trustee's office.

Java looked up and down the street. His indecisiveness was joined by ire when he saw Harley Rawlins walking behind June Bug and High Pockets with a drawn gun directing them to the jail.

The eyes of these two-men looked at him imploringly and all he could do was stand helplessly. Java stood arms akimbo and tried to stifle his anger.

Later His eyes really widened when he saw the man whom he assumed was John Lee Johnson, himself. The big man sauntered across the street with the indifference of a Sunday worshipper after a big meal.

Java noticed his weapons and his immense size. When John glanced his way, there was no emotion one way or the other. Java was unsettled by his indifferent attitude. It was obvious he was an ass kicker looking for an ass to kick.

Sonny Stevens who was standing next to Java leaned in and whispered, 'Latigo' in his ear. Java's eyes moved to the right in thought. He moved his hand to his chin and rubbed it in contemplation.

Java nodded and his eyes narrowed. This was the time to brace John Johnson 'in front of the world.' He turned and looked at the half-lidded eyes of his thoughtful cousin. "Go get Latigo."

Latigo was in the midst of a big game and was dealing the cards when he saw the beckoning hand of Sonny Stevens. He gave a steely look toward Sonny but he stopped dealing and slapped the cards on the table.

He grated back his chair dramatically and looked at each man with emotionless eyes. He stood and adjusted his hat brim. He sauntered to the batwings and each man in the saloon looked at him as they might an avenging angel.

'All-Night' Roy looked around at the three-other card players and said, "Well, what in the hell are we sitting here for?"

The card players scooted back their chairs and rose up in unison and walked stridently after the feared Latigo Wilson.

Latigo exited the batwings. The Rocking P riders gathered on the porch, parted for him like Moses and the Red Sea. Java leaned in close and pointed to the big Texan who had his back to them.

John was standing across the street with his back turned toward Latiogo. He was talking to Deputy Levi Brown who had become one of his favorites. Levi was telling about something that had happened during one of the early campaigns in the War. He was demonstrating with his hands when he looked over John's shoulder and saw the threatening figure.

John caught his eyes and noticed how he had quit talking. He followed Levi's eyes as he slowly turned. He saw Latigo Wilson for the first time.

John looked at Latigo and smiled. He could not help himself. He glanced over at Levi and over at Harley. They seemed very nervous, but he was far from nervous. He stepped into the street and the deputies behind him began to arrange themselves to stay out of the line of fire.

Latigo Wilson began to take singular steps down the steps. Each step increased the melodramatic tension. Each step accompanied by harsh spur jangle. His eyes shadowed beneath the hat brim seemed to glow.

Latigo finally reached street level and began to stride slowly toward John. He finally stopped and his face moved into a scowl.

John began to grin again. He asked across the way, "Who in the hell are you?"

Latigo Wilson took umbrage at John's smile. "It don't matter who I am. " He cocked his head to one-side and studied John's smile. "And what in the hell do you think is so funny?"

John grinned broader. "I think you are." John nodded toward Latigo's boots. "Where did you get those silly boots?"

Latigo's eyebrows knitted closer as he burned in anger.

John glanced at his sleeve garters. "I only knew one other man who wore sleeve garters and he liked men."

Latigo gritted his teeth.

John nodded at his spurs. "Mister, I'm not sure but I think you ought to be in a circus."

Latigo angrily snapped, "I'm going to blow you to hell, you smart mouth. So, either drop those holsters or die."

John shook his head 'no' in amusement. "What is your name?"

Latigo grated out his name.

John nodded amusedly, "Well, it's like this, Latigo. We both know I ain't going to bluff and we both know that I am just seconds away from killing you. You might have the Indian sign on those hombres over there." He nodded toward Java and the Rocking P riders. "But you don't on me."

Latigo just licked his lips and narrowed his eyes.

John stepped one step to the side and said, "I ain't got a lot of time to waste on a tinhorn gunfighter. You either go now and live or I'm going to have to kill you."

Latigo amazed everyone when he turned promptly and began running down the alley between the Texas Saloon and the Purvis Mercantile Store. His spurs glaringly jingled as he ran down the alley. The sound of the spurs became less and less until they could no longer be heard.

The deputies standing beneath the wood tiled roof of the

sheriff's office chortled. Seth, who normally was quiet, guffawed and grabbed his sides.

Java Stevens did not laugh. He stood stunned. He looked at Sonny and over at 'All-Night' Roy. He and his men had gaped mouths as they listened to the last vestiges of Latigo's fleeing spur music.

The Rocking P riders backed into the saloon serenaded by the loud, mocking laughter of the deputies.

Java sat down at a near table and swallowed. He absentmindedly reached for a deck of cards and began to shuffle nervously.

Sonny and 'All-Night' Roy sat down on each side of him. Java looked at each one of them in a searching stare. "Have either one of you ever saw something like that before?"

'All-Night' Roy said, "Well, it's like this, Java, he wasn't much of a gunfighter. He wasn't much of a card player. Hell, I lost on purpose to him so he wouldn't get mad at me." 'All-Night' Roy paused and made a point with his finger. "But that bastard sure could run."

Java gave him a wry look and shook his head. Java shrugged his shoulders. "They've got the jail and they've got the Trustee's office. If we leave here, they've got the saloon."

'All-Night' Roy added, "I don't give a damn if they got the sheriff's office and the Trustee's office and that whole side of town. Just don't give up the saloon."

Java gave him a sarcastic look.

Java asked, "Do either of you have any suggestions?" He looked pointedly at 'All-Night' Roy. "Good suggestions."

Sonny said, "I say we take the boys we have here, and we got some good ones, and just go up and down the street and position ourselves and just cut loose on 'em."

Java sat still for a long time and deliberated on Sonny's words. The idea of firing on the troopers down the street was a serious matter.

Java fiddled with the cards as he thought. He looked up at the clock. "If we leave now we can be at the ranch in two-hours and see what Bill wants to do."

Sonny mulled over that and said, "Bill Purvis will hit the ceiling if you go back now."

Java kept shuffling the cards lazily and thinking. "Yeah, but if we cut down on those damned troopers, that'll bring in the whole dad blamed army too." He shuffled some more. "And if they send in troops, Bill will disavow all knowledge of it and we'll be up Salt Creek without a paddle."

Sonny nodded his head, "Yeah, see what you mean. But he's going to raise hell either way."

Java tossed the cards en masse onto the table. "Tell the men to mount up. I ain't making this call."

Java stood and looked at Sonny. "Get someone to hide behind the bar and see if they can hear anything."

The two-sheriffs watched the Purvis brothers' crew, ride out of town. They galloped down the main street and past the Trustee's office where they hooted at the troopers stationed there.

Sheriff Nelson turned to Sheriff Buchanan and asked, "What do you think?"

Sheriff Buchanan pulled back from the window with attentive eyes. "I think someone is hiding behind the bar is what I think."

Sheriff Nelson smiled. "You've been around, Sheriff."

Sheriff Buchanan replied, "You go over and arrest the guy behind the bar and meet me and the deputies down at the livery stable."

Sheriff Nelson did not have to be told twice. He walked over to the Texas Saloon. He moved up to the bar and looked at the nervous Otis Quigley. Without saying a word, he walked around the end of the bar and looked at the scrunched up cowpuncher balled up in a leg space. He pulled his Colt out and gave a 'come with me look.'

The startled cowhand slowly crawled out and stood shocked

that it had been that easy. The sheriff merely said, "Let's go, Butch, I have to book you on vagrancy."

At Chili's stable, deputies guarded all entrances and windows. Sheriff Buchanan had all his deputies either seated or on duty watching. John and his crew were there as well as Lieutenant Gardner.

The sheriff began to talk. "We've talked (meaning Sheriff Nelson, Lieutenant Gardner, John Johnson, and Levi Brown) and we have decided on this particular strategy. I want to let Captain Levi Brown discuss with you what we should do and what we should not do." He paused and pointed at Levi. "He is not only a captain in the U.S. army but a scout, telegrapher, expert rifle shot, and a lawyer."

Even the other military deputies, who had ridden with him were astounded by his credentials. He had never spoken of them and always maintained a quiet attitude.

Levi, taking his cue by the head nod of the sheriff, stood and began. "This is a ticklish situation. We must be very careful on what we legally can do." He pointed to Lieutenant Gardner. "You need to adhere to what I'm saying especially because you're going to be in the eye of the storm.

"We are going to serve a 'subpoena' on the Purvis brothers telling them to come to a hearing at the Trustee's office at eight in the morning. We also will hand the Purvis brothers a 'subpoena ducestecum' asking that they bring with them the books dealing with the purchase of cattle and all financial records.

"Lieutenant, you can escort a member of Sheriff' Nelson's staff out there but you yourself cannot administer this 'subpoena.' It is beyond what you can legally do. Especially since this area is under the command of General Weyland.

"You (meaning the lieutenant) must stay back after escorting the deputy out there and let him do all the talking. If the Purvis brothers react in a negative way, you can do nothing." He held up a finger, "Unless they fire on you."

Levi continued to talk. "This deputy cannot be any of the Federal men who are on Sheriff Buchanan's staff nor the sheriff himself. We are legally soldiers just like Lieutenant Gardner and his troopers.

"It should not be John Johnson, Russell Johnson nor Seth Johnson or Harley Rawlins since they would be viewed as inflammatory. That leaves Sheriff Nelson or Big Willard.

"These two-men are the only ones who are not affiliated with the Federal government nor are considered inflammatory."

Levi looked at the sheriff indicating that he had finished and then sat down on his bale of hay.

Sheriff Buchanan looked over the thoughtful faces. "The Purvis brothers are not going to like getting these summonses. They are going to kick and fuss and moan.

"This will probably push them to the breaking point and that is what we are counting on." He pulled his pipe out and packed it down and struck a match and let it sizzle. He languidly shook his match and not finding a place to toss it reluctantly put it in his shirt pocket, which brought a few needed chuckles. "Here's what I forecast. The Lieutenant will lead Big Willard out to their ranch as a show of force." He puffed and continued, "He has no idea that the troopers are handcuffed so to speak. We know that but Bill Purvis don't know that.

"Bill Purvis will accept these summonses. When Big Willard and the troopers leave, he'll throw a fit and get madder. I guarantee he will because I have another document that Sheriff Nelson and I have drawn up that will really singe his backside." A stiff smile spread across his face. "I would imagine tonight around three-in-the-morning we can expect a violent wakeup call from the Purvis brothers.

"I suggest that all of you allow yourselves to two-beers and quit. You are all professionals. You are the most talented group of men I've ever worked with. So, don't be foolish and mess up all this praising I've been heaping on you."

"After leaving here, go to Sheriff Nelson's office and pick up your assignments. They'll tell you when to get up in the morning and where you are to hide and what weapons you need and rounds."

The sheriff puffed some more and concluded, "Are there any questions?" He looked over the group of capable men. He did not get a question. "Have a good day and you are dismissed."

Sheriff Buchanan walked up to Big Willard and handed him three-legal documents. They were official looking and had been prepared by Levi Brown. "Here are the two 'subpoenas' and the one 'subpoena ducestecum.'"

Big Willard nodded, "You think Bill Purvis will soil his britches when the troopers ride in"

Sheriff Buchanan sighed, "I don't know, but if he does I sure in the world would make a quick exit, I'll guarantee you that."

Big Willard gave a hearty chuckle and turned and followed the lieutenant out the maw of the stable.

Sheriff Buchanan turned and saw John huddled with his group near the back entrance. He walked to him and placed his arm on his shoulder. He looked into the faces of Harley, Seth, and Russell as he deliberated his words. "I know this has to be tough on you boys to restrain yourselves like you have, but that's why this is going to work." He sighed, "We've come this far. Let's finish this thing right."

John inhaled and nodded affirmatively. "You're right on two-counts. It's not easy controlling myself." John pointed at his friends. "And it's not easy for them. But I gave my word and I would abide by the law and I'll keep my word." John grimly smiled at the sheriff and continued, "The second-reason is that you're right. I've never been around this many talented men in all my life."

John turned and looked at the deputies dutifully and professionally checking weapons and studying a map of the town that had been hastily drawn by the ever-talented Levi Brown.

The sheriff removed his arm slowly from John's shoulder and

shook hands with all his crew. "You boys had better get some food in you and a couple of beers. Tonight's going to be a barn burner."

As he walked away, Russell looked at John and asked, "Do you really think the Purvis brothers will hit town tonight?"

John studied and stayed silent for a long time. He turned to Russell in particular, although his whole crew was listening. "I forgot a to mention one other reason why I have had some self-possession." He looked at their inquiring faces. He slowly raised his hand and pointed at the back of Sheriff Buchanan. "Him."

Harley added, "You know between Sheriff Buchanan and Sheriff Nelson there's a lot wisdom there."

Russell pulled his .36 out and checked it. "I think what both of you're saying is that the Purvis brothers are goin' to hit town tonight."

There was a community smile as they broke their huddle.

Bill and Michael Purvis were looking a lot of tracks on a side road that took a dip into a shallow dry wash. They had several of their ranch-hands down investigating. Red Wind, an Osage Indian, was the expert tracker in the county and he observed from his horse.

Michael looked at Red Wind's wrinkled-coppery face. Red Wind, it appears to me that there were at least twelve or thirteen riders here."

The two-Rocking P riders, who had knelt down investigating the tracks, looked up at the heavily lidded eyes of the tracker. They thought there were more riders than Michael had guessed.

Red Wind's inscrutable expression betrayed a twinkle in his eyes. "No, Michael, three-riders and one other rider who joined them later. They are fooling you. Those riders," he paused and pointed toward a cluster of mesquite trees a half-a-mile away. "Would ride in that direction and would return riding over their exit tracks. Making you think they were many."

Bill Purvis shook his head. "This is the work of those damned deputies."

Bill flipped a five-dollar gold piece to the wizened old Indian. "Thanks, Red Wind."

As the Rocking P riders mounted up to join Michael and Bill. They caught sight of a cloud of dust coming from another road that led to the junction. It was Java and his crew. Bill tilted his hat up with his index finger and watched them thunder down the road.

Java caught sight of Bill, and he and his men forgot the road and cut across the tawny sand in a short cut.

As Java's men pulled up around him in a swarm of dust, Bill's eyes were moving to each face but in particularly Java's to ascertain the cause of this mass exodus from town.

Java did not give him a chance to ask. He gave Bill a quick rundown of Sheriff Nelson riding into town with a string of deputies and troopers. He explained how they had cordoned off the Trustee's office and had secured the sheriff's office. When he got to the part where John Johnson had faced down Latigo Wilson, Bill Purvis exploded. His face turned several shades of red and purple before he spoke.

"Java, I've got several things to ask you, but this one in particular. "Why did all of you leave town?" If you wanted my advice couldn't you have stayed at the saloon and sent a rider or even two riders?"

Bill waved his arms around and said, "You brought the whole crew!"

Java said, "I thought if I stayed in town we would have a shootout with those troopers."

Bill's exploded in anger. "I want every damned one of you to get to the ranch house and stay there."

Java and his men, cowed by the harsh words, rode dejectedly away. They rode into the ranch yard and dismounted soberly awaiting more verbal lashings.

Bill and Michael rode into the ranch yard and ignored them. Java, usually in on the private talks, was left out this time. He sat humiliated on the ground next to a fence post. He watched the two-Purvis brothers climb the steps and enter the house.

Java was still sitting a half-hour later when he heard horses coming down the ranch road. He spit out the weed he had in his mouth and looked through the slats of the fence. He stood in an alarming posture when he saw the troopers move down the road.

He swung his face around to see if there was a reaction from the ranch house. There was. The hulking Monk Danielson came out first followed by Bill and Michael Purvis. Several of the Mexican house servants could be seen peering out the windows.

Java's eyes moved back to the troopers who moved down the road in perfect formation. He noticed riding next to the officer in-charge was a man wearing a derby hat with enormous shoulders.

The soldiers suddenly pulled up just before entering the yard. But the man with the huge shoulders and chest kept riding. He rode up to the hitching rail and sat there on his mount and looking at the principals on the porch.

Monk Danielson, the powerfully built bodyguard of Bill Travis, eyed Big Willard. He recognized immediately the implicit threat of this man. Big Willard also took in Monk. They both appraised the other. They became instant adversaries.

Bill Purvis walked hesitantly down the steps with his eyes on the distant troopers. He looked up sharply at Big Willard. "Who in the hell are you and what're you doing on my property?"

Big Willard answered coolly. "My name is Deputy Big Willard and I am here to give you some 'subpoenas.'" He paused dramatically and then said rather pointedly, "one for each of you two-birds."

Bill Purvis walked closer and peered up at the looming figure. He gratingly asked, "What kind of name is Big Willard?" He looked at the big brawler for a second and then harked up some spit and spat to the side in contempt'

Big Willard ignored the obvious insult and smiled benignly back at him. Well, it's a name that's not in trouble with the law."

He paused and added, "I am not guilty of murder or stealing land that does not belong to me."

Bill Purvis ignored that remark and looked at the summonses that Big Willard held in his hand. "Who has the authority to give me 'subpoenas'?"

"The sheriff of Bailey County." Big Willard paused and looked at his fingernails. He took his time in answering as he looked at his cuticles. "He also is the justice of the peace." Big Willard's voice then took on an edge. "Just take the damn things."

Monk Danielson made a threatening move down the steps but was held back by the hand of Bill Travis. Bill irately looked back up at Big Willard. Bill's face took on a sneer. "You may be a big and tough man wherever you came from but you haven't met Monk yet."

Big Willard smiled broadly at Monk. "No, we haven't met, but I sure intend to rectify that soon. I have a special way to greet birds like him."

Monk made throaty noises.

Again Bill held up his hand to avoid a confrontation. He looked at the papers. "I don't recognize the authority of Sheriff Nelson and his judgeship."

Big Willard shrugged and answered, "It doesn't matter whether you do or not." He smiled menacingly at Bill Purvis and at Monk Danielson. His voice took a higher register when he punctuated the air with these words. "We do."

Michael walked down the steps and joined his brother. He saw the 'subpoenas' in Big Willard's hand but his eyes went to the oversized document sticking conspicuously from Big Willard's coat pocket.

Michael asked, "What's that?"

Big Willard acted surprised but both Bill and Michael could tell he was 'messing' with them. He raised his eyebrows as though he had made a bad oversight. It was obvious that he was acting.

He dramatically pulled the paper out of his pocket and read. "This document reads as follows: If the two-aforementioned subjects," Big Willard nodded at the two-brothers, "That would be you." He grinned an imperious smile at them but continued, "Ignore the 'subpoenas' and fail to show up for the hearing tomorrow at eight at the Bailey County Trustee's office, you will be charged with contempt and be found guilty by default of the charges leveled against you and you will be considered 'outlaws' by the Bailey County authorities." He pulled the subpoena ducestecum from his pocket and dropped it to the ground. "It orders you to bring your ledger books with you too. So, I would take some time and go get those books and doctor them up some before the sheriff and the commission sees them."

Bill Purvis was livid. His whole body trembled. He snatched the 'subpoenas' from Big Willard's hand and tore them up. He kept grinding them and ripping them. He pointed up at Big Willard and through gritted teeth seethed these words. "I got a 'subpoena' for you, big man, you and those damned troopers have five-minutes to get out of my yard." He paused and shook his finger at Big Willard in a waggling, out-of-control way. "You in particular will pay for your insolence."

Big Willard ignored Bill's ranting and let his eyes fall on Monk Danielson. This is what really motivated Big Willard. Big Willard, who had been in innumerable fights, knew what buttons to push. Big Willard had mentally cut out Bill Purvis who stood in Big Willard's mind just soundlessly making black mouth shapes with occasional glimpses of tongue and teeth. His eyes bored into Monk's and Monk could sense his challenge.

Big Willard broke off his stare and started hearing again the tail end of Bill's cussing. He gave Monk another hard-challenging glower and then Big Willard abruptly turned his horse during one of Bill's cussing rampages and rode to the troopers.

Bill Purvis was still cussing and kicking at the shreds of

'subpoenas' at his feet. He shouted curses on Big Willard and the troopers who turned wordlessly and rode away in perfect formation.

In Baileysboro, the citizens had returned to the streets. It was almost a celebration. Buckboards were racing into town from the out skirting ranches to validate that the Purvis brothers no longer controlled the town. Merchants, customers, ranchers, townsmen were all shaking hands with Sheriff Nelson and the efficient deputies which seemed omnipresent. The saloon was filled with happy people again.

But at the Purvis Mercantile Store, Ferlin Henderson was not happy. The customers were not coming into the store and he imagined it was a tacit boycott of sorts. Ferlin, a skinny man, with a handlebar mustache that was out of control watched the streets through his store window with anxious but also fearful eyes.

Sheriff Buchanan and Sheriff Nelson had it fixed that he would overhear a bogus conversation that would implicate the troopers and deputies. He would 'accidentally' overhear their secretive plans of attacking and laying siege to the Purvis ranch at ten o'clock the following morning.

Sure enough the merchant did overhear the bogus conversation in the corner of his store. Ferlin, who owed his money and success to Bill Purvis, was chomping at the bits to get this information to the Purvis brothers as soon as possible.

He asked his wife, Irene, a dumpy lady with multiple chins, if she would watch his empty store while he got his buckboard and made a surreptitious trip to his boss' ranch.

When he sneaked out the door and made his way to his backyard shed, Levi Brown, who was watching him from a hiding place grinned. He felt confident that his plan was working.

As Ferlin slapped the reins and gave a cursory backwards glance, Levi flashed a mirror signal to one of the other deputies and this information was rushed to the two-sheriffs.

Bill Purvis had composed himself since his earlier fit of rage. He sat stolidly behind his desk. A large bourbon bottle sat prominently in the middle of it. He had a stiff slug and sat deciding on the best course of action. Seated in front of him were Michael and Java. The upbraided Java, whose past sins were now forgotten in the greater drama of things, sat soberly mulling over how he could get retrieve his self worth to the Purvis brothers.

Bill took another drink of bourbon and looked intently at the map of the town sprawled out on his desk. "I'm not sure if we should raid the town or let this play out." He remarked.

Michael and Java wanted to raid the town and rid it of the unwanted deputies and troopers. Michael said, "These damned deputies are a pestilence and they sure don't act like deputies I've ever seen."

Bill Purvis held up his hand to interrupt. "They aren't like any deputies you have ever seen. They are Union soldiers and that is the irony of it all."

They sat and mulled over several plans and wavered on most of them. Carlos, the Mexican butler, tentatively got Bill Purvis' attention from the hallway. Bill looked up with a 'what's the matter look.'

Carlos looked troubled. Bill went to him and Carlos made a motion with his head indicating that someone wanted to talk with him. Bill's eyes moved beyond him to see a sweating Ferlin Henderson. Ferlin looked distraught standing in the shadows of the hall. Bill could see he was busting a gut to tell him something. He grabbed Ferlin by the elbow and hustled him into a small side room. As soon as he shut the door behind him, Ferlin began to spill his information almost without pausing.

Bill sat and listened and it all made sense but he wondered aloud how that they could be so careless to allow Ferlin to overhear. When he posed that question to the shaken store merchant, Ferlin seemed deeply offended that he could be so easily fooled. He explained that it was two-deputies talking in the corner of the store and that it appeared to him as though they were trying hard to keep their voices low. But he heard enough to know the gist of their plan.

Bill's eyes burned angrily. His chest was full of outrage that his ranch could be put to a siege and that he could be pursued as an outlaw. He slammed his fist on the table. His normal suspicion of a setup and receiving misleading information was blinded by his fury. His thoughts were muddled as he remembered the grinning and insolent Big Willard.

He kept his composure enough to dismiss Ferlin. He did not want to reveal his own plans, so he tried to placate the upset store manager with 'we will look into words.' He walked him to the front door and tried to reassure him as he gave him a quick 'goodbye.' He watched Ferlin ride away and Bill stood on the porch until he was out of sight. He could stand his simmering anger no longer. He had had enough. He socked his gloved fist into his open gloved making a definitive leather sound as he walked back to his brother and Java,

He walked back into the meeting saying these words, "Hell yes, we'll hit the town tonight. I want every single deputy and trooper shot to blazes. I'll fix it that the military authorities here in Texas will blame that idiot Bushrod Elkins." His neck was lined in blue, rage veins. "A bunch of hicks from Arkansas taking me on. I'll see the Union boys here in Texas chew their asses before this is over with."

That brought a laugh from Michael. He slapped his brother on the shoulder and said, "That's my brother talking."

Java took a sip of bourbon and shouted," And we'll do it without Latigo Wilson." That brought some real hee-haws.

# CHAPTER TEN

IT WAS A QUARTER-MOON. IT was two-thirty in the morning. Michael Purvis was moving with fourteen-men across the mesquite dotted plain. The moon's wan light extended the eerie shadows of the crooked mesquite tree limbs.

There was little noise. Each man's face was tight and filled with anxiety. All the momentum had been with John Lee Johnson and his men up to this time. All those deputies and troopers seemed to have the upper hand, but the Purvis ranch hands were determined to get back the edge.

They moved through the spooky green-moonlight and made their way around to the south entrance of town near Chili's livery stable.

Java's group, the other attacking party, had twenty-men including Monk Danielson who was pulling a grulla packhorse. The packhorse had two-oversized canvas bags filled with cans of coal oil and rags.

They were headed for the north entrance of town where the Trustee's office was. The objective was to trap the deputies and troopers in the middle and squeeze them with no means of escape. They had the firepower and the numbers. They were ready to go from building to building systematically destroying the enemy. Each man had at least one-rifle and one holstered weapon and one stuck in the belt. Another motivating factor, they would be richly compensated. Bill Purvis was putting everything on the line.

Michael's group had farther to go than Java's so they had synchronized their watches when the two-groups split on their separate responsibilities. Michael was to attack the sheriff's office and work his way to the Trustee's office. Whereas Java was start at the opposite end and work his way to the jail.

Michael's group stayed well north of the arroyo that ran behind the sheriff's office. Even by the moonlight, his men could see the blobby shapes of the backsides of buildings. They could hear the desultory barking of dogs. But there were no other sounds.

As they began to make the bend and head toward Chili's stable, the tension grew thicker. Their own sounds became more magnified: the hooves swishing sand, the occasional blowing of a horse and the jingle of bridles, the leathery sounds of saddles.

They had every confidence that the deputies would be caught napping. But each man knew there was going to be bloodshed and not all of it would be the military men.

When they did fully make the bend and faced the main street of town. Michael spaced them quietly using his .44 as a pointer.

Michael glanced at the black, yawning entrance of the livery stable but saw no one there. His eyes then moved to the jail on the right side of the street. There was a dull, smoky-yellow light against one isolated window. The other window was pitch black.

He pulled his watch out and held up it to catch the moonlight. He could see he had an extra minute. He looked at down at his men. They were in two-groups of seven lined up in two-lines. Each line fully covered the width of the street.

He quietly snapped his pocket watch and put it away and then he rode out in front of the two-lines and slowly motioned for them to follow him.

The hollow sounds of hooves seemed to reverberate in the

street. As they passed each building, their eyes strained attempting to see. Although things looked normal enough, the singular lack of noise was disquieting. Rain barrels in alleys were solitary but there were no foreign shapes behind them. The doorways and windows were Bible black and blank. It was graveyard quiet.

The viridescent moonlight and the one-yellow, oily, window light exposed the silly ass grin on Michael's face but also the tension and excitement around his eyes. He pulled his .44 from his holster and aimed at the light. He fired a roaring round into the sheriff's office and the sound of crashing glass erupted.

His men were leveling their weapons to fire at the door and windows when all hell broke loose. Muzzle flashes of Spencer rifles ripped the night air with orange and yellow flumes. Michael whirled his head and saw shots coming from under the buildings in stoop places, from under porches, from darkened rooftops, from alleys, and store buildings. It was as though he opened a Pandora's box filled with fireworks.

Bullets were zinging and whistling and zipping the air and his men were taking serious hits. The sounds of thud and slunk were heard all around him. He turned in panic. He yelled at his men to fire. They began to fire at the muzzle flashes but the enfilading gunfire was too much. It was like a maddening sleet of lead balls.

Michael's eyes widened, when he saw 'All-Night' Roy take three immediate slugs. Roy twisted with the force of the shots. His body was rocked this way and that way. He gurgled in pain and shock. He fell awkwardly from his saddle raising a dust cloud puff. Michael ducked his head and hugged his horse. He looked around him and there were more empty saddles than filled ones. He cussed his luck and yanked his horse's neck around violently throwing his horse's mouth foam in a spray. He gave the spurs to his horse and galloped down the street leaving Chili's Livery far behind.

Jaybird Roberts and Fuzzy Williams saw him leave and both in anger started to fire at him for his cowardice but they both holstered and rode down an alley past a startled deputy. They

319

were not sure where they were going, but they sure did not want to be late.

When Michael, initially, shot the first shot at the dim light in the office window, it was Seth, who had jumped up from his prone position in the alley with a lamp blackened face. He fired three-consecutive shots that rocked 'All-Night' Roy. He cussed when 'All-Night' Roy fell because he wanted to shoot him some more.

It was Russell and two-deputies who came from the black interior of the livery stable and began peppering the Purvis raiders from the rear.

Sheriff Buchanan and Levi Brown had devised the angles to do the most damage and it had certainly taken its toll on the harried Purvis riders. The Purvis riders could find no respite, no avenue of escape.

The deputies kept up the damaging bombardment until only two-riders survived other than the three who escaped. These two-riders threw up their hands and looked around with shell-shocked faces. Their eyes were wide in total astonishment at their unexpected predicament. They looked at their comrades lying dead in all manner of contortions.

Down the street, Java's men passed the dress shop on their left and a feed store on their right. They had seen but not paid any particular notice to the heavy stacks of burlap bags of cattle feed that were columned on both sides of the street, but when the shooting started down at the jail, the trailing riders took note over the shoulders that the bags of feed were now strewn across the street with Spencer rifles aimed over the tops.

Java's eyes widened when he looked down the street and saw Michael's men being rocked by bleaching gunshots that seemed to come from every weird angle and shadow.

Java turned his horse viciously and shouted, "Trap."

But it was too late. The troopers, at the end of the street effectively blocking his exit, began a steady barrage of shots.

John and Harley boldly exited the front door of the vacant building next to the Trustee's office and began a salvo of gunfire.

Java's fretful eyes moved behind him and over at the two-men vexing him from under the dark shadows of the sloping porch of the empty building. He screamed at his men to fire. They began firing back and the windows of the Trustee's office were shattered.

The Purvis riders were returning fire tit-for-tat until Sheriff Buchanan and Sheriff Nelson and the remaining deputies cut loose from the other side of the street. The sudden crescendo of gunfire sounded like heavy holiday firecrackers.

This heavy crossfire was dropping riders like horse turds. Java's mouth opened in exasperation and he decided to ride down the alley between the empty building and the Trustee's office. He thundered down the alley, hugging close to his saddle, he fired a single round at John and Harley as he passed by. He knew the attack on the deputies was an abject failure, but he still had his pride and if he could bring down John Johnson he could still salvage something from the raid.

He jumped from his horse and stealthily made his way back up the alley shadowed by the two building to the back door of the vacant building. He tried the door and it opened easily and he blindly made his way through this back room and to the door that would access his way to the front room and then the porch. He gritted his teeth in anger and slid along the walls using his gloved left-hand as his guide.

When he found the doorway that would lead him to the front room, he slid his gloved hand around the door facing and then pushed his left boot through. As he began to ease his whole body sideways into the darkened room, he was unexpectedly grabbed by his shirt and pulled through roughly.

Java felt like a pair of women's underwear in a cyclone. He was whirled around roughly. Next he saw a fist coming from the darkness that felt like a freight train when it collided with his chin.

As Java fought through unconsciousness, he heard John say, "You didn't really think it was going to be that easy did you?"

While this was going on, Monk Danielson had worked his way around the back of the Trustee's office and was dousing the back porch with profuse shots of coal oil. He had emptied one can and was reaching for another when he heard a voice say, "I hate a fire bug."

He whirled, and there in the darkness, he saw the large man with the derby hat. Monk uttered, "You."

Big Willard walked closer and smiled at Monk. Big Willard's eyes cut down at Monk's gun belt and his gleaming .44. He looked back up at the face of the smiling Monk.

Monk looked down at Big Willard's holster and his .44. They wordlessly unbuckled their holsters and tossed them aside,

Monk looked at Big Willard curiously and said, "You know I'm close to thirty and you're the only man in my life that has had the guts to brace me. I think I like that."

Big Willard smiled, "Soon as I saw you, I knew we needed to get this over with." Big Willard smiled broadly. "There can only be one hoss, you know?"

Monk looked down at their weapons. "When I work you over, you ain't going to go for your weapon are you?"

Big Willard shook his head 'no.' He looked back at Monk, "You?"

Monk shook his head 'no.' " I've killed big men, little men, fat men and slim men but I ain't ever cheated."

Big Willard nodded and said, "Let's get the show on the road."

Monk nodded and threw up his large fists. He charged in with straight hard jabs.

Big Willard countered most of those and threw back some straight jabs.

They circled each other like two large behemoths. Monk

charged in again and threw some scorching hooks and landed some hard body shots.

He smiled and Big Willard smiled back. "You did well, Monk, but that ain't good enough."

Big Willard slipped under a right hook and landed a whopping body shot. Monk smiled and said, "That one had some zap to it." But if Monk felt pain, he did not admit it.

They kept circling and looking for open shots. Monk decided to go for broke; he threw a hard punch that landed solidly off the noggin of Big Willard that sounded like billiard balls breaking.

Big Willard shook it off and kept circling and then he threw a looping right over Monk's jab and nailed him hard in the temple.

Monk growled in anger and he threw rights and lefts and they were coming at different angles.

Big Willard caught some of those on the top of his head and shoulders. He fired an uppercut that stunned Monk and sent him wheeling backwards. Big Willard kept moving forward and for the first-time in Monk's life he was back-pedaling.

Monk caught Big Willard with two-quick punches to the face that stung.

Big Willard caught several more stiff jabs but threw his overhand right that nailed Monk in the nose and blood spattered around his face like a flattened tomato.

Monk's hand went up to his nose and saw the blood. He nodded admirably at Big Willard, "I'll say one thing for you, Big Willard, you're one tough son-of-a-bitch."

Big Willard smiled and said, "You're not so bad yourself."

When the last gunshot sounded in the street, Big Willard cocked his head to one-side and held up his hand for Monk to wait a second.

Monk looked at him mystified. "What is it?"

Big Willard doubled up his fists again and said, "The shooting's stopped."

Monk said, " So?"

Big Willard said matter-of-factly, "Well, that means I got to knock you out now."

Monk dropped his fists. "I ain't ever been knocked out before."

"Well, you're going to be."

Monk sighed and said, "Oh, hell, I surrender."

Monk picked up his gun belt and handed it to Big Willard and asked for a handkerchief.

Big Willard accepted his holster and handed Monk a handkerchief. They walked down the alley nonchalantly.

Monk said, "You know you ain't half bad."

Big Willard said, "If I buy this saloon here in town, maybe I can pay your bail and show you how to make some good money."

The rest of the late night and still even at dawn, the two-sheriffs, the deputies and the troopers laid the dead bodies of the Purvis ranch hands in front of the jail in the street. The surviving Purvis riders were taken to jail and were herded into the crowded cells.

The town doctor, Doctor McClain, worked diligently going from man to man. He stitched and sterilized the best he could. He enlisted the efforts of several townsmen to serve as his assistants. Levi Brown supervised the whole affair of rounding up the Purvis outfit. He sent the hale and hearty ones to jail and put up the wounded Purvis gang in a empty building that served as a field hospital. Levi ran an efficient system and there were no escapes, nor did anyone go untreated. Even the burials were systemized.

The news of the wild shootout was quickly circulated and townsmen and local country residents quickly appeared to look and marvel at what had transpired.

Sheriff Nelson was answering questions fielded by many curious and excited citizens. After he had talked as much as he felt was necessary, he called Sheriff Buchanan aside. "When it gets eight o'clock, let's get some men and go arrest Bill Purvis."

Sheriff Buchanan opened his watch and looked at the time it was six o'clock. "What about Michael Purvis?"

Sheriff Nelson inhaled and looked at the road leading out of town that went by the livery stable. "He not only got away but he's got a sizeable jump on us, but maybe we can track him down."

Sheriff Buchanan asked, "Do you have any leads?"

"He and his brother used to go hunting just south of here. It's about twenty-miles or so. There's an adobe hut there and he most likely will hide out there for a while." He paused with a twinkle in his eye and added. "He don't have many options."

Levi Brown, who was standing close by picked up on Sheriff Nelson's comments. He began running his hand under his chin and thought. His eyes were narrowed as he looked in the direction in which Michael had fled.

Sheriff Buchanan who was turning his head to look down the street caught the perplexed look in the talented deputy's face. "Anything you want to say, deputy?"

Levi exhaled and nodded, "Yeah, last night, Henry Johnson and Kiowa Bob were in the saloon and they were taking some shots at the Purvis bunch. When Michael skedaddled out of town they took off after him." He looked pained as he took a quick glance across the street at John and his men. "It's been on my mind but I just hadn't the opportunity to tell John."

The sheriff sighed, "We have to tell him."

The two-sheriffs and Levi walked across and informed John what had happened. John was confounded by the information. He knew he had to honor his pledge to the general, colonel and sheriff that he would not let his emotions entangle him in a personal vendetta but he also was duty bound by familial loyalty.

Sheriff Buchanan could see his dilemma and offered this sage advice. "John, no one is asking that you stay in town and not be involved in this final mop up. "As soon as it is eight o'clock, Sheriff Nelson is going after Bill Purvis. Me and half of the deputies will be going with him." He thoughtfully paused and said, "I reckon you can go if you will allow yourself to be passive."

The sheriff getting no response from John, continued, "Levi will take the other half and go after Michael. Russell, Seth and Harley can go with them. We will try and head off your uncle and Kiowa Bob."

John looked troubled. He pulled out his pocket watch and caught the time and sat down on the edge of the boardwalk. Soon Harley and Russell joined him. He sat gloomily staring off into space. He was battling his emotions. He wanted to do as the sheriff had advised but it sure was hell going against his nature.

Seth, catching the distressed look in John's face, knew the big man was worried about his Uncle Henry. He knew John was saddled with the burden of doing nothing at all, or lose all he had gained by impulsive action. Thus Seth decided to act for him. He knew he had not been given that charge by the sheriffs. But he felt he owed it to John.

He got up causally and stole away as nonchalantly as he could. He moved building by building until he found his pinto and mounted up. He checked his .44's. He then gave his horse his head and galloped down the south road.

He knew that Uncle Henry and Kiowa Bob had a three-hour start but he could read the signs well on the sand road. He kept a steady pace.

Michael rode his big sorrel hard down the sand covered road. His horse was pounding the road and sending billowing clouds of dust behind him. He knew his big horse was lathering and beginning to weaken badly.

Knowing his pace was grueling, he pulled up in a bosk of mesquite and dismounted. He took some canteen water and poured into his hat and let his horse slurp it.

As he watched down the road for his pursuers, many thoughts were going through his mind. He thought of the phrase 'How the Mighty Have Fallen.' He licked his lips and wondered about his brother and how he was faring. Bill had always been the one who was resourceful. He was the one who had the answers. It bothered him that his brother would be waiting for men to return who would never return. It was difficult to perceive that his brother would be on the run.

He searched in his pockets and found about fifty-dollars and that was all he had between him and wherever in hell he was going.

He knew the deputies would soon be coming and hounding him. Those damned deputies that seemed to presage Bill's every move and then trump it. He knew that he and his brother were through. They had been at the top of the world and now they were at the bottom of it.

He poured more water in his hat and let his horse drink. When the horse finished, he glanced once more down the hot road and saw puffs of dust.

He decided to cut across the plains and take his chances on gopher holes. He mounted and turned off the road and cut across the wind swept plain strewn with gypsum weed and mesquite.

One-hour later he came upon the adobe hut that he had used so many times for hunting. It had a stream behind the building and he watered his horse and got a fresh canteen of water and then led his horse into the hut and tied him to a handle on the stove. He went to the open window and placed his Sharps beside it and then checked his .44. He wished he had some men with him. For the first time he realized how much he had depended on money and power. For the first time in his life he felt stripped and powerless. It was an empty and demoralizing feeling. He thought of John Johnson, and how he had brought him to this station in life. He hated the man. If he lived, he would kill him or die trying.

His thoughts were interrupted by a sudden shadowy figure moving from one mesquite tree to another. He lifted his Sharps and fired a roaring shot that seemed to reverberate across the empty horizon.

The shot tore a chunk of bark off the tree and the ricochet whined drearily. He loaded his Sharps and he felt sweat begin to form on his forehead.

As he put his finger in the trigger guard and began lifting the rifle, a booming report of a .44 was heard and debris of adobe splintered on the edge of the window aperture.

Michael ducked and hunkered down by the window. He licked his lips and took a few furtive glances out the opening. His eyebrows moved up when he thought he heard Henry Johnson's voice. He surmised the other man had to be Kiowa Bob.

This cat and mouse game continued for hours. One shot by Michael followed by several by his two-adversaries.

Michael pulled his pocket watch out and checked the time. It was ten-fifty one. He knew if these two-men kept him bottled up the deputies would arrive soon and he would be sewn up.

As he sat on his haunches against the wall next to the window, he pulled his .44 out and checked his loads. He decided he would get on his horse and just ride out blazing and take his chances. Hell, one was an old man and the other way past his prime.

He scooted across the floor as a slug went through the window and took out a lump of adobe in the back wall. His horse nickered nervously.

He stood quickly and booted his rifle and jumped into the saddle and rode out. He saw Henry Johnson stand from his hiding place and Michael fired a quick shot that nailed him. Henry staggered and fired but the shot whizzed over Michael's head.

Kiowa Bob yelled curses on Michael as he pulled his Colt from his holster and fired. The shot hit Michael flush on the top of his shoulder and blood splattered.

Michael pulled up sending a spray of sand and dust. He cussed and turned his mount and took aim. He fired a roaring round and the gun barrel belched an orange flame. The slug caught Kiowa Bob in the side and he twirled and collapsed on the sand.

Michael looked to his left and saw Henry Johnson supine on

the sand. He had a crimson splotch on his chest. He looked back quickly to Kiowa Bob who was still moving and attempting to stand. Michael grinned callously and leveled his weapon. Before he could pull the trigger, he heard a shot and felt the furrow of air as a shot zipped by.

He pulled his eyes off Kiowa Bob and looked at the rider headed toward him with an outstretched pistol. Michael gave a disdainful look at the struggling Kiowa Bob and then decided to duel it out with the man on the pinto.

Michael grinned even in pain. He gigged his horse and he rode straight at the interloper. Both Michael and Seth had their pistols out and were riding toward each other in an intense gallop.

They were on a direct course. Each horse was chuffing. Each rider was aiming. The sound of desperate horse hooves churning sand and dirt pervaded the scene. They fired simultaneously. Seth was hit high in the chest and he lurched in the saddle. He lifted the pistol with both hands and blasted another two-shots. One missed and the other caught Michael in the throat.

Seth fell unconscious from his horse to the sand. Michael rode for about thirty more feet and then pulled up. His hands were clutching at his throat.

Michael reached for his canteen and tried to drink away the pain but there was no relief. He looked at the unmoving Seth who was a mere dark-silhouette in the dust. He spat blood and dismounted falling to his knees. His horse shied from him smelling the blood.

Michael put his hand on his throat. He tried to speak but no words came out. He felt the blood gurgling and he reached for his handkerchief and poured canteen water on it. He dabbed at the poker hot wound. He shook his head in frustration and began knee-walking to his horse,

As he reached for the stirrup of his skittish horse, he felt a rough hand on his shoulder. He turned slowly; his eyes, occluded momentarily by the bright sunlight made out a dim and menacing shadow. His eyes and mouth widened when he focused in on the pitiless eyes of Kiowa Bob.

Michael's eyes soon lowered to Kiowa Bob's moving hand. He watched in terror as the half-breed pulled out his knife. He felt Kiowa Bob roughly grab him by the back of the head. He gurgled as the sharp cutting edge scraped against his scalp. Michael's mouth was filled with blood and rivulets of gore streamed down his face. Michael's eyes widened. His eyeballs were distended. The excruciating pain caused him to jerk and convulse. He reached out from his body with wiggling fingers begging for mercy. He then saw Kiowa Bob dangle his bloody scalp before his eyes. Michael shook his head 'no' not believing his body's defilement. Michael wailed in a primal agony. Kiowa Bob looked down the road where his dead friend lay. He shouted in Kiowa and then savagely cut Michael's throat.

At ten o'clock, Bill Purvis knew something bad wrong had happened. His eyes moved agitatedly beneath furrowed eyebrows. He ran his hand over his whisker-stubble. He looked anxiously for his riders --any rider to come and tell him that he had won or lost. But there were no riders. There was no noise. Only the greasy West Texas sun which beat down on him from a white sky.

He stood for a good while gazing down the road. He finally saw two-horsemen headed his way. He swallowed and pushed his hat up with his thumb and pulled his rifle up and held it across his chest. He felt like he recognized Jaybird Roberts and Fuzzy Williams.

He could see that it was them eventually.

Jaybird and Fuzzy rode close to the porch. Bill walked to the edge of it and peered down at them and asked authoritatively, "Where is everybody?"

Jaybird looked at Fuzzy., He glanced back up at his former boss. "They ain't coming, Bill."

Bill had never heard Jaybird call him 'Bill' before and he felt the sting of impertinence. He ignored that for the sake of information. "What do you mean they aren't coming back?"

Jaybird snorted, "Well, it's like this. They are either all dead or in jail."

"What about Michael?"

Jaybird shook his head in disdain. "He turned yellow and ran."

Bill grasped the rifle tighter in anger. "You watch your tongue, you dim-witted bastard."

Jaybird turned his horse sideways and looked up Bill. He gave him a contemptuous smile. "Hey, , Bill, if you want to play act and pretend you're still running the county, then go ahead." Jaybird pointed up at him and continued, "You ain't running 'doodly.' If I was you, the only thing I would be running would be for the territory line."

Fuzzy laughed and sneered up Bill.

Bill whirled the rifle around and said, "Get off my ranch. Or I'll kill you where you stand."

Jaybird coolly replied. "You might kill us all right, but it ain't your ranch any longer. All this belongs to John Lee Johnson."

Jaybird and Fuzzy rode away with mocking laughter trailing over their shoulders.

Bill's eyes bulged. He looked down the road and over at the two jackanapes pulling into the bunkhouse.

Bill whirled around and went traipsing into his study. He put on his gun belt and then walked into the hallway and yelled for Carlos the house servant. Getting no answer, he walked to the kitchen. His eyes widened when he saw no cook. He walked briskly to the backdoor and saw his all his Mexican help walking in the far distance with burros.

His rolled his eyes to their edges and he turned rapidly and went to the front porch again. He picked up his Sharps and looked down the empty road.

Jaybird was watching Bill through the dusty panes of the

bunkhouse. He was kneeling on a bunk while his pal was going through everyone's belongings.

Jaybird was talking audibly even though he might as well been talking to himself. "You talk about a worm in hot ashes."

Fuzzy grunted as he opened saddlebags and pulled out anything salvageable.

Jaybird shook his head. "He once paraded around like a peacock telling everyone what to do. He don't look so high and mighty now, I can sure tell you that."

Fuzzy mumbled and knelt down to look under bunks.

"Damn, he's nervous. He's standing there with that rifle like he can hold off John Johnson and all those deputies."

Fuzzy laughed when he found a roll of money. He gave a quick glance at Jaybird while he stashed it in his underwear top and then went back to pilfering more saddlebags.

Jaybird laughed out loud and said, "He keeps going in and out of the house. He's probably looking for someone to boss or order." Jaybird laughed again and said, "By the way, Fuzzy, I saw the money you stashed in your underwear top."

Fuzzy's eyes bulged some but he shrugged and responded, "You don't hold it against me for trying do you?"

Jaybird got up from the bunk and said, "Get all you can get now. We got to get out of here."

They went to their horses and gave a mock military salute to Bill as he frowned at them from the porch. They mounted up and thundered away.

Bill watched their trail dust and almost envied them. If he ran to New Mexico Territory, he had almost as many enemies there as he had in Bailey County. He knew if he surrendered, the citizens that he had run rough shod over would gloat in his fall. He knew he could not stand to see himself debased in front of all those people he had ruled as a tyrant. He shuddered at the thought of being hanged.

He saw the deputies coming down the road. They were followed by a troop of cavalry. He grasped the rifle and then realized he was foolish for brandishing such a weapon and giving them the excuse to kill him.

He placed the rifle against the porch wall and backed into the door opening and then turned and walked briskly to his office.

As he sat down, it dawned on him that this had been the office of Ed Johnson. He looked around at his seat of power one last time. He inhaled and tears glistened in his eyes. He raised his .44 and placed the barrel in his mouth. He trembled briefly and pulled the trigger. His head was partially blown away as he collapsed forward on his desk.

Fifteen-minutes before Bill Purvis had taken his life, Sheriff Buchanan and John were riding side-by-side down the hot road. They were bringing up the rear of the deputies led rightly by Sheriff Nelson. They were positioned between the formation of deputies and the troopers who were bringing up the rear.

They had ridden silently most of the trip but Sheriff Buchanan cut his eyes over at John and said, "I guess you saw Seth take off after your Uncle Henry and Kiowa Bob.

John gave the sheriff a sad smile. "Yeah, I saw him."

"I was surprised you let him."

John thoughtfully nodded. "I could've stopped him I guess, but he's wanting to belong and stopping him might have hurt his feelings."

The sheriff sighed and they rode silently for a few more minutes. "He's "not really your cousin is he?"

John told the sheriff about the night Seth wanted his name changed. When he finished, John added, "He came from nothing and he wants to be something and he might not be a cousin by blood but he sure is by heart."

The sheriff replied, "I understand and appreciate that kind of feeling. It's just that I've heard that Michael is pretty salty with his Colt."

John looked over at the sheriff and said, "I'm worried. I'm

worried about Uncle Henry and Kiowa Bob. They're both old. I'm worried about Seth because he's worth one hundred Michael Purvises on their best day. But I have faith in him. He may not be all that tall but he throws a pretty long shadow."

The sheriff said, "This may be unfair of me to ask you this, but why don't you pull out of this posse and head back to town."

John looked at him squarely. "I'm torn. I can tell you."

"The way you and Russell have handled yourselves in all this is to be commended. The folks around here won't be accusing you of murder or revenge. If Bill Purvis is there we'll arrest him, and if he's not, we'll go after him." He paused and said, "You don't want to be there, John."

John did want to be there but he peeled his horse from the formation and galloped back to Baileysboro. But he did not stop in the town. He kept on riding south following the numerous horse tracks down the hot, sandy road.

He had been in the saddle for four-hours when he met the deputies coming back. He saw Seth and Kiowa Bob being pulled in separate travois. He saw his Uncle Henry and Michael tied over their horses. He dismounted and the deputies stopped for him in respect.

John walked to his uncle and leaned on the body and softly touched his face. He fought tears. Russell dismounted and hugged his cousin. They walked over to see Seth. He was lying seemingly unconscious. John dropped to his knees and placed his hand on Seth's brow. He looked at the bloody wound that was seeping through the field-dress bandage that one of the military deputies had made.

Russell said, "I got to tell you, John, I don't know if he's goin' to make it or not."

John stood up and looked at the small form in the travois. He leaned down and said to the pale face. "Don't "die on me yet. You're going to be a rancher in about a month. Besides that you can't cross the great river yet, you can't sing worth a damn."

They both had to check tears when Seth smiled.

John checked on Kiowa Bob who gave him a peculiar smile and when he passed the scalped corpse of Michael Purvis he understood why he had received that smile.

Deputy Levi Brown gave a heliograph signal to a faraway deputy and who in turn messaged another deputy. The news of Michael's death and Henry Johnson reached Baileysboro fast.

The two-sheriff's had reached town with Bill Purvis' body and they deposited it with Doctor McClain who in turn placed it in his spring cellar on a crude slab.

When the sheriffs and the deputies and troopers heard that Michael Purvis had been killed, there was no celebration. In fact for the most part there was disquietude. The death of Henry Johnson, for the most part, clouded any feeling of success.

Sheriff Nelson turned off from the men assembled outside the Doctor's springhouse and rode to his office along with Big Willard. As they rode along, Big Willard asked him about the possibility of Otis Quigley selling his saloon.

The sheriff said, "You know he's been wanting to go live with his nephew in Amarillo for sometime. Let's just drop in and see what he'd take."

Big Willard said, "If the place is clear and free, I'd give him nine-hundred dollars."

Sheriff Nelson answered, "Otis" don't owe nobody. He probably will ask a thousand, but you can always dicker you know."

They rode in silence for a few minutes and Sheriff Henry gave Big Willard a sidelong look. "He really needs a new toilet."

Big Willard's head swiveled quickly to the sheriff. "A "new toilet!" Big Willard exclaimed. "What in the hell does a new toilet have to do with a sale of a saloon?"

The sheriff was silent for a spell and he answered. "The toilet he's got now is rickety and sometimes blows over."

Big Willard looked strangely at the sheriff and replied, "Listen, I like a good toilet story just like the next fellow, but why are we discussing a damned toilet for. I don't care if his toilet is wobbly or not. I'm just interested in his saloon not his outhouse,"

The sheriff answered, "The Taylor brothers can build you the best damned outhouse in the country for twenty-five dollars. A good two-holer with a foundation."

Big Willard pushed up his derby hat with his thumb and looked at the sheriff out of the corner of his eyes.

The sheriff continued, "Now they could dig you a hole about forty-feet deep too."

Big Willard shook his head. "A skinny man who fell through that hole could end up dead with a drop that deep." He gave a sly look toward the sheriff, "Hell, even a fart would echo."

The sheriff replied, "I never cared for fart jokes." He gave a sly look back at Big Willard. "Skinny men who fall through holes shouldn't be there in the first place."

Big Willard smiled, "Sheriff, if you have a message, I sure in hell am not picking it up?"

"Well, it is like this, Big Willard, the county would pay half for the toilet. The hole is too deep that is true, but not if the two-bodies of the Purvis brothers were buried down there and covered up with about five-feet of dirt."

As Big Willard rocked along with the rhythm of his horse, he dryly asked, "What about the smell?"

Sheriff Nelson replied, "A man or woman who goes to the toilet to inhale needs to be in an institution."

Big Willard said, "If you can get Otis to sell at nine-hundred dollars, I'll gladly take you up on your offer to build that new toilet."

Sheriff Nelson looked at Big Willard and smiled, "And it will be our secret where the final resting place of the Purvis brothers is."

Big Willard sighed and nodded, "Yeah, and those damned Taylor brothers."

They rode along further and Big Willard asked, "Now I want to ask you something else that does not deal with two-holers."

The sheriff looked at him curiously. "What you got on your mind?"

"I want to pay Monk Danielson's bail."

This time the sheriff's head swiveled quickly. "He worked for the Purvis brothers and he was trying to burn down the damned Trustee's office."

Big Willard smiled. "Yeah, but he did a piss-poor job of it. I figure a man like yourself who is an expert on toilets might see the wisdom of letting a man like that go especially since he's a proven inept criminal."

The sheriff nodded with an amused look on his face. "I gather that the toilet deal goes hand-in-hand with Monk's bail?"

Big Willard gave the sheriff a roguish grin.

Sheriff Nelson shook his head and asked, "Why him?"

"I like him. He can fight and he sure in the world can take care of the place if I have to be gone."

The sheriff was about to shake his head 'no,' when Big Willard added. "He would really be watchful about the maintenance of the county toilet too."

The sheriff exhaled loudly and said, "Twenty-five dollars ought to do it."

Big Willard said, "It's real funny how his bail matches the cost of the toilet."

The sheriff slapped his reins and added as they picked up speed, "Ain't it though."

# CHAPTER ELEVEN

WHEN JOHN RETURNED FROM THE posse, He went to the saloon and was joined by the other deputies and troopers. There was a big dinner table spread in the middle of the room. The local townsmen and several ranchers, who had been fearful of losing their spreads to the Purvis brothers, had feted the deputies and troopers to a big Texas style supper.

Big steaks and chuck wagon beans, along with piles of boiled potatoes and large chunks of cornbread and sliced onions and tomatoes adorned the table.

John took a few bites and excused himself and made his way to Doctor McClain's clinic. As he was walking along the cinder alley way, he heard a soft and kind voice coming through the open window.

He peeked around the edges of the window and saw Private Ray Harp feeding Seth some chicken soup. Private Harp had tears in his eyes and his voice was broken as he begged Seth to open his mouth and take more nourishment.

John turned with his back to the wall and sighed. He knew Seth was in good hands. He walked back to the Texas Saloon with a much bigger appetite.

The next day John and Russell buried their uncle at his old home place. A thin-faced minister with a bad suit said some kind words and read from the Bible. The deputies listened dutifully with their hats in their hands. The troopers lifted their Spencers and fired several shots of tribute.

They had dinner on the ground. The small Baptist Church provided mounds of food. A group of cowhands from a spread, that once was threatened by a Purvis brothers' takeover, played the guitar and fiddle and entertained them.

Mostly they slept and spent the day recovering from the rigors of the trips and the unending action.

The next day, the commission met in Charley Danton's office. The members of this official group were Charley Danton, Sheriff Nelson, Lieutenant Gardner, and Judge Washburn from Earth, Texas.

John and all the deputies and troopers were playing cards in the saloon. He anxiously awaited their decisions.

Sheriff Buchanan was shuffling cards and he gave John a certain look that meant for him to turn around and look at the bar. When John turned around he was shocked to see Big Willard running the place and standing beside him was Monk Danielson wearing an bar apron.

John shook his head---what a bond those two had secured by 'duking' it out behind the Trustee's office. They were laughing and acting long lost brothers.

The sheriff dealt the cards and said, "Would you have ever imagined?" He sighed and said, "I have a hard time figuring out things sometimes. Have you ever seen some ole ugly guy and he's got a woman on his arms that has more curves than a goat path and a face that belongs on an angel? Or some handsome guy married to some ole gal that has an ass that is the size of barn and is uglier than lye soap?"

John laughed and tossed in his cards. "I would go check on Seth but Ray Harp stays with him night and day."

Sheriff Buchanan smiled and tossed in his cards. "It's a strange world, John."

John nodded and allowed himself to smile. He looked up at Monk Danielson who had brought them free beers. Monk introduced himself and lifted a beer for a toast. "Here's to new friends."

They all raised their mugs and chugalugged.

They whiled away the next two-hours with poker and listening to the rinky-dink piano. Soon the batwings opened and Levi Brown stuck his head in. He motioned for John.

Every deputy and trooper arose and followed John out the exit and down to the Trustee's office. Judge Washburn, a portly white-haired man, was waiting on the front porch under the sloping, wood-shingled roof.

The other commission members were lined up behind the judge next to the wall.

The judge reached into his inner-coat pocket and pulled out their decision. He looked at John and John nodded back at him to let him know he was 'John.' Pulling out a pair of spectacles and placing them on, he cleared his throat and began reading in an official voice.

"John, you and Russell will receive your father's ranches in total without penalties. Your Uncle Henry's ranch will be of necessity have to be purchased. The duress of his sale was considered but it was decided that for the sake of the county and its integrity that you will have the first chance to buy it at the price determined by Charley Danton."

He paused and looked over the assemblage of troopers and deputies and a growing number of townsmen. "The horse ranch of the Rawlins family will also have to be purchased.

"The two-other ranches that were acquired by the Purvis brothers were made on the profit of the cattle chiefly raised on your spread, therefore, those two-ranches are now yours.

"The Purvis Mercantile Store, the Purvis Hotel and the Purvis

Feed and Seed Emporium are also now considered your property because they also were bought by the sale of cattle to the U.S. army and those cattle chiefly came from your father's ranch."

The crowd broke out into a clamorous cheer. John was pushed up the steps and through the door into Charley Danton's office. Charley handed John the figures and it came out at an even seven thousand dollars. John sighed and pulled out a bank draft from his pocket and wrote out the check and placed some money he had in his pocket on the desk.

He walked out owning a lot of land and property but he had only the five-dollar gold piece in his pocket that he received from Henry Fagan over in Tennessee.

He walked with Levi Brown and Sheriff Buchanan to the saloon. As they walked, they all caught sight of Ferlin Henderson and his wife, Irene, who had the pie-shaped face, standing in front of the Purvis Mercantile Store.

John could see they were waiting for him. Sheriff Buchanan turned aside and entered the saloon, but Levi followed him with narrowed eyes at the merchant and his wife.

John trudged up to them and nodded courteously. He noticed the trembling hands of Irene. It never bothered him if someone who was supposed to be afraid of him quavered, but if it were someone that should not be afraid, it bothered him a great deal.

Ferlin was extremely edgy. His eyes would go from John to Levi who had fixed his eyes on him. Ferlin said, "I was wondering what you were going to do with us?" He licked his lips and looked away from the steely look of Levi Brown.

John again took note of the shaky hands of Ferlin's dutiful wife. "I was hoping you would stay and run the store."

Ferlin's eyes widened in disbelief, "You're not going to fire us?"

John shook his head 'no.' Levi said over the back of John, "You did run to Bill Purvis when you saw trouble brewing, now didn't you?"

He swallowed and looked again at John to see if he were going to change his mind about keeping them. He nodded and said, "I am always loyal to the man who pays my salary."

John held out his hand and Ferlin held out his tentatively. John said, "I like the fact that you were steadfast to him even when things were not looking too bright for him."

They shook and Ferlin stood thunderstruck and looked over at his wife. She dabbed at her eyes and gazed up at John.

John was about to turn and go with Levi into the saloon but an afterthought caught his mind. "I want you to do two-things for me."

"Yes, of course, anything."

"I want you to notify all the other people that run the hotel and the feed and seed emporium, that they still have jobs."

Ferlin looked relieved and exhaled. "I'll do that immediately." He looked at Levi and back at John. "And what is the second-thing?"

"I want all those signs that say 'Purvis' on them painted over and just put 'Bailey County' up there."

Ferlin swallowed and nodded, "But of course."

John nodded at Ferlin and tipped his hat to his chubby wife and he and Levi turned and walked away and into the batwings of the Texas Saloon.

As they entered the saloon, the rinky-dink piano was sending loud Irish tunes over the entrance out into the street. John saw old Doctor McClain leaning on the bar. He walked straight to him and asked, "I want to see Seth as soon as possible."

The doctor nodded and said, "He's been asking about you and Russell and some woman named Bonnie." The doctor chugalugged his beer and said, "Come over when you get through here and see him but just don't stay too long. He's out of the woods but not too far."

John nodded and followed Levi to Sheriff Buchanan's table.

John could see into the expressions of the sheriff and the deputy that they wanted to talk with him.

He could see a sense of urgency, so, he sat down with his eyes gravitating back and forth in a slow pan.

Levi Brown began talking, "John, we don't have much time. We need to get out of here and headed back to Fort Smith. We are definitely out of our jurisdiction here and we don't want to run afoul of General Weyland. Those in his command would be greatly offended if they knew that General Beasley had sent us here. There would be a lot of unnecessary bickering and we just want to leave before there is too much said."

John looked at both the sheriff and Captain Brown. "I owe you both a debt."

Sheriff Buchanan gave him a twinkling eye and said, "Well, I want to ask you something before we go."

John shrugged and nodded at both of them.

The sheriff inhaled and leaned back in his chair. "I have had several long talks with Russell. He informed me about your promise to a Union captain about delivering a pocket watch to his brother in Ironton, Ohio."

John did not betray his perturbation at Russell but he did lick his lips and give a small grimace.

The sheriff caught his look but did not belabor it. "He also said you met a young woman near the Missouri line that you were wanting to see again soon."

John tilted his head and said, "Sheriff Buchanan, we are good enough friends for you to level with me before giving me this long running start."

The sheriff gave a stiff smile and looked over at Levi Brown. "I wish you would take it from here, Captain."

Levi leaned in with his hands clasped. "Yesterday, two-couriers rode into town from Colonel Daugherty. They informed the sheriff and me that there is trouble in the Nations."

He paused and looked at John for any reaction and not getting any he continued, "The Indians who run these towns do not have any legal authority to arrest white men. They can only appeal for military help." He paused and spread out his hands. "There are some white men who have taken over a town and are terrorizing the citizens." He sighed and looked at John. "We have used up all our time here and we have to get back to Arkansas. We won't be able to help them at this time."

John's eyebrows moved up and he pushed his hat brim up with his thumb.

The sheriff looked at Levi and back at the big Texan. "So, Marshal Johnson, we'd like for you to look into the matter as you make your way to Northern Arkansas and Ironton, Ohio."

John looked at both men. He sighed resignedly and asked, "What's the name of the town?"

Levi and the sheriff, as if on cue, stood and pushed in their chairs. They both reached over and shook his hand warmly.

Sheriff Buchanan said, "The name of the town is 'Quiso' see you in about two-months."

They both smiled at him. Levi snapped him a quick salute. "You didn't really think you could hide here in Texas, now did you?"

They departed and he sat looking at the moving batwings. He grated his chair back and followed them.

When he exited he was stunned to see every trooper, that included the driver and the guard of the armored coach, lined up in a straight-line. After the troopers, stood the deputies, they each walked up and shook his hand. Each soldier and each deputy would then snap to attention and give him a formal salute. After each one had shaken his hand and had given him the salute, that particular t individual would go mount up and await the others.

Lieutenant Gardner leaned in and said as he had finished his salute. "See you in about two-months,"

John watched them ride out in perfect military formation. Trailing them was Sheriff Buchanan who suddenly stopped his horse and gave him a friendly wave. He turned his horse rapidly and rode after the troops.

Russell and Seth, who had observed all of this, walked up to him and asked what was going on.

John put his arms around each of them and said, "Let's go see, Seth." He paused and sighed. "We got a whole lot of things to do."

During the next week, John gave Harley a clear deed to his father's ranch. He and some new cowhands refurbished his old home place and bid adieu to Harley as he took a buckboard to go fetch his wife.

Russell assumed his father's ranch. He took on the role of foreman and merged his ranch with John's three-ranches.

Seth, who still was mending from his wound, was given Henry Johnson's ranch and he immediately merged with John and Russell forming a mammoth ranch.

Big Willard had changed the name of the Texas Saloon. It was now the 'Big Willard's Saloon.' He built a ring and bleachers in the back of his saloon and Monk had assumed Big Willard's former role of fighting for fifty-dollars and a thousand-dollar maximum.

His toilet with the forty-feet shaft was the talk of the county and many a cowhand and citizen would use the facility and then light a match to see if they could see the bottom.

John continued to sell fifty-head of cattle to the U.S. army for ten-dollars a head each month and with that was able to break even in expenses. The money he made from the mercantile store, hotel and feed store were reinvested for growth.

The beginning of the second-week, he took a break and was sitting on the steps of his father's ranch when he saw a rider hurriedly moving down the ranch road.

The man, who reined up in a cloud of dust, walked up to him and handed him a letter from Colonel Daugherty. It appealed to him to go to 'Quiso' as soon as possible and help the inhabitants of the Indian town to maintain law and order.

John bade the deputy to spend the night and he escorted him to the bunkhouse. As they were walking John asked about Levi Brown and Sheriff Buchanan. The deputy replied that Sheriff Buchanan had resumed his office in Fort Smith and that Levi Brown was working undercover in the Nations.

The next morning the deputy rode out in a gallop with the assurance that John was on his way to 'Quiso.'

John watched him ride down the ranch road in a cloud of dust and then assembled his two-cousins and newly hired men. He explained to them what was asked of him.

Russell and Seth went to the barn and saddled his horse and gathered in a gentle gelding as his packhorse. They placed a canvas bag over the gelding filled with a two-week supply of coffee, beans and jerky. They put in ten-pound block of salt and twenty-five pounds of feed for the horses.

John thanked them both and mounted up on his massive black horse. He pulled the watch out that he was obliged to deliver to Cyrus Schofield. He looked at it and sighed. He lingered awhile longer looking at the prosaic landscape filled with mesquite and caramel-colored dirt. He knew that over the horizon that Martha Taylor was waiting for him. He repocketed the watch and inhaled deeply.

He nodded at each cousin in particular and all the men in general and he took the tether from Russell to the packhorse. He coaxed the big black horse and he went trotting down the ranch road.

They all watched him ride away. Russell and Seth watched his broad back for a long while. Russell sighed and walked away. Seth kept looking until John's image disappeared into the shrinking, perspective of the landscape.

He knew that whomever it was in Quiso that was causing problems and misery would soon be dealt misery. He thoughtfully looked at the barn and walked away.